# MIDWINTER

## WHITE HAVEN WITCHES (BOOK 12)

# MAGIC
# TJ GREEN

Midwinter Magic

Mountolive Publishing

Copyright © 2023 TJ Green

ISBN eBook: 978-1-99-004763-3

ISBN Paperback: 978-1-99-004764-0

ISBN Hardback: 978-1-99-004765-7

Cover design by Fiona Jayde Media

Editing by Missed Period Editing

A big thanks to Elsa who sorts out my tax returns as I navigate the complicated waters of Portuguese income tax. You are so patient and helpful with my very messy accounts, and you make my life so much easier! This book is for you xx

# Contents

# One

Avery Hamilton stood at the window of her shop, Happenstance Books, admiring the town's Yuletide decorations.

White Haven was decorated with winter greenery, seasonal lights, and other Christmas-related decorations. However, the view was filtered through a veil of thick, velvety snowflakes that blanketed the street, suppressing everything into hushed silence. It felt timeless. Magical. In fact, as she gazed out, she felt as if the rest of the world had faded away, and that there was nothing except White Haven and the upcoming celebrations.

"Hard to believe that the Yuletide parade and feast is tomorrow," Alex Bonneville, her boyfriend, said, handing her a mug of coffee and then leaning against the window frame. "Let's hope the snow stops falling by then or no one will see a thing!"

Avery laughed. "It always does. It's the magic of this time of year. White Haven is always blanketed in snow, and yet the day of the parade is bathed in crisp, winter sunshine." She returned to the counter with her coffee, turning her back on the snowy scene to appraise her shop's decorations.

As usual, Sally, her shop manager and good friend, had made Happenstance Books warm and welcoming, twinkling with candles and fairy lights, and smelling of cinnamon and frankincense. In addition, thick branches of pine were festooned across the top of bookshelves, and glittering pinecones nestled within them.

"How are your pub decorations coming on, Alex? You know that Stan will be inspecting everyone today." Stan was one of White Haven's councillors and their pseudo-Druid, and he organised all the solstice and seasonal celebrations. "We don't want to upset him."

Alex rolled his eyes. "Anyone would think our lives depended on it. Don't worry, Marie has risen to the occasion, and the pub is groaning with decorations. You'll see when you swing by later. I'm on the evening shift tonight."

"Great. I'll come and have dinner with you."

Alex's eyes clouded for a moment, as if he was struggling to think of something, but then he shrugged it off. "I'd better go. I need to run over the Yuletide menu. We're fully booked for lunch, so we better make it good!" He leaned in and kissed her cheek. "See you later."

The door clanged shut behind him, setting off the bells that hung over the door. Their sound was startlingly loud in the quiet shop, as if they were trying to remind her of something she'd forgotten. She ran through her plans for the day.

At the moment, the shop was closed. She and Alex had risen early for once, for reasons neither could understand. They both preferred late nights to early mornings. Maybe it was the unusual, hushed silence that hung over the town, and the brilliant white light that filtered through the blinds. There was a quality to snow that was hard to ignore. It turned the once familiar landscape into alien shapes as it settled on walls, trees, and houses. Avery might not be able to see the beach and harbour from here, but she knew that the sea would be a flat pewter sheet stretching to an unseen horizon, the foaming surf churning up the snow-white beaches. The fishing vessels might even be trimmed with ice.

But what was she forgetting? Her shop manager, Sally, and Dan, her shop assistant, would be arriving soon, and then they would open for the day. They would need to check that all of their decorations were ready for inspection, and then they would prepare the reading corner. Dan always loved the chance to read Christmas classics to the children and their parents who visited the shop. *Hopefully Sally would bring mince pies.*

And then, what else? She'd contact Briar Ashworth and El Robinson to see if they wanted to eat at The Wayward Son, too. But she was sure there was something else to do...

Her reverie was broken by Sally and Dan's bickering voices as they arrived using the back entrance to the shop. They clattered around in the kitchen for a few minutes, and Avery took the opportunity to walk around the shop, still trying to focus. She tidied up messy books, straightened displays, and picked up random objects. Snow globes were dotted on some of the shelves, and she shook one absently, watching the glitter swirl around a castle on a hill in the centre. A castle made of ice.

The door to the kitchen flew open, and her friends struggled into the shop, Sally carrying a large Christmas Bunch, and Dan a set of stepladders.

"Good grief," Dan complained, "did you have to make it so big?"

"Yes! It wouldn't look the same if it was small!"

"If it falls on someone's head, they'll have a serious injury!"

"It won't fall!"

Avery giggled. "You two! What are you like?"

Dan shot her an impish grin. "I wouldn't complain so much if Sally would have just given me a mince pie!"

"They are for later!" Sally reminded him. "It's not even ten o'clock yet!"

"So? Elevenses can be any time I want. I'm an adult."

"Says the man wearing a *Jingle Balls* t-shirt!"

"If I could just interrupt for one moment," Avery said, trying to head off more bickering, "I would like to say how gorgeous that wreath is!"

Sally was flushed, her normally neat blonde hair tumbling over her face, but she gave Avery a beaming smile. "Thank you! I intend to win Stan's competition!"

"It is impressively large, and I'm sure we have a good chance!" Avery also thought Dan was right. They needed to secure the Bunch well. If it fell on Stan, it would be a disaster.

The Christmas Bunch was a traditional Cornish Christmas wreath made of two hoops set at right angles, decorated with seasonal green leaves and a candle in the centre. It was made to be suspended from the ceiling. Sally had added baubles and beads, too.

"We must make sure," Avery continued, wrinkling her nose, perplexed, "that the candle doesn't set fire to the wreath. We do not want to burn down my house and shop."

Dan had already placed the step ladders into position, and taking the Bunch from Sally, he wrestled it on to the hook just beyond the front entrance. When it was finally in place, he lit the candle. "Don't worry, Avery. It will be fine. It's a good distance from the greenery."

Sally clapped her hands with delight. "Perfect! I knew a real one would look much nicer than a fake!"

"Now can I have a mince pie?" Dan asked as he folded the steps up.

"You may, if you make coffee, too."

Dan grumbled as he headed to the backroom, and Sally laughed. "I do love teasing him."

"As long as you keep making mince pies, you can tease him all day long." Avery settled behind the counter. "So, when's judging day for the wreath?"

"The day after Yule, seeing as tomorrow Stan will be whirling around White Haven, making sure it's ready for the parade." Sally leaned on the counter. "I really think that he needs help. He never stops!"

"Will he open the fayre tonight, too?"

"I'm not sure, but I can't wait." Sally grinned. "I'll take the children this year. They will love to see the castle lit up. How is Clea this morning? Will she go to the fayre tonight with you?"

Avery had returned to sit behind the shop counter, and startled by the question about her grandmother, she almost knocked over the cold dregs of her coffee. "Shit! How could I have forgotten her? I'll go and check."

She raced into the backroom of the shop, straight past Dan who was making a fresh pot of coffee, and up the stairs to her flat. She paused on the threshold of the living room, once again feeling as if something was wrong, but everything looked fine. The Christmas tree was decorated in the corner, the TV was on with the sound turned low, and Clea's door was partly open. But the smell of burnt toast wafted from the kitchen, and Avery walked to the archway that separated the kitchen from the living room.

Clea, still dressed in her fluffy bathrobe, was at the sink, scraping off the blackened edges from the toast. Avery crossed to stand next to her. "Gran! I'm so sorry I didn't wake you. Are you okay? Let me make you more toast."

Clea looked up at her, her smile vanishing into her wrinkles as she patted her hand. "I'm all right, my dear, don't you worry. You have the shop to worry about. I'm going to watch a bit of breakfast TV. Join me for lunch though, later?" She headed to the counter to butter her toast.

"Of course." Avery's head felt woolly, and she looked around at her familiar kitchen, wondering if she had a hangover.

*Had she and Alex got riotously drunk the night before?* Surely not. She would have a pounding headache. Her kitchen had the remnants of her and Alex's breakfast in the sink, and their belongings were strewn around the living room, and yet, everything felt so wrong. She drifted to the window, but the view was as muffled as her head. Snow swirled thickly, obliterating her view of the garden and the town. She could barely see the lane behind the house, and the sea was completely hidden.

Drawn upstairs by a compulsion she couldn't understand, Avery headed to the attic floor where her bedroom was situated, leaving Clea to potter. Standing on the threshold, she frowned at the shadow filled space. Her and Alex's bedroom was the room on the other side of the fireplace. On this side was the big, wooden table cluttered with books, the shelves around it stacked with candles and herbs. She inhaled the scent of incense and felt her spirits lift. *But why had she so many herbs up here? Shouldn't they be in the kitchen? And why so many books?*

She should turn this space into another seating area, a lounge for her and Alex for when they needed privacy from Clea. Perhaps she would do that later. She walked around the room, her finger running along the thick, wooden shelves.

And then Avery paused as she saw another snow globe. This one was the size of a football, and inside it, perched on a snowy branch, was a raven, its yellow eyes fixed on her with an intense glare. She couldn't even remember why she owned such a thing. She shook her head, perplexed, deciding it was time to return to the shop.

Briar knew she'd have difficulty getting home that evening if the snow continued to fall so thickly. She'd had enough trouble walking to work that morning.

She had set off from her cottage on one of the side streets, wrapped in layers and wearing her sturdy leather boots that were now drying out in front of the heater in the herb room of her shop. However, the snow did not deter customers. They entered the shop in an endless flow, her products evaporating off the shelves. She was thankful that she had plenty of stock.

She needed to get a shop assistant. She'd been promising herself one for years, and couldn't work out why she hadn't organised one sooner. *Especially at this time of year.* She would miss lunch again, she knew it. She would have to make up more of her hand lotions and seasonal candles that evening, too. However, she would still take time to see her friends in Alex's pub. She could always work late after that. But she needed to see her friends first; it would cheer her up. While she loved Yuletide and Christmas, it always reminded her of her lack of family. She shook her head and smiled at one of her regulars. *This was not the time to be depressed. Her friends were family, and they would celebrate it together.*

"Penny for them, my lovely," a middle-aged woman called Carla asked her. "You look worried."

"Sorry!" Briar brushed her hand across her brow, pushing a thick lock of her hair away. "Just thinking of my friends and wondering what we'll do to celebrate Christmas. You know, I'm sure I had plans, but I can't for the life of me think what they were."

"It's just stress, love." Carla frowned as she glanced around the shop. "You need help in here. It's a big shop to manage all on your own."

"I know. Maybe I should put a sign up in the window advertising for help. Someone must want some extra Christmas cash."

"Excellent idea. Although, the castle has employed most available people at this time of year." Briar must have looked as confused as she felt because Carla said, "For the feast tomorrow? Don't tell me you forgot that!"

Briar had totally forgotten, but instinct told her it wouldn't be right to admit it, so she lied. "Of course not! I'm just preoccupied with work. I can't wait."

Carla smiled, her frown clearing. "Every year I think it can't get any better, and every year it does! I'll see you there, I'm sure, despite the crowds." She placed her purchases in her bag and left, and as the door shut behind her, the chiming bells seemed to emit a warning.

Instantly, Briar remembered the feast. The costumes, the delicious food, the band, the dancing, the Yuletide fight between the kings, all of it taking place in the castle on the hill. *How could she have forgotten that?* But instead of feeling excited about it, dread crept through her.

It made no sense. *Why would she dread a feast?*

El was going to be late to work, but she watched the ice encroaching on the sea, mesmerised.

Her warehouse flat overlooked White Haven's harbour, offering a panoramic view of the harbour, the beach, the edge of town, and the sea. The view was always captivating, but it was even more so today.

Although snow had fallen in the town before, she was sure it had never felt quite so cold, and the sea had surely never iced up. The harbour already had a solid layer of ice that locked the shipping vessels, rowing boats, and yachts inside it. This would last until spring, and the snow would fall thick and heavy until March, at least. But the Winter Fayre would be fun. Hot chestnuts, mulled wine and cider, and the braziers that lined the streets would burn brightly, staving off the chill. And of course, the council would issue the sleighs today. Soon the streets would ring with sleighbells, the air misting with the breath of reindeer.

El paused, confused.

*Reindeer and an icy sea until spring? Thick snow for months? Where had those thoughts come from?*

But then a fluttering pennant caught her eye up on the cliffs above White Haven, and she gazed upwards, the snow clearing for a moment to reveal the castle on the cliff top. It sparkled despite the gloomy, cloud laden sky. The icy walls gave off a bluish glow that reflected the snow and its surrounding.

They would be preparing for the feast in there, the multiple fires in the kitchen no doubt blazing as food was cooked, and today the shops and town would be inspected for the parade. It had to be right, or everyone would suffer.

Pulling her coat on, she knew she had to hurry. She needed to join Zoey in her shop to make sure everything was perfect.

Despite the heavy snow, Alex loitered on White Haven's streets, eyes sharp as he took in the decorations around him.

Every shop was adorned to perfection. Every window gleamed, every pot was filled with winter plants, every display sparkled. He should be excited. Tomorrow, starting at four o'clock in the afternoon, the Yuletide parade would march from the square, down the main street to the harbour, and then up to the castle. The streets would be lined with well-wishers, and street vendors would sell roasted chestnuts and candy floss. The feast would complete the day. Alex paused, confused.

The feast.

*Damn it.* He wouldn't have Jago, his chef, working in the pub for another couple of days because of it. He had been poached, as he was every year at this time, along with many other great cooks in the town, to help with the Yuletide extravaganza. As a result, more pressure was put on other staff.

But it would all be worth it.

Alex raked his hands through his hair. He was missing something. Something important. This should be a fun time of year. It *was* a fun time of year normally, and yet...

He shrugged the thought away and set off again, finally rounding the corner into the square. As usual, a huge Christmas tree dominated the space, the lights sparkling through the swirling snow.

For a second, Alex's spirits lifted, until the wind parted the snow like a curtain to reveal a huge ice sculpture of a regal woman seated upon a glacial throne at the edge of the square. A crown was placed upon her head, her hand clutched a staff that was planted in the ground next to her, and her swirling skirts hid all sorts of impish figures and animals that cavorted at her feet.

Alex halted, riveted at the sight of the queen's sculpture, and it seemed that her eyes bore into his as if she could see his soul.

As Reuben Jackson approached his home on the hill above White Haven after his early morning surf, he slowed the car to look at what appeared to be a white wall around the town that was nestled in the valley below.

He was so confused that he found a layby to park in, exited the car, and stood on the grass verge to get a better look. Snow was falling, becoming thicker by the minute, whipping over the moors and covering the thick, tufted grass.

His eyes weren't betraying him. Beyond the swirling snow, it was as if thick cloud had settled into White Haven. It had been dark when he'd left to go surfing on a neighbouring beach that morning, so he hadn't noticed a thing. He reasoned with himself, arguing not to be paranoid, and that it was just a low cloud. But the longer he stared at it, the more worried he became. It was too thick. Too solid.

Shivering in the icy chill, he returned to his car, and continued past the turnoff to his house, instead turning onto the road that would take him down the hill into White Haven. Except the road that would lead him there turned back on itself. In minutes, he found himself back on the lane leading to his house.

Confused, he stopped the car again. He had lived there all his life and had never once got lost in the meandering back lanes that wound through the fields and moors around his home. He turned around and tried again. This time he ended up on another lane entirely that wound past Stormcrossed Manor, Briar's family home.

*Okay. Something was definitely wrong.*

He tried again, heading down the lane, this time at a crawl. The white blanket of cloud rose before him, the lane heading straight into it. He stopped the car and exited, progressing on foot. He took his time, sniffing the air as if for danger. For magic.

For a few paces, everything was normal, and then he was suddenly turned about, facing his car and the fields again. He hadn't felt a thing, either. No tingle of magic, no disorientation, just a gentle righting. He turned to face the cloud again, worry balling in the pit of his stomach.

However, the longer he stared at it, the more he wondered what he was staring at. *Why was he staring at a low hanging cloud?* He had to get home, check on his staff in Greenlane Nurseries, and make sure that work was going smoothly. The wall seemed to rebuff him, telling him that everything was okay.

Reuben stepped back, retreating to the car where he felt more in control of his thoughts. He pulled his phone from his pocket, found El's number, and called his girlfriend. But the phone rang and rang and no one answered. Then he tried the rest of his coven—Alex, Briar, and Avery.

Not a single one answered. Nor did their voicemail messages kick in.

*This was not normal.*

He focussed within himself, calling on his familiar, Silver. He was a huge water horse that had appeared during the fight with the wizard and Wyrd who had tried to destroy White Haven over Samhain. Sometimes he surfed with Silver, but he hadn't that morning.

Usually, Silver arrived quickly. They had bonded well. This morning, however, he was taking his time. When he finally manifested, his shimmering, watery body icing up quickly in the freezing temperature, he pawed the ground impatiently.

"*You took your sweet time,*" Reuben complained. "*We have a problem. White Haven has vanished, and my coven isn't answering the phone.*"

Silver snorted, throwing his mane up as he eyed Reuben with disdain. "*I know we have, you fool. Where do you think I've been? All of the familiars have vanished, too.*" Silver spoke, but only Reuben could hear his voice, inside his head.

Reuben had been worried and confused, but now was getting more angry than afraid. He fisted his hands. "*What now? Is El okay?*"

"*I have no idea how any of them are. I can't reach them.*"

Reuben pointed at the thick, white wall that edged White Haven. "*Look at that! Can you see it too, or is it just me? I can't even drive through it!*"

Silver studied it. "*Interesting. Does it feel magical up close?*"

"*Interesting? It's infuriating! And weird.*" He considered his familiar's question. "*No, actually, it didn't feel like magic, but the closer I got to it, the less I seemed to care about White Haven. It muddied my thoughts, so that has to be magic. Who has done this? Is that bloody wizard back?*" Reuben's magic swelled as he considered his next course of action.

Silver shook his head. "*He can't be! We defeated him. I have no idea who's behind it, but they are powerful, because even my magic can't penetrate it.*"

"*Let's be logical. I can't get in this way, but there are other roads into the town. I'm going to try all of them, and if that doesn't work, then I'll find a boat and try to get in by sea.*"

"*And if you can't?*"

"*Then we have a massive problem.*"

## Two

D etective Inspector Mathias Newton, the head of the Cornwall Paranormal Division, wasn't often called to Bude, the bustling seaside town on the north coast of Cornwall.

It was situated close to the border between Cornwall and Devon, and it took almost an hour and a half to drive there from Truro where he was based. He certainly didn't relish the early call. The previous night had been their team's Christmas outing. He, Moore, and Kendall had been rallied into joining the other teams, and as far as he was concerned, it was a painful experience. He'd have much rather been drinking in The Wayward Son. As a consequence, he'd had too many beers, knowing he had a room to sleep in at Moore's house. He had slept in a single bed belonging to Moore's youngest child so he didn't have to worry about taxis or driving, and had woken with his face pressed into a pink teddy bear.

Hoping the painkillers would kick in soon, he studied the dead body on the beach, and wished he was back in bed—preferably, his own. First impressions suggested the corpse was frozen solid. He even had a slight film of ice over his body like a casing. His blue eyes were fixed open, the eyelashes rimmed with frost.

He pulled his coat firmly closed against the wild wind that ripped in from the Celtic Sea, and turned to the local PC, a young woman with mousy brown hair who looked barely out of school. "You say you know him?"

"Yes, sir. Michael Hammett. Forty-six years old. He's a regular surfer here. Lives in the town. I was only talking to him last night in the pub!"

Newton frowned. "You're friends?"

"Not really. As I say, just a local, and I get to know all of those." A flicker of regret passed across her face. "He was a nice man. Everyone liked him. Mad good surfer. Loved this beach."

Newton was relieved she wasn't a good friend. It would have made life complicated. "Well, he's dressed in regular clothes, so he obviously wasn't about to go surfing. Who found him?"

"Mrs Janice Vingoe. She lives in one of the houses along the road there." She pointed to the road above the beach. "She walks her dog here. She's a bit shaken up, so she's in the café having a cuppa."

*That was good. A local would know more than a visitor.* "Fair enough. Who's with her?"

"My colleague, PC Downes."

The young officer looked stoic in the face of such an unusual corpse. "Did she see anything odd last night or this morning?"

"I'm not sure. She was quite tearful, so we haven't really got much information yet."

Newton took pity on her. She looked half frozen despite being wrapped in a thick coat, but she'd secured the area and done all the right things. "Go and join them for five minutes to get warm, but then you'll have to come back and watch the area, okay?"

She nodded and hurried to the café situated a short walk away on the beachfront. Able to speak freely, Newton sighed and turned to DS Moore, his red-haired sergeant. "What do you think?"

"Poor bugger looks like he's been stored in a freezer, except for the fact that he only went missing last night. So how does that happen?"

"Excellent question. Fingers and toes would freeze quickly, but the trunk? I know it's cold, but it's hardly Arctic conditions. We'll have to ask Arthur. I imagine it would take a day or more to freeze a body solidly like this." Newton had already donned his gloves and he crouched and poked the victim again, hoping that Arthur, the Forensic Pathologist, would arrive quickly. The body seemed as solid as a rock. Then he noticed something else. He stood and stepped back to assess the area. The body was at the edge of the rocks that were damp from the tide. *It wasn't obvious on first inspection, but now...* "Moore, there's a film of ice all around this area. The sand is frozen, too."

Moore frowned, his forehead wrinkling as he considered Newton's observation. "A couple of metres radius, I reckon. Okay, that *is* weird."

Newton stood, sticking his hands deep into his pockets. "Now it makes more sense that we've been called. But what caused it? A local weather event?"

Moore cocked a sceptical eyebrow. "There's local, and there's *local*!" He looked beyond Newton. "Someone's coming this way, Guv. A woman."

Newton positioned his back to the stiff wind, and watched a woman with curly red hair, wrapped in an enormous puffer jacket, cross the wet sand towards them. She looked vaguely familiar, but he couldn't work out why. They both headed towards her, beyond the yellow cordon.

She stuck out a gloved hand. "DI Newton. I'm Gray Pengelly, one of the witches of the Cornwall Coven, and head of the Bude Coven." She smiled at his surprise. "I know of you from Avery and Caspian, and I met you at Samhain last year."

He shook her hand. "Of course. You must remember Moore then, too?"

"I do."

"I presume this isn't a social call."

"No. It's about the body over there."

Newton folded his arms, instantly suspicious. "How do you know about it so soon?"

"It's a small Cornish town. News spreads quickly. Especially bad news." She cast her eyes down to the sand, and then to the body behind them. "It's Mike, isn't it?"

"Michael Hammett. You know him?"

"Vaguely. He's a local, and a good surfer. Everyone knew him."

"So I gather. Do you know who killed him?"

"No!" She looked startled. "But I heard he's frozen, is that right?"

Newton groaned. "How the hell did you know that? If that young constable..."

Gray held a hand up. "Not her. Jan is in the café, distraught. That means she's gabbling. News reached me."

Newton exchanged a worried glance with Moore. "Do you have an idea as to why he's frozen solid and covered in a layer of ice?"

"Not exactly, but I thought you should know about a weird event that happened here last night. I don't know if it might have any bearing, but all things considered..." She paused, and they waited, giving her time to formulate her thoughts. "There's a Winter Fayre in Bude. Just a collection of merchants selling Christmas gifts, food stalls, and alcohol. It's very popular. We run one every year for a few days over the winter solstice. I help my cousin. We sell scented soaps, candles, lotions..."

"Potions?" Newton smiled. "Things with special properties?"

She grinned. "Something like that. Anyway, it started to get very cold as we were closing. That would be close to 9:30 last night. I mean it was *very* cold. I could see frost spreading along the stalls and creeping across the ground—literally before my very eyes! It was...weird. I sensed something. We both did."

"What was it?"

"A presence. Something old—as old as time. And..." she struggled for the word, her brow wrinkling and lips tightening. "Mischievous. Like a naughty child with a mean streak."

"A spirit?"

"No. Something more than that. But I didn't *see* anything. Just this weird frost. We cast a spell—a banishing spell. It took a few attempts, but it finally stopped." She looked up at Newton, her hazel eyes clear, warm, and brutally honest. "Unfortunately, we don't know what we banished."

"I take it," Moore asked, "that your cousin is a witch, too."

"Yes. A member of my coven. There are three of us in total. We both knew that it was something supernatural, but stupidly didn't anticipate that it would return. As soon as I heard about Mike, well," she shrugged, "I knew. But there's something else. We have friends who live in Devon. This happened there too, just last night."

"The frost or a death?

"Both. In fact, two people died there. Frozen solid, too."

Newton turned to Moore. "Why haven't we heard about this?"

He shrugged. "I can make some calls."

"Yes, please." Moore pulled his phone from his pocket and turned away, leaving Newton alone with Gray. "So Gray, any suggestions as to what it could be?"

"No, but it's strong, whatever it is, and the fact it came back means that it's determined, too. Our spell should have sent it away for good, but clearly it was only temporary." She kicked the sand, regretful. "If we'd have done a better job, Mike would still be alive."

"And if you hadn't banished it at the time, more might be dead." Newton shook his head. "You did what you could. The supernatural *something* is to blame, not you."

He studied the wind-whipped waves, his thoughts already focussing on the investigation. He needed to speak to the witches—his witches—soon, but in the meantime... He studied Gray, pleased that she was calm and logical. "I'll take a statement and your contact details. I presume you have no objection if I need to call you?"

"Of course not. Anything I can do to help." She looked around and then up at the sky as snow started to fall. "I presume we can do this inside, before we freeze to death?"

"Of course. Let's head back to the café." *And caffeine. Lots of caffeine.*

Shadow reined Kailen to a halt on the moors above White Haven. Thick snow was falling, and the landscape looked stunning.

Kailen was her fey-bred horse who had crossed over from the Otherworld with her. He snorted, breath pluming in the cold air as they waited for Gabe who rode on Stormfall, the other fey horse, to join her. She yawned, tiredness overcoming her, despite the invigorating race. The last few days she had risen late after their time in France fighting Black Cronos, but as soon as she was up, she saddled her horse and headed out.

Fortunately, their home hadn't been attacked again in their absence. She had studied the burned loggia, a flare of anger burning deep within her. They may have destroyed Black Cronos's base, but their existence still infuriated her. Horseback riding calmed her down, and she was relieved that the horses hadn't been hurt, either. Dante, the blacksmith who lived in a small hamlet a short distance away, was fond of horses, and had looked after them in their absence.

Shadow leaned low on Kailen's back, head close to his neck, inhaling his animal scent, already feeling her stresses ebbing away, and absently studied the horizon, trying to get a glimpse of White Haven, but everything was so white.

As Gabe finally reined in next to her, he groaned. "You're too quick for me, Shadow."

"I shouldn't be too quick for Stormfall. You should trust him more."

"I've never been as comfortable on horseback as Nahum." His eyes raked across the horizon, snow landing on his dark hair. "It's hard to see anything in this weather. It looks like it's settling in."

"I can't even see White Haven," Shadow admitted. "I thought I'd go into town later, see El and the others. Or maybe tonight."

"Let's get a little closer. Maybe I can beat you to the next rise." Gabe grinned at her and took off like a rocket.

Never able to resist a challenge, she raced after him, but as the snow fell thicker and thicker, they were both forced to slow. It was becoming treacherous underfoot. When they finally halted again, Shadow looked back towards the farmhouse, but it was hidden by the snowfall.

"We'll never get the car out in this weather, Gabe. Thank the Gods it wasn't like this a few days ago. We might have been stuck in London." They had to get a connecting flight from London to Cornwall upon their return.

"It wouldn't have been so bad." He grinned at her. "And I can always fly later. No one will see us in this."

"Surely it won't still be falling this heavily tonight." White Haven should be visible immediately below them, but the blizzard had whited it out. "I can't see the town at all. Not even a glimpse of the church steeple. They must be inundated in snow."

"Come on. Let's get a little closer."

However, they had gone only a short distance when Shadow felt a looming surge of power and magic ahead. "Gabe, wait! Can you feel that?"

He cocked his head at her. "No. I'm just wondering why we're pushing on in this weather. We should go home."

She ignored him and edged Kailen forward, all her senses on full alert. The silence was almost suffocating, and combined with her lack of vision, it was unnerving. But her skin prickled with goose bumps. Ahead of her, something waited. Something as old as time, and full of dark intent.

She withdrew one of her daggers that she always carried. They were as much a part of her as wearing clothes. "Are you sure you can't feel that, Gabe?"

He frowned, eyes distant as he concentrated. "I feel an absence of something. Does that sound odd?"

"That's not how I would describe it." However, another step had her feeling as if her world had turned upside down. For a second, time seemed to slow, and then she was back on the rise, Gabe next to her, their horses hard to control. They wrestled them calm again, soothing them with whispered words.

"Tell me you felt *that*!" She whirled to look around.

He nodded, wary now. "Some kind of magic."

She was tempted to try again, but instead had a better idea. "Come on. Let's get to Ravens' Wood."

They took their time as they crossed the fields and moors, keeping White Haven always to their left, and when the ancient forest's dark mass rose ahead, Shadow led the way in. Snow filtered through the canopy, turning the ground white, and it seemed to make the dark, shadowy interior even more forbidding. Especially as all traces of the paths had now vanished. *No matter.* Shadow didn't need them. She spent so long exploring this place, she thought she could cross through it blindfolded.

They pressed on in silence, heading steadily towards White Haven Castle where Shadow knew she would get a good view of the town. She wondered if she might see dryads, but it was too cold. They would be hidden in the darkest interior. Besides, they knew she was angry with them for trapping Eli and Zee into a guardianship arrangement.

Gabe spoke, as if he'd read her mind. "You're radiating fury again. The dryads won't speak to you in that mood."

"I'll drag them from the trees if I have to, but I don't want them. Not yet."

However, when they reached the tree line and stepped on to the land where the castle should be, all they could see was a wall of thick, white cloud with snow swirling within it. Again, Shadow felt dark, icy power.

Gabe dismounted, hand resting on Stormfall. The horse was wild-eyed, and Gabe eased him back beneath the trees and tied him to a branch. "They sense something, too. Shall we try to get close again? Or better still, I'll try, and you watch. An experiment."

"Okay. But if you vanish completely, I'm coming after you."

"If I vanish, you'll do no such thing. You'll get my brothers and find help."

He strode forward, snow settling on his broad shoulders as he left the cover of the trees. Shadow didn't take her eyes off him. Within another few steps, he vanished, and then promptly returned to the spot he'd left.

Shadow blinked. "That was surreal."

Gabe looked down at himself. "Well, I'm intact. What did you see?"

"You were there and then you were here." She paused, hearing the cracking of branches behind them, and she whirled around. "Show yourself!"

"Steady on!" a familiar voice called out, and then Reuben, the water witch appeared, hands raised. "It's just me!"

Shadow slid from Kailen's back, so relieved to see him that she hugged him. "I thought you'd be trapped in there!"

"You've noticed the big, white Wall of Doom, then?"

"It's hard not to," Gabe pointed out, as he shook Reuben's hand and pulled him into a brief hug. "How long has it been there?"

Reuben was tall with a surfer's build. All lean muscle and flat stomach, with tussled blond hair and an almost permanent tan. He normally looked upbeat, his sardonic sense of humour always bubbling beneath the surface. Now, however, his expression was grim. "Since this morning. It certainly wasn't there last night."

Gabe glanced behind him. "El isn't with you?"

"No, she stayed at her own place last night."

All three stared at the snow-filled wall again, mesmerised by it.

"How far does this thing go?" Gabe asked.

Reuben rubbed his face, perplexed. "All around the town. The whole place! I haven't tried approaching by sea yet." He explained how much he'd investigated it already.

"You're a water witch," Shadow said. "You must feel more of an affinity to this. It seems to be made of snow."

"I do not feel an affinity with it at all!" He looked offended. "It feels dark. Have you noticed that if you get too close, you almost forget what you're trying to do?"

"No, but maybe my fey magic isn't so easily swayed," Shadow pointed out. "How did you resist its command?"

"I just backed off, quickly. This is about as close as I can risk getting. I wondered if the forest might be in it, but as we all know, it has its own magic."

Another thought struck Shadow. "You don't ward the town, do you?"

"Like cast it in some kind of magical enchantment? No. Seems over the top. We still want the town to feel normal."

"It's lucky that it didn't encompass the hills around it, or we'd be stuck in there, too," Gabe observed. "But who's behind it, and what's their purpose?"

Shadow leapt on to Kailen's back, sick of the wind-driven snow. "I suggest we discuss it at home, and make a plan to fight back."

Cassie was utterly perplexed.

"I didn't imagine it!" The old man clucked with annoyance as Cassie took notes. "I may be old, but I know what I saw!"

"I don't doubt you, Mr Featherington. I come across many strange things as a Paranormal Investigator. I believe you." She looked him square in the eye, her tone firm, and he seemed to relax.

"All right, then. My wife thought I'd gone mad."

"You did the right thing by calling me. Show me where you saw him."

The man leaned on his stick as he hobbled across the room of the tiny cottage at the edge of the village, and then, leaning on the back of the chair, he used the stick to jab at the hedge across the lane. "Over there. It looked like he was skipping along it. It were weird. Gave me a chill down to my bones."

"And it was at what time?"

"Close to midnight, I reckon. I was dozing in the chair, and the lights were off." He lowered his voice. "I sleep in the chair a lot these days. My wife snores."

Cassie gave him a conspiratorial smile. "I would do the same. So, can I just run over the description again?" He nodded. "It was a slim man, all sharp elbows and knees, a pointed chin, and he wore white clothes and had very white skin. Correct?"

"Yes. And he was like an adult, but like a piskie, too. He skipped on the hedge, like it were a road, and frost just spread behind him. It was Jack Frost, that's who!"

"Jack Frost?" Cassie tried to keep the incredulity from her voice. "From the fairytale?"

"Yes! There was a blizzard around him."

"But it was snowing last night."

His voice rose along with his very bushy eyebrows. "I know what I saw. He had his own little blizzard. Like a storm cloud." His voice dropped, and he gazed out of the window. "I didn't dare move. I just knew if he saw me that I would be dead."

A chill raced through Cassie. "Why do you think that?"

"Because a fox raced through the undergrowth, and he saw it and killed it. You search under that snow, and you'll see the body." The old man fumbled for the chair, and Cassie helped him sit. "He pointed an icy finger, and it just caught the poor creature. Froze it solid."

"All right." Cassie tucked her notebook back in her bag. "I'll go and check. Mind if I leave my bag here?"

"No, love. Go ahead. I'll put the kettle on. There's a spade next to the front door, ready to shovel the snow."

Cassie was pretty sure that the old man could barely pick up the shovel, never mind use it to shovel snow, but pulling her scarf tightly around her neck and her woolly hat firmly on her head, she stepped outside into the thickening midday snow. It was showing no signs of abating, and she would need to get back to the office soon, or she might be stranded. Already, snow lay thick along the lanes. The thought of being trapped in her car was horrifying.

She wavered for a moment on the doorstep, and then taking a deep breath, took the spade and headed across the lane. Her initial inspection showed nothing unusual, just deep snow along the base of the hedge and piled atop it. For a few minutes she dug through it finding nothing at all, but she worked her way along the hedge, aligning herself with the window. Every now and again, her client yelled from the window, "To the left! Closer to the hedge!" She knew he was trying to help, but the snow was trickling into her collar, her hair was wet, her gloves were soaking, and her fingers were numb.

But then she hit a lump. Although she loved the paranormal, she really hoped it was a rock and not a dead fox. Proceeding slowly, she gently moved the snow away, and found the very stiff and very dead body of a fox, mid-stride. His nose and paw were lifted as if it was sniffing the air and debating which way to go. It wasn't as if it had keeled over and died. The poor thing had literally frozen to death mid-step.

This had happened in seconds. *How cold would it have been to do such a thing?* It certainly wasn't natural. She stepped back, eyes narrowed as she imagined what Mr Featherington had seen. A creeping figure stalking over hedges in the middle of the night, working malevolent mischief. Panning across the landscape, she tried to work out where he would be going. *To the village, perhaps.*

She mentally corrected herself. She couldn't presume it was anything, let alone a "*he*." She needed to take photos and measurements. Try to detect unusual energy. And then she'd visit the village to see if anything was amiss there.

# Three

Alex's mouth felt abnormally dry as he watched Stan inspect the pub. He didn't know why. The whole place looked perfect.

Banners bearing the queen's emblem were on the back wall, a decorated Christmas tree sparkled in the corner, and lights and pine branches swagged over the fireplace and on shelves. Every single table shone, the bar gleamed, and glasses sparkled on the shelves behind the bar.

Stan swept through the lounge imperiously, inspecting the small courtyard garden at the back that was deep under snow drifts. "Will this be swept clear tomorrow?" he asked, eyes meeting Alex's.

"Of course. As long as it stops snowing, obviously." Alex tried to keep his tone as even as possible, and yet a hint of sarcasm crept in. Stan was never normally this exacting, but of course whenever the queen was involved in anything, it always made life complicated.

"I believe your chef, Jago, is at the castle helping to prepare the feast."

"Yes. He's one of the best chefs in White Haven."

"Then you should make sure that you do nothing to make his life more difficult there."

"More difficult? What do you mean?"

"Please don't speak to me in that tone. As you know, I have the queen's ear. One word, and this pub will belong to her. It's one of the old laws of White Haven, as you must know! Then it's up to her what she does with it. Potentially all of your staff will be looking for new employment. It will be hard to find a job though, especially for you, under such disgrace."

Alex recoiled at Stan's words. His staff were all lined up next to him. Simon, his manager, Marie, his lead bartender, some temporary Christmas staff, and the kitchen staff who'd had to step up to cover Jago's absence. He could feel them staring at him, willing him to appease Stan. The silence stretched out, but Alex bit down his anger. "There was no tone, and I apologise if there seemed to be. The courtyard will be swept clean, and everything will be perfect on the day."

"Excellent." Stan nodded, an odd expression crossing his face. "I appreciate your hard work. However, I must move on. There are plenty more places to see." He lingered a moment, looking apologetic. For a second, he looked confused as his eyes met Alex's, and inexplicably Alex felt a kind of kinship with him. A knowing that went beyond a casual friendship. But then it passed, and Stan swept out of the pub.

A collective sigh ran through the entire staff once the door had banged shut, but Simon rounded on Alex. "You can't help yourself, can you? Just be civil to him!"

"I was civil, but come on. Asking if the courtyard will be swept on the day? Of course it bloody will be. I'm not an idiot!"

"And that is just the sort of tone that will lose you the pub."

Marie swiftly herded the other staff out of the way, leaving Alex and his manager glaring at each other. "I will not lose the pub, I can guarantee you that, and you do not have to fear for your job. I know when to play nice, Simon, and you've worked for me long enough to know that."

"Perhaps that time might be drawing to a close."

Alex stepped closer to him. He and Simon had never been close, but he was good at his job, and the staff liked him. Unfortunately, lately, Simon seemed more wary around him than usual, and it made Alex uneasy. "What's wrong? You know that working anywhere else in this town will be just as hard. The queen's eyes are everywhere."

"I was thinking somewhere other than White Haven."

The thought had never struck Alex before, and it sounded preposterous. *Outside White Haven?* He struggled to think of a place, and for a moment, city names flashed in his head and quickly vanished again. He couldn't think of a single worthwhile place to go. "Where?"

"I..." Simon faltered, face wrinkling with confusion. "I don't know. It was just an idea I had."

"Well, it was a stupid one, more stupid than my *tone*. Beyond White Haven is a vast, white tundra. You know that! There is nowhere else. Only the queen and this place can keep us safe from the wolves that circle us. Only our friendships can keep us safe from the queen."

Newton was on his way from the crime scene in Bude to another case in Polperro, thinking wistfully of his own bed, when Reuben phoned.

"Thank the Gods!" Reuben exclaimed before he could even answer. "You're okay!"

"Of course, I'm okay, you bloody idiot. Well, apart from a crushing hangover. Please stop shouting."

"So you're not in White Haven?"

"No. I'm on the road with Moore. Why?"

"You didn't wake up to anything strange?"

"I woke up to a pink teddy bear covered in my drool that was trying to suffocate me with affection. You should wash it," he added in an aside to Moore, who was driving. His headache was threatening to return. "Are you drunk, Reuben?"

"No. Are *you*? Why are you talking about pink teddy bears?"

"It was our work Christmas party last night and I slept at Moore's house, in his daughter's bedroom. Can we discuss this later? I have the mother of all hangovers, and I'm on the way to another crime scene. I was going to call you later about the first one I was at, actually."

"What kind of crime scene?"

"Is this a bloody inquisition?" And then, through his pounding headache that he thought was going but was now returning with a vengeance, he caught Reuben's panicked tone. "Is something wrong?"

"Yes! White Haven has vanished!"

Newton kneaded his temple. "I'm putting you on speaker phone. Go on."

"The whole place is surrounded by a thick wall of swirling snow."

Newton looked at Moore, and then through the windscreen. "It's snowing, Reuben. You have heard of snow, right?"

"No! You don't understand. A thick, impenetrable wall of snow and cloud. I can't get into the town. No one can! Not me, not Shadow, and not the Nephilim."

"Are you serious?"

"Yes! How soon can you get to the farmhouse?"

Newton was convinced that Reuben was setting up a practical joke. It sounded ridiculous. However, he decided to humour him, despite his incredulity. "I have a crime scene to visit in Polperro, and then I'll be with you. In the meantime, don't call me again. And make sure there's plenty of coffee and a bacon sandwich waiting—for both of us.

We'll be there at lunch. Why don't you call Kendall, in the meantime? She's in Harecombe, and should be able to get to you quickly." *For your bloody joke*, he mentally added, and rolled his eyes at Moore.

Reuben continued, unperturbed. "Okay. And I'll call Ghost OPS in, too."

"Bloody white wall of snow," Newton grumbled to Moore as he ended the call. "Look at it! It's a bloody blizzard. Honestly..."

Moore concentrated on driving, hunched forward over the wheel, progressing slowly. "We're going to investigate another death. What if he isn't joking?"

"You really think White Haven is locked behind snow?"

"Weirder things have happened."

"Not *this* weird!" He closed his eyes, unwilling to discuss it anymore, and he knew the journey would take a while. "Wake me up when we're there. With luck, I might feel better."

Ben scribbled notes as he took another call, listening patiently to a worried parent on the other end of the line. He reassured her as best as he could before ending the conversation, after promising to investigate.

"You know," he said, as he put the phone down and swivelled his chair to look at Dylan, "that's the third call this morning about the same damn thing."

"Kids seeing Jack Frost?" Dylan laughed. "Look at the weather! There's a full-blown arctic blizzard out there. We have central heating, and still our windows are icing up. It's a miracle we haven't lost power yet! I can't believe you sent Cassie out to the old guy's place."

"She wanted to go!"

Dylan turned away from the computer screen to face Ben. "We should have stopped her. I'm worried she'll get stuck. Or one of us should have gone with her, at least."

"She went prepared. Besides, it wasn't this heavy earlier."

"She'll get stuck on those back lanes. Maybe we should head out now and find her."

"So then we all get stuck? I don't think so." Ben checked his watch. "Besides, she already texted to say she's on her way back. She won't be too long now. How do we explain an old man seeing Jack Frost though, as opposed to a kid?"

"Senility."

Ben huffed, exasperated. "Why are you being so cynical? This could be a thing."

"It's a fairy story."

"You like fairy stories and myths, it's *your* thing."

"Yes, I do, but this is a *child's* story."

"But the story could have its roots in an actual creature." Ben headed to the kettle on the counter to make coffee. "After my experience last month, I'm unwilling to discount anything. You shouldn't, either. We have been trained to keep an open mind."

"Sorry, you're right. But say it is Jack Frost who's running around causing mayhem and scaring kids by leering in their windows like some peeping Tom. How do we detect him? In this weather, trying to detect anything will be impossible. What even is he?"

"I guess he's a type of fey creature. Like a piskie. Or an imp." Ben grinned. "I used to read the Rupert Bear stories when I was a kid. He was in those."

Dylan had been cataloguing videos, one earphone still clamped to his ear, while the other one was shoved on his head, but now he pulled them off and swung his feet up on the desk. "That has potential, as a theory. I can look at the myths behind the story, and I'll chat to Dan about what he knows. But why is it *here*? Cornwall is not normally known for its blizzards, nor in fact England as a whole. Is he here just to make mischief?"

"That is what he's known for. Or perhaps he is carried by weather patterns. Maybe he has no choice as to where he goes?"

Dylan sniggered. "I can't even believe we're having this conversation. We'll be talking about Santa on his bloody sleigh next."

Ben's eyes widened. "What if they're connected?"

"Can we deal with one thing at a time, please? I think your experience over Samhain has addled your brain."

"I travelled back in time! It was seriously odd."

Ben still dreamt of it. It was like PTSD. He woke up in cold sweats, the animalistic chants of the ancestors running through his head, memories of wolves snapping at his throat, and the feel of the wizard's hands clutching his head. Cassie had studied his brainwaves weekly. It was disturbing to find himself the subject of an investigation. Fortunately, his brain was working just fine.

Dylan watched him, looking deadly serious all of a sudden. "Are you still having nightmares?"

"Yes, but they're less often now." He handed Dylan a mug of coffee and returned to his desk with his own. "You know, I felt like I dealt with it quite well at the time. I guess survival mode kicked in."

"That makes sense. But your brain needs to keep processing it now that you're back. I mean, your reality was completely upended. I can't imagine what it must have been like. How's Stan doing?"

Stan, White Haven's pseudo-Druid and a council member, had travelled back in time, too. "I haven't spoken to him for a few days. He's been busy with the Yule celebrations, but he was okay. I think he's actually dealing with it better than I am." Ben laughed. "He's so excited to know there's real magic and witches in White Haven, I think it's eclipsed everything else. I'll call him later." Ben hoped that neither he nor Stan were having a delayed reaction that would lead to an outburst of weird behaviour. He liked Stan, and had developed a new respect for him after their experience together.

"Why don't you call him now, and I'll call Dan?" Dylan suggested as he reached for his phone.

However, neither answered their calls, and Ben sighed. "No time like the present. Let's research Jack Frost now."

*The house was horribly loud*, Zee reflected, *now that all of his brothers and Shadow were at home for Yule.*

They were gathered in the lounge with Reuben, the games console abandoned, and a Christmas film playing on the TV at a low volume. Everyone's voices were raised as several conversations were taking place at the same time. All of them were about the white wall of *something* that surrounded White Haven. Far from having the restful Christmas that they had all wanted, it seemed they had something else to deal with now.

"Can you all stop shouting?" Zee yelled, trying to be heard above the cacophony. "You're giving me a headache!" One by one, they fell silent, looking at him expectantly. "Thank you. Now, can we please decide what we should do first?"

"Isn't that exactly what we were doing?" Shadow asked sarcastically.

Zee resisted the urge to throw something at her. "In just one conversation, please. There must be a way to get in. Maybe we should call
Caspian and see if he can fly in?"

"That is a brilliant idea," Reuben said, jabbing a finger at him.

"Actually, it's terrible," Eli countered. "He would have no idea
what he was flying into. It could kill him. Has anyone called him?"

"It's next on my list," Reuben told him.

"I suggest one of us do it now. For all we know, he's planning to do
exactly that after being away for a few days with us."

"I'll do it," Gabe volunteered, and headed into the kitchen.

Zee perched on the arm of the sofa, eyeing Eli with unease. Both
of them worked in White Haven, and had been planning to head in
later. Eli had taken half a day's leave, and Zee was scheduled on the
afternoon shift. The wall had thrown their plans into disarray. "We
have magic, surely we can get through this wall-thing. Can't you create
a gateway, Reuben?"

Reuben scratched his head. "I honestly have no idea. It's something
I've never tried before! I don't even know how to go about doing it."

"Can your familiar help?" Niel asked. He was sprawled in front of
the fire, prodding at the logs occasionally.

"No, he's as confused and worried as I am. He can normally speak
to the other familiars in whatever weird way they have, but he can't
reach *them*, either. This is powerful magic!"

"What if one of your witches," Ash suggested, "or all of them, in
fact, raised the wall themselves? Perhaps they thought they needed to
keep something out?"

"No way! I would be involved!" Reuben exclaimed. "They
wouldn't shut me out."

Eli shrugged. "Just a suggestion. Why don't we see if we can fly in, or over it? We wouldn't even need to wait until tonight. No one will see us in that!" He pointed at the snow.

Zee volunteered immediately. "I'll go. I'm really worried about them."

"We all are," Barak countered. "It would also be a way to see how far the bad weather reaches. This could be localized snow, related to whatever's happened in White Haven."

"It's not," Eli said immediately. "It's being reported all over the news. The entire country is affected, particularly Cornwall."

Niel turned to Reuben. "Did Newton say anything about the crimes he was investigating?"

"No, other than he needed to speak to us about it. Apparently, Kendall is in Harecombe, but I haven't called her yet, and I don't know why she's there."

"Well, it has to be paranormal, or they wouldn't be dealing with it at all." He paused, thoughtful. "Your business employs locals, right? Is anyone there today who lives in White Haven? I mean, I'm wondering if people can get out but can't get in."

Reuben shook his head. "I've checked. No one is in from White Haven. Only the two guys who live in Mevagissey are there. I've sent them home, actually, because of the weather. The way this is falling, we're all going to be blocked in, and the lanes will be impassable."

"What about Beth?" Nahum asked. "Briar's young niece. She's a Seer. Has she predicted anything?"

"Bollocks!" Reuben exclaimed. "I meant to call Tamsyn. I'll do it now."

Like Gabe, he left the room to phone her, and Zee stood up. He felt restless, and the house was getting stuffy. "I'm going to fly now, before the snow stops. Anyone want to come?"

"I will," Eli said immediately, already rising to his feet.

"Why don't we all go?" Niel suggested, looking pleased despite the situation. "It will be good to fly in daylight for once, even in a blizzard."

Zee laughed. "I thought you would have had enough of that after France?"

"Hopefully I won't be avoiding weapon fire, this time," he pointed out. "But I have a feeling that the wall will cover the entire place. Like a bubble. Why leave a way in?"

Gabe returned then. "I've updated Caspian. He'll come over later, when Newton arrives—using witch-flight."

"Good. In the meantime, we're going flying, brother." Niel told him the plan. "Want to come?"

"Of course. We're taking weapons, right?"

"It would be stupid not to. And you better take me too," Shadow said, standing and stretching in anticipation.

Gabe shook his head. "In this weather? You'll freeze! Stay here and keep Reuben company."

Shadow scowled, and was clearly about to start complaining when Reuben walked in, perplexed. "Surprisingly, Beth is fine. I know that's good news, but I didn't expect it. I'd still like to see her, so I'm going over there."

Eli looked torn with indecision as he stood in the doorway. As an apothecary, he had a deep understanding of herbs and their magical properties, and Briar had taught him a few simple healing spells. "Do you want me to come, too? We were all going flying over White Haven, but..."

Reuben's car keys were already in his hand and he was halfway out of the door. "No, it's fine. You fly with your brothers. I'll go alone. I want to make sure Tamsyn's okay anyway, in this weather. That house still needs work, and I hate to think they might be freezing in there. I'll be back later, hopefully..."

Shadow was on his heels. "Then I'll come with you, seeing as Gabe has abandoned me."

"Shadow!" Gabe remonstrated.

She flashed him the bird, and sashayed out the door, hips swinging.

Niel sniggered. "You'll pay for that later, brother."

Detective Sergeant Abbie Kendall pulled up her coat collar, adjusted her scarf, and wondered why anyone would call her in about *this*.

"They're just ice sculptures, Ms Brown. I'm not sure why you think there's anything unsavoury about them." She shuffled her feet in an effort to keep warm. "I mean, they're enormous, and I appreciate that their sudden appearance is odd..."

"But that's exactly it! Where have they come from?"

"Perhaps this is someone's idea of a practical joke?"

"But it's not normal!"

"Ice sculptures are very normal."

"Not when they appear in a matter of hours! The council certainly hasn't sanctioned these."

Kendall took a deep breath, willing herself to be patient. Ms Honoré Brown was the Arts Councillor for Harecombe, the town next to White Haven. She was in her fifties, Kendall estimated, with a sharp, honey blonde bob that was currently covered by a large felt hat with a brim. She was well dressed, her wool coat cut to perfection. Kendall imagined that very few people ever tangled with her, because she had an air about her that was intimidating. Consequently, she was outraged about the fact that overnight, half a dozen very large ice sculptures had appeared across the town. They studied two of them that marked the entrance to the harbour next to the road. Kendall quite liked them. She would have liked them even more if she could admire them from inside a warm café.

"Maybe it's a gift by a grateful citizen," Kendall suggested.

Ms Brown—Kendall didn't dare call her Honoré, she looked far too superior for that—harrumphed in an unladylike manner. "Perhaps, but they really should have asked."

"Is there any damage anywhere?"

"No, but that's not the point. I would still like to know who's behind it."

"Has anyone reported hearing anything? Any rumbling engines in the middle of the night? I mean, a lorry or van must have delivered them. Or any other disturbances?"

She shook her head, but her severe bob didn't move. It was clearly hair-sprayed into submission, but it wouldn't be if they stood outside for much longer. "I wouldn't mind so much if the subject manner wasn't so...questionable."

"But there's nothing sexual about them."

"I know that! But they're odd. Mystical. *Weird*."

Kendall subdued a smirk. Ms Brown would not be pleased to hear there was a coven of witches living in Harecombe. However, she had to concede that she was right about the subject matter. The sculptures were of a centaur, satyr, castle, tower, mermaid, and a very impressive one of a woman wearing a crown who sat on an enormous throne. They were incredibly detailed, and flawless.

"Okay, Ms Brown, here's what I'll do. I'll access the footage from your security cameras, but to be honest, even if we see someone, it's unlikely we'll see their details in this weather. The snow has been falling since midnight."

"And that's the other thing. It hasn't been this cold for that long. Where have they been stored?"

"A huge freezer, perhaps?" Kendall had been prepared to laugh it off, but the more she thought through the details, the more uneasy she became. It did seem unlikely that a mere mortal could have done this overnight. A team of men, perhaps, but then someone would have surely seen or heard something. *Unless this was Caspian's idea of a joke.* That seemed unlikely, especially as she had found out he had only recently arrived back from France.

"Ms Brown, thank you for calling us. I will investigate it. As soon as I know something, I'll call you. I suggest you now go home, keep warm, and leave the rest to me."

She looked as if she might complain, but instead she nodded, muttered her thanks, and marched across the road to her huge, four-by-four vehicle.

Kendall shivered and decided to find a café to warm up in, but she had barely taken half a dozen steps when a shout made her stop and turn.

"Over here, Kendall!"

Through the flurry of snow, she saw a huge building edging the wharf, and a man standing at an open door. "Caspian?"

"Come on in, before you freeze!"

"I think it's too late for that!" She hurried across the road and through the glass door, entering a large, spacious foyer. The warmth of central heating enveloped her as Caspian shut the door and faced her with a smile. Kendall didn't know Caspian well, although of course she had met him and knew he was a good friend of the White Haven Witches, and a powerful witch in his own right.

He was tall, and good-looking in a mature sort of way. His dark hair was sprinkled with grey, and he had deep blue eyes edged with lines. He always seemed severe, but his smile dispelled that. He certainly looked good in a suit.

"I see *Ms* Brown has been nagging you. I presume it's about the ice sculptures." He emphasised the "Ms" with a twinkle in his eye.

"Of course. There's devilry afoot."

His eyes darkened with worry. "I don't know about devilry, but something is. Have you got time for a coffee?" He nodded his head upwards. "We can chat in my office."

"Sounds wonderful."

Five minutes later, with her coat off and a coffee in hand, they stood in Caspian's corner office overlooking the harbour.

"This is quite the view!" she told him. "And it's a beautiful office!"

"It was my father's. I moved into it after he died last year. I've redecorated it since then, modernised it. Tried to erase his presence."

She hesitated, surprised at his admission. "That bad?"

His lips tightened. "Worse, but you don't need to hear that. We need to talk about the ice sculptures and whether they are connected to what's happening in White Haven."

"White Haven? What's wrong there?"

He looked surprised. "You haven't heard?"

"No! I've been stuck listening to that woman wittering about ice sculptures. Is everyone all right there?"

"Hard to say, considering what's happened. I'll update you, and then we'll decide what to do about those." He nodded at the sculptures below. "Unfortunately, I think they're part of a much larger problem."

# Four

Reuben watched Beth playing in the snow with her brother, Max, and her mother, Rosa, and didn't know whether to be pleased or disappointed. "So, she's okay? No weird visions or anything?"

"None at all." Tamsyn looked up at him, her beetle-dark eyes flashing with intelligence. "You seem disappointed!"

Reuben huffed. "I'm pleased, obviously, but under the circumstances, I thought she might be experiencing something. What about you? Have you had any premonitions?"

"Nothing either, sorry."

He, Shadow, and Tamsyn, were in Tamsyn's kitchen that overlooked the wild garden at the rear of Stormcrossed Manor. He had explained about the mysterious white wall around White Haven, trying not to alarm Tamsyn in the process. He didn't know why he was worrying, though. She was as tough as old boots. It was Rosa, Briar's cousin, who had delicate sensibilities.

Tamsyn turned her back on the scene to head to the kitchen counter. She picked up a plate of warm biscuits, their scent filling the kitchen with cinnamon and shortbread. She held out the plate to both of them. "Biscuit?"

"Thought you'd never ask," Shadow said, beating Reuben to the plate first.

Shadow's presence seemed to fill the small kitchen, as she didn't bother to hide her fey energy and appearance in front of either of them. It was something she was doing more and more lately, Reuben noticed. Amongst friends, at least. It was unnerving. She glowed with Otherworldliness. Her hair shimmered, and her violet eyes were even more striking. She was lithe and graceful, and even though Reuben didn't fancy her in the slightest, his eyes were drawn to her. He wondered if he said anything, would she threaten him with her dagger? He knew she wouldn't actually use it on him...or would she?

Tamsyn obviously saw it, too, and decided to address it in her usual, forthright way. "Young lady, you need to reel it in. Your energy is disturbing my thinking. And his."

"What am I doing?"

"Don't come that with me. You know exactly what you're doing. You're being fey." Tamsyn fixed her with a steely glare.

"I am fey." Shadow tossed her head, her hair cascading down her back.

"And you have powerful magic that is disturbing to us mere humans."

Shadow snorted. "Fine. It feels good to release it sometimes, that's all." Within seconds she had applied her glamour, and the kitchen seemed darker because of it.

"Thanks, Shadow." Reuben gave her an apologetic smile. "It really is disturbing. You're just...too much!"

"I think it's the wall. It's affecting me."

"Are you serious? How?"

She shrugged and sat in a chair at the table. "I can feel its magic. Ever since me and Gabe got close to it this morning, I feel that it's calling to me. It's weird." She broke off a piece of biscuit and licked her fingers.

"And of course, we're closer to the wall here than at the farmhouse. I can feel it even more."

Reuben shot Tamsyn a concerned look as they sat on either side of her. "You didn't mention it in the car."

"I was trying to ignore it. It felt better when I released my glamour."

"So, your magic is kindred?" Tamsyn suggested. "It calls to you."

"I think it does. But it's weird, because it feels nothing like Ravens' Wood. That place is full of Otherworld magic in places, and it's ancient. But the magic from the wall is just as old, but it's dark. Ravens' Wood is never dark."

Reuben almost choked on his biscuit. "You must be kidding. It's so creepy at night! It feels like anything might happen in there."

Shadow tucked her hair behind her ear. "That's just the fey Otherness you can feel, because it is so unlike the human world. The wall," she jabbed a finger towards White Haven, "is darker. In fact, the more I think about it, the more I think it wants my magic. No, maybe not *want*. Perhaps just recognises it. But if it does, why didn't it allow me in earlier?"

"Because it's like an animal," Tamsyn said without a trace of doubt. "It's watching and waiting, biding its time."

"You seem remarkably calm about this," Shadow pointed out, "considering that Briar is trapped in there."

"Me running around like a headless chicken will not stop what has happened. We need calm heads." She stared at Reuben. "That applies to you, too. You're worried about El and your friends, but we must focus."

"I know! Why do you think I'm sitting here instead of launching every spell I know at the place?" He took a deep breath, knowing that Tamsyn meant well. "I just wish we knew *something*. How can a giant wall just appear? Who's behind it? How long will it be there for? I mean, is this forever? Just for Yuletide?"

"Just for the winter?" Shadow countered.

Reuben's stream of questions that had been bubbling in his head for hours continued. "And why White Haven? What do they want? Why can we remember that it exists if we can't see it? Why hasn't it been wiped from our memories completely? More people will arrive over the coming days for the celebrations. What happens to them? Do they just forget? Turn around and go home?"

"Reuben!" Tamsyn held a hand up. "Enough. My head is spinning. Those are all excellent questions, but the most important ones are who's behind it, and what do they want? I think we all suspect the answer to the second question."

Reuben and Shadow answered together. "*Magic.*"

The morning had passed unbearably slowly for Avery. Happenstance Books had passed its inspection, and Stan had given her a wavering smile as he exited. He had seemed more tense than usual.

As the door clanged shut behind him, the bells once again jangled particularly loudly. A collection of dead leaves from the wreath hanging on the wall above the door fluttered to the floor, and stricken, Sally ran over to collect them. "This shouldn't be dead! How could any of us have missed it?"

But Avery and Dan had no answers, and thankful it hadn't been seen, the wreath was unceremoniously dumped in the bin.

Avery tried to shake her unease off as she returned to her flat to have lunch with Clea. Even that felt odd. Unusual, as if it was a new habit.

Except that she knew she did this every day. Clea lived with them. She cared for her aging grandmother with her faulty memories as best she could. Clea was sitting on the sofa, knitting, the cats seated on either side of her.

"Not watching the lunchtime news, Gran?" Avery asked.

"There's no picture. Must be the weather." She nodded at the window. "It's still thick. Getting heavier, I think."

"At least we're warm in here." That was an understatement. The fire was blazing, and the room was stuffy, and yet Clea still wore a thick cardigan over her dress. "Have you eaten yet?"

"No, my lovely. I've got some soup ready for both of us, though. You just need to switch the hob top on."

Avery left her to her knitting, put the saucepan on a ring at a low heat, and walked up the stairs to the attic space. Something was still niggling her. As she stood on the threshold looking at the pots of herbs, baskets of candles, and rows of books, she knew that she had forgotten something. *And why on Earth had she put four huge, old leather-bound books on the table?* She didn't remember seeing those that morning.

She pulled the top one towards her and turned the first few pages. The rich scent of old paper wafted over her, and her fingers tingled. But every single page was blank. Hurriedly, she checked the other books. They were the same. Four ancient, leather-bound books, and not a single word in any of them.

She drifted around the room, picking up items and putting them down again. Some things, like the grimoires, made her fingers tingle, including the candles and the gemstones in their pretty bowls. However, the room felt sad. A pile of incense sticks drew her attention, and she pulled one from the pack, thinking to light one. The room seemed to need it. But there wasn't a lighter or a box of matches anywhere. Not one. She couldn't light the candles or the incense, or the fire.

And there was the raven in the huge snow globe, still staring at her with its beady yellow eyes. "Stop it, you weird bird!" She picked up a scarf from the back of the chair and threw it over the globe. That was better, but she still couldn't shake her uneasiness. She was hungry, that was all. *Time to join her Gran for lunch.*

Gabe wasn't surprised to see banks of thick, white clouds and swirling snow below him, capping off the valley, and sitting barely higher than the fields around it. It was inevitable that whoever had trapped the town would seal it from all directions.

He had lost sight of his brothers in the driving snow, but he knew they were close by. Despite his disappointment, he enjoyed flying in the daylight. It was exhilarating. He climbed higher, using the thermals to carry him, and then swooped down, the feather-light snowflakes caressing his skin like kisses. He dropped lower, always ensuring he kept a good distance between him and the wall. He didn't want to risk getting caught up in strange magic and being turned around unexpectedly. He cleared the boundary to fly over the sea, and saw a sheet of ice below him. It was so cold, even the sea had iced up for a few hundred metres beyond White Haven's coast.

A flash of golden wings caught his attention, and Ash glided alongside him. Ash had hurt his left shoulder only days before in Egypt. It had been injured so badly that his wing wouldn't unfurl. In circumstances that Gabe would rather forget, Ash had been forced to use Belial's jewellery to save his life when he was plunging to his death in a similar snowstorm only a few nights before. It had made his wings change colour. Instead of the range of browns that they were before, the feathers were now all shades of a golden sunset.

"How are your wings feeling, Ash?"

"As good as new. Stronger, actually. But they are a little bright." He twisted to look at them, half amused, half worried.

Gabe studied the huge sweep of his glittering wings. "They stand out in the snow, but it might give you an advantage in sunlight. You might actually get away with daylight flight."

Ash laughed. "I think I'll save that as a last resort. But now we have more pressing concerns. White Haven is impregnable."

Gabe pointed to the icesheet below. "It's far too cold. These are arctic conditions. It's abnormal. Look how far the sea ice stretches. And are those patterns within it?"

Both dropped lower for a better view, and Gabe groaned. "Fish. Hundreds of them, trapped inside the ice. That's horrible."

"But inevitable, I suppose." Ash pointed to another section of ice. "There's something sticking up over there. Odd shapes that look like ..." He trailed off, his voice lost in the howl of the wind as he dropped even lower.

Gabe followed, and they landed on the ice carefully, wings still outstretched in case they needed a quick escape. But they needn't have worried. It was thick enough to take their weight. Up close they could see that sea creatures had been carved from the ice. Giant whales, leaping dolphins, mermaids, narwhals, and a huge octopus.

"Wow." Gabe huffed, his breath billowing like steam. "This is weird."

Ash didn't speak, instead weaving his way through the ice sculptures until he stood in front of the largest one of a woman twice their height, her skirts whirling around her ankles. She had an imperious glare that seemed to follow them wherever they walked.

"Gabe, I think we're looking at who's behind all this."

"Is she a witch?"

"I don't know, but I think it's time we found out."

Dylan finished cleaning the whiteboard in their office and placed the titles *Jack Frost* and *Big White Wall of Doom* in the centre of it. Reuben had recently called, updating them on what had appeared around White Haven. The news had added an extra level of urgency to their work.

"Let's brainstorm."

"That's a bit old-fashioned for you, isn't it?" Cassie said, through a mouthful of biscuit. "I thought you'd be working on spreadsheets and things!"

"To be honest, I'm sick of staring at the computer screen, and debating the merits of a fairy story seems like fun."

"Does the Wall of Doom sound like fun?" Cassie asked sarcastically. "Because our friends are trapped behind it! Besides, you wouldn't say that if you'd seen the dead fox." Cassie shuddered as she took a seat in their lounge area, propping her feet up on another chair. She'd taken off her sodden boots to reveal bright red socks with reindeer on them, peeking out from beneath her jeans. "That was horrible. I love foxes. They're so beautiful, and this one was glassy-eyed and...horrible."

"Sorry, Cas." Dylan felt terrible for making light of it. "Makes you wonder though what other creatures could be frozen under all that snow. Hedgerows shelter so many of them."

"I'm hoping that they're all safely in their burrows! Like I should be."

Ben had been seated at his desk, rummaging through notes, but he moved to sit next to Cassie and faced the whiteboard. "You'll be stuck here tonight, I reckon. Surely you're not risking driving in this?"

"No. I'll sleep on the sofa if I have to. *Again.*" She'd slept over once before when a huge thunderstorm hit the coast.

Ben rolled his eyes. "Have my bed. I'll even change the sheets! I'm not feral."

Her eyes slid to his desk where a mound of papers and coffee cups were piled. "You're almost there. You two live like pigs."

Dylan had to agree with her, but thought he should look outraged anyway. "How dare you. I wash and shower."

"Do you know what a vacuum is? I have to clean this office. God knows what state your bedrooms are in."

"Can we move on?" Ben said, glaring at her. "Although, I would like to say that since my experience of going back in time, I have a newfound appreciation for all things modern. My room is clean! And I wash up regularly."

"That must happen when I'm not here, then!"

"I think," Ben said pointedly, "that we have bigger things to worry about, like giant walls that have trapped our friends!"

"Children, please!" Dylan tapped the board. "Focus. Let's start with Jack Frost. Tell me what we know!"

Ben referred to his notes. "Well, he has various personas, depending on what culture you reference. He is known in some places as Old Man Winter, others refer to him as a giant, while still more call him an imp. Others think he's more teenaged, while some cultures refer to him as a trickster. Whatever he is, everyone thinks he makes mischief.

Unless, of course, you look at Hollywood. They sometimes portray him as fun, but we should discount that."

"Great," Cassie groaned.

"It's par for the course," Ben said, not looking the least bit put off. "We're paranormal detectives. We'll figure it out. Maybe he changes, depending on the culture. If he's a trickster, he can do that. He's very big in Scandinavian countries—not surprisingly. According to my research, he originated in Norway. He's believed to be immortal and forever young. In Norse mythology, they call him *Jokul Frosti*."

"Not Old Man Winter, then?" Dylan said, scribbling furiously. He listed the names on the upper half of the board, arrows shooting from the centre.

"Well, he's essentially a nature spirit. Russians call him Grandfather Frost. In general, though, he's seen as trouble, with darkness at his core."

"And a murderer," Cassie added. "He killed the fox just because he could."

Dylan wagged his pen. "*If* we believe what the old man saw. How reliable was he?"

"Reliable enough. He certainly wasn't senile, just old."

"Did he give you a description?"

"He said he was skipping along the hedgerows, like a sprite. Described him as skinny, wearing white clothes, with white skin. He did admit that the snow was falling very heavily, and it was dark, so his view wasn't clear."

Dylan nodded, jotting the description at the side of the board. "Sounds like many descriptions in fairy stories. Angular. What about your calls, Ben?"

"Similar, though I was told bluish skin, high cheekbones, and piercing eyes. Although," he rummaged through his notes, "a couple of other reports said he was athletic. Handsome. Well dressed."

"Interesting," Dylan said. "That definitely suggests he's a trickster, if people are seeing different things."

"Or there's more than one of them," Cassie suggested.

"But if it's the same creature, he's quick," Ben added. "He must be able to flit about magically!"

"That would make sense," Dylan said, making another note. "Sounds like he covered a lot of ground last night. Is it like witch-flight, do you think? Can he just manifest anywhere?"

"Perhaps." Cassie reached for another biscuit. "Shadow says piskies just pop in and out of vision all the time—except that we don't normally see them."

Dylan tapped his lip with his pen. "Okay, that would make him hard to fight. Did you get any readings on him?"

"No. No heat signatures—not surprising—no energy vibrations, zero evidence that he'd been there at all."

"Any area in particular that you can narrow down from your calls, Ben?"

"A few spots along the south coast, a couple from the north, too." He stood and walked to the map pinned further down the wall, and jabbed his finger in a few places.

Dylan huffed. "Damn it. I was hoping there was a place we could focus our efforts on. It seems he's all over the place, though. Makes sense if you want to cause as much chaos as possible. I guess that brings us to the Wall of Doom. He must be connected to that."

"Has to be," Ben agreed. "But according to Reuben, no one can pass through it. That suggests no one can get out."

"Maybe our friend, Jack, can," Cassie suggested, "with his special magic."

"Do you think he made the wall?" Dylan asked. "I mean, it's possible, right?"

Ben sat down again. "Anything's possible, but I somehow don't think he'd have enough power. Perhaps he's working with another spirit. We really need to get to White Haven and study that wall. But..."

All three turned to the windows. Snow still fell heavily. It was impossible to see further than a few feet.

"The roads will be impassable," Cassie pointed out. "They were bad enough when I got back an hour ago. We're not even that close to White Haven. We'll have to wait until it's clear."

"Which means we hit the books again in the meantime," Dylan said. "But I'll tell Reuben what we think so far."

# Five

B riar walked down the street into the town centre at the end of the working day, heading to Alex's pub. It was dark, and the lights festooned across the street provided a festive glow through the falling snow. Fortunately, it wasn't falling as thickly anymore, but underfoot it was deep, the surface already crisping with ice as the temperature fell further.

The lights that hung from the lampposts were giant snowflakes and reindeer, and the sound of bells drew louder as she approached the square. As she rounded the corner, she couldn't help but smile. Dozens of reindeer were gathered around the Christmas tree, bells jangling around their necks, their animal scent pungent. Lined up along the street were a variety of sleighs for any groups from two people up to ten.

*How could she have forgotten?* The fayre always heralded the reindeer. The town folk would be bundled up in sleighs to be taken to the castle. Attendance wasn't obligatory, but it was encouraged. Games were organised, and carol singers and a brass band performed there, too. Briar checked her watch. Another couple of hours yet until they had to be there. Plenty of time to eat beforehand.

She skirted the queen's ice sculpture on the edge of the square, aware of pressure between her shoulder blades as if from an unseen observer, until she passed out of view. With relief, she entered the pub and headed to the bar. The place was busy, the tables packed with Yuletide revellers, and Briar gratefully slid onto a vacant barstool and picked up the mulled cider that Marie placed ready for her.

"Your friends are already in the back room at the reserved table. Alex will be with you soon." Marie looked her usual self, chirpy and teasing as she moved away to serve another customer. Her presence was reassuring. Normal. It was strangely comforting.

But when she joined El and Avery, the uneasy feeling that had stalked her all day returned. Avery stirred her mulled wine with a stick of cinnamon while she talked to El, who was sipping her beer. She broke off to greet her. "Briar! We were just talking about going to the fayre. You are coming, aren't you?"

"Of course." She removed her scarf and gloves, and then eased out of her coat before sitting down. "I take it your inspections went well?"

El shrugged and rolled her eyes. "I have been told to make sure to clean the smudges from my windows. I can't help it if my customers goggle at my beautiful jewellery."

Avery glanced around nervously. "Keep your voice down, El. You don't know who's listening."

"Spies, you mean?" El huffed but lowered her voice anyway. "I feel all at odds today. Nothing feels right."

Briar leaned forward, hands gripping her mulled cider. "I know what you mean. I feel that something is missing. Something fundamental! Maybe it's just because I'm tired. I've been so busy today that my feet throb, and my head aches. I don't know why I have so many herbs in my backroom. I know I need them for the shop, but the scent is so overpowering!"

"I feel exactly the same!" Avery whispered. "I have an attic full of weird stuff, and having Clea around seems odd."

"She's your grandmother!" El pointed out. "It shouldn't feel *that* odd. But I know what you mean. I sort of feel lonely."

Briar looked at El, suddenly struck by her earlier statement about spies. It seemed crazy, and yet, as she looked around the crowded pub at the laughing customers, she was aware of an underlying tension, as if everyone was trying a little too hard. Eyes darted nervously around the room, and then slid back to their own group. She had known many of these people for years, and yet, they seemed like strangers.

The words were out of her mouth before she could stop them. "I feel like I'm dreaming. No, like I'm in a nightmare. Everything feels wrong."

El took a sharp intake of breath. "Don't let anyone hear you say that! The queen's guard will have you up in front of her before you can blink. You know she will not tolerate any criticism."

"The queen?" Briar sat back, wondering if this is what she'd been missing all day. *Of course, The Queen.* Their imperious majesty who ruled over them from the castle on the hill. She'd passed some of her guards on the walk to the pub. *But why had she only just remembered her?* She had just walked by her ice sculpture in the square, and knew half of the town's artisan workers were at the castle preparing the great Solstice Feast.

With shaking hands, Briar sipped her drink. She was stressed and tired, that was all. She needed a good night's sleep. "I think I'll skip dinner and go home. I've just realised that I'm really tired."

"You'll do no such thing!" El's hand snaked out and gripped Briar's arm, pinning her to the chair. "You must go to the fayre. It will look strange if you miss it."

"El! What's got into you? I can miss it. It's encouraged, not manda-tory. It's not like we have to sign in when we go!"

"Outliers get spotted. It's best not to stand out, Briar. What's got into *you*, today?"

"I don't know. Maybe I've got the flu." Briar shook El's hand away, suddenly scared. Her friend had an intensity about her that seemed at odds with Briar's memory of her—*if she could trust her memory*. "I can't be here anymore. I'm going."

"Please don't," Avery pleaded.

"Stop worrying. I'll see you tomorrow."

Briar couldn't bear another second in the pub. She felt sick. Hot. Confused. Everything was wrong. Before either of them could utter another word, she grabbed her belongings and fled the pub. But once outside, she faltered.

The wind buffeted down the lane leading to the harbour, the snow swirled, and for the briefest moment, she saw a huge castle on the hill, its spires lost in low cloud, its many levels tiered like a wedding cake. It was like a palace in a fairy story. Her breath caught in her chest. It was white and looked to be made entirely of ice. Lights gleamed from windows, but they weren't welcoming. Instead, it looked forbidding.

But in seconds, the snow fell like a curtain again, and it vanished from view.

Briar looked around her. No one else seemed to have noticed, and if they did, no one cared. Keeping her head down, and her scarf pulled up, she hurried down the narrow street, feeling paranoid that everyone was watching her, despite the crowd's jovial conversations and shouts of laughter. She wanted to be home, but she knew she had so much work to do to be ready for tomorrow. Someone from the castle would be coming to collect a selection of candles, and she needed to make sure that they were perfect.

However, the streets were more and more crowded, and as she neared the square, the sound of the reindeers' jingling bells grew louder. Hawkers called out their wares, mostly roasted chestnuts and mulled wines. She would have preferred to avoid the central space, but the narrow lanes leading off it were also busy, and some shops were still open. Cafés and restaurants were full, and she found herself funnelled into the square, regardless. She tried to keep to the edges, avoiding the queen's sculpture.

Until she felt like a coward. *What was she afraid of? It was just a sculpture.*

Briar halted by a man selling chestnuts and bought herself a bag, their heat warming her gloved hands. She casually leaned against the wall behind his stand to study the statue. It was huge, and skilfully made. The queen sat on an imposing throne; icicles formed the back and arms of the chair, their sharp points pricking the night. A huge crown, tall and spikey, was perched regally on her head, but her dress was lush, swirling out from her tiny waist, full skirts billowing at her feet. Caught in the hem were tiny creatures—hedgehogs, squirrels, stoats, imps, and gnomes. They peeked out as if afraid to show their faces. It was charming and whimsical, and yet the queen's face showed no charm at all. She was imperious, superior, her expression as icy as her statue. And the eyes seemed alive. As if she was actually watching everyone...

Briar shuddered and decided to return to her shop, but as she pushed away from the wall, a man stood in front of her. She had to tip her head back to look up at him, her gaze sweeping up his long, lean body. He wore a suit, well cut in pale grey, a frockcoat made of grey, silky fur, the collar of which was angled up—more out of style than to protect his neck. When her gaze reached his face, she found very deep blue eyes staring down at her, set above high cheekbones and full lips, with a shock of white-blond hair rakishly styled. He was handsome in a too smooth kind of way. A smile spread across his face, and mischief danced in his eyes as he held his hand out and greeted her. "I don't believe we've met. I'm Jack."

Despite his tame demeanour, everything about him shouted danger, but Briar shook his hand, regardless. "I'm Briar. You're new in town?"

"Very." He leaned into her, and it took every ounce of Briar's determination not to step back. His eyes glittered. "I like it here, even more so now that I've met you."

"Well, aren't you charming?" Briar smiled, her heart beating so loudly that she thought he must be able to hear it. "I presume you're here for the solstice celebrations. Everyone loves Yule."

"Of course. I love winter, too. The colder the better."

"It will be cold for months now," she found herself saying, although she hadn't realised it until it was out of her mouth. "Until spring. The winters are long in White Haven."

"Excellent! As if it was made for me. May I accompany you to the fayre tonight?" He extended his arm and nodded at a waiting reindeer and two-person sleigh.

"I'm afraid not. I was going back to work, sorry."

"But the queen likes everyone to go, you know that. I know her, you know. We're old friends. I might even be able to introduce you to her." His arm was still extended, his eyes fixed on hers, and Briar wasn't sure whether it would be more dangerous to go with him or refuse. She decided it was the latter.

"Well, as long as we're only there for a couple of hours. I have candles to prepare for the palace, and they must be finished tonight." She slipped her arm into his. "It will be a pleasure."

"I assure you, the pleasure is all mine."

In seconds she found herself tucked up in the sleigh, Jack seated next to her, and furs pulled over their knees. With a crack of the whip and an encouraging shout from the driver, the reindeer trotted out of the square and up the hill to the castle.

When Newton and Moore finally arrived in the courtyard at the Nephilims' farmhouse, it was dark out, and hideously cold. So far, the roads were just about passable, but they wouldn't be for much longer.

The journey had taken much longer than it should have done, and although they had left the crime scene in the murky midafternoon light, it was now early evening. The trek had been so bad that they had barely spoken, both concentrating on the road. They had bought a spade and blankets in Polperro, which turned out to be a good decision. They had used the spade to dig themselves out of a couple of spots, but neither were prepared to give up and wait for the snow to stop. The way it was coming down, it could last for hours.

Newton sat for a moment in the darkness, watching the thick, swirling snow as he contemplated his next actions. "Moore, you should go home."

"I don't think I'll get home, Guv. My wife texted earlier saying it's terrible round by us. Besides, I think you need me. They're all safe and sound, so I'm not worried about them."

"We might end up sleeping on the floor," Newton pointed out, as the snow obliterated their tracks in seconds.

"I'd rather that than be stuck on a lane with one blanket and a murderer on the loose." He rubbed his chin, regretful. "I honestly didn't think it would get this bad."

"The snow or the deaths?"

"Both."

Newton sighed deeply and rolled his stiff neck. His muscles felt like concrete. "No, neither did I. I didn't anticipate having *two* suspicious deaths to investigate. Two remarkably similar deaths." A young woman had been found on a lane behind a pub in Polperro. Her body had been found next to the bins when a café owner who shared the same rubbish bins discovered her that afternoon. She was a young barmaid who'd supposedly been on her way home the night before. She lived alone, so no one had reported her missing.

"Perhaps the extreme weather is to blame, and we're just seeing weird stuff where there's none."

"Except that the victims are both young and fit as far as we know, and there's no reason the young woman would lie down in the snow for the night, not with her flat only a short walk away. You don't just die of the cold on a short walk home. And there was no sign of an attack otherwise."

Moore sighed. "I know. Just trying to offer other potential scenarios. And we can't ignore the supposed wall, either."

"Which we have yet to see." The route to the farmhouse had taken them past the road into White Haven, but the heavy snow had blocked the view, and they didn't want to take a detour. "At least Kendall confirms it. I just wish Reuben had been joking."

Moore nodded to where Kendall and Reuben's cars jostled up against Gabe's SUV and Nahum's estate car. The bikes must have been under cover. "It will be a full house."

Newton felt strangely reluctant to leave the warm comfort and relative silence of the car, but they couldn't sit there all night. "Come on. Let's join the party."

In the short time they were in the farmhouse, the cacophony of voices exacerbated Newton's headache.

Niel, the huge blond Nephilim who looked part Viking, ushered them down the hall to the kitchen. "Beer, hot toddies, mulled wine, or coffee? I am prepared for anything."

"May the Goddess smile upon you," Newton said with feeling, as he took in the vast array of drinks and snacks spread across the far counter. "A hot toddy. Large."

"Make that two," Moore added, shrugging off his coat and leaving it on the pile on one of the kitchen chairs, before pacing to the window. "We might need a bed, too, if this blizzard continues."

Niel grinned. "All in hand."

"You look a bit too chirpy to say that White Haven has vanished."

"We flew in the daylight today. It's been a long time since we did that, and despite the circumstances, we all enjoyed it. However," he sighed as he fixed their drinks, "there's no doubt that this is a huge issue."

Newton sat at the table, soaking in the warmth, still reluctant to join the melee in the lounge. "Before we get sucked into our current dilemma, tell me how it went in France. I take it everyone survived unscathed?"

Niel snorted. "I don't know if I'd say *unscathed*. There are changes. Ash has golden wings now. Belial's jewellery is all wrapped up in spells, Jackson had some horrible news, but the important thing is that we all survived. There's other news too, but that can wait." He looked amused.

"Fair enough."

"What about Black Cronos?" Moore asked, beating Newton to the question.

"Decimated—we hope. The count is dead. Although, there is still speculation about that..." Niel shrugged. "We're taking the win for now. Or rather, we were, until today..."

Newton had plenty of questions about Black Cronos, but he pushed them aside for now. "You saw the wall, too?"

"We all did. It encapsulates the town, from the bay to the very edge of the suburbs. Only the upper valleys on either side have been left out. Hence, we're okay, and Reuben and Stormcrossed Manor are unaffected, too."

"So, no doubt a few other cottages are also locked out." Newton tried to fathom what other consequences there might be, but he was so tired he could barely think straight. "It means my home is inside it. Who could have done this?"

Niel passed them their drinks, placed a bowl of crisps and dip on the table, and he and Moore joined Newton. "Well, there are some commonalities. Ice sculptures seem to be a thing. And Cassie found a fox that had been frozen mid-step. That's not normal."

"Ghost OPS are here?"

"No, they phoned us. They're stuck in Falmouth." He updated them about their reports, and what the Nephilim had seen on the iceshelf beyond White Haven's coast. He cleared his throat, looking embarrassed. "So, a name kept coming up in all of Ghost OPS's reports. You're not going to like it."

Newton exchanged a worried glance with Moore. "Go on."

"The theory is that Jack Frost is involved."

"You have to be fucking kidding me!"

"No." Niel leaned back in the chair, sipping his own drink. "What do you think all the debate is about in there?" He nodded to the lounge.

Newton exchanged an incredulous look with Moore. "Everyone is taking this seriously? It's a child's story!"

"That has its roots in myth. It seems that Jack Frost is a troublesome sprite in some cultures—that means he's fey. Shadow is pretty sure it's fey magic at play here."

"Kendall is buying this?"

"Oh yeah. She arrived with Caspian and Estelle. It's a full house. There are other theories, too."

"Better ones?" Moore asked, looking as shocked as Newton felt. Unfortunately, he looked excited too, and Newton thought that at any given moment he might start waxing lyrical about fey borderlands again.

"No, worse." The oven timer pinged, and Niel stood up. "Time to join the others with snacks. You guys can help me carry stuff through. Then you can hear the full range of madness."

# Six

Caspian had travelled to the Nephilim's farmhouse in Kendall's car, and Estelle had accompanied them.

Even though Estelle now spent little time at work as her responsibilities had been handed over to other staff, she still went in on occasion to deal with some tasks. When Barak told her about White Haven, she had gone to see Caspian and volunteered to help. A large part of Caspian presumed it was because she would be spending time with Barak anyway, but he also liked to think she wanted to help because of their better relationship.

Now they were crowded into the farmhouse's lounge, and if it wasn't for their current dilemma, it would have felt festive. The Christmas tree in the corner glittered with lights and decorations, more fairy lights hung around the walls, and a few presents were under the tree. It made him realise he really needed to decorate his own house for the season. He had already updated his altar for Yule with berries, pinecones, and winter flowers, but it wasn't enough. He was hosting his coven's celebrations, and he intended it to be a big affair, especially seeing as this was about reinvigorating his coven to make it work for everyone.

However, that was something he couldn't dwell on now. The room was full, and the conversation heated while they ate and drank. Newton and Moore had found seats among the Nephilim, who were spread across the room on the sofa, armchairs, and on the rug in front of the fire. Estelle was sitting by Barak, and Shadow sat cross-legged on the floor, close to Gabe, who sat in the armchair. Kendall looked at ease next to Zee, who she seemed to know well from the pub. And Reuben...well, he was brimming with anger, worry, and frustration as he chatted to Nahum. His missing coven and girlfriend had struck him deeply, and Caspian wished that there was more he could do to help. He caught Gabe's eye, exchanging a glance that said it was time to begin.

Gabe's authoritative voice made the various conversations halt. "Tone it down, everyone. Time to share information, and decide what we're doing next. Caspian and Kendall, do you want to start with what you've seen today? Or do you just want to start off with your theory, Caspian?" Gabe cocked an eyebrow at Caspian's admittedly slightly out-there theory.

He sighed. There were caveats to what he was going to say, but he'd stick with the basics first. "I may as well jump in at the deep end. I think the Snow Queen is behind all of this."

Newton snorted and Caspian winced, already feeling Newton's ire. It didn't help that Newton was tired, his home inaccessible, and that he was in the middle of investigating two deaths. Newton glared at the roomful of people, including his two sergeants. "First Jack Frost, and now the Snow Queen! Am I in the middle of some practical joke? Are you two in on this?"

Moore rolled his eyes, well used to Newton's outbursts. "Of course not. I've been with you all day!" He turned to Caspian, his deep voice calm and thoughtful. "What's your reasoning?"

Caspian looked to Kendall, thinking it might sound better coming from a police officer, but she gestured for him to continue. He sensed she did not wish to suffer Newton's wrath. "Well, as you know,

Kendall was investigating an issue in Harecombe. Multiple ice sculptures are there, all of which have appeared overnight. It's happened in a few places—Ghost OPS can confirm that. But the one common sculpture is of a queen—one in Harecombe, one on the sea ice off of White Haven's coast, and another two in small towns further down the coast. Ben took several calls about them today."

Silence fell, and Newton looked around the room before finally staring at Caspian again. "This is the base of your argument? Ice sculptures?"

"There's lots of corroborating evidence to support her presence." Caspian started ticking things off on his fingers. "For a start, there's the inexplicable wall around White Haven that is undoubtedly magical. The excessive blizzard conditions and subzero temperatures. Multiple ice sculptures that appeared overnight and have no rational explanation. Various sightings of a creature called Jack Frost. A fox frozen solid mid-step by a man who is believed to be Jack Frost. And your suspicious deaths, which I gather are unusual in nature."

Newton groaned. "Yes, unfortunately. Initially, we questioned whether they were weather-related. It's cold out—that doesn't have to mean it's paranormal. But the young woman in Polperro was on her way home from her restaurant job after closing. She lived only a short distance away. That just doesn't make sense at all. The surfer, also odd. He was virtually encased in a block of ice. And I can't ignore what Gray saw—one of your coven's witches."

Caspian's eyes widened with surprise. "You were in Bude?"

"Yes. She was with another coven member—a woman called Katya."

"Her cousin," Estelle said, nodding as she recognised the name. "She makes soaps and candles, like Briar."

"That's right," Newton agreed. "They were at the Bude Winter Fayre the night before, selling her stock. They had a weird experience when magic swept around the stalls, bringing a sudden, sharp dip in temperature. Gray was convinced there was a presence there. An ancient presence."

"But who was it?" Moore interjected. "Was it the Snow Queen or Jack Frost? And why do you think both of them are behind this, and not just one of them?"

Reuben had been unusually quiet up until then, not that it had quelled his appetite. As usual, he was steadily eating anything close to hand. Now, however, he leaned forward, eyes bright. "Because in some fairy stories they are linked, and to be honest, with sculptures of a queen everywhere, and Jack Frost sightings piling up, it seems logical they are together now. But they are powerful, magical beings, so I'm not sure what they want with White Haven."

"Magic," Shadow said, without hesitation. "White Haven has lots of it, you know that."

"But they have their own magic," Reuben persisted. "They have constructed an impenetrable wall around White Haven. To do that must mean they're strong enough, so why do they need more? Our magic certainly could not do what they have done. Not at that scale, or for the length of time."

"I haven't even seen it yet," Caspian said, "so I'm unable to comment, but I did sense magic around the sculptures—faintly, but it was there. I'll look at the wall as soon as it's practicable."

"Unfortunately, although this sounds horrible," Reuben continued with a frown, "Beth, Briar's niece, is fine. She doesn't seem to be experiencing any premonitions at all. Either her training with Alex to block them is working, or something else is at play. I was hoping she could give us some insight. Tamsyn isn't getting anything, either. But Shadow has a theory."

Shadow shrugged. "It's just what I feel. The wall feels like fey magic. It's different to the witches', and I think it recognises me. I hope if I get close again, it might let me in."

Gabe virtually growled. "Shadow! You are not going in alone! For a start, we don't even know what's beyond it. White Haven could be somewhere else—"

"You mean like it's been moved somehow?" Kendall gasped, incredulous. "That seems impossible!"

"It seemed impossible that a wall could be around it yesterday!"

"Even Wyrd and the wizard couldn't get rid of it," Shadow reasoned. "It is there, it's just blocked off. I'm wondering if the few days of snow that we've had helped precipitate it. I also want to know what they're experiencing inside."

Reuben shook his head. "Don't. I'm worried sick about them."

"We all are," Ash said, a look of regret crossing his face. "They're our friends, too. I've heard of the Snow Queen, and I admit that I'm confused. She's a type of witch, yes?"

Reuben looked at Caspian and Estelle. "I guess she is. The stories seem to say so. What do you think?"

Caspian nodded, deciding it was time to expand on his theory. "Yes, I believe so, although when I say the Snow Queen, it's probably misleading." He paused, wondering how to explain. "The Snow Queen was popularised by Hans Christian Anderson. He was the one who made the name up and wrote the fairytale. But there are other female mythical figures that he probably based her on—you know, winter-weather Goddesses. I've been reading up on them. Greek myth has Chione, a Goddess of Snow."

Ash laughed. "I haven't heard of her name for a long time! She was no myth! She created havoc in our time."

"Thanks Ash, it's good to know I'm not completely heading in the wrong direction. Skadi is the Norse Winter Goddess, Morana is the Slavic Goddess of Winter and Death. Poli'ahu is the Hawaiian Snow Goddess. Cailleach Bheur is the Scottish Gaelic Winter Goddess—although, she's also described as a hag who ages backwards. There are more, and they all vary. The singular fairytale draws all of these together. So," Caspian sighed, "when I call her the Snow Queen, I actually mean a Winter Goddess of some sort who has decided that she needs White Haven."

"Okay, now I'm less sceptical," Newton admitted. "A Winter Goddess who seems intent on a power grab makes more sense."

"Really?" Niel shook his head. "You're a funny man! The Snow Queen sounds bonkers, but a Winter Goddess is fine? Humans are so weird."

Everyone sniggered, and it lifted the mood—even Newton's. "Yes, all right, I admit that sounds odd. But you know what I mean! The Snow Queen sounds like a fairy tale. I'm used to the Gods and Goddesses being terrifying. Having met the Raven King and the Green Man, you can see my point!"

"To be honest, Newton, in the fairy tale, the Snow Queen was a mean bitch," Estelle pointed out.

Barak edged forward. "It started snowing a few days ago, and only really got this heavy overnight. Do you think our Winter Goddess was behind it all?"

"The entire south of England is affected, so it's hard to say," Reuben pointed out.

"There were deaths in Devon," Moore said, consulting his notebook. "Two deaths caused by the cold. Both frozen solid, both unusual. One man was frozen in his back garden, within feet of his door. First thoughts were a major heart attack, but now... Sounds to me like Jack and his Goddess are causing havoc."

"They arrived with a blast of winter. Interesting," Ash mused. "Can they only travel in wintry weather, or do they manipulate the weather to move? I mean, they must have arrived here from somewhere. I ask because it could be important. Warmer weather could force them to leave."

"That's an interesting suggestion," Caspian said. "We know a weather witch. Our friend, Eve, from the St Ives Coven. If we can find out more, then it might be worth contacting her. Perhaps I should call Jasper, too." Jasper was another witch in the Cornwall Coven who they could always turn to for advice. "And I'll call Gray to ask her about what she felt at the fayre. I'd like to hear her experience first-hand."

Newton looked confused. "Aren't you going to all meet at the solstice, anyway?"

"That was the plan, but it may be too late by then, and if this weather keeps up, we won't be able to anyway." Caspian looked through the windows to where the snow continued to fall steadily. It looked like it would last for days.

"I'll call Eve," Reuben said. "I'd like to chat to her. You call Gray. You know her better."

"Then I'll call Jasper," Estelle suggested.

Caspian smiled at her. She normally hated coven business, so this was generous of her. "Thank you."

"What can we do?" Gabe asked. "I feel powerless!"

"I'll tell you exactly how you can help me," Newton said to Gabe and his brothers. "This Jack Frost is killing people. I want him stopped! I don't know how, but we must. Ice sculptures are one thing, but these deaths are something else. They're spiteful and needless, and right now I want to kill *him*!"

Newton's outburst further sobered the room. They were all looking forward to celebrating the solstice, and the Nephilim had enough worries with Belial and Nahum's recent news. This certainly wasn't the homecoming they wanted.

"I wonder if we could catch Jack Frost?" Shadow asked.

"Ah, sister," Niel laughed. "I can always rely on you to cut to the chase."

She shrugged. "No harm in trying. And I'm also serious about trying to get through the wall."

"Shadow!" Gabe glared at her.

"I'll go prepared." She stared at the others. "I think you're right about a Winter Goddess. It feels right. Is there a way to find out which particular one we're up against?"

"Not right now," Reuben admitted, "but it's something we should work on. Is there a Winter Goddess in your world?"

Shadow shook her head. "I've already considered it, and there isn't."

"Okay." Reuben nodded, running his hands through his hair. Caspian felt his frustration. "I'll look for a spell to penetrate the wall. If it's made of ice and snow, then that's water based. In theory, as a water witch, I should be able to manipulate it, and then that means you won't have to go alone. But I admit, I don't even know how to start."

"We'll help," Estelle reassured him. "If Jack Frost is a sprite who is passing back and forth easily, there is a way."

"Don't worry," Gabe said to Newton to try to reassure him. "We'll do whatever we can."

"Actually," Caspian said, thinking of Eagle, his familiar, and how woefully he'd underutilised him since Samhain, "I can fly using my familiar. But I'll need a quiet space. Our familiars give us extra perception and enhance our magic. I might see the wall differently."

"I didn't," Reuben pointed out. "Although admittedly, I use my familiar slightly differently to you."

"Well, Caspian, you can't do bloody *everything*!" Newton pointed out, exasperated. "Help Reuben, make phone calls, fly... What's next? Pull a feather duster from up your arse?"

The whole room exploded with laughter, including Caspian. "Perhaps I'm overcompensating. We're four witches down, and I'm trying to be as useful as possible!"

"But you're not four witches, you're just one," Estelle said softly. "And there's plenty of us to help. Why don't I just knuckle down and study our family grimoires? There must be something in there that can help."

Kendall practically jumped out of her seat. "I can help! I mean, you could tell me what to look for, right?"

Estelle nodded. "Of course, if you're happy to help, that's great. Then Barak can focus on flying alone while I'm occupied." She smiled at him. "You're far more agile without me."

"I think it's a brilliant idea," Shadow said, unexpectedly supporting Estelle. "We can hunt Jack Frost, or find a way in."

"Okay!" Newton sounded brighter as their plans were worked out. "In that case, I have one more request. I want to see Tamsyn. If she's a Seer, then maybe she can use a crystal ball, or help Beth see something."

"We've been trying to stop that," Reuben pointed out. "But I'd like to see her again, too. I can do it after phone calls and before I search through my grimoire. We'll all just need ferrying around either by the Nephilim or witch-flight."

All the Nephilim just shrugged as Ash said, "We can take anyone anywhere they need to go before we go hunting. Just wrap up!"

"And I have one more question," Newton said, looking suddenly weary. "I, Kendall, and Moore need a bed for the night. There's no way we can drive anywhere in this weather. I have a feeling this place will be cramped—despite your generous offer, Niel."

"I have a solution," Reuben offered. "If Caspian or the guys don't mind acting as a ferry service, you can all come to my house later. There's plenty of room there for all of you. I can leave my car here. I have others at my house."

Caspian smiled. "And there's room at my place, too. Or I can just take you wherever you need to go—as long as I've been there, of course. Although, you might not thank me after you've experienced witch-flight."

All three police officers brightened at the offer of a bed. Clearly, sleeping on the floor did not appeal.

As a general discussion broke out and Niel and Moore headed to the kitchen to get rid of the plates, Caspian's gaze drifted to the window. *What was happening out there in the cold, dark, freezing weather? What was Jack Frost, the mischievous and deadly sprite, up to? And who was the Winter Goddess that was causing so much trouble?* Despite his best intentions, Caspian thought of Avery, and his heart tightened. *Was she okay?*

Avery sat between Alex and El in a comfortable sleigh, a pile of furs pulled over their laps and up to their chin, as the reindeer pulled them up the hill towards the castle.

They were all worried about Briar, and Avery kept replaying their last conversation in her head. Unfortunately, Briar's worries were also their own. Everything *did* feel odd. White Haven, as lovely as the place looked, and as much as she loved her home, felt *off*. It was too perfect.

The snowfall was gentler now, feather-light snowflakes drifting onto the deep snow that smothered the landscape in a soft white blanket. She could see the town clearly as they ascended the hill. Everything was picture perfect. The lights, the Christmas trees, the shop windows, the stalls selling chestnuts, mince pies, and hot drinks. But she felt tense, despite it all. And she was sure someone was missing. El looked particularly worried, casting glances about her as if she'd forgotten something.

However, the calm, muffled silence, the jingle of the reindeers' bells, and the muffled laughter of people in other sleighs was soothing. It lulled and caressed her. The sensation was exacerbated by the fact that the weather had knocked out all mobile communications.

Nothing worked. There was no radio, TV, phones, anything... They had all tried to call Briar, but the line was dead. And then just as they were planning on going to her house, they were hustled along with the crowd to the waiting sleighs. The palace staff were buzzing around, nodding in greeting but firmly persuasive, and before they could resist, they were on their way to the fayre.

Alex nudged Avery. "Briar will be fine. We'll visit her once we're back. Like she said, she's busy, and probably in her shop. If not, we'll go to her house."

"Thank you. She just looked so upset." She smiled at Alex. He looked good. His long, dark hair was tied in a top knot, his jaw was stubbled with a day-old beard, and he smelled clean and fresh. Just taking him in was reassuring. She wanted to go home and snuggle up to him and block the world out. And then Avery had another thought, and she gasped. "My gran! I've left her at home. She'll wonder where we are!" She clasped her head, a band seeming to tighten around her temples. "How could I have forgotten her? This is awful! I'm a terrible granddaughter."

"Clea will be fine. She might have a bit of memory loss, but she'll be okay."

"But she should be with us! She'd have loved to come. Why didn't I think of her?"

El had been looking at the view, lost in her own thoughts, but now she stirred and turned to them. "I feel like I'm forgetting someone, too." She patted her heart through her jacket. "I have an ache, like I'm missing part of me." El's blue eyes welled with tears, and she hurriedly brushed them aside, glancing nervously at the driver. He sat at the head of the sleigh, wrapped in a thick cloak and with a hat pulled firmly over his ears. It was unlikely that he would hear them, and yet Avery appreciated her worry. "I feel flat. Incomplete," she continued. "And I snapped at Briar, which is unforgivable."

Alex leaned across Avery, also lowering his voice. "I'm trying to push it to the back of my mind, but I feel weird, too. Like I'm forgetting something. It's like an itch I need to scratch. But apart from us three, and Briar, obviously, everyone seems fine!"

Avery shook her head. "Not fine. The pub felt tense, under all that jolly chat. Didn't you feel it?"

Alex squeezed her hand and kissed her cheek. "I trust you, but I didn't sense that. Maybe I was just busy."

"You should both know why some people are on edge," El said, virtually hissing at them. "I know we feel like something's wrong, but surely you can't forget the queen! All these celebrations are for her! She demands loyalty and is unforgiving if she doesn't think she's getting it."

Once again, Avery reeled. It was as if all thoughts of her had vanished, and then as soon as the name was mentioned, they all came rushing back. The imperious woman who lived in the palace on the hill. The woman whose whims dictated their own. Her brain was screaming at her that it was all wrong. She looked to Alex for reassurance, but he just nodded and agreed with El.

"That's true," he nodded again, "but most people love her and wouldn't have White Haven any other way. This is the way things are, we just need to accept it. And that."

He lifted his chin and looked up as they rounded a bend in the road. Above them, shining in the light from hundreds of torches, positioned on the cliff above the town, the fayre spread at its feet, was the castle made of ice-covered stone. Snow was piled against its walls and pillowed on the battlements. Lights gleamed at its many windows, the highest turrets lost in low clouds.

Avery shuddered. Tomorrow, on the solstice, they would all be seated at the feast in its Great Hall. The culmination of the solstice celebrations. *It should be exciting, so why did she feel terrified?*

The driver pulled into the turning circle next to the sprawling fayre that was situated on a broad strip of land beneath the castle and stopped in the line of sleighs. In seconds they had clambered out under the watchful eye of the palace guards. Avery plastered a smile on her face and slipped her hand through Alex's arm. Time to fake her enjoyment.

She had a sinking feeling that her life depended on it.

# Seven

**D**ylan pushed his chair away from the computer and stood and stretched, feeling as stiff and achy as if he'd aged twenty years.

Dylan was tall and rangy, and prolonged sitting didn't agree with him, even though he'd trained himself to tolerate it. "I cannot sit at this damn computer any longer," he complained to Cassie and Ben. "And if I drink any more coffee, I might have a heart attack. There's only so much reading I can do. We need data!"

"I thought you liked reading," Cassie said, stifling a yawn. "You did your post-grad studies in it!"

"I studied folklore, not reading, but you know what I mean. If nothing was going on, I'd love nothing more than to curl up in front of the fire with a good book. But weird things are happening! Out there! In the dark..." He widened his eyes and made spooky noises, satisfied when Cassie laughed.

"Idiot."

"I agree," Ben said, standing and stretching, too. He'd been sprawled out in the seating area on a low couch, papers spread around him. He continued to take the odd call, but for now, things seemed to have quieted. "We need to get outside."

Cassie snorted. "But look at the weather!" She paced from her desk to the window. They'd left the blinds partly open, and she stared at the blizzardlike conditions.

Dylan stood next to her, arms crossed, eyes narrowed. It was impenetrable, and while they couldn't drive, they still had options. "I know what we should do. Either ask Caspian to take us to the wall using witch-flight, or ask the Nephilim to fly us there."

Cassie gaped at him. "Why didn't we think of that earlier? Bags the Nephilim! I don't care that it's snowing. *I want to fly!*"

"Excellent." Ben was already punching numbers into his phone. "Let's see who's available."

Dylan checked his watch. "They'll probably all be at the farmhouse."

"Perhaps it's just a weird snow thing," Cassie said hopefully. "These things could stop when this blows over. And then White Haven will be fine again."

Dylan patted her shoulder. "Sure, it will. And pigs will freeze in trees."

"Aren't you the slightest bit worried about our friends?"

"Of course I am. Why do you think I'm bent double like an old man after hours of reading about Snow Queens, Winter Goddesses, and the trickster Jack Frost? I think Caspian is right. It has to be a Winter Goddess, but what does she want?" They had been fully brought up to speed with Caspian's theory earlier that evening.

Cassie shook her head, tucking her hair behind her ear. "We shouldn't jump to conclusions. It could be another witch. But you're right. We need data."

Both turned as Ben ended the call and he grinned at them. "Three Nephilim are on their way. Niel, Eli, and Zee."

And then the electrics cut out, leaving them standing in darkness.

"Great. That's probably half the county without power," Cassie groaned. "There'll be no heating! And no lights on the lanes."

Dylan laughed as a surge of excitement stirred his blood. "We're not going to need them where we're going, Cassie. Let's lock and load."

Briar had to admit that Jack was a very attentive companion, and he was undoubtedly handsome. His unruly shock of almost white hair, the colour of driven snow, framed his sculpted features, and his dark blue eyes seemed to see into her very soul.

Briar's hand was still tucked into his arm as they strolled through the fayre, his bare hand resting on her gloved one. There were so many stalls that they formed narrow alleys, edged with bunting, and the scents that emanated from the food sellers was captivating, as were the other wares on sale. The whole place was so colourful that Briar could barely take it all in.

Some stalls sold toys carved from wood or painted tin. They were of animals, people, fauns, and Satyrs, all wearing colourful clothing. Then there were stalls selling leather goods—purses, bags, coats, and belts, while others sold pretty pottery, silverware, jewellery, soaps, candles, woollen garments, and rugs. And the food! Chocolates, pastries, and sweetmeats, not to mention the huge pig that was roasting on a spit in the centre of the food stalls.

Jack directed her to his favourite stall, buying her a pastry to nibble on, all the while nodding in greeting at the stallholders. Briar smiled and laughed, but she had to quell her growing unease. She thought she would recognize some stallholders, but all were unfamiliar, and she realised that they were all from out of town. There wasn't one recognisable face there, except for the townsfolk, of course. There were plenty of familiar faces walking around. They all looked excited, and yet beneath it all was wary tension.

And over all of it loomed the castle, a huge white edifice towering above them. The sight of it stirred something deep within her. A knowingness.

"You look cold," Jack said, his eyes staring deep into her own. "You need a hot drink."

"That's a great idea, and then I should go home."

He pouted, and his long lashes fluttered against his pale cheeks. "Not yet. A little longer. Hot chocolate?"

"Thank you."

Briar took deep breaths and studied her surroundings, willing her heart to stop racing. This was supposed to be fun. There was an area she hadn't spotted before where people were playing old-fashioned games, like throwing hoops over posts, and along the edges of the market, where the ground dropped away to the town, people were having snowball fights. And then she saw Stan. He looked horribly flustered, eyes scanning the crowd and the stalls. He smiled, however, when he recognised her, recovering quickly, and he walked to her side. Briar calmed down when she saw him, comforted by his familiar face. He was clad in his cloak, and carried his staff.

"Briar, how lovely to see you. You're alone?" He peered over her shoulder, confused.

"No, I'm with a new friend. Jack. I was heading home actually, but, well..."

Stan's eyes widened with horror. "Jack!"

"Do you know him?"

"He's...coming back." Stan beamed at him. "Jack. I didn't know you were back in town!"

"You know me, Stan," he said, passing Briar her drink. "I come and go."

"So, you two know each other?" Briar asked, keeping it light, aware that despite the freezing cold, Stan had a sheen of sweat on his brow.

"We are mutual friends of the queen," Jack informed her.

"Oh, you're too kind," Stan muttered. "I merely serve her will. I'm honoured to be charged with making sure the solstice procession goes smoothly, and that the shops are decorated appropriately. Briar's looks magnificent."

"Yes, Briar has told me of Charming Balms Apothecary. I must visit it. Tomorrow, perhaps?"

"Of course." Up until now their conversation had been about everything and nothing. Jack gave little away of himself. "Although, I think you'll find my shop very boring."

"How can anything that you do be boring?"

"Ah, well," Stan said awkwardly, "I must go. I actually have an appointment to see the queen. She wanted an update on events."

Jack grinned, his smile dazzling Briar. "That's perfect. We'll go with you. You can meet the queen."

"I can't! Look at what I'm wearing!" Briar looked down at her long, deep purple woollen coat over her thick, ankle-length skirt and boots. Any excuse would do. "I'm hardly fit to see royalty!"

"Not at all. She will be thrilled to meet you." And without waiting for her reply, Jack tucked her hand into the crook of his arm, and falling into step with Stan, they progressed to the palace.

"So, what I need to know, Eve, is whether you have the power to undermine whatever this spell is around White Haven," Reuben said, leaning back in his armchair, feet up on the coffee table.

Eve sighed, and he could hear her moving around her flat. She lived above a gallery surrounded by her artwork, and he imagined that as a weather witch whose art was influenced by the weather, she must be loving the blizzard. "I wish I could say that of course I can, but it's hard to know without being there and seeing it. But you've confirmed what I've suspected all day. This is no normal storm, Reu."

Reuben sat up, almost sloshing his beer over himself. "Really? What makes you say that?"

"I can feel it. It's too concentrated. Too intense. There's design behind it."

"Whose?"

She gave a short sharp laugh. "I don't know—yet. From what you've said, it's a Winter Goddess, or another witch. Jack Frost is an interesting suggestion. Some kind of sprite, you say?"

"So Shadow thinks."

"And they all want magic."

"Perhaps. We might be leaping to giant conclusions and be very wrong about everything."

"There are a few spells—"

The phone call abruptly ended and the lights went out, leaving Reuben lit only by firelight.

"Bollocks."

By now, the witches and the police officers were the only ones in the farmhouse. Newton and his sergeants were tidying up in the kitchen, trying to keep busy, and Estelle was unpacking her grimoires. The Nephilim had all headed out. Three of them were picking up Ghost OPS, and the others were flying over the area. Their plans were admittedly vague. Try and spot Jack Frost the sprite flitting about the countryside. *Sure. That would be so easy.*

"Hey, Reuben," Caspian entered the room, holding a witch-light. "I presume we're not worried that we're under attack?"

"I hope not. We have super reinforced protection spells around this place."

He sat, relief washing over his face. "Good. How are you holding up?"

Reuben considered lying, but what was the point? "I'm feeling pretty crap, actually. A whole day has passed since I discovered the damn wall, and we're no closer to getting in at all."

Caspian extinguished the witch-light, leaving them bathed in firelight. "We *are* getting closer. We have a good idea who's behind it, and our friends are out there now, helping. Why don't I take my grimoires to your house later, and we'll hit the books together? Estelle will help."

Reuben worked well with Caspian, and it was partly thanks to him that he'd found confidence with his magic when they'd worked together to defeat the pirates. "That would be great, thanks. Right now, though, I want to see the wall again."

"So do I. I know where the Nephilim are taking Ghost OPS. I've already arranged to meet them there. The edge of Ravens' Wood."

"We're not actually going into the wood at night, though, right?" Everyone knew that the wood was very unusual at night.

Caspian laughed. "No. But I'd like to investigate a couple of places by the wall—you know, to check for weak spots. I guess they will, too. We should go up by Tamsyn's place, too, if the wall is close by."

Reuben nodded. "Excellent. And then we can drop in on Tamsyn again, just to make sure Beth is okay. We need to take Newton and Moore, too," he added, remembering his earlier request. "Maybe you should take them first, then they can chat while we do other stuff. Did Gray have anything to add?"

"Nothing beyond what Newton said. What did Eve say?"

"That she'd help if she could, of course, and that the storm is unnatural. Someone's driving it."

Caspian's expression darkened. "Which makes it dangerous to be out in it. Unfortunately, we have no choice."

"Sorry to interrupt," Estelle said, walking into the living room and placing her grimoires on the coffee table. "I need a couple more books from our library. Would you mind quickly taking me? I'll phone Jasper after that."

Reuben shook his head. "Too late, I'm afraid. The phones are down."

Estelle groaned. "Damn it. I'm sorry."

"We'll manage, and of course I don't mind," Caspian answered. "Reuben, let Newton know I'll take him in ten."

El was only at the fayre for minutes with Avery and Alex when she knew she needed to be alone.

"Guys, I'll make my own way home, and see you tomorrow."

"Why?" Avery asked, alarmed. She began furtively glancing around. "We should stay together."

"It's a fayre! I just need some alone time, Avery. My head is all over the place, and my paranoia isn't helping. You two enjoy yourselves. I'll be fine!" She stopped Avery before she could say another word.

Alex didn't argue, but he leaned forward and kissed her cheek. "Be careful, El."

"Of course. Have fun!"

She breathed easier when she was on her own, not having to focus on conversation when her thoughts were elsewhere. For a while she drifted around, taking in the sights and sounds, reflecting on how alien and yet familiar everything felt. She bought two huge cookies to munch on as she walked, analysing her feelings and why she felt so unsettled. And then she saw Briar with Stan and a man with startling white hair heading towards the castle.

El was about to call out to her friend, but inexplicably thought better of it. She couldn't say why, other than a bone-deep feeling that nagged at her. Instead, she followed them. For a while, the crowd helped hide her, until Briar reached the path leading up the hill to the castle gates. El hesitated, debating what to do. Fortunately, they weren't the only ones taking the path. A few palace staff were weaving back and forth, as were a couple of well packed carts carrying supplies to the castle. Groups of people were also winding their way up the path to stroll along the grounds at the edge of the castle and take in the view. The only light was from the flaming torches that lined the way, and El casually followed a group of people, pulling her hat down low and her collar up.

Briar's new friend seemed animated, laughing and pointing out things to them as they walked. The only thing that stopped El from worrying too much was the fact that Stan was with them. But while others headed to the right or left at the top of the path, Briar's group continued straight on, disappearing through the huge gates of the palace, into the courtyard beyond. The guards saluted as they passed. It seemed the young man was well known, and important.

Making a quick decision, El headed left, following a group of people along the route that led to the rear of the castle, taking them along the cliff edge, and a view of waves frozen mid-crash against the rocks. The sea was lost to view, however, in a huge bank of cloud that sat off the coast, and El turned her back on it to study the palace.

Up close she could see the big blocks of stone beneath the thick ice that coated them. There were no windows on the ground floor, though, so it was impossible to see inside. On the upper levels were hundreds of windows, all gleaming with light. *What was her friend doing in there?*

A shout drew her attention, and she saw another pair of large gates set into the wall. One of them swung open, and large carts rumbled through, horses snickering and tossing their manes, before disappearing into the dimly-lit courtyard beyond. Before she'd even considered her actions, El ran after them, slipping through the gateway.

The courtyard was large, and clearly a working part of the palace. Stables lined one side, as well as doors to the kitchen, storerooms, and other areas. She ran to the nearest doorway and sheltered in the dark recess to watch.

It was only when she stopped to draw breath that she wondered what the hell she was going to do next. But there was something wrong with this place. She knew it. She could feel it in her gut. She clenched and opened her hands, looking at her palms. They tingled, as if something should be happening. *Idiot.* She needed to focus.

Several staff were milling about, shouting to each other as they unloaded the wagon to take supplies inside. There was no snow in here; instead, it was churned up mud. The biggest door off the court-yard led to a bright room. Grooms unhitched the horses and guided them to the stables, and others carried boxes to what appeared to be a storeroom. But it wasn't just a yard for the stores. On the far side of the courtyard was another row of buildings, and unfortunately a few soldiers. *The barracks.* Knowing that if she stayed where she was that she would be seen, she fumbled to open the door behind her, but the door was locked.

She crouched, hoping that her black clothing would keep her hidden. But she couldn't stay here all night. She wanted to get inside and search the castle for clues of...something. But this way wasn't going to work until the yard fell quiet. She needed to stick to the shadows, leave the yard, and return later.

She had crept to within a few feet of the gate when another horse came cantering inside, almost knocking her over. She stumbled back, and the rider saw her and shouted. Within seconds, she was surround-ed by palace staff, strong hands restraining her.

The man dismounted, eyes narrowing. He was clad in the dove grey uniform of the palace guards, and from the number of lines on his epaulettes he was a senior officer. "I believe you're trespassing."

El lifted her chin, refusing to show fear. "I was curious. I meant no harm. I was actually just leaving."

"The queen's orders are clear. Trespassers are not tolerated." He gave a quick nod to the men restraining her. "Take her to the dun-geons. The queen will deal with her tomorrow."

# Eight

S hadow slid from Gabe's grasp onto the icesheet that butted up to the huge, white wall.

She immediately sank knee-deep into thick snow. "Herne's blistering horns! It has snowed a lot since this morning!"

"No shit!" Gabe murmured, eyes raking the surroundings. "It will get even deeper before the night is out. This is a good idea though, Ash." He looked across to where Ash, Nahum, and Barak had just set down. Ash had suggested that it could be one of the ways the sprite exited.

"And it's even colder here!" Shadow's fey blood normally kept her warm, but these bitter temperatures were testing her fey magic. Wind swept in from the sea, and she pulled her cloak around her, still gripping her swords. She'd brought both, for good measure.

They spread out, warily investigating their surroundings. Barak and Nahum walked towards the wall, but Shadow looked at the sculptures, impressed at their detail. She hadn't visited with the others earlier, so this was new for her. Despite the snow that had gathered in thick banks around them, the sculptures remained uncovered, glittering with the faint light afforded them.

She paused in front of the queen on her throne. "I see what you mean, Gabe. She is a mean bitch."

Gabe laughed. "She must be for you to say so. It's in her eyes, right?"

"Everything. Her jaw, her eyes, the tilt of her head... She would be merciless. If she's like this for real, we're all in trouble."

"Nothing scares you," Gabe said, leaning close to her ear, his breath warm on her skin. "It must be bad."

"She doesn't scare me, but," she cocked her head, "one should never underestimate one's enemy."

"Can you feel any fey magic?"

She closed her eyes and focussed, trying to block out everything around her. There was something faint, but the ice dampened everything. She opened her eyes again, the queen staring down at her. "Nothing significant. Might be fun to provoke her, though." She clambered onto the queen's lap and loped off her head; it rolled across the rapidly freezing snow.

Ash emerged from behind the sculpture of a giant octopus, its tentacles rippling across the ice, half hidden beneath the snow. "Throwing down a challenge, Shadow?"

"Yes. I think she should know we're on to her." She looked at the wall and shouted, "We're coming for you!"

Her voice echoed across the icy expanse, making Nahum and Barak stare at her. And then an ominous *crack* resounded through the muffled silence.

"What was that?" Gabe said, sword raised as he turned around.

"The icesheet?" Ash asked, wings expanding.

And then another crack rent the air, and a huge tentacle whipped up from the ice and clipped Ash, sending him flying. In seconds, more tentacles lashed out, and the other sculptures came to life—Satyrs, centaurs, and a huge bear.

"Herne's flaming balls!" Gabe yelled as he faced a charging Satyr. "What the hell have you done?"

"I guess she doesn't like being disrespected!" Shadow didn't have time to say anything more. Swords whirling, she faced the icy centaur that galloped her way. His sword flashed, hooves thudding over the ice, shards of it flying up. She skipped to the right, bringing her sword across his flanks, and gouging a deep cut in his side. He skidded past her, rearing up and kicking out, and she flew backwards.

The next thing she knew, a tentacle had wrapped around her waist and was crushing the life out of her.

Briar was intimidated by her grand surroundings. It might be an ice palace, but it was still impressive—although freezing cold.

After crossing the grand courtyard, they walked up the sweeping stairs and through the huge front doors that were opened by immaculately dressed guards. All bowed low to Jack. Briar's expression remained impassive, but it was obvious that Jack was well respected. Maybe even feared.

Beyond the front door was a series of huge reception rooms with sets of double doors. To the left of the first reception room was another large antechamber, with enormous doors on the far side that were shut tight. The Great Hall lay beyond them, where the feast would be held the next night, on the solstice. Briar had vague memories of the interior, but had barely time to think about them as Jack led them onwards through the reception rooms directly ahead. All were mostly devoid of people except for guards, until they reached one which had a line of people waiting nervously, their arms full of papers. Jack escorted them past all of them, sweeping through the final set of enormous doors, and into the throne room.

Briar gasped. The hall was magnificent. It was illuminated by chandeliers made of icicles, the walls were of pale, white stone clad with ice, and huge ice pillars supported the vaulted ceiling above. The floor was made of white marble. It was all so startling white, it was dazzling. But more dazzling than all of it was the woman sitting on the enormous throne at the far end.

Her gaze felt as if it could cut Briar in two, and she'd barely glimpsed her, when a strange force made her eyes drop to the ground as they halted just inside the doors. Briar had never bowed to anyone in her life, but she bowed now, following Jack and Stan as they were granted an audience.

"Welcome, Jack." The queen's voice cracked like a whip. "How good of you to see me. I see you've brought Stan, and a new friend. Come closer so that I may see her properly."

Whatever pressure the queen was exerting seemed to release, and Briar lifted her head again. Her hand was still in Jack's arm; although she had tried to pull it free, he kept a firm grip on her. All three walked down the centre of the room, finally halting within a few feet of the queen.

All the way down, Briar drank in her appearance. She was young and slender, and beautiful in an intimidating way. She was paler than Jack, her skin almost appearing translucent, but her ruby red lips were full, and when she smiled, she revealed even, white teeth. Her hair was raven dark, and her eyes were almost black. She wore a shimmering grey and white gown, the neckline plunging to show a generous, snowy-white cleavage. It wasn't until Briar was up close that she saw the gown was made of grey lace in a snowflake design laid over white satin. Everything enhanced her delicate pallor.

But there was nothing delicate about her demeanour. She was utterly terrifying. It radiated out of her. She cast Stan a dismissive, withering glance, not that he would have seen it. He kept his eyes fixed firmly on the floor. Briar she similarly ignored, narrowed eyes sweeping over her, before cutting to Jack. Briar looked down, watching them out of the corner of her eye.

She beamed at Jack, extending her hands so that he stepped forward, finally releasing Briar. The throne was on a dais, and he stepped up, carefully avoiding her full skirts to clasp both of her hands in his. He raised them to his lips and kissed them.

"My Queen. As always, you look radiant. It is my honour to serve you."

"An honour I accept. It has been hours since I last saw you. Have you been busy?"

"Making sure that preparations for the solstice and the feast are going well. I am pleased to say they are. The town is resplendent." He nodded at Stan. "Everything is in hand."

"Well, councillor?" Her peremptory tone had Stan looking up, very briefly, before fixating on his shoes again. "Will we have any issues on the day?"

"No, Your Majesty. The parade is planned, and everything is ready. All of the shops look perfect. Everything will be ready for your arrival."

*So, the queen would be in White Haven for the parade?* Briar supposed that was normal, but it still seemed off, and again she felt that something was very wrong.

"Excellent," she continued. "You know the penalties, should you fail."

"Yes, Your Majesty."

Briar felt her eyes rest on her. "And who is this you have brought to see me? You know I don't like surprises, Jack."

Briar lifted her head, trying to appear as meek as possible.

"This is Briar Ashworth, the owner of Charming Balms," Jack said, looking down on Briar as imperiously as the queen. "She has skills with lotions and herbs."

The queen's eyes widened. "Ah! That shop. Yes, I recall it." She leaned forward, examining Briar as if she was a butterfly pinned to a board. "Interesting. You feel well, Ms Ashworth?"

"Perfectly well, thank you, Your Majesty." Briar had the feeling she was caught in a game; that there was surely subtext that she was missing in this exchange.

"How do you like my palace?"

"It's beautiful, as is the fayre. Jack has been very kind to show me around."

"Has he?" She stared at Jack. "How unusual. Well, Miss Ashworth, we have things to discuss."

Briar stared at her, so shocked that she asked questions she knew she probably shouldn't. "We do? What?"

She didn't answer, instead speaking to the other two. "Thank you. You may leave now. I presume you have work tonight, Jack?"

"As always, Your Majesty."

And then something very peculiar happened. The queen froze, her eye fixed on something only she could see, and Jack tensed. Her sharp tone returned. "Jack. Something stirs on the South Gate that needs your attention."

"Your Majesty." He bowed, and without a backward glance, bounded down the steps and towards the doors.

Briar and Stan made to follow him, Briar hoping she wouldn't want to talk to her anymore, but the queen said, "No!" They both stopped, barely daring to look at each other as they turned around.

She studied Briar carefully. "You will stay here tonight. As I said, we have much to discuss."

Briar's pretence at meekness vanished in her panic. "But I have a home, my business!"

"All can wait. You should be pleased. Not many are invited as guests to my palace."

Briar fought to keep her breath even and her heart from pounding. "Of course. It will be an honour. But—"

"There are no buts. Stanley, you may leave."

Stan looked as if he might protest, but then thought better of it. He shot Briar an anguished glance, and then scurried from the hall, as guards flanked Briar.

Alex felt the mood shift, and noticed uneasy expressions on the faces of the stall owners and the palace guards.

The snow that had been falling gently up until now suddenly thickened as the wind whipped up, howling down the fayre's alleyways and causing people to hunch forward. He grasped Avery's arm and pulled her away to the waiting sleighs.

"What are you doing?" Avery protested, trying to pull her arm free. "I was about to buy something!"

"Another time. We're getting out of here."

"Why?"

Keeping a fast pace, he said, "Can't you feel it? Something's wrong."

White light flashed along the wall of clouds that smothered the sea from view, and the snow thickened to a blizzard. Shrieks sounded behind them, but Alex didn't slow down, and he gripped Avery's arm even tighter.

"We can't go yet! We don't know where El is!"

"El will be fine. She's clever. She'll make her own way home."

"But Alex!" Avery finally wrenched her arm free. "What if she's not?"

But along with the flash of light, he heard a deep-throated rumble, and he knew they had to get away from the palace. "Avery, I swear we'll come back and find her if we have to, but right now, we have to go!"

They were slightly ahead of the crowd, and crossing the last remaining ground, he pushed Avery into a sleigh, and leaped in next to her. The driver shook the reins, and they were off.

The blizzard was so strong that the wind whistled, whipping Alex's hair free from its top knot and whipping it around his face. He pulled Avery in close, wrapping his arm around her. Hunching low in the seat, he pulled the furs over their faces so that only their eyes were showing. The palace and fayre vanished from view, leaving only snow. It was so thick that they lost sight of the driver and reindeers, and also anyone who might be behind them.

Alex had no idea how the driver saw the route, but he didn't hesitate. He was vaguely aware of the twists and turns in the road as they leaned from one side of the sleigh to the other. When they dropped within the lee of the hill and the outskirts of the town, the wind ceased, and the sleigh slowed down. Here, things seemed more normal. Christmas lights glowed within flats, houses, and shops, and Alex's racing heart calmed.

Where the road split into two, the main lane heading down towards the town centre, Alex shouted for the driver to stop. They were closer to their house there. He obligingly stopped, and Alex tipped him before they exited and he quickly whirled around, heading back to the fayre. Alex and Avery walked home, Avery brooding all the way.

"Avery, you know that was weird up there!"

Avery pouted, eyes sullen. She could pack a mean argument when she wanted to. "It was...odd. Probably just a sudden storm. But El could be stuck in line now, waiting for a sleigh. She could be freezing."

"She's an adult, not a child. We'll call her later. Hopefully the phones will be back on soon. But it was more than odd, and you know it!"

She rounded on him. "So, what was it?"

"Not here!"

The streets appeared deserted, but with thick snow still falling and their vison obscured, Alex didn't want to chance it.

When they reached home, Avery ran up the stairs, shouting, "Gran. I'm back! Are you okay?"

Alex locked the door and headed into Avery's shop, wanting to make sure that everything was all right in there. There had been some big gusts of wind, and Avery had large windows at the front of her shop. A hushed silence and the faint scent of incense greeted him as he wound between the bookshelves, but the shop felt calm and safe, settling his nerves. He stood at the window as he had that morning, looking onto the lane outside. All day he had felt off, and this evening, he wasn't imagining it. The storm felt animalistic. Wild. Untamed.

And then Avery's panicking voice shattered the silence around him. "Alex! Come quickly! It's Clea!"

*Nine*

Cassie stepped from Eli's arms at the edge of Raven's Wood, aware of the watchful forest behind her, but trying to ignore it.

She shivered as she glanced longingly at Eli's broad, warm chest, wishing she was still pressed against it, but those kinds of thoughts wouldn't do at all. Instead, she slung her backpack off and started to pull her instruments from the bag as Niel and Zee landed with Dylan and Ben.

"Herne's frigid balls!" Dylan was obviously gobsmacked as he studied the wall around White Haven. They had swept over the top of it so they could understand the scale of it before setting them down. "This is immense! It's so cool!"

"*Cool*? Our friends are stuck in there!" Eli pointed out. He didn't bother to fold his wings away, no doubt wanting them ready in case they needed to escape quickly.

"You know what I mean." Typical of Dylan, his camera was already pointed at the wall.

"Anything in the thermal imaging?" Niel asked.

"Lots of blue. Not surprising."

"Maybe we should try prodding it," Ben suggested.

"With what?" Despite the situation, Zee laughed, rolling his eyes at Eli. "A big, pointy stick?"

"Didn't you say that JD had given you some cool weapons? Maybe one of those."

Eli stared at Zee, pursing his lips. "You told him about them?"

"Just idle chat on the way over."

"They're not for general knowledge. Or use!"

"Still here," Ben said, firing up his EMF meter. "And not deaf. I am not *general knowledge*. I can keep secrets!"

"Yeah, dude!" Dylan lowered the camera to glare at him. "What the fuck?"

Cassie looked at all of them. "What weapons? Don't leave me in the dark!"

Eli huffed. "A very creative, clever friend of ours has made alchemical weapons. They're surprisingly effective—and therefore dangerous. And no, you can't have one, before anyone asks."

"Spoilsport," Cassie said, turning her attention back to her instruments.

"I like the idea," Niel said, pacing a wary distance from the wall. "Man, I can feel that thing. It's humming like electricity."

"It didn't feel like that earlier," Eli admitted, getting a little closer to it. "What does that mean? Does it get more active at night?"

The sudden whine of Ben's EMF metre backed up Niel's observation. "Wow. These readings are climbing. There is something very weird going on here."

Cassie was busy taking temperature readings, but they didn't fluctuate. She was suddenly aware that Eli had stepped closer to her, which stupidly gave her the warm fuzzies. She really had to get over her Eli crush.

He frowned, oblivious to her whirling thoughts. "We could *not* feel any of this earlier. What's happening?"

Niel withdrew his sword. "Something is changing."

"Why?" Cassie asked. "How different is it?"

Eli shrugged. "It was just *there*. Like the solid mass it is now, but it had no energy or magic to speak of. Not like now. The only thing anybody felt was that when you stepped too close, it just turned you around again."

"This I have to experience," Dylan said, walking forward before anyone could stop him.

This time, the response was stronger. Dylan had got within a few paces of it when he was suddenly thrown backwards, clean off his feet. Zee's response was lightning fast. He flung out his wing, catching Dylan before he crashed into a tree.

"Holy crap! I felt that in my balls." Dylan struggled to stand, but his knees gave out and he fell in the snow.

Zee pulled him back to his feet. "Any weird thoughts? Memories?"

Ben immediately ran the metre over him. "You're spiking too, now."

Dylan rubbed his head. "I feel disorientated. Why are we here again?"

"I think we all need to step away," Eli said, ushering them all back, and Cassie quickly did as he suggested.

But they had taken only a few paces back when the entire wall flashed with a rippling light, and they were all thrown backwards.

The entire icesheet seemed to have come alive, and Gabe spun around, sword flashing, as tentacles whipped around them, and centaurs and Satyrs charged at them.

"Shadow! What have you done?" Gabe hacked at the tentacle that was wrapped around her waist.

She grunted as she slashed with her swords. "Provoked a response, and that's good! That will teach the bitch to mess with our friends!"

"Really? I'm not sure she's getting that lesson!" The ice was as hard as iron, and it was a sign of Shadow's fey blade that she had managed to lop the queen's head off so cleanly. The tentacles were thicker and far harder to hack through. He had barely made any progress when he was swept off his feet and thrown across the ice.

He landed with a thump, and saw a Satyr charging at him, sword raised. Gabe stayed low, rolled, and swept out with his sword. The Satyr anticipated his move and jumped over him, bringing his sword down as he did so.

Barely keeping out of his reach, Gabe regained his feet, and charged the creature. It was like hitting a brick wall. They crunched to the ground, and the ice shelf started to crack beneath them. Gabe brought the hilt of his sword down on the Satyr's head, smashing it into thousands of icy pieces.

He staggered to his feet and looked around. Ash was battling the octopus, and had managed to free Shadow. Together they hacked it into chunks, its writhing tentacles finally slowing. Nahum was fighting with a centaur, but Barak was dealing with something else entirely.

A gateway had opened up in the wall, and thick snow blasted through the opening. Out of its midst stepped a slim figure with a shock of white hair and a dozen guards flanking him. He took one look at the situation, and seemingly out of nowhere, conjured spears of ice that he hefted at Barak.

The big Nephilim spun his sword in his hands and raised his wings as a shield, shattering the icy spears. Shards of ice scattered across the ground as Gabe raced to join his brother. The centaur tried to block him, his hooves rearing up as it still fought Nahum. But it couldn't fight both of them effectively, and while Nahum kept it distracted, Gabe drove his sword through its neck, virtually beheading the ice creature.

"Cheers, brother," Nahum said, breathing heavily.

They lined up next to Barak, Ash and Shadow also racing to their side.

The ensuing fight was furious and fast paced. The young man and the guards shed their human veneers, becoming sharp-faced sprites with jutting jaws and grasping hands that pulled icy weapons out of thin air. But there was no doubt who the lead sprite was. The creature that had been the blond man was bigger and faster than his companions, although all were startlingly quick.

The clash of swords and grunts of fighting were interspersed with the keening of the wind and hampered by the blinding blizzard that whipped around them. An icy spear grazed Gabe's ribs, but he charged down the offending sprite, cutting it in two with a sweep of his sword. Shadow lunged at Jack—at least that's who Gabe presumed it was. Jack Frost, the winter sprite who was causing such chaos.

The ice under their feet cracked even more, and the whole sheet groaned. Water seeped through, adding to their danger.

Jack Frost and his sprites were strong opponents. They threw out icy clouds around them, and every time Gabe stepped close, his skin became so cold it was like being burned. Fortunately, his Nephilim blood repelled it, and Gabe desperately tried to reach Shadow's side.

Barak loomed out of the blizzard. "Gabe, I'm heading for the gate. It's still open. I'll slip through while they're distracted. Just keep them fighting and then fly off. I want them to think I've gone, too."

Gabe started to protest. "Barak, we'll come with you—" But he'd gone, a whirl of darkness in the greater dark of the night.

Gabe both hated the idea and admired it. Barak was right. If one of them could sneak in, they could help the witches. Too many of them would mean they would be quickly spotted. He doubled down on the fight at hand. A sword swept out of the snow, skimming his head. He needed to focus—and get to Shadow. A retreat meant he had to take her with him, no doubt kicking and screaming.

For the next few minutes, the battle only seemed to intensify. He lost track of where the guards were, and the snowstorm was distracting. His feet ploughed through puddles of sludgy ice, and he barely had sight of his brothers. But hopefully there was time enough now for Barak to have slipped inside.

He yelled, "Retreat! Now! Shadow, to me!"

To be honest, it was a believable course of action. The sprites were furious opponents, and the blizzard was only aiding them. They were not going to win this fight. Gabe wished he'd thought to pick up JD's weapons.

He yelled again, "Retreat! Where are you?"

A shout drew his attention, and he saw Ash's golden wings, and close by, Nahum. Beyond them, he finally spotted Shadow, fighting at the ice floor's edge with Jack, their swords a blur. He yelled again. "Retreat! To the forest!"

He pounded through the snow, grabbed Shadow mid-battle, and launched into the air. His brothers disengaged and followed. Jack sent a pocket of super freezing air at them, hail whirling in its midst. But they were too quick, and he soared high, Shadow complaining all the way.

"What are you doing, Gabe Malouf? I nearly had him!"

"You did not, and you know it."

As he circled, he glanced down, catching a glimpse of the closing gate. He hoped Barak had made it inside.

Newton hadn't been to Stormcrossed Manor for months, and he was pleased to see that it looked more habitable now than on his last visit. He just wished he hadn't arrived there by witch-flight.

"Here you go," Tamsyn said, passing him a steaming cup of tea. "Ginger tea will sort that nausea out."

He sniffed it tentatively. "Do I have to?"

"No. Just keep feeling sick. It's fine by me."

Moore accepted his with a great deal more grace than Newton. "Thanks, Tamsyn. Much appreciated. My gran used to make ginger tea when I was sick as a little boy. It always worked."

"A sensible woman, then, your gran. And so are you." Tamsyn patted his cheek whilst rolling her eyes at Newton. "You should pay more attention to this one."

"Fine! You're as bad as Briar." As soon as he said her name, he wished he hadn't. "I just hope she's okay." He forced himself to sip his tea. He needed to be sharp if he was going to get through this.

"So do I." Tamsyn sank into the chair by her fire. "But I think she is. I can't feel that anything is amiss, and I think I would. But her presence is not as strong as normal."

They were gathered in Tamsyn's small sitting room that Newton had never seen before. It was in Tamsyn's area of the house, and next to her kitchen that hadn't been updated since forever. It looked like the sitting room hadn't been, either. The wallpaper was of huge, overblown roses, faded and worn, and her sofa was the worse for wear, too. But the paintwork was fresh, and the place was clean. An old cast iron fireplace was filled with a crackling fire, and it was warm and cozy, especially in the candlelight. There was no electricity or phone reception there, either.

Moore leaned forward. "You sense Briar?"

"We have a connection, and it gets stronger with each passing day. I think it's my Seer skills, though, that enable that. When Reuben came by this morning, I hadn't noticed any change, but I feel it now." She rubbed her heart. "She's alive, but things aren't right at all."

"Have you tried to *see* her? Or has Beth?" Newton asked.

Tamsyn eased back in her chair and sipped her tea. "I'm not like Alex. I can't look into crystal balls or summon the void. Not like him. Visions come to me—or they used to. Beth is the same. But I tell you what I am still seeing." They looked at her expectantly. "The white stag."

"Which means what?" Newton asked.

"I don't know."

Newton groaned. "Great!"

"I thought they brought good luck?" Moore asked.

"There are a few interpretations. They represent a spiritual quest. For those that sight them, it could also mean that a momentous moment is close. It can also signify the Otherworld. Maybe that's what it means now. Maybe it knew this was coming. Maybe it was a warning."

Newton exchanged a puzzled glance with Moore. "You mean it predicted this? The white wall?"

"Perhaps." She shrugged, her frail shoulders barely lifting the thick cardigan she wore. "Its interpretations are many, so it's confusing. My powers aren't what they were either, so... Maybe it's telling me something, and I'm missing it."

Newton was over mystical mumbo jumbo and questions without answers. "Your granddaughter is inside that wall. What are we going to do about it?"

"I wish I knew."

The patter of feet had them all turning around to look at the door to the hall. Beth and Max appeared, clad in their pyjamas and ready for bed, Rosa behind them. "They've come to say goodnight. Come on you two, you've met Officers Newton and Moore before."

Newton didn't bother correcting her on his title. It seemed churlish. Especially when the children looked so much better than they had only months before. He knew Beth had experienced sightings of Wyrd at Samhain. Like Reuben, he wished she was seeing something now.

But just as the kids had kissed their grandmother goodnight and were heading back out of the door, a strange crackling noise seemed to envelop the house, and ice spread along the windows. Newton and Moore leapt to their feet.

Something was out there, and Newton suspected it was Jack Frost.

After Caspian had finished ferrying everyone around, he took Reuben to the outskirts of Ravens' Wood to join the Nephilim and Ghost OPS, and found them sprawled on the ground, winded and confused.

Zee was wedged into the branches of a huge birch tree. Eli was floundering in undergrowth, half on top of Cassie, and Niel was flat on his back with a branch on top of him. For a moment, he couldn't see Ben, but then spotted him a few feet into the forest, winded and groaning. Dylan looked the worst off. He was lying crookedly against an enormous tree trunk, blood pouring from a head injury. Caspian ran to help him, leaving Reuben struggling to regain his feet after the witch-flight.

"What the hell is going on?" Reuben said, hands on knees as he retched. "Why are you all on the ground?"

Niel groaned as he lifted the tree trunk and threw it aside. "Just communing with nature, you bloody great oaf. What do you think we're doing?"

"I'll rephrase it. What happened with the wall?"

"It went *poof!*" Niel staggered to his feet, checking himself over for injuries.

"It did a bit more than that," Eli groaned. Underneath him, Cassie squeaked, and he rolled off her. "Sorry, Cas!"

"Hey, Dylan," Caspian said, gently rousing Dylan. "Are you with us?"

Dylan blinked and moaned. "Ouch. Something hard hit me."

"That would be the tree, and I think *you* hit *it*. Let me see your head."

Dylan twisted slightly and moaned again. "Fuckity fuck. Everything aches."

"You have a big cut on your head. You hit a gnarly chunk of bark." Caspian patted the tree. "Sorry."

"You're apologising to the tree?"

"It's Ravens' Wood. Best to be safe." Caspian suppressed a smile. If Dylan was joking, then he was okay. "I'll sort your wound out when we get inside. In the meantime..." He pressed the hood of Dylan's jacket onto his cut, and fixed Dylan's hand over it. "Press right there."

Zee shouted from up the trees, branches creaking. "Guys, you need to get back in the tree line. Something's happening!"

Caspian looked over his shoulder, eyes widening with shock. He'd been so focussed on his friends that he'd barely looked at the wall, but it was crackling and popping again, as it slowly advanced towards him. He grabbed Dylan and dragged him into Ravens' Wood, and the others retreated, too. With horror, they watched as the wall butted up against the wood's perimeter and stopped.

"If it's doing that here," Eli reasoned, "then it's happening everywhere, but how far will it go?"

"Thank the Green Man and the old Gods for the wood's magic," Dylan said, slightly breathless. "At least we know the wall can't penetrate this place."

"But what set it off?" Ben asked. He pulled twigs from his hair, and brushed off snow as he joined his friends. "Was it us? All we did was take a few readings."

"Yeah, you didn't even poke it with a pointy stick," Cassie said.

Reuben looked confused. "A pointy stick? Are you all mad?"

"Actually, no," Niel admitted. "It was though, admittedly, an odd strategy we thought we should test."

Caspian hadn't been close to the wall before, and found it both fascinating and terrifying. "I thought you guys couldn't feel magic? I can feel it now."

"It's changed," Reuben told him. "Its energy felt stable earlier, calm. Now, it's all riled up and aggressive. Something has upset whoever is making it. The Winter Goddess, I presume."

"Actually," Shadow called from overhead. "It was probably me."

She scrambled from the canopy high above, down through branches, until she landed next to them. "We were worried for a moment when we couldn't see you." Her eyes raked over them all, hand on her sword hilt. "You're all okay?"

"Could be better, sister," Niel growled. "What did you do?"

"I lopped the head off the Snow Queen's statue. I don't think she liked that." She smirked.

Caspian took in her dishevelled appearance. "There was a fight?"

"Of course. Gabe dragged me off. He's flying overhead now. There's nowhere for him to land here. But you all need to leave. There's something happening on the far side of the valley. It looks like Stormcrossed Manor is caught in a kind of localised storm. If you stick to the tree line, and work your way out, you'll come to the road. That will be the quickest way to clear ground. I'll head that way." She pointed overhead again. "Gabe will pick me up. And there's something else you should know. Barak is inside now—or at least we hope so, anyway."

A roar of "*What?*" came from everyone.

But before explaining further, Shadow was gone, leaving the others scrambling to follow.

Barak soared through the gateway set into the wall of icy cloud that surrounded White Haven, and found himself in a peculiar, twisting tunnel that was far longer than he expected it to be.

It didn't help that like the outside it was dark, filled with whirling snow and strong winds that disorientated him. The good thing was that they also hid him from sight. However, he could hear the patter of running feet, and make out sprites sprinting to get inside before the gate closed. He thanked the Gods that the tunnel was high. He finally soared outside, straight into the middle of a blizzard. He gained height, aware of another sheet of ice on the sea where the gate exited, and that headed inland towards the harbour. A gust of wind pushed him west, and he banked around in shock as the sheer ice wall of an enormous palace reared up in front of him.

*What in Herne's hairy bollocks was that?*

He flew as high as he dared, not sure how low the false sky would be. It wasn't visible, that was certain. It was lost in dense, thick cloud. When he was sure he was hidden, he maintained his height and studied the palace that loomed out of the darkness like a beacon.

It was huge, stark, and chilling. It suggested an iron will, and intolerance for weakness. His heart sank. *The Snow Queen's epicentre of power, no doubt.* He had fought a battle in another icy castle only days earlier. *Was he going to have to fight another?* His heart sank even further at the thought.

On the ridge below it, where the carpark would normally be, was a huge fayre made up of lots of stalls. Currently, it was being battered by the storm, and people scurried to a row of sleighs waiting at the side. It warranted further investigation, but he needed a moment to take stock of other changes. Under cover of the blizzard he dropped lower, flying over White Haven.

The streetlights illuminated a few people walking the streets that were decorated for Yule and Christmas as they normally were. Restaurants and pubs were open, and looked to be busy. He flew even lower over The Wayward Son, pleased to see that it looked as normal. El's flat, however, was dark, as was Briar's shop.

Just as Barak was about to head to Avery and Alex's place, a flash of light lit up the clouds, and the air sizzled. A colossal roar like thunder resounded around him, and the storm intensified. And the palace... *Well. That was the centre of it all.* It stood bleak on the cliff top. Barak was drawn towards it like a moth to a flame.

Waves of energy rippled over the building, looking like the northern lights. That was weird. *Had she brought the north with her? Had she taken White Haven there?*

# Ten

Avery shook Clea's shoulder. "Gran! Clea! Can you hear me?"

Clea didn't respond. Her eyes were shut tight, and she lay on the sofa, unresponsive, but her eyes moved beneath her lids, as if she were dreaming, or having a nightmare. *Or had she had a stroke? Was this what happened?*

Avery sat back, her frustration growing. When Alex arrived in the living room, she leapt to her feet, fury blazing from her. "I told you I shouldn't have left her, and now look what's happened! And we left El! What if something happened to her, too?"

"Avery! Your gran is old, El is not. And we don't know what's happened. She could be drunk on sherry!"

Avery itched to hurl something, her palms opening and closing as if something should happen. Instead, she picked up a cushion and threw it at him. "How can you be so cold?"

He caught the cushion and frowned. "I'm not cold! I'm being practical."

He tried to squeeze past her to see Clea, but Avery blocked him. "And what can you do that I can't?"

"You shouted for me, remember? You wanted a second opinion!"

"You are infuriating! Something is wrong."

"I know it is. That's why I made us leave the fayre. What's the matter with you? You're all contrary."

"I am not contrary!"

"You are. You've contradicted yourself, and me, several times to-day." He adopted a singsong voice, cocking his head from side to side. *"Something's wrong, something isn't."* It took a while to rouse Alex to anger, but he was obviously getting there now.

*Good.* She wanted to provoke him. She was seething, and worried, and he was just so... "Fuck you, Alex Bonneville. Look at my grand-mother. She's just lying there, and I keep forgetting her, and you don't give a shit! You're all pub, and staff, and work, and you don't care about me!"

"That's a fucking lie, and you know it!" Alex's hands were clench-ing, just like her own.

"Are you going to hit me?"

He stepped back, appalled. "I would never hit you!"

"So then what's going on with your hands?"

"What's going on with yours?"

She looked down, shocked. "I'm angry. I'm trying to control my-self. *And something's wrong!*"

"I know!" He roared it out.

As he shouted, a huge rumble erupted around them, the blizzard howled like a demon, and a wave of power flashed out from Alex, knocking her into the coffee table. She stumbled and fell over it as flames erupted from his hands.

"How the fuck are you doing that? Are you a freak?" And then memories came flooding back. Memories of magic, elemental power, ghostly ancestors, and familiars. Avery was more furious than upset and she leapt to her feet, hands extended. Without effort or thought, she pushed her hand out and waves of wind made Alex stagger back-wards. "You could have hit Clea!"

"I didn't know what I was doing!"

They both paused, breathless and confused, the coffee table between them. More feelings and memories raced through Avery, and she could see that Alex was experiencing the same. She tingled as a familiar energy and power started to race through her core.

"Shit, Alex, we're witches!"

Alex turned horribly pale, and he vaulted over the coffee table to hug her. "How did we forget that? I could have killed you. I'm sorry."

But she had barely time to take in his warmth and scent. "Helena! That's why Clea is here!"

The previous month, while they were battling Wyrd and the wizard, they had needed more witches to help them. Clea had allowed Helena's spirit to inhabit her body to use her magic, and it had worked better than they had anticipated. Helena had argued for more time to remain in human form, and they had struck a deal. Helena could inhabit Clea's body for a few days once a month, and Clea would leave the rest home to live with Alex and Avery for that time. They had decided to say that Clea was on a successful experimental drug that was improving her cognition. That was why Clea – really Helena – was living with them. Helena had been Clea for the last twenty-four hours. Avery sighed with relief. At least that made sense now. No wonder it didn't seem normal for her grandmother to live with them. It wasn't.

Before Alex could respond, the sound of shattering glass came from the attic, and then a huge squawk. In seconds, a flurry of wings whirled down the stairs and landed on the dining table. It was a huge raven. And not just any raven, either. It was her familiar.

"Raven. You're back."

"I've been here all along, you great fool," he squawked. "Stuck in the crystal ball up there." Raven was a cranky, wise old bird that was short on patience, and had a gift for speech that the other familiars hadn't. Sometimes Avery wasn't sure if that was a good thing or not.

"Nearly twenty-four hours, too! Do you know how uncomfortable that was?"

"Not as uncomfortable," Helena bit out from behind them, "as being stuck in Clea's muddled head, and trying to make her talk. I haven't done so much knitting in my life!"

Avery couldn't quite work out what was happening. It was like looking on her room with fresh eyes. A blizzard raged outside the window, she had just been to a fayre, and there was an ice palace at the top of the hill. The past few hours felt like a dream. "What's happening to us?"

Raven rustled his enormous wings. "A Winter Witch has cast a spell on White Haven, and she is so powerful that she suppressed your magic—and mine. But not anymore. We need a plan. Or else we'll all be stuck here forever."

El was furious with herself for getting caught. *Stupid, stupid, stupid!*

She'd been cocky and reckless in her curiosity and concern for her friend, and now she was stuck in this hideously cold cell, her arms bruised by the powerful grip of the guards. They had literally frog-marched her down long corridors and steep stairs, and now she was in the bowels of the castle with dripping walls, cockroaches, and rats.

El looked with distaste at the pile of filthy straw in the corner of the room. The only light came from a torch down the passageway that filtered through narrow bars on the door of her prison. This was grim. And she would have to face the queen tomorrow.

Her frustration turned to fear as she considered that outcome. She would be taken down to the main square and made an example of.

She would be publicly whipped, an example to the town not to upset the queen and break the rules. If she was really unlucky, she would most probably lose her shop and spend her days seeking charity from her friends or becoming a beggar on the street. But charity was not encouraged to be given to those whom the queen had punished. It would earn the giver the same outcome.

El rarely succumbed to despair, but she could feel it creeping through her now. Dread settled into her stomach like a stone. And she still had the overwhelming feeling of loss. She pounded on the door. "Let me out!"

But no one responded to her—except for the skitter of a rat in the corner.

She shouted, hitting the door until her fists ached, and then kicked it. Exhausted, she finally sank to the floor on the meagre straw, ignoring the scratching that came from within it, and finally gave in to her tears.

Briar stood before the window in the luxuriously appointed room she had been escorted to, staring at the blizzard that assaulted the fayre, as she considered a way to leave.

After Jack ran out, she had been escorted swiftly from the queen's presence, along corridors and up the stairs. She was relieved to find that her room was not clad in ice, but had a roaring fire, a richly furnished bed, fancy furniture, and a chair before the fireplace. If she was a prisoner, and she must be because the door had been locked behind her, she must be a valued one.

*But why?*

Briar was no one special. She was a shopkeeper, admittedly one with a successful business, but why would that matter? If she had realised Jack knew the queen, she would have tried any way possible to have avoided coming with him. But as she considered the intensity behind his deep blue eyes, she knew he would have never taken no for an answer. That's why she agreed in the first place. He was dangerous. Things would have become ugly. The glitter of control behind his eyes told her that.

Which led to another question. Why did he particularly ask her to go with him? Had he sought her out to begin with? He must have, because the queen, apparently, had much to discuss with her. And then of course, there was the curious exchange in the audience hall. Briar tried to recall her exact words; she had a feeling they were important. *Something stirs on the South Gate that needs your attention.*

What on Earth was the South Gate? Was it another entrance to the castle?

At least she was warm after being cold for hours, and the ominous rumbles had finally stopped. It was as if a monster had raged in the dark.

Just as she was debating what to do, she heard footsteps outside the door, and the jangle of keys. The door opened and a guard stepped inside. "The Queen demands your presence. Follow me."

He led her upstairs to the second floor, rather than down to the audience room, stopping in front of a pair of huge wooden doors guarded by two men. After a brief rap, a young woman answered. Briar presumed she was a Lady-in-waiting, considering her immaculate dress of fine silk and wool. She appraised Briar with cool eyes, and nodded at the guards dismissively.

They were obviously in the queen's private quarters, which were as cold as the audience hall, despite its rich tapestries and fine furnishings.

Several doors led to other rooms of which Briar saw only a glimpse. The queen stood before vast windows made of arched stone columns, with doors that led out to a balcony—thankfully closed. Her back was to Briar, and she seemed lost in thought. She was tall, her waist narrow above her full skirts, and from behind, Briar could see the elaborate way her hair was dressed, her raven dark tresses glinting in the candlelight.

"Your Majesty," the young woman said. "Briar Ashworth is here."

The queen turned, her grim expression sending a jolt of fear through Briar. "You are not what I expected."

Briar stuttered. "I'm sorry? What do you mean?"

The queen strode across the room, her cold hand outstretched. She gripped Briar's chin and lifted it up, making Briar stand on tiptoes as she tipped her face from side to side. "You seem so insignificant, and yet you hold so much within you."

Briar jerked backwards, her skin burning with the icy imprint of the queen's fingers, but the queen didn't let go. Her grip was like a vice. "You wield huge elemental power, and I need it."

"I, what?"

The queen laughed, throwing her head back, white teeth flashing, before fixing her with her coal dark eyes. "You. I need *you* and the power that resides in here." She prodded Briar's stomach and then her head. "You are the key to everything, and I need to suck you dry to keep the wolves from the door."

Terror raced through Briar so swiftly that she trembled and her knees weakened, but the queen's other arm snaked around her waist and pulled her close, like a lover. Slowly she lowered her lips to Briar, her icy breath forming a mist that stole across Briar's skin. Briar brought her arms up between them, pushing the woman back, but it was like pushing a wall. The queen watched her through emotionless eyes, and Briar felt as if she was falling into a void. Their lips met, so cold that all thought of warmth and light fled from Briar's memory.

There was only darkness and ice.

Newton recoiled in horror as Beth screamed and screamed. "What the hell is happening to her?"

Rosa, her mother, didn't help matters. She shrieked and picked Beth up, but Beth flailed and kicked and kept screaming.

Max watched his sister, transfixed, eyes wide with horror, hands over his ears. Tamsyn ran to comfort Beth, but it was Moore who was the most helpful. Beth squirmed and kicked in Rosa's arms, her screams frantic and terrified. She kicked Tamsyn, knocking the old woman over, and Rosa could barely hold her. Moore covered the room in quick strides, sweeping Beth out of Rosa's arms and into his own. He wasn't a big man, but he was stronger than Rosa, and he clutched Beth to his chest, pressing her head into his shoulder, murmuring soothing words to her as if she were one of his own children. Newton helped Tamsyn to her feet.

An icy wind blew around the house, seeming to find its way into every nook and cranny, and the candles flickered. Long shadows stretched across the room, and Rosa ran to her son instead, wrapping her arms around him as they both sank to the ground.

Newton thought he'd known terror, but he hadn't experienced anything like this. Beth's screaming turned into a flurry of words that were barely understandable, her breath coming now in sobs. Moore kept comforting her, arms wrapped tightly around her, and his eyes met Newton's, his expression full of despair.

Tamsyn ran to her great-granddaughter, and gripped Beth's head between her two bony hands, locking eyes. "Beth, what is it? Slow down, my love, slow down. What do you see?"

But Beth wasn't seeing Tamsyn. Her gaze was elsewhere. With breathless sobs she finally stopped screaming and said the worst thing Newton had ever heard.

"The queen is killing Auntie Briar."

Reuben stood on the lane at the bottom of Stormcrossed Manor's long drive, watching a maelstrom of hail filled fog whip around the house and over the grounds. He could feel the magic in it, even from a distance.

Ash and Nahum landed next to him and Caspian, Ash's golden wings the only brightness in the cold, dark night.

Nahum said, "It's swallowed the whole house. I can't see through it."

"It could be the sprite causing it," Ash suggested. "We lost sight of him when we fled the icesheet."

"But why attack that place? Why not mine?" Reuben asked. He looked at Caspian. "Can we stop it?"

Caspian considered the question for a long moment, before warily looking towards the Wall of Doom that had encroached further down the lane. "The only thing I know that can cancel ice is fire and warmth, but I'm not sure that between us we have enough power. But of course, we can try. We *have* to try." He looked at the two Nephilim. "Have you tried to get inside?"

Ash shook his head, ruffling his feathers as he did so. "It has a similar energy to the wall. It repelled us."

Reuben was determined to get in. His friends were trapped in White Haven. His girlfriend. He wasn't about to let more friends and Briar's family get hurt, too. "Let's build a shield of fire ahead of us, see if we can force our way through."

Caspian nodded, fire already balling in his hands. "I like it. But let's put it behind us as well to create a bubble."

Eve had done much the same thing when she was fleeing the tunnels underneath West Haven, taking Cassie and Dylan to safety with Jasper.

"Great." Reuben was eager to do something.

"What about us? Can we come?" Nahum asked.

"Best wait here. When the others arrive, check the perimeter. If that deadly sprite is behind this, try to catch him." Reuben paused. He hadn't asked anything about their encounter on the icesheet, and it might be important information. "What happened on the ice?"

Nahum summarised everything—the ice sculptures that came to life and the ice-wielding sprites. "If there's anything like that in there, you'll be in trouble."

"Not in a wall of bloody fire we won't be."

"And if the ice puts out your fire?" Ash asked.

Reuben nodded at Caspian. "He's got curses in his blood, and I'm a water witch. We'll improvise."

"Always with the curses," Caspian said, clearly amused, before spelling a wall of flames in front of him. "Get cosy."

Reuben stepped next to him, shoulder to shoulder, adding his power to Caspian's. He extended the spell until they were enveloped by flames, at least a couple of metres away from their bodies. "I think that's a bit close," Reuben complained, as searing heat replaced bitter cold.

Caspian responded by enlarging the circle they were within and Reuben breathed easier. "That's better. Ready?"

"Ready."

They advanced steadily up the drive, but the fire flickered as they reached the icy maelstrom ahead of them. "Plan for if the fire goes out?" Reuben asked.

"Positive thoughts, please, Reu."

Reuben focussed on strengthening his magic, feeling it mix with Caspian's as it had many times before. After the initial flicker the fire steadied and they continued, but it was harder going once they were fully within the ice storm. Reuben felt as if he were walking through treacle. The howl of the wind penetrated the roar of the fire, but they persevered. The fire sizzled and flickered, and soon they were enveloped in steam.

"This isn't working," Caspian said, slick with sweat. "We're going to cook to death. I have a feeling we're being hit by something, too. Weapons of some sort. Maybe those ice spears Nahum told us about. Let's stop. Weigh up our options. I don't even think we need to go much further."

"I know! I could call Silver, my familiar!" Reuben suggested. "He's a water horse. He might be able to carry us through this! But we'll need to drop the fire spell."

"We can shield ourselves with a protection spell instead."

"But, it depends on how busy he is."

Caspian's eyes narrowed, sweat dropping into them. "What does *that* mean?"

"He was searching for my coven's familiars."

"Which is what I should be doing, too!"

"One thing at a time, Cas!" Reuben thought he might die from heat exhaustion. "If we drop the fire, then we have to raise the protection spell immediately."

"I can do that. You call Silver. Ready?"

Reuben braced himself. "Ready."

As soon as the shield of fire vanished, the howling wind ripped Reuben's breath from his body. He was immediately blinded by pelting hail that stung any exposed skin. "Caspian? Where the fuck is the protection spell?" He stuck his hand out, grasping Caspian's coat. "Caspian?"

"I can't..." Caspian gasped. "It won't let me!"

Reuben roared into the wind. "Silver!"

Nothing happened. But he could feel icy fingers jabbing his skin and trying to tear his clothes from his body.

"Silver!" Reuben tried to block out everything except the powerful, shimmering form of his horse. But he didn't appear.

He could barely breathe, the cold was so harsh. He kept hold of Caspian and pulled him to the ground, until both were enveloped in deep snow. Reuben drew on his water magic, and instead of trying to repel the ice, he drew it to him, skilfully weaving the snow and water around them. There was so much of it that Reuben was flooded with power. He wished he'd have thought of it sooner. It was feeding his power exponentially. He raised his hands and constructed a wall of sheer ice around them.

The wind dropped, and his vision returned—some of it, at least. The driveway was pitch black, and he was sure he could see darting figures in the dark—ethereal, unnerving... A short way ahead was the house, a light burning in the hall window. He slowly stood again.

"Herne's horns! Caspian, are you okay?" He looked down at his friend, who was shivering in the snow.

"My eyebrows are almost burnt off and now my balls are freezing and so far in my body I doubt that I'll ever see them again. Apart from that, I'm fine."

Reuben tried to calm down and think clearly. "We need to call on our strengths. Water for me, air for you. Silver won't come. The house is close, though."

"I think there are sprites out there." Caspian examined his hand. "Welts. I'm covered in them."

"Me too, in places no sprite should ever be. We need to get to the house. I'll keep the ice around us, you use air to move it—or something like that. One last push."

Caspian stood again. "One last push."

# Eleven

A lex sipped his whiskey, deciding it was the only thing that could fortify him for Raven's news and their returning memories.

He, Avery, and Helena, who was in Clea's body, were pacing or sitting around the attic spell room talking to Raven, who commanded their attention from the big wooden table. He and Avery had taken the time to change their wet clothing, and get drinks and snacks, preparing themselves for what lay ahead. The electricity had cut out in the height of the storm, leaving them in candlelight.

Alex sat down and pulled his grimoire towards him, needing practical action. "Raven, run through it again, please. How are we in this mess?"

"Last night, at midnight, a snowstorm descended on White Haven. It had been building all day—"

"I remember that," Avery said. "It was getting bad while I picked up Clea from the rest home. It was affecting all of Cornwall."

"Exactly." Raven rustled his feathers. "You brought Clea here, and she allowed Helena to possess her again. The night progressed as normal. But the storm was never normal. You felt it, I remember you saying so."

Alex nodded. "We did. We commented on what a strange energy it had, but we just thought it was storm energy."

Helena leaned her elbow on the table, resting her chin in her hands. "But it was more than that. The Winter Witch disguised it well."

"She's a pro." Raven snorted, which Alex would have thought was impossible if he hadn't just heard it. "She's brought her sprites with her, and one is particularly deadly. Anyway, at midnight, while most people were sleeping, she released the full power of the storm, and her magic with it. She has wrapped an impenetrable wall about this place, and unleashed a memory spell with it. She's suppressed memories and implanted new ones."

"Making us forget we were witches and suppressing our magic." Avery played with her magic as she listened, summoning flames in her hands, and lighting candles and incense. It seemed to reassure her to use her magic again. "I can't even fathom how powerful she is to do that. Are you sure she's a witch?"

"She's not a Goddess, I'm sure of that," Raven answered. "A Goddess would have no need for us. Therefore, she's something else, and a witch fits."

"A Winter Witch," Helena said thoughtfully. "Intriguing. So, why is she here, and how come you know so much about it, Raven?"

"She may have trapped me in Alex's crystal ball, but I could still see what was going on within White Haven. But she has suppressed us, too, because we are connected to you. Briar's familiar, Deer, and El's, Bear, are both struggling to return and communicate. I can't contact them. And my normal freedom is limited. I still can't get out of White Haven."

"But she couldn't stop us knowing that something was wrong," Alex said, as he recalled recognising that something was off all day. "What released us—unblocked our memories?"

"Your argument and pent-up frustration. It burst it. It helps that we are further from her centre of power, the palace."

Helena tapped the table. "You still haven't said why she's here."

He cocked his head and fixed her with one beady eye. "I don't know why, but I suspect she is losing her own magic. This place is rich with it."

"How can a witch lose her magic?" Alex asked dumbfounded. "That can't be right!"

"Age, perhaps? Or the source of her power has changed? Maybe," Helena said thoughtfully, "she does this every year, somewhere. The important thing is how we stop her!"

"We need to gather our coven," Alex said, starting to pace again. And then he stopped and stared at Raven. "You haven't mentioned Reuben. Where is he?"

"Not here."

"He stayed at Greenlane Manor last night," Avery reminded him. "Does that mean he's locked outside?"

Raven nodded. "From what I can gather, only the immediate town is caught within the spell."

"And we forgot he ever existed!" Avery looked appalled. "That's why El was so upset. She was missing Reuben and didn't even know it! That's so cruel!" Wind whipped up around her, making the candles flicker wildly. "I hate this woman already. What a bitch! I'd even forgotten Helena." She whirled around to look at her. "Even though you were here all along."

"But I couldn't remind you, could I?"

Alex focussed on Reuben. "Hopefully, Reu knows what's going on. And the Nephilim are back, and Caspian, so he'll have help breaking the spell and getting in—somehow." His initial excitement faded. "Unless their memories are affected, too."

Helena's cool, calculating gaze returned as she tapped her grimoire. "She can't possibly keep us here forever. It would create havoc in the real world. There must be a short-term objective. If she takes our power, she needs to do it quickly. There must be a ritual she's planning. Or maybe she takes us one by one. When she's done, she gets out, leaving us without magic. The fact that she suppressed our power means we can't retaliate. Or couldn't!"

"There's always magic," Raven pointed out. "You can't just suck it dry. It's everywhere and forever, if you know how to use it. You will never be without it."

A quiet, creeping dread descended on Alex. "That's true. It's not like we have a well that runs dry. That applies to her, too. But not everyone can wield magic, can they? Or know that actual magic exists, or the paranormal world. We may think we will always be able to use our magic, because we're witches, and it runs in our blood. But what if she can strip us of our ability to wield it? Like turning off a switch!"

"If she needs to act quickly, why hasn't she attacked us already?" Avery asked. "That brings us back to your suggestion, Helena, of her needing some kind of ritual."

"It can't be a coincidence that she's turned up the day before Yule. Maybe her feast has something to do with it," Alex suggested. "It does seem to be a very big deal." He turned to Helena. "Can you still travel around as a ghost?"

"No. I mean, I could leave Clea's body, but with things the way they are, I don't know if I could get back in. I should probably stay put." She pouted. "It's very annoying."

"Okay. We can still find Briar and El, bring them here, and plan our attack. I'm sure we can bring their memories back, and their magical abilities."

Avery nodded. "Like us, they knew something was wrong. Perhaps something has provoked them, too. They may be trying to find us. But we left El at the fayre. Maybe she's still there. And that reminds me!

Why did the storm flare up again? What was the disturbance about? Knowing what we know now makes me think something made the queen angry. Alex, we should go and find them and bring them here. We need to stick together."

"Let me," Raven said. "I can at least check where they are. I need to stretch my wings after what I've been through, anyway."

Alex let him out the window, poured himself another whiskey, and sat down, thinking through the implications. "We need time to plan and gather information, therefore we can't do anything tonight. That means that tomorrow we are going to act dumb. We cannot let on that we know anything, or that we have magic. To *anyone*! There might be spies."

"There are definitely spies," Avery pointed out. "The queen's guards are in the town, and they must be her staff that are driving the sleighs." All of Avery's nerves and anger seemed to leak out of her, and she sat at the table with a thump. "This is so slick. No mobile phones. No transport, except for her own sleighs. It's only just struck me that I haven't seen a single car on the road today."

"And there's no TV or radio," Helena reminded them. "I was trying to watch it today. Clea loves The Chase! We have no communication from the outside world, and only select things from the modern day have survived. Plumbing, electricity...although, the storm seems to have got rid of that." She raised her eyebrows. "I wonder if that will be out for good now."

"She's returning us to a more primitive state. It's old-fashioned," Alex mused. "And no one has even noticed. Why is she posing as a queen?"

"Perhaps she is one, wherever she's from," Avery said. "She seems to have a retinue. And it's the perfect way to have everyone do your bidding. As appalled as I am that this is happening, I'm also intrigued.

Who is she? She's posing as a copycat Snow Queen, but that's a fairytale."

"Or is it?" Alex asked. "A fairytale with truth at its root. Raven called her a Winter Witch. Perhaps she's both. A Winter Witch who is the Snow Queen."

"Say it is us that she's after," Helena suggested, "what happens to the rest of the town? And that's presuming a lot. Does she know about the magic in general here, or you, specifically? And does she know about me?"

Alex's head ached. There were so many questions, and so few answers. "She must have researched us, or else why is she here?"

Helena sighed. "There's more than one coven in Cornwall, or all of England. Or even the world, for that matter. Admittedly, White Haven seems to have more than its fair share of magical entanglements. You know, I think the locals here make a big difference. They believe in the old ways. They're passionate about them. It all adds to the magic of the place. And it's been like that since my time."

"Which suggests it's not just us," Alex said. "It's White Haven."

Helena's familiar, mischievous smile spread across her face, looking even cheekier as it was on Clea's elderly features. Dimples appeared in her wrinkles. "I guarantee she does not know about me. I feel it. And look at me!" She swept her hands down to take in her woolly jumper and skirt. "I look harmless. What an excellent disguise."

"But your magic is strong," Alex reminded her. "You need to tamp it down. Mask it."

"I can do that. You need to take your Wolf out. It's the perfect night to stretch your legs."

"That's a great point. I'll sit in front of the fire, later on, when it's quiet. He'll come to me more easily."

"I'll work on spells with Helena in the meantime," Avery said. "But say she does know about us, and then they come for us. What do we do?"

"We resist, of course," Helena said, looking aghast. "But not until we're up close and personal to her. We aim for maximum damage." She smiled maliciously.

"I agree with you." Alex always found Helena's presence a mixed blessing, but she was valuable in a sticky situation, and this was stickier than most.

Barak decided to linger by the palace. So far, no one seemed to have noted his arrival. There were no shouts of alarm. No search parties had set out from the palace.

He flew back to where the gate had been and saw that it was fully shut now, and all traces of its existence had vanished. The icesheet was pristine and empty, and ran all the way to the beach, the cliffs, and the harbour. It was a churned-up mass of spiky ice below the cliffs, as if the pounding waves had frozen quickly. But if there was one gate, there might be more. He would investigate in time, but he decided to take advantage of the blizzard conditions and examine the castle more fully.

There were two huge courtyards, one at the rear that looked like a working area, and one at the front that was far fancier. There were no windows on the ground floor, but plenty on the other levels. Lights shone from many of them. But it was a set of windows that opened onto a balcony that caught his eye. They were majestic, overlooking the town, the balcony roof held up by fluted columns. It was meant for grand gestures. Somewhere to be seen. Somewhere for the queen or Goddess or whatever she was to watch over her domain.

*If that's who was behind everything.* Barak needed to find out and confirm their suspicions. He considered the high roof, battlements, and towers. He could break a window and find a way in up there, perhaps.

His attention was caught by movement within the room beyond the balcony. Barak flew closer, curious. The room was luxurious, and a regal woman was in the centre of it, wearing a huge, full-skirted dress, with raven black hair. She looked to be embracing someone. He considered his chances. *Was this the woman represented in the sculptures? Was she behind everything? If he struck now, would it be over? Could he kill her, while her back was to the window? Was there a spell of protection on the place?* If he called it wrongly, and this wasn't who was behind it all, he'd alert everyone to his presence needlessly.

And then his breath caught in his chest as he saw a figure struggling in her arms.

*Briar.*

All thoughts of stealth vanished. Sword outstretched, he charged at the central window, shattering it as he plunged through the glass between the stone frames, wings close to his sides. Even folded, the apex of his wings were above his head, and they took the brunt of the force of the impact, protecting his body. He rolled through the shattered glass and bounded to his feet. Magic filled the room, as rich and heady as wood smoke on an autumn evening.

The woman turned, a snarl on her lips, transforming her features into an unearthly mask. Her eyes were dark holes that threatened to burn through him. One arm still gripped Briar in a deadly embrace, but she flung up the other. An icy blast flew from her fingers, engulfing Barak in a subzero mist that burned his skin—despite the fact that his wings should have protected him from the cold. He took in a sharp intake of breath in shock, and the cold poured into his lungs; he fell to his knees.

Then something unexpected happened. The queen was focussing so much on Barak that she was ignoring Briar, who was limp in her arms. But she was stirring now, blinking as reason seemed to return to her.

Barak had to buy her time.

He flexed his huge wings, drawing him back to his feet, and with every beat, warmth returned to his body. The queen shrieked, dropping Briar on the floor without a second thought, and stalked towards him.

At the same time, the doors of the grand apartment flew open, and half a dozen guards ran in. But their human faces quickly vanished, becoming pale-faced sprites instead.

Barak charged at her, sweeping his huge wings out. They fell together in a ball of tumbling feathers, layers of skirts, and sharp, scratching nails. He pinned her to the floor, trying to stab her with his sword. She gripped his face with her hands, almost paralysing him with cold, pulling his lips close to hers.

Barak called on his father's healing energy. A flash of fire rippled beneath his skin, and the woman screamed. Barak pressed himself on to her, her flesh searing beneath his, locking eyes as he waited for the life to ebb from her.

That is until something struck him from behind. Sharp jabs pierced his feathers and skin, and he twisted to try to see what was happening. The queen took advantage of the distraction, and with superhuman strength, threw him off her, and regained her feet. A row of guards with raised spears raced to form a defensive line between them, Briar behind all of them.

The queen pushed them aside, radiating fury as she shouted, "Who are you?"

She was so angry, and they were all so focussed on Barak, that they didn't see Briar rise to her feet, or see the green light that now blazed from her eyes.

Barak raised his sword. "I am a Nephilim, destroyer of worlds."

Memories flooded through Briar as she struggled to her feet, the icy grip of the queen's magic fading. Memories of her friends, of old loves, of family. Of how White Haven should be. Of the Nephilim and her friend, Barak, who stood before her, facing off against sprites and the queen.

She thought of her magic and the Green Man.

Briar flexed her fingers, feeling power flood through her. And anger. *How dare this bitch try to steal her magic?* Briar might be surrounded by stone, but it had come from the earth once, and it would feed her power, as would the Green Man, who was growing increasingly restless.

As Barak fought the charging guards, Briar hit the queen between the shoulder blades with a powerful blast of fire that made her stagger forward. Thick, green vines shot from her fingers, binding the queen, and dragging her to the ground. She stamped her feet, and cracks ruptured the stone floor, spreading out like a spider's web across the cavernous room and rocketing up the walls.

The queen screeched again, a chilling, banshee-like sound. But as thick as the vines were, they quickly turned to ice and shattered. Briar blasted her again, more vines shooting across the floor to smother the queen, but this time every vine withered and died as soon as it touched her. The queen responded instantly, shooting icy darts at Briar. Briar threw up a protection shield, and then cast a spell to knock the queen off her feet. Spells and magic flew back and forth, both women weaving around the room as Barak fought his opponents simultaneously.

Then there was a shout from the door, and both women turned in surprise. Another guard stood there, wearing a different uniform, and he shouted his command at the queen. "Do not kill her! It is too soon! The king demands it."

As more guards filed in behind him, Briar knew that they would not win this fight.

They had to get out.

Briar ran towards Barak, then slipped on ice beneath her feet. Icicles shot up to form a cage around her, the bars as thick as an iron fence. She tried to melt them with fire, but the icicles reformed as fast as Briar could respond—until a huge, black bird appeared out of nowhere and dived at the queen, trying to blind her with its jabbing beak and flapping wings.

Raven shouted, "Get out!"

Barak yelled, "Balcony, now!"

Briar blasted a hole through her cage, ran to the shattered window, and vaulted through it, while Barak decapitated a sprite and dodged the spear of another. He raced to her side, wrapped his arms around her waist as she clung to him, and jumped off the balcony. Within seconds they were soaring into the thick blizzard.

"Barak! Where are we going?"

"If Raven is here, then Avery must be okay. We'll head there."

Caspian was exhausted by the time they virtually fell through Storm-crossed Manor's front door. They sealed it behind them with a spell, hearing the scrabble of sharp fingers on the door.

"Bloody hell, Reuben. I didn't think we were going to make it."

Reuben looked drained, his skin white despite his tan. "I hope the others aren't trying to follow us. That was insane!"

Caspian pressed his face to the glass window in the door, and then jumped back as a sharp-faced sprite with razorlike teeth snapped at him. "Fuck! We were right. There are creatures out there."

"No shit! We need to ward this place." He shouted, "Tamsyn? Newton!" Neither responded. "Come on, Caspian, we need to find them. You don't think they're stuck outside, do you? They can't survive this!"

A smash of glass had them both jumping back as balls of ice shattered the windows like bullets.

Caspian cast the strongest protection spell he knew, and a blue, shimmering field sealed the broken pane. "We need to cast a much bigger spell."

Reuben was walking down the hall when they heard Newton's shout and running feet. Newton almost sagged with relief when he saw them. "Thank the Gods. How did you get through that?"

"With sheer, bloody-minded persistence and a fuck ton of magic," Reuben declared. "Is everyone all right in here?"

"Well, we're all inside and safe, if that's what you mean, but Beth's just had an episode, and well," his gaze drifted to the window behind Caspian, "you can see what's kicked up out there."

"How long?"

"Ten minutes, maybe? And getting stronger." He turned and led the way down the corridor and into a small sitting room, summarising the situation as he walked. Caspian's chest was tight with worry when he heard what Beth had said about Briar. *If it was so bad out here, what was happening in White Haven? Was Briar alive?*

The mood was decidedly edgy. Moore sat with Beth on his lap, her face pressed against his chest, his hands resting on her head. Her eyes were closed, her soft face streaked with tears. Tamsyn sat next to him, her hand on Beth's leg, jaw tight.

Rosa was seated in a large armchair, arms around Max. For once, the young boy didn't want to throw off his mother's embrace. His eyes were fixed on his sister. All of them looked up at him and Reuben as they entered, hope kindling in their eyes. Caspian wished they could deliver it.

Tamsyn struggled to her feet to hug Reuben. "You came back. Thank you."

"Of course I did." His voice was rough as he hugged the old lady. He towered over her and had to bend almost in half. Tamsyn seemed to have become everyone's grandmother. "How are you?"

"I'm fine. It's Beth I'm worried about. And Briar, of course. Newton told you..."

"Yes."

Caspian kept his eye on the window while they talked. He could see the darting figures in the snow, getting bolder and bolder as they crept closer to the house. If they didn't act now, they would break in and kill them all.

"Reu, we need a protection spell first. The sprites are getting closer." Caspian frowned as another figure became visible. In fact, it was as if the snow moved aside for him. He walked towards the house, sparks dancing at his fingertips, a swathe of ice forming on the ground around him. It was a young man with a shock of white hair, and he was wearing an unexpectedly elegant suit. "I think Jack Frost has arrived."

"Jack Frost!" Rosa murmured. "What is happening?"

Caspian immediately started to cast a protection spell, hand outstretched, his magic blooming across the window and along the wall. He worked quickly, pushing his hands outward. The spell grew in strength and power, rippling across the house. Reuben stood next to him, aligning their magic once again. They were so used to each other now that they connected quickly. Reuben focussed on the other side of the house, and between them, in a matter of seconds, the house was sealed in. And it wasn't a moment too soon.

A jagged spear of ice flew from the sprite's fingers, crashed into the protective wall, and vanished.

Eyes narrowed, the sprite advanced, his acolytes behind him, hurling weapons of ice. Sounds of repeated attacks echoed through the house. Caspian felt every wave of attack, but their protection spell was strong. He smiled victoriously at the vicious-faced man. If looks could have killed, Caspian would surely be dead.

Reuben waved. "Hey, shit face." He put two fingers to his eyes and pointed them back at Jack Frost, who was now only a few feet from the window. "I'm watching you."

The man snarled, his anger transforming his boyish good looks into something far uglier. Never taking his eyes off the two witches, he lifted his hands, raising up a wall of sheer ice, sealing the house inside it, and blocking himself from view. Jack Frost might not be able to get in, but he was making sure they couldn't get out, either. *Except...*

"Can you still use witch-flight?" Reuben asked him, echoing his own thoughts.

Caspian frowned. "I'm not sure I can. This feels like the magic around White Haven, so I don't think I should risk it. I don't know what the repercussions could be. It might injure me, just send me back here, or maybe even kill me."

"Then you absolutely should *not* risk it," Reuben answered.

"I'll certainly try to think of a spell to counter it, but for now we need to warn the others not to come in after us, and let them know we're safe. If the phones won't work, we need another way. Like our familiars."

"What others?" Rosa asked, clutching Max, who was now squirming in discomfort.

"Our friends, Zee and his brothers," Caspian told her, knowing she knew Zee.

"What can he do to help?" Tamsyn asked, eyes widening suspiciously. "What are you keeping from me?"

"Later, Tamsyn. Right now, I need a quiet space."

"Use my kitchen. You know where it is. But I have questions..."

Caspian grinned at Newton, knowing he would be furious with him. "I'm sure Newton can answer them. Then we need to speak to Beth."

# Twelve

S hadow realised that the longer they waited at the end of Storm-crossed Manor's drive, the more likely they would be blocked in.

The wall that encompassed White Haven had advanced up the lane, but had at least stopped for now. However, the ice cloud—a lame description of the magical cloud of whirling hail that surrounded Stormcrossed Manor—advanced down the drive towards them and across the garden on either side, stealing along the hedge.

They were all lined up there, anxiously hoping that Reuben and Caspian had made it to the manor. Zee, Eli, and Niel had arrived with Ghost OPS, and she and Gabe had arrived a few minutes earlier, joining Ash and Nahum, who had told them what had happened. Ghost OPS was already doing what they did best while the others paced, weapons in hand.

"What if they're trapped in there?" Niel argued, bristling with intense anger and a need to act. She knew how he felt. She was experiencing the same emotions. The fight on the icesheet had whetted her appetite for more, not slaked it. "We should try to get inside."

"Brother," Ash said gently, "I know you crave violence and want to help our friends, but that way lies madness, especially until we know what we face. You didn't see the sprites like we did."

"They're fucking sprites! We're Nephilim!"

"They carry a lot of magic."

"And," Gabe added, "we have no idea what we're dealing with. If Reu and Cas are safe, then we'll put ourselves at risk for nothing. We're better off forming a plan to hit them stronger later."

"When it might be too late!" Niel said, glaring at Gabe. "Have you decided how you're going to tell Estelle where Barak is?"

"Oh, I'm telling her?"

"You are our de facto leader!" Niel bowed. "And welcome to it!"

Gabe blanched. "Fuck off, Niel. And no, but I'll handle it."

"She'll handle you, more like. Take a last look at your balls, my friend, before she force-feeds them to you."

Shadow intervened. "I know what we're dealing with, and sprites are no easy fight. They are fey, vicious and strong. There are a few different types in my world. Huge, green ones with muscles like yours, these blue-skinned cold weather sprites, and little imps that are no less deadly in their own right. I'm beginning to think the queen is fey, or at least has affiliations with them." *And whatever that meant, it was bad. Very, very bad.* It was something she needed to think on. The sprites had been a shock when she saw them. *Jack Frost was one thing, but hordes of them? And how had the Witch-Queen managed to get them here?*

The sound of beating wings and an unearthly screech made them grip their weapons tighter as they looked upward, but it was Cassie who shouted, "It's Eagle, Caspian's familiar!"

Zee stepped forward, arm outstretched, and Eagle landed on his forearm, sharp talons gripping his bare skin. *Impressive.* He didn't even wince as he asked, "Is it Caspian? Is he all right?"

Eagle merely screeched once, very loudly.

"He's not chatty like Raven, is he?" Nahum said, amused. "One screech for yes, two for no. Understand?"

Eagle screeched again.

"My name is Zee," Nahum said. "Yes or no."

He responded with two screeches.

Nahum grinned. "Excellent. Are Caspian and Reuben safe in the manor?"

One screech.

"Are Newton and Moore there?"

Another single screech.

"Is everyone safe inside?"

Another screech.

"Should we try to reach you?"

Two furious screeches answered that one immediately.

"Are there sprites surrounding you?"

One screech.

"Can you get out again?"

Two screeches.

"Not even using witch-flight?"

Another two screeches.

Nahum looked at the group. "They're safe at least, and we shouldn't try to get to them. I suggest we get home and strategise."

Gabe nodded, his eyes sweeping the surroundings. "Yes. There's nothing we can do right now." He stared at Eagle. "Stay in touch. We'll work on a solution."

It screeched again, wings flapping ready to leave, but Shadow had one more thing to add. "Caspian should not trust the sprites. Not by an inch. They'll kill anyone without hesitation."

He screeched once more and soared into the sky.

Kendall was normally self-assured and confident, but she was starting to feel distinctly useless as she helped Estelle search her grimoires.

They were sitting on the rug in front of the fire in the farmhouse living room, surrounded by candles. The electricity was still out, and the house was starting to feel cold because the heating had gone off. At least the fire provided warmth, and they had plenty of wood. If they weren't all in mortal danger, Kendall would have enjoyed being trapped inside a house in blizzard conditions. Especially if she had been trapped with a hot man, instead of Estelle. One of the Nephilim, perhaps, with their impressive build and seductive smiles. *No, not Eli.* She should absolutely banish that man from her mind. She took a deep breath and focussed on the book in front of her.

There were two ancient volumes they were searching through. One belonged to Estelle's family, and had been passed down through the generations. The other was her private book that she called her Book of Shadows. In addition, stacked on the coffee table, there were a few old books on myths and legends. Estelle was quiet as she searched the family grimoire methodically, making notes on a sheet of paper, and marking some pages with strips of paper to act as bookmarks.

Kendall searched Estelle's book. It felt intrusive, as if she was reading a personal diary. Her fingers tingled sometimes as she turned the pages, evocative scents lifting off the page and drifting across the room to mingle with incense. Kendall had never wished to be anything but a police officer, and was thrilled to be on Newton's team, but now she harboured distinct urges to be a witch and cast spells. To feel magic under her skin.

She was used to White Haven's witches, but she'd never been alone with any of them. Estelle was different. More serious and intimidating. She had lit every single candle with a spell, and searched her grimoire magically, the pages whispering as they turned on their own. Kendall could feel the magic lift the hairs on her arms. Everything felt unreal, like she was caught in a spell, too. And then she laughed. She *was* caught in a spell. The Snow Queen's spell.

Estelle was hunched over the table, but she rolled her neck as she looked up, disturbed by Kendall's laugh. "Are you okay? Sorry, I've been distracted."

"I'm feeling all magical sitting here, reading this. I was thinking how it felt like I was in a spell, and then realised that we actually are!"

Estelle grimaced. "Unfortunately, yes, we are. It doesn't feel like it, though. I can't detect obvious magic, but it was like Eve said to Reuben. It's the intensity of the storm. We'll work it out." She looked at the list that Kendall had made. "Looks like you've found some useful spells."

Kendall shuffled and stretched her arms out, trying to ease the ache in her shoulder blades. "I found some, but I don't think I'm making any headway at all. Are you sure you're not better off searching your own book?"

"I'm overfamiliar with mine. There are a few spells that will be effective, but you might see something with fresh eyes that I won't." She gave her a tight smile and tapped the grimoire. "It's hard going, isn't it? This book has such fancy writing, and *old* writing, it gives me a headache to read. It's the old-fashioned terms, and weird names for herbs that add to the confusion."

"It must be nice, though, to have something that connects you to your family history. Something so palpable."

Estelle brushed her dark hair back. Strands had escaped from her ponytail, and she pulled it out, letting her hair fall loosely around her shoulders. "Sometimes it's nice, and then I come across my father's writing and want to throw the book through the window. I won't, of course." She grinned. "His spells are good, even though he was such a bastard."

Kendall didn't know much of Estelle and Caspian's background, but knew their father was problematic. "Well, at least he had his uses," she said lamely.

"True. Let's run through what we have while we wait for the others to return." All business, she turned to her list. "I have found spells to create gateways—something that hopefully works on the wall around the town. It's unclear what the spells were initially used for, but might be worth trying. I just hope it isn't a gateway to somewhere unpleasant." She cocked an eyebrow. "We certainly don't want to let anything in!"

"Like what?"

"Demons, trolls, spirits, any other weird creature from another dimension. I don't think they create portals, though. One distinctly says it's to create a gateway *through* something. Then there are spells that use heat. Spells to subvert will. Spell breakers—but that requires one to understand the nature of the spell, and I'm not sure I do. Spells that track back to the spellcaster. But that's also tricky, because we don't really know who she is. Of course, we really should be using Eve, because she's the weather witch, and is more likely to break this spell than us." She sighed. "There are a few others. I need time to go through them. Really think them through and test them. Caspian and Reuben should be able to help. What about you?"

"I found a few fire spells, and a few Yule solstice spells." She grimaced, "I told you I was useless."

"Mmm. Yule spells. That *is* a good idea. I was so fixated on weather and the wall. Remind me what kind of Yule spells? I've written and recorded so much over the years."

Pleased that she'd made a useful suggestion, Kendall pulled her notes close. "Well, Yule is the longest night. The time when the Holly King hands over his rule to the Oak King for six months. I thought it probably means the Green Man is getting stronger, yes?" Her thoughts were muddy. "If the Green Man is the Oak King? Or is he both? Anyway, Yule is about lighting the Yule log, and keeping the flame burning for another year."

Estelle's eyes widened and a smile spread across her face. "Oh, my Goddess! You are right. The Wheel will turn. Darkness will be banished as the year flips towards the summer. Find me the pages on my Yule celebrations. I'll look in here."

"You think I have a point?"

"Yes, I do." She turned pages while she talked. "This time of year is meant for stillness and quiet introspection. The land is sleeping, renewing its energy for the coming year. It's a time for feasting and relaxing. Traditionally, food is stored better in winter. There should be plenty of meat and vegetables, which allow for feasting. If our enemy is a kind of winter witch, she would be strongest at this time of year. What if she's trying to make it last longer?"

"Or forever," Kendall said darkly.

"Then it's even more imperative that we stop her. Focus on Yule spells, and make lists of herbs and correspondences."

Kendall looked out of the window at the blizzard conditions. To live in this forever would be unthinkable. Everything would die. With renewed enthusiasm, she picked up her pen and turned back to the book.

Avery stared at Briar in shock, and then hugged her again. "I can't believe what that bitch did to you! And you!" She turned to Barak and hugged him, too, struggling to get arms around him. "And I can't believe you're here!"

"And half naked," Helena added, her eyes roving across his broad, muscled chest. "Clea is having palpitations. This is giving her memories to dine out on for years!"

Barak gave one of his huge, infectious laughs. "Glad I can help out a few ladies today!"

Alex rolled his eyes and headed to the bedroom. "I'll try and find a top that might fit you. It will be tricky!"

"Actually," Barak raised his hand to stop him. "We can't stay here. None of us can. If the queen knows of your existence, and your link to Briar, which is highly likely, we all need to get out of here. Now."

Briar nodded, her lips set in a determined line. "He's right. She knows I'm a witch, and that I have control of my power again. Likely she knows about you, too."

Briar and Barak had arrived only minutes before, banging on the door to Avery's flat. They had entered hurriedly, covered in snow and casting wary glances behind them. Raven still hadn't returned.

"Leave here?" Avery looked around her cosy attic. Her safe space that was filled with her favourite things and magical knowledge. "I have protection spells! They can't get in!"

"You hope."

"And what about Raven? What if they break in and ransack the place?"

"What if they break in and arrest us?" Helena shuddered. "I have been through that. I will not suffer it again."

Avery felt foolish and sentimental. And scared. "You're right. But what about El?"

"I'll search for her," Barak offered. "If you have magic, you can use witch-flight to take everyone to Newton's place."

Avery smacked her hand on her head. "Newton! Is he here?"

"No. He was staying at Moore's, so he's locked out of White Haven. He'll be happy for you to stay at his place, I'm sure."

"I have so many questions to ask!"

Briar squeezed her arm. "Me, too. We can do it all at Newton's. That should be safe. He's not a witch. Why would the queen want him?"

Alex nodded at Briar. "You're right. Newton's home will be a good place to go. Let's take everything there. Can you use witch-flight, Avery? Will the queen's magic interfere?"

"No. The rest of our magic works fine." She started to think practically. "If she's gathering troops, then we have only a small window. Let's take as many magical supplies as possible, and the cats, and grimoires. We may be able to sneak back later."

Barak nodded. "And I can keep watch from above. But I must be careful. They'll be looking for me now."

"Why don't I fly to El's?" Avery asked, worry about her friend eating at her.

"No." Barak was insistent. "Go to Newton's now. You have time for a few trips. I'll search for El. Okay?" He kept his eyes fixed on hers.

Avery took a deep breath. "Okay."

# Thirteen

Gabe followed his brothers and Ghost OPS into the farmhouse—all except for Nahum and Ash, who had wanted to spend more time in the air, assessing the threat of the weather, and Shadow, who had headed to her own place in the outbuildings.

"You all need to give me five minutes," he warned the rest of them. "I want to speak to Estelle alone."

"I think we all need showers, anyway," Niel said, "if there's any hot water left."

"Is there a shower available for us, too?" Cassie asked hopefully.

Niel started up the stairs. "Of course. Follow me. And good luck, brother."

"And be nice," Eli added. "She'll be upset before she's angry."

Gabe sighed as he walked down the hall, pausing on the living room's threshold to find both women looking at him. The room felt hot after being outside, but it looked inviting, and Gabe wanted nothing more than to lie on the sofa and sleep.

Estelle was already looking over his shoulder. "What did you find?" She asked, eyes narrowing. "Where's Barak?"

"Kendall. Give us five minutes, please."

She jumped to her feet. "Beer?"

"Yes, please."

Estelle's lips were pinched so tight that her skin was white, and her voice rose with panic. "What's happened to Barak?"

"He's okay, as far as I know." He raised his hands to calm her down as he crossed the room to her side. "But he managed to get through the wall—I think. He's inside."

"You *think*?" Her magic was building, balls of power glowing in her palms. "What the fuck happened?"

Gabe summarised the situation on the ice. "He didn't give me a chance to stop him. And honestly, it was a great idea."

"But you don't even know if he made it! He could be trapped in it. Or dead!" Her voice faltered, her breath coming in quick, sharp intakes.

"He made it, I'm pretty certain." Gabe sank down into the armchair, suddenly weary. He'd been flying and fighting for hours. "Sprites were running through the door after he passed through it. I've played it over in my head. We had to fly out of there because the icesheet was breaking up, but I saw him go through it. He would have made it before they did."

"And if it rejected him somehow?"

"It's possible, I guess, but unlikely. It was a big, pillared entrance. A kind of gate." The more he thought of it, the surer he became. He stared at her, not taking his eyes from hers. "He's okay."

"Fuckity fuck!" Estelle exploded. "That stupid, idiotic moron!"

"Brave, strong, and brilliant," Gabe countered, wincing as she used some kind of magic on the fire that made it flare up. "And very resourceful. But you know all of that."

She yelled again, glaring at the ceiling. "Herne's blistering bollocks! I can't believe he's done that! I could strangle him!" She levelled her fierce glare at Gabe. "He's on his own in there! Why didn't you go with him?"

"I couldn't get close to the gate. None of us could. He used us as a distraction. And he's not alone. He's with the White Haven witches!"

"If they're there!"

"I'm sure they are. Besides, he's a Nephilim. We're hard to kill."

She pressed her hands to her cheeks. She was trembling. "I know, but..."

"You love him, and you're worried. He'd be worried sick if it was you who'd gone through the gate, and I'd let you. He'd have probably punched me by now, he loves you so much." He turned his face, offering a cheek. "Want to take a shot?"

Estelle froze at his words, eyes drifting across his cheek before meeting his eyes. "What did you say?"

He tapped his cheek. "Want to take a shot? I can take a good one, so make it count."

"Before that, you idiot!"

He smiled at her. He knew exactly what she meant. "He loves you. He must have told you. It's written all over him. He's like this big, grinning, goofy idiot every time he sees you. And I know you love him. It's in the way you look at him."

Estelle's eyes filled with tears. "Of course I do, but we've never said so, not in so many words... I didn't want to jinx it."

"Maybe he didn't want to, either." Gabe leaned back, hands behind his head. He liked seeing this more vulnerable side to Estelle. It made her more human. It also softened her features. "He was probably worried it would scare you off. But I'm not telling you anything you don't know. Deep down, you know he does!"

She sniffed. "Not really. Sometimes I just think he's being really nice, and it will all end. And I'll be alone again." Real tears threatened this time.

Gabe blinked back his shock. *Was Estelle so damaged that she couldn't see Barak's love, even when it was right in front of her?* He wanted to hug her. Tell her it was all okay. *She'd probably hex him, though.* He settled for leaning forward and squeezing her hand. "Trust me. He loves you, and he's going nowhere without you."

"Easy to say now when he's stuck behind the Wall of Doom!"

He smiled. "Well, I don't know about you, but it's given me extra motivation to get in there now."

"There is that." She pressed her hand to her heart. The room, with only the crackle of the fire and the deep, hushed silence that the snow created outside, invited confidences. "I actually ache for him. What madness is that?"

"It's love." Gabe had felt similar emotions for his wife and daughter, and when other close brothers in the past had died. The ache for his past life and lost civilisations was constant. And now he felt it for Shadow, too.

It was as if Estelle had read his mind. "Do you love Shadow?"

"Yes, of course. She's maddening, and infuriating, but we work. She was like a thunder bolt. Took me by surprise." He grinned. "She's constantly challenging, but I'd have it no other way. We're lucky, aren't we?"

Estelle sniffed again, her hands wiping tears off her cheeks. "Thank you, Gabe. You've been very kind."

Gabe had expected anger, shouting, and blame, but not this. "It's just the truth. It's important, you know." He'd been dreading talking to her. Now he was glad he had. He looked at the open grimoires on the coffee table. "Any ideas?"

"Yes. Sort of." She straightened her shoulders, all business now. "Kendall had a great idea. I want to run it past Caspian and Reuben. Where are they?"

"Ah. That's the other thing. They're stuck at Stormcrossed Manor."

"You have got to be fucking kidding me!"

He winced. *Now the shouting would start.*

Newton stood in Tamsyn's kitchen with Reuben and Caspian, exasperated with the situation, and worried sick about Briar. "There must be something we can do!"

"Like what?" Reuben asked, arms crossed as he leaned against the counter. He looked tired. His hair had dried and was sticking up over his head in a very dishevelled manner, and other than a vague, half-arsed attempt to smooth it down, he didn't bother. "There's a big ice wall around us, and potentially a horde of very angry sprites beyond that. It nearly killed us to get here."

Caspian was sitting at the table, eating Tamsyn's buttery cookies. He brushed the crumbs off his lips. "He's right. We'll give it thought, obviously. I'm sure there's something we can do."

"Are you sure witch-flight won't work?"

"There's something about this magic that I don't trust. It feels sort of sticky." Caspian looked a lot more groomed than Reuben, but that wasn't unusual. He, like Reuben, had dried off, and was looking composed and thoughtful. He reached for another biscuit. "Witch-flight works by using the element of air. It's my element, obviously, and I can dissolve myself into it to take myself anywhere within a reasonable distance. But essentially, I use air to carry me from one place to another. Walls, buildings, and other obstacles don't matter. I move through them. But the barrier around White Haven, and now this house, feels different. It's sticky. Like fly paper. I have a feeling that if I try to get through it, I'll be trapped. Whether that's in my body or dissolved in air, I don't know. Sorry. Dissolved is a weird word to use, but it's the best I can think of."

Newton gave in to his hunger pangs and reached for a biscuit, too. "So, it's a different type of magic?"

"Maybe?" He frowned and looked at Reuben. "Do you get what I'm saying?"

"Totally. Do you think it's fey magic?" He joined them at the table, the candlelight casting a warm glow on their features. "I'm trying to think how Shadow feels, vibrationally, and I think it's similar. But she's not a witch."

"So where have the sprites come from?" Newton asked. He was feeling increasingly frustrated, and cold. The heating wasn't working, and the only warmth came from the ancient AGA-style oven in the corner of the room. "They are not of this Earth! The queen, or Winter Witch, or whoever the crap she is, must have brought them with her, which means she came from somewhere else, too." He groaned and crunched aggressively on a cookie. "We should be out there. There could be more deaths tonight. That vindictive Jack Frost does it for fun. Bastard."

"Reuben and I were planning to work on spells together tonight, anyway. We might not have our grimoires, but there are spells we already know well. Tamsyn has herbs here. We can improvise, right?"

Reuben nodded. "Sure. Ice is water, and that's my element. It certainly responded to me when we marched up the drive. That works in our favour. And of course, there's Beth."

Newton stared at him. "You want to use the child?"

"I'm not sure 'want' is the right word, but she's finally connected to Briar. I think we have to try. The thing is that I have no psychic mojo like Alex."

"She's only just calmed down!" Newton shook his head. "I don't like it. She was terrified. There must be another way. What about your familiars? You reached the Nephilim on the lane. And then there's your crazy horse!" Newton had seen Reuben's horse before and would never forget it. It was more unnerving than the acerbic-tongued Raven. "They crossed millennia. They must be able to pass through a bloody wall! They're not really here, are they?"

Reuben rolled his eyes. "They're on another plane, but they're here. But," he cocked an eyebrow at Caspian. "That's a good point. Eagle did reach the Nephilim! Do you think we could use them to find the others in White Haven? I could talk to El."

"You said Silver couldn't find them."

"But if he can? He's been trying to all day." Reuben stood, chair scraping across the floor. "I'm going to find a quiet spot now that I'm fortified with sugar. Be back soon."

Caspian stood, too. "Good luck. Perhaps I should try to contact Estelle? In the meantime, Newton, you check on Beth and Tamsyn, just in case they have any more news."

Newton was left alone, in silence. He checked his watch and groaned. It was close to ten o'clock, but felt much later. And it was still Tuesday, which seemed impossible. So much had happened in the day. He'd started it with a hangover, dealt with two mysterious deaths, almost got stuck in snow, White Haven was trapped behind the Wall of Doom, and now he was encased in ice at Stormcrossed Manor. And he was exhausted. He was looking forward to a warm bed at Reuben's, but now... He pressed his fingers to his eyes. *What a catastrophic mess.*

But his friends in White Haven were in a bigger mess than he was. They were stuck in there with a megalomaniacal queen who was attacking Briar—if Beth was to be believed. Unfortunately, he did believe her. She'd been too accurate before. They needed to get in, and that meant they needed knowledge. He heaved himself to his feet and went to find Tamsyn.

Cassie was starting to feel human again after her flight in the blizzard. It had been a brilliant experience, crushed against Eli's huge, muscular chest, with snow and wind snatching at her clothes and hair.

She may have been cold, but she would not have exchanged the experience for anything. The shower had thawed her out, and now they were all gathered in the farmhouse's kitchen around a table piled with food and candles. There was no hope of any of them going home that night. It would be mean to ask the Nephilim to take them home by flying again, and they needed to be together anyway, to pool their resources and knowledge.

All the Nephilim were there, other than Barak, as was Shadow, Dylan, Ben, Kendall, and Estelle. Chairs had been dragged from other rooms, and somehow they had all managed to fit around the table. Fortunately, although the electrics were out, the gas still worked fine. They had devoured food that Niel had prepared. It was simple, just a full English breakfast of bacon, eggs, beans, toast, mushrooms, sausages—complete with coffee, tea, beer, wine, or whatever else they wanted. And also eggnog. The disgustingly gloopy, yellow liquid was in a bottle to the side, and was surprisingly popular. Shadow had imbibed a very large measure of it.

"Herne's balls," Dylan said, pushing his plate away. "I feel human again."

"Fortunately, I do not," Nahum said with a wink as he topped up his plate. "I still have room for more."

Cassie was used to the Nephilim and Reuben with their gargantuan appetites, but it was still a shock to see the mountain of food on their plates. However, now that they had eaten, other matters pressed on her mind. "So, what are we going to do?" she asked the table in general.

"I don't think there is anything we can do right now," Gabe admitted. "We can't get into Stormcrossed, which is frustrating because Estelle has no witches to help her, and we have no way of getting into White Haven, either."

"Yet," Estelle said, reining in her impatience, and no doubt her worry. "But this is still early in our research. Kendall reminded me that Yule is tomorrow. That's a huge solstice celebration for witches, and a major turn on the Wheel of the Year. This is what we need to focus on to get inside." She picked up her mug of coffee and sipped it. "The more I think on this, the more certain I am that the woman behind this is a witch. Caspian was right. A Goddess is too powerful to need us or our magic. This is someone human—"

"Or fey," Shadow cut in. "Sprites are fey. The wall feels more akin to my own magic. I think the woman is perhaps a human who straddles the world of fey and people. *Somehow.*"

"Or," Ben suggested, "she is both. Half fey, half human." He shrugged as everyone stared at him. "Why not?"

Shadow cocked her head, fixing him with her brilliant, violet eyes. "That's an excellent suggestion."

"I know, right?"

"Are you sure," Zee asked, "that the sprites aren't behind this and there is no *Witch-Queen*? Just for shits and giggles?"

"It's possible," Shadow admitted. "They are quite capable of planning attacks, but this is too sophisticated. Too organised. And big! Although, the lead sprite seems very efficient. And powerful."

"Jack Frost, you mean?" Dylan said, smirking. "He has a name."

Kendall laughed. "A storybook name."

"Ben talked to loads of people who called him that. It originated somewhere. So did her name, so for now, can we call her the Snow Queen? Winter Witch or not, she needs a name."

Ash smiled, and his golden eyes glowed even more in the soft candlelight. "Stories aside, they exist, and they are causing havoc and deaths. I hate to think what is happening in the town. They knew when we were on the icesheet. Within seconds of Shadow lopping off the queen's head, we were attacked. They exited right on top of us. Which means, we know of at least one gate we can get in through."

"And it means she was monitoring that area somehow," Estelle mused. "Maybe through the statue?"

"Those bloody ice sculptures came to life!" Nahum said. "That means they are spelled in some way. So yes, Estelle, there was a spell on them to react when under threat. Unfortunately, I haven't seen any others on the perimeter to suggest another gateway."

Ben reached for another strip of bacon. "Maybe we don't need to find any other way in. We just need to find a way to open that one!"

"But it didn't connect to the land," Gabe pointed out. "So, unless sprites can swim..."

"Jack makes his own ice, remember?" Cassie pointed out. "He could make his own path. Perhaps the others can, too."

"But the gate is interesting," Eli said thoughtfully. "Although there aren't any ice sculptures, there could still be another gate that opens on land. Why advertise it?"

Kendall nodded with excitement. "I like that idea. Is there a way to detect it with your instruments?" She looked at Ghost OPS.

"The EMF might help. Or perhaps the camera?" Ben looked at his team. "We could look again tomorrow. In the light. Try to pick up anomalies. Is there a spell that could help, Estelle?"

"Perhaps. I need to focus. I'm looking into so many things now, I'm spread thin."

"I'll help again," Kendall said eagerly. "But can't you contact Caspian with your familiar?"

"Unfortunately, I don't have one. Or if I do, I don't know what it is. I was planning on finding it, with Caspian's help." She sighed. "Perhaps he'll be able to visit me, or Reuben's horse will. At least then we can work together in some way."

Niel snorted. "Good luck with that. All his eagle could do was screech!"

"Okay. Essentially, there is nothing that we can do tonight," Gabe summed up. "We need sleep and daylight. Unless anyone has any brilliant ideas? My only suggestion for tonight is that we have a lookout. We can swap every hour, just to make sure the wall doesn't spread to us, or we get surrounded by Jack Frost's army of sprites."

"We can't stop him if he does attack," Ben pointed out.

"No, but we can evacuate so we're not trapped."

"Ah, true!"

"Right." Gabe stood. "Let's sort out beds, and then we'll brainstorm again in the morning."

# Fourteen

Barak circled above El's flat, observing that there was hardly anyone on the streets below. The earlier blizzard had made sure of that.

Ice creaked in the rigging of the fishing boats, frozen in the harbour. Restaurants and shops were closed, and barely any light could be seen behind curtained windows. The fayre below the castle had closed. The whole place looked like a ghost town.

Barak flew lower, certain he couldn't be seen, and frustrated that he could see no light in El's home. He hovered outside the living room window, and then her bedroom. But the blinds were open, and she wasn't in there.

*This was bad news. If El wasn't with Briar or Avery, where was she? Had the queen already caught her?*

He swept over the town again, his heart sinking at everything he saw. The electricity had cut out, so none of the streetlights or decorations were lit. As the temperature dipped even lower, ice coated the streetlamps, windowsills, bunting, chimneys... Everything glittered in a cold, hard way. Tucked in dark corners were the queen's guards, stationed in teams of three.

Then he heard shouts, the rhythmical stamping of boots, and the whinny of horses as more of the queen's troops arrived in town. At least two dozen of them. Barak's mood dipped even further. He was right. They were going to search the town for Briar and the other witches. The guards split up, some heading to El's place. Keeping his distance and looking through a huge landing window, he watched in horror as they marched into the converted warehouse and hammered on her door. The good news was that her protection spells held, and they couldn't get in. And of course, she didn't come to the door. That made the guards even more furious. They started harassing her neighbours. He considered intervening, but there was no point. However, that posited another question. The queen couldn't have El, or she wouldn't be searching her place.

The troops also headed to The Wayward Son, Briar's shop and cottage, and another team headed for Avery's place, too. Barak watched as they attempted to raid every single place, and every time failed. Their frustration grew. They started banging on neighbours' doors and interrogating everyone. The soldiers spread like a virus through the town. It was horrific.

People were scared, and Barak realised that some might be scared enough to suggest friends they may know. Work colleagues. Newton, perhaps. Everyone the witches knew could be in danger—and they had lots of friends in town.

*The question was, how many soldiers could Barak attack on his own? And if he did, would it make life worse for everyone?* He decided to return to Newton's place, rather than discovering the answer on his own.

Briar sipped one of Eli's invigorating herbal teas as she studied the supplies they had managed to collect in the short time allowed them.

They had broken into Newton's place, closed all the curtains and warded the building, and were now in his kitchen.

"I feel awful for breaking into his house." She studied the familiar layout with sorrow. It had been a while since she had been here, in more romantic times. They were long gone now, and wouldn't return, either. However, she still had fond memories of their time together. "I hope he's all right."

Alex laid out their grimoires on Newton's table. "He'd rather we be here and safe than not, and I'm sure he is."

Helena nodded in agreement. "He's clever. He'll probably be with Reuben and the Nephilim."

"But what if that super-bitch is creating havoc out there, too?" Briar groaned. "What am I saying? Of course she is. Barak said so."

Avery had pulled the curtain back slightly to keep watch. "I see him. I'll go and let him in."

Barak was grim-faced and still gripping his sword when he entered. "The good news is that your protection spells held. The bad news is that it made the guards furious, and they have harassed your neighbours about you all and started dragging people out onto the street."

"They *what*?" Alex asked, appalled. "We have to do something!"

"Like what?" Barak asked, sheathing his blade. "I nearly attacked them myself, but there are lots of them, and ultimately it will only make things worse. We're best laying low until we have a plan."

Helena leaned against the kitchen counter, arms crossed. "You're right. It will add fire to them and might even put our friends at more risk. Besides, if their memories are affected like ours, they might not remember things in detail."

"But she seems to have done her homework," Avery pointed out. "She obviously knows about every single one of us, and that means she'll know about Sally and Dan, and Marie and your bar staff, Alex. They will absolutely target them."

"And unfortunately, they will use them to get to us," Helena said. "Unless we get to them first."

"Neither Marie nor any of the bar's staff know anything about my magic," Alex said. "Although, that's not the point, is it? They could still use them to get to me."

"Well, Sally and Dan know everything about us!" Avery exclaimed. "Though they had completely forgotten about magic this morning, just like all of us. Sally has kids! I know where she lives. I could go to her house."

"Woah! Slow down," Barak instructed. "If you rescue Sally, then you rescue her whole family. Are you bringing them here? Newton's house has limited space. It's not our farmhouse or Reu's manor. And you can't bring the kids here, they'd be terrified. Besides, chances are, if they widen their search, they'll come here, too."

"Exactly," Helena said. "And her family doesn't know about you, right? Sally kept it a secret. That's the way it should stay. Besides, you have lots of friends who know you are different. Old Mary, for example. Are you going to rescue her, too?"

"Bollocks! You're right. But I feel helpless!"

Alex hugged her. "We all do, but we'll think of something."

Briar floundered, her mood veering between anger and terror for her friends. "Stan could be at risk. She knows we know each other. We arrived there together with that snake, Jack! And I'd almost forgotten about him with everything that's going on. That sneaky, smooth bastard. I knew he was dodgy."

"Jack?" Helena asked, confused. "Who's he?"

"Ha!" Barak grunted as he raided the fridge for food. "Jack Frost. Vicious sprite extraordinaire. He's a sly, slippery bastard."

"But that's interesting that we don't know about him," Helena pointed out as she filled the kettle to make a drink. "He has been deliberately left out of our implanted memories, for some reason."

Alex eased back in his chair, pushing his hair off his face. "I can't work like this. We need a plan, and we need to know what's happening out there, and what happened with you, Briar. And we need to find Raven!"

"He helped us escape, so I hope he's okay," Briar said, dread flooding through her once again.

"And I need a t-shirt," Barak reminded him.

"I'll grab you one. In the meantime, let's organise our stuff and catch up. Then we plan."

El was freezing cold. Water dripped down the walls of her cell and puddled on the floor, and the straw beneath her was damp, providing scant insulation from the packed earth.

She sat in the middle of the room, hands wrapped around her knees, watching the door. But no one came. From further down the corridor she thought she heard crying, but although she had shouted a few times, no one replied. They were obviously scared, and she couldn't blame them. So was she. And she was confused.

Apart from the fact that she was in this nightmarish hellhole, she still had the feeling that something else was wrong. It was persistent. A constant nag in the back of her mind. Exhausted, she lowered her head to her knees, her eyelids drooping with exhaustion.

Until a squawk resounded outside the cell.

Her head jerked up. "Hello? Who's there?"

A large raven flew though the bars of the door and landed on the ground in front of her. "Shh! Keep quiet, you foolish girl!"

El nearly screamed. Birds didn't talk. *Actually yes, they did. Parrots did. Weren't ravens supposed to be mimics, or was that something else?* And then she became annoyed. "You squawked!"

She could have sworn the raven grinned. "I've been looking for you everywhere. I didn't expect you to be here! What have you done?"

El blinked. "I think the cold has muddled my thinking. Maybe I'm asleep. Are you in my dream?"

"No! I'm right here. You need to snap out of it!"

"Out of what? The cell? Are you mad?"

The raven rustled its feathers and stamped its claws. "Pay attention. You are a witch!"

"I'm a *what*?"

"A witch! You have power! Lots of it. You can blast that door off with your little finger."

"Who are you? Who sent you? Is this a trick of the queen's?"

"No! Where is Bear when I need him?"

"Bear?" El's eyes widened with horror. "I don't want a bear in here!"

"I can assure you that you do. Now, calm down and listen. You are a witch. Do you feel different in some way?"

"Well, yes actually. I felt weird all day. My palms itch. I feel all tight within myself."

"That's your magic. The queen has cast a spell and made you forget. She's smothered your power, but Avery, Alex, and Briar are now free of it. Understand?"

A bolt of surprise shot through El, quickly followed by certainty. She rubbed her palms over her eyes, trying to blink tiredness away. "Sort of. Yes, for some reason, it seems right. But..." she wiggled her fingers. "Nothing's happening. Are you sure I'm a witch?"

"Yes, but you have to *know* it. Really feel it to be able to break her spell."

El was suddenly excited. "But I don't know how!"

The raven fixed her with its beady eye. "You don't remember?"

"No. Nothing beyond knowing I live here, and that there will be months of winter ahead. I know about the queen, how dangerous she is, and how important the upcoming Yule Feast is. And Briar! I saw her go into the palace with the strange, blond guy. You said she's okay?"

"She is now. But your memories are linked to your magic. She's suppressed your knowledge of who you are. The others broke their spell by becoming angry, or in danger of their life."

"I *am* in danger. I'm locked in a freezing cell, and apparently will get hauled up before the queen tomorrow."

"What did you do?"

"A guard caught me snooping in the courtyard at the back. I was looking for a way to find Briar."

"So the queen hasn't seen you yet?"

"No."

"Good. That's very good! And to be honest, you look a state. She might not even know it's you." El patted her hair, distracted. She *felt* a state. She knew she had dirt smeared all over her face and clothes from where they'd thrown her on the floor. Raven continued, "But that's not the point. We need to get you out before that happens."

"Er, sorry, this is ignorant, but who exactly are you?"

"I'm Raven, Avery's familiar. Alex has Wolf. You have Bear—who I can't reach. Briar has Deer, and Reuben... Oh, my. You don't even remember Reuben, do you?"

"Reuben?"

"Your boyfriend." For once, Raven lost his sharp tone. "You know, love and all that."

Just hearing his name made El's heart ache. "I can't remember my boyfriend?" Her breath started to come short and sharp, panic filling her. "I can't remember what he looks like! What he sounds like! Oh, fuck! This is horrible!" She stared at the bird. "I don't even know how long we were together!"

"Years, I believe."

"Why isn't he here?"

"He lives in a big house on the hill above White Haven. He surfs." Raven shuddered. "Unpleasant."

It was too much for El. She burst into tears. She didn't normally cry. She knew it wasn't who she was, but to have someone that meant so much blocked from her memory... "What if I never remember him?"

"Then get angry! Don't cry. Break the spell!"

"I *am* angry!"

"So act like it. You should have seen Avery. She's a firecracker. She nearly took Alex's head off, she was so furious. And Briar! She was spitting green vines like a fountain."

"What sort of magic do I do?"

"Fire and metal, swords and knives. You, my dear, are impressive. But," Raven cocked his head, "I hear guards. We need to shut up. I'm going to find Avery and tell her what's happening—but I'll be back."

The silence after he left was profound. The guards' voices receded down the corridor, and the dripping of water echoed in the darkness. El stared at her hands. *If she knew she was a witch, why didn't that information trigger anything?*

Feeling more miserable than she'd ever felt in her life, El curled up, desperate to try and keep warm, and despite everything, fell asleep.

Alex didn't think the night could get any worse, until Raven arrived with news of El's captivity.

He'd just opened a beer and was hoping to have a brainstorming session, but he couldn't abandon El. "We have our magic now. We can use a shadow spell to get into the castle and rescue her."

"Bollocks to that!" Avery said. "I can fly straight in and get her. Or at least to the gate."

"No, you won't!" Raven squawked. "There's a huge protection spell around the castle. You won't get past with magic."

Barak shrugged. "Then I'll do it. Show me the way."

Raven laughed, and the sound grated on Alex's nerves. "After what you did with Briar? There are lookouts on the roof—lots of them."

"Considering the days I've had recently, that's nothing to worry me," Barak said, already reaching for his sword that was lying on the kitchen bench.

"She's tripled the guards on the palace, and Jack is back. I saw him on my way here. He looks angry. I watched him for a while. He spits ice from his hands like its nothing. There are too many of them. You'll get captured, too."

"He's right," Helena said, fingers drumming on the table. "We can't risk losing you. We all need to act together. We're stronger as a team, and we'll stand more chance when she's outside the castle." She stared around the table. "We know what they'll do with El. Our implanted memories tell us that she'll be brought to the square to set an example with any other rulebreakers. The guards will fine her. Maybe whip her. She might even lose her life if the queen is feeling vindictive—and after tonight, she will be. The queen governs with fear. As long as we obey her, and follow the rules, we are all happy."

"But if the queen recognises her?" Briar said, voice rising indignantly. "She'll kill her like she was going to do with me!"

"To be honest, she's barely recognisable," Raven said. "Her makeup is smeared. I could tell her to rub it off. Cover herself in mud. Rub it in her hair, too. As far as the queen knows, she's with us, and like Briar has regained her magic. El could be anyone right now. If she makes up a story as to why she was in the courtyard..."

"She could have been stealing food or something," Alex suggested lamely.

"That's good," Barak nodded. "She could make up a false name. Then they'll take her to the square, and once she's out of the palace, we can rescue her together."

"There's a big if here." Alex sighed, easing back in his chair. "If we're wrong, she's dead."

Raven flew to the window. "I'll go back to the palace now and tell her our suggestions. If I'm not back straight away, don't worry. I'll stay with her for a while. I might even see if I can eavesdrop in the castle."

"Won't the queen recognise you?" Alex asked. "You did attack her."

"I'm just a bird. One of many, and there are many of us up there close to Ravens' Wood—even though it isn't in the queen's spell."

Alex breathed a little easier. "Okay. We'll have to work with that for now."

"Wait!" Avery leapt to her feet. "I'll come with you—mentally, I mean. I'll connect with you, see through your eyes."

"That's a good plan, but find me out there. I'll be waiting."

Helena opened the window, and Raven left.

"Before I go, how do we tackle tomorrow?" Avery asked. "We can't go to our businesses, but Sally and Dan could be at risk."

"I can," Helena said. "First thing, as a customer. Sally will open up as normal, right?"

"But Sally knows that you live with me—and I won't be there! How can we explain what has happened?"

Helena fell silent, musing on the problem. "Okay, I'll lie and say you two stopped with El overnight, and that I took a sleeping tablet and slept all night long. That way if the guards come knocking, it will explain why I didn't answer. They'll want to search once it's open, and that's fine. I'll let them. Sally will vouch for me that I'm senile, and I'll act it. It means I can mingle, too."

Alex nodded. "That's a great idea."

"There might be news of El," Helena added. "You can take me when we're done planning, Avery. I'll get up as normal in the morning."

"And the fact that I'm not at work?"

"I'll say I don't know! I'll sit and knit and look vague."

Barak looked uneasily between them. "It's risky. If they find out that you're lying, you could be hauled to the square, too."

Helena laughed and patted Barak's arm. "A little old lady like me? I'll improvise. You can take me once you've finished with Raven, Avery."

Alex knew that if anyone could pull it off, Helena could. She was clever. Sharp. "In the meantime, I'll find Wolf, and perhaps do some scrying, too. I can survey the town. Check in on our friends while Avery is with Raven."

"And me?" Barak asked. "What if I search for other gates on the perimeter of the town?"

"That's a good idea, but be careful."

"And when you're back, you can help me and Briar search grimoires," Helena said, her eyes sliding to Barak's chest again.

Barak winked. "Yes ma'am. But you know I'm spoken for, right?"

"A girl can look!"

Helena's flirting was too much for Alex, and he rose to his feet. "Time to find my wolf!"

# Fifteen

Reuben was trying to put on a brave face, but the more time that passed, the more frightened he became for El's safety. He pushed his fear to the back of his mind, but when he was alone and it was quiet, it was the only thing he could think about.

He was in the living room of the second wing in Stormcrossed Manor, the one that Rosa had decorated and usually used. However, she was still in Tamsyn's wing of the house, and he had the place to himself. He lit the fire with a finger of flame he conjured in his hands, watching it spread across the kindling and lick along the logs. The wood was dry and it burned quickly, the warmth reaching out to embrace him.

For a moment, he let his mind drift. He saw shapes in the flames. Faces of imps and sprites with hate-filled eyes, sharp chins and cheekbones, but then they vanished, replaced by cities and towers that crumbled and rose again, reformed with every curl of fire. He wished he had Alex's ability to cross to other planes or to scry. He wanted to be floating over White Haven.

To see El.

If anything happened to her, he would be lost. She was everything to him—a steady rock that loved him for all of his tomfoolery. After Gil died, she had been a constant reassuring presence—other than the time he had nearly killed her, of course, through his anger and grief.

When he had raised the waves so high that they had nearly drowned her on the beach. He could not have hated himself more for that.

He loved her individuality—the way she dressed, her makeup, her clever wit, and magic. The way she supported him when he thought his magic was weak and he was a terrible witch. In fact, he was a better witch because of her. She was home. His house felt better when she was in it, although he respected her choice not to live there.

Without her, he felt like half a man. Diminished. Lost.

And now that spiteful bastard Jack Frost had trapped him and separated him from his other friends, too. He wanted to wring his neck. To shatter him. His fists were clenched so tight they ached, and he took a deep breath. He needed to use his anger to focus and fuel his magic. He called Silver again, but he suspected that the new magic around Stormcrossed Manor was the issue. He would have to contact him the way the others did. By meditation.

He closed his eyes and sank into darkness. He envisaged the landscape around him. The gentle rolling moors, the fields, the streams that ran through it, the valley that held his hometown, and beyond that, Ravens' Wood. Then he thought of the sea, his favourite place.

He could hear it. The crashing surf on the rocks, the ice that splintered on the beaches, the churning depths. The feeling of exhilaration and fear as the current pulled him under and spat him out again. And Silver's pounding hooves and foaming mane as he rode the surf.

And suddenly, there he was. Huge and shining in his mind's eye, racing across Greenlane Manor's grounds. Reuben plunged into him, at one with his familiar, seeing the world though his eyes. He felt powerful, the horse's muscles rippling as he galloped across the snow-covered lawns, leaving no trace of his passing.

*"There you are! I thought I'd lost you."*

*"You'll never lose me, Reuben. I'm having issues with the sprites' magic, that's all. I've been waiting for you."*

*"Thank you. I wasn't sure I could do this."*

*"Of course you can. Stop doubting yourself. And I'm always here, although other magic may try to block us, it can never sever the connection."*

His calm words eased Reuben's fears. *"That's good to know. Have you found Bear yet, or El? Or the others?"*

*"Not yet, but I'll keep trying. The wall around White Haven is dense with magic and protection spells. Everything is warded—including other planes of existence. It's clever. And I've realised something else. Winter is woven through it."*

*"What do you mean?"*

*"The season itself, and everything that it entails. The darkness, cold, long nights, and sharp winds. It will be hard to break."*

*"Then we break the one who cast it."*

*"An interesting suggestion. Finding a way through the gate would be easier."*

*"There's only one, then?"*

*"Hard to say. Perhaps."*

Reuben groaned. *"Can you travel to the Nephilim's house? I want to talk to them. Well, try to."*

*"We can travel there together."*

Greenlane Manor receded as Silver raced across the winter landscape in a blur. They skirted the wall, its magic easier to perceive in this form. It was a dark mass of energy, ice whirling within it. It reminded Reuben of the wall they had placed around Stormcrossed Manor in the summer, but much, much stronger. It was a gargantuan feat of magic, and they passed it in seconds as they travelled at a high speed through the winter beauty.

The snow sparkled despite the heavy cloud cover and constant snowfall. The temperature had plummeted, and hoar frost was thick on hedges, trees, and brambles. Reuben would have liked to admire the natural beauty if he hadn't got other things on his mind.

They approached the farmhouse by the field in front of it. Reuben could see their protection spell all around it, sparkling like a rainbow—the weaving of his coven's magic. Silver raced through it, and it felt like a warm summer breeze as it shimmered over them and allowed them inside.

Reuben laughed. "*That's weird seeing it like that.*"

"*You're seeing it through me, that's why. I see things differently.*"

"*Like I'm spirit-walking?*"

"*Not exactly. It's complicated.*"

"*Of course it is.*"

He felt Silver's amusement. "*You can do it more often, if you like.*"

"*I might do just that,*" he said smugly. "*So, how do I speak to the Nephilim like this?*"

"*I can't speak to them directly, but I have ways of manifesting so they can see me. I think if we can connect physically, you should be able to talk to them. I can't guarantee it, though.*"

"*It's worth trying.*"

Silver shook himself, and it was as if they had stepped from one reality into another. The physical world came into sharper focus. The farmhouse was in darkness.

Reuben huffed. "*Damn it. They're asleep.*"

"*Not all.*"

A dark shape materialised on the roof and flew down to meet them halfway across the field, snow settling on Niel's huge wings and shoulders. He landed a short distance away, sword in one hand, and his double-headed axe in the other. His eyes were hard.

"*I do not know them all,*" Silver said in Reuben's head. "*Who's this?*"

"*Othniel, but we all call him Niel. He's a great cook!*"

Niel, however, wasn't waiting for introductions. "What in Herne's bollocks are you?"

Silver pawed the ground and shook his mane, and water flew off him.

Niel grimaced and stepped back. "I didn't ask for a shower! How did you get through our protection spell?"

"*Is that all you've got?*" Reuben said to Silver, growing impatient. "*What is this achieving?*"

"*I don't know!*" Silver was exasperated. "*I'm trying to prove I'm friendly.*"

"*Well, it's not working!*" Reuben yelled as Niel lunged at them, sword and axe whirling. His sword whipped through Silver, but it achieved nothing other than cause water to splash again. But Silver didn't retreat. He charged at Niel, encompassing him completely.

Niel roared with anger, slashing wildly.

"Stop!" Reuben yelled, the words finally bursting out through Silver's mouth. "It's me, in my familiar! Reuben!"

"What the fuck?" Niel yelled back, now soaked and looking around for the source of the voice.

He kept trying to get away from the horse, but Silver followed him.

"It's me! In my familiar!" Reuben repeated. "Stop moving! We need to connect."

But Niel had kicked off the ground and was now hovering over the horse. "What the hell are you? And where did that voice come from?"

"*I have an idea,*" Silver said.

He shimmered and changed shape, and suddenly Reuben realised he was standing in his own shape, completely made of water. "*Wow! That's cool!*"

"*Well, I can't hold it for long, so be quick.*"

Reuben looked up at Niel, grinning, or hoping he was. He wasn't sure he had any control of his shape at all.

Niel grimaced. "What the hell? *Reuben*? You look...weird." Niel dropped to the ground and stepped forward, and so did Silver. Reuben reached out to touch the tip of Niel's wing.

"Can you hear me?"

Niel stared at him suspiciously. "Well, this is just weird as fuck! How do I know you're not an agent of the queen who's managed to sneak through our shield?"

"Don't you think I would be busy trying to kill you right now, you great oaf?"

Niel raised his sword. "Careful! Prove yourself."

"Fine! I suppose that's reasonable. You are Othniel, but are called Niel, and you're a great cook."

"Well, everyone knows that! Tell me something more personal."

Reuben laughed. "Tricky. You've got a soft spot for a thief called Mouse."

Niel's blade whipped up beneath his throat. "Not funny! So, it's really you, you surf-mad idiot?"

"Less of the idiot, please! You believe me, then? And you may as well lower your sword. You cannot hurt me, and I cannot hurt you. I am in Silver's body. He is a vessel, that's all."

"*Although,*" Silver added mentally, "*if you channel your magic through me, we absolutely could hurt him.*"

"*Let's not do that,*" Reuben answered hurriedly. "*I just want to find out what's going on.*"

Niel prowled around him, still wary. "Where is your body?"

"Physically, still stuck at Stormcrossed Manor. Look, Niel, can we get on with it? Silver can't hold this form for long. It's not natural for him, and it's hard for me!"

"Really? Then you're a shit, Reuben! Never mention Mouse's name again."

*"Perhaps,"* Silver said smoothly to Reuben, *"we could move on?"*

Reuben decided he was not made to have three-way conversations with one of them in his head. *Although, maybe that was two in his head? Whatever.* "Niel, I just want to know what's happening. Is everyone okay?"

Niel finally lowered his weapons. "Everyone is sleeping. It's been a full day. Have you got any information?"

"Lots. Look, I think Silver needs to be a horse again, but we can communicate—at least for a short while. Let's make this quick, and I can leave you to your watch. Perhaps we will find a way to work together."

Avery soared across the palace, safe within Raven's body, and horrified at the hive of activity around the Snow Queen's palace.

Guards patrolled everywhere. On the battlements, in the courtyards, and on White Haven's roads and lanes. The frenzied door knocking that Barak had described had stopped, so that was one good thing, but the palace remained busy.

*"Where was Briar fighting with the queen?"*

*"The room beyond the enormous balcony."* Raven flew to the stone balustrade that edged it. *"She has fixed it already."*

*"How badly was it damaged?"*

"*Barak crashed through the huge, central window. I was searching the area when I saw them and flew in to help.*" Avery could feel Raven's anger. "*I flew at her. Tore at her hair and face. She was badly scratched, but she might have been able to heal herself.*"

"*Thank you. You saved them.*"

"*They saved themselves. I just gave them a little time.*"

"*I don't understand how this place is even here.*"

"*Neither do I, yet. But we will discover her secret.*"

"*But we're running out of time. Yule is tomorrow, and the huge feast is tomorrow night. I know it's significant, but why? Never mind. We'll think on it later. Take me to see El.*"

Raven flew around the side of the castle and through the courtyard, darting between the bars of a door close to the barracks. No one took any notice of Raven as he swooped inside. "*She's through here,*" he directed. But when Raven flew through the bars in another door, he squawked with dismay.

El had gone.

"I need to know what Beth has seen," Newton said to Tamsyn and Moore. "We need to wake her up."

"I'm not sure that's a good idea, Guv," Moore answered, his hand still resting on Beth's head as she slept, leaning against his chest. "You saw how upset she was."

"But she connected to Briar. She's the only one who has, so far. The familiars can't connect, although Reuben and Caspian are trying now. We need clues!" He stared at them both, exasperated. "You know we do! We are fighting blind here."

They were in Tamsyn's small living room. Rosa had taken Max to bed, after much persuasion. He was exhausted and needed to sleep, and Rosa didn't look much better. Rosa was out of her depth, and scared for her daughter. It was obvious she hated all of this, but equally knew she had to deal with it. Newton was glad she wasn't in the room now.

Tamsyn took a deep breath and let it out slowly. "You're right, of course. Sometimes she's calm after these events pass. She can remember, but is no longer as frightened. And I'm as desperate as you, Newton. I've grown close to Briar. I can't bear to lose her now." Her small hands closed into fists, her fierce spirit blazing from her eyes.

"Do not talk of losing! This is a setback. We've got through worse. We've faced vampires and mad wizards before now, and we survived that."

"Why don't you make her a drink, Tamsyn?" Moore suggested. "A hot chocolate, perhaps? Something to comfort her."

Tamsyn nodded and hurried to the kitchen.

"Thanks, Moore. You have a way with kids." Newton nodded at the sleeping child.

He smiled. "Maybe she's missing her dad. My youngest loves a cuddle on my lap."

Newton rarely stopped to think of Moore as a father. "You risk a lot to be on this team with young kids at home."

"I'd risk a lot as a copper anywhere. We all do. Don't think you're getting rid of me."

"I wouldn't dream of it. Not many would handle this as well as you. I just hope Kendall is holding up okay."

"She's tough, and is with the Nephilim and Estelle. She'll be fine. Tamsyn, however, is not holding up as well."

"Isn't she?" Newton asked, shocked. "She's as tough as old boots!"

"That tough exterior hides a lot. She's too quiet. She's terrified at the prospect of losing Briar. She connects with her more than Rosa—that's obvious. She and Rosa snap at each other. I saw it tonight, even with Max here."

"Rosa doesn't like the supernatural."

Moore snorted. "She needs to get over that!"

Tamsyn returned with hot chocolate and biscuits, and Moore roused Beth. She stirred and blinked, her hair falling over her face, but Tamsyn smoothed it aside.

"Hey, Beth. I've made you hot chocolate. Cookie?" She held out the plate.

Beth reached for it, squirming as she made herself comfortable in Moore's lap. "Thank you, Grandma."

"I'm sorry to wake you, honey, but I need to ask you some questions. Is that okay?"

Beth nodded as she crunched. "About Auntie Briar?"

"Yes. Can you remember what you saw? It's really important. I wouldn't ask you otherwise."

She fixed her eyes on Tamsyn. "The lady with the dark hair wanted her magic, but Auntie Briar woke up and stopped her."

All three froze as Tamsyn said, "Auntie Briar is all right?"

"Yes. The Green Man woke up—eventually. And the big, black man with wings arrived, too. He took her away."

Newton was so relieved that he sagged on to the floor, cross-legged. "How do you know, Beth? Did you see it all?"

"I dreamt it. But the lady is very angry."

Tamsyn squeezed her hand. "Where's Auntie Briar now?"

Beth shrugged. "I don't know. Everything has gone again. I can only see snow."

"What about her friends?" Moore asked. "Uncle Alex? Auntie El?"

She shook her head. "I don't know."

Newton leaned forward. "What about the lady who attacked her? Do you know who she is?"

"No, but she was very pretty." Beth frowned as she dipped her biscuit in her mug of hot chocolate. Newton wished he had one; it smelled amazing. "But I don't think her face was real."

Newton glanced at Moore and Tamsyn. "What do you mean?"

"I think there was another face under it." She patted her own face. "It was...different."

"Like a monster?" His eyes darted to the window. "Like the things that were here earlier?"

"Like Jack Frost? He's naughty." She thought for a moment. "A bit like him. I think she's upset too, though."

"Why?" Tamsyn asked.

"The king will die tomorrow, and she's sad. She wants him to stay."

Newton was now more confused than ever. "What king?"

"The Holly King. When he dies, so does winter. She wants winter to last forever."

Newton needed to find Reuben and Caspian, and tell them to get the word out.

*Now.*

# Sixteen

S hadow stood on the patio outside the farmhouse kitchen early on Wednesday morning, drinking coffee and studying her surroundings.

It was just after dawn, and snow was still falling, although not as thick as the day before. The wind had died down, too, and apart from the occasional bird call, it was quiet. Outside, at least. Niel was clattering around in the kitchen, and the sound of running water and doors opening and closing carried down to her.

She was mulling over the information that Niel had given her. Reuben had visited in the night with news of their predicament—and Beth's vision. Today would be full of action, and they had a lot to do. They needed to find a way through to Stormcrossed Manor, and to White Haven. At least the farmhouse was unaffected, for now. And still Shadow couldn't shake the nagging feeling she had about the magic around White Haven, or the sprites. *How were they here? Who was the queen? And what was this about the Holly King?*

The side door opened and closed, and Estelle joined her, carrying her own mug of coffee. There were dark circles beneath her eyes, and that familiar, guarded expression was back on her face.

"You didn't sleep," Shadow said.

"Is that your way of telling me I look like shit?"

Shadow gritted her teeth. "Herne's balls, Estelle! Always so prickly!"

"How would you feel if Gabe was stuck in White Haven, or your brother was locked in Stormcrossed Manor?"

"I would be angry and worried, obviously. I wouldn't necessarily be a complete bitch to everyone around me, though!"

"I wanted fresh air, but I'll go elsewhere!" Estelle turned as if to leave.

"Estelle!" Shadow sighed. "Don't go. I'm worried about Barak, too. And everyone in Stormcrossed. We'll get them out. And actually, you don't look like shit—just tired, like the rest of us." She leaned against the fire-damaged loggia post. "I hardly slept. Gabe snored like a dragon all night, and I've been puzzling about this weird magic I can feel. It reminds me of home, and I don't understand how it can be here."

"Like a dragon? Attractive!" Estelle smirked, and her shoulders dropped as she made a visible effort to relax. "Are you saying the magic is like Ravens' Wood? Isn't part of that from your world? Although, to me, it feels like it's been here forever."

Estelle hadn't been involved in the magic that made Ravens' Wood, so like everyone, she thought it had always been in White Haven.

"It has been, in a way," Shadow explained. "The roots are from a forest long gone, and the Green Man made it grow again. It's nowhere near as big as the original forest, but he brought a few dryads here to populate it, so I understand what you're saying. Ravens' Wood has a touch of the Otherworld about it. But not like this. Not what I sense now. Especially the sprites!" She shook her head, perplexed. "They are absolutely from the Otherworld! They shouldn't be here. I mean, I know there are portals here because a couple of teenagers crossed to my world a few years ago in an attempt to rescue their lost grandfather. But the portals are few and far between, and I have no idea where they are. This is different. There are lots of sprites here. That means whoever is behind this is powerful enough to cross worlds."

"She's made her own portal. And is powerful enough to take you back, perhaps?"

"I used to want to go back, but not anymore. Not to stay, anyway. My life is here now—with this bunch of idiots."

Estelle laughed. "But even so, it must be tempting."

"If I could return easily, perhaps. But that's not what is worrying me. If this witch-fey woman has come through, what else could?"

"I presume dragons are on your mind for a reason?"

"Yes! No one wants *them* here. That would be a disaster. But there's other news, too. Did you speak to Niel?"

"No. He was too loud in there." Estelle rolled her eyes.

"Reuben visited him last night in his freaky horse familiar. Twice."

"Caspian visited me as well, but we couldn't communicate. Not properly, anyway. It was frustrating."

"Well, Reuben could, through his horse. He told Niel that Beth had a vision of Briar being attacked, but Barak saved her."

"He's *alive*? You could have opened with that!" Estelle's eyes blazed with anger.

"Sorry. I was distracted." Shadow winced. She really didn't think that through at all. "Yes, but that's all I know! She saw him save Briar, and that was it. I'm really glad he's okay. Both of them."

Estelle laughed, her mood instantly lightening. "That's great news. Thank you. I could kiss Reuben! And Beth!"

"Please don't kiss *me*. Anyway, I'm preoccupied because apparently this queen wants to save her consort—the Holly King."

Estelle's mouth dropped open. "I knew it! This is a Yule thing!"

"We all know it's a Yule thing..."

"Do you know the story of the Holly King and the Oak King?"

"Not really." Shadow was familiar with folklore, but although some stories were similar to her own world's stories, others were not. "Isn't he like the Green Man?"

"Sort of, but they have distinct roles. The Green Man is a wild, woodland spirit who is present all year round, but is stronger in the spring and summer. You know that?" Shadow nodded. The Green Man crossed cultures, but had a more physical presence in the Otherworld. "Well. The Holly King and the Oak King are seasonal. The Oak King is the Summer King, and rules from Yule to Litha. At that point, the Holly King takes over and rules until Yule. He is the Winter King, taking the world from summer to winter, bringing short days and long, dark nights."

"The Winter King to go with the Winter Witch. Is there not a Summer Queen to take over from a winter one?"

"No, not in our folklore. They're sometimes described as vying for the attention of the Goddess."

"But we're pretty sure that whoever is behind this is not a Goddess."

"No. But say she is a Winter Witch, and he is her consort, then she will be alone without him."

Shadow shrugged. "For six months, though. In theory, that has been a cycle forever!"

"What if she wants to stop it?"

"It sounds like she does. Beth says she wants winter to last forever." Shadow rested her hand on the hilt of her dagger, an instinctive touch of reassurance. "Are we in the middle of this because she wants her king to stay all year? Is this like some Romeo and Juliet thing?"

Estelle rolled her eyes. "No! Those were lovelorn teenagers who ended up killing themselves. Don't you know anything?"

"I know disco."

"Anything useful?"

"Disco is useful." Her swaying hips always made Gabe want sex. "But that wasn't what I meant. They were kept apart by their warring families. What if the seasons are like that? Desperate to keep the Winter Witch from her king?"

"You're personifying the seasons."

"You're personifying winter and summer already!"

"Fair point. They are, according to some myths, brothers," Estelle conceded. "Each has half of the year. Perhaps this suggests that she..." Estelle stopped dead, eyes wide.

"What?" Shadow asked.

"The Green Man is everywhere and nowhere, impossible to pin down. He's nature! I said that he's distinct from the Oak King and the Holly King, but actually some stories link him with the Oak King, because the imagery is the same—a face surrounded by verdant greenery and oak leaves. Say that an aspect of him is the Oak King. That means a little part of him is in Briar."

"Are you saying that the Winter Witch is in White Haven because of Briar? That's crazy!"

Estelle put her hands on her hips. "Why is it crazy?"

"Because like you just said, the Green Man is everywhere. He's nature. He's not a thing you can box up!"

"But what if Briar is unique? She contains a little bit of him. What if that's enough for the queen? Maybe she needs him to save the Holly King."

Shadow started pacing. "Okay. Maybe there is something in that. Maybe she just needs a bit of the Green Man to strengthen the Holly King so that he can fight the Oak King and win?"

"Or if he *is* the Oak King, perhaps she wants to drain his energy so that the Holly King wins."

"Would that work?"

"I don't know!" Estelle looked exasperated. "I'm trying to get my head around all this. But it could, right?"

"So, she's wanted Briar all along, and that's why she's here and has sealed off White Haven. And Yule is today. Tonight, in fact. The queen—or witch, whatever—has already tried to kill her once. She'll be furious that she escaped, and she'll seek retribution. We have to get in there today, or it's too late."

"For once, Shadow, we agree. Let's go and update the others."

Helena, locked in Clea's body, waited to hear movement in Happenstance Books before she went downstairs on Wednesday morning, savouring her time alone.

She still marvelled at this strange, new modern world that she was now a part of for a few days each month. She liked it, too. Showers, hot running water, central heating, vacuums, TV, phones, the radio, makeup, and so many other things. It was like being transplanted onto another planet. However, it was strange being in Clea, who was so much older than she was when she was killed.

Her back ached, and her knees, and she became breathless if she tried to climb the stairs too quickly, and every now and again she felt her heart pound unexpectedly. There must be spells to help with that, and she was determined to find them. Briar could help. But despite all of that, she liked being Clea. Liked the ability to touch things, feel the cold and heat, scent cinnamon and nutmeg. *Perhaps she could spruce her wardrobe up, too. That might make her feel younger.*

Avery had taken her to the flat in the middle of the night, along with her own, ancient family grimoire. They had spent hours at Newton's home searching for spells to counter the queen's magic. They had decided that if it was safe enough, they would try to release Sally and Dan from the spell so they could understand what was really happening, and hopefully help them.

Of course, that came with risks. While under the spell, they would go along with anything and would therefore not risk the queen's wrath. Additionally, they wouldn't say anything that might give them away and risk their families, too. But they needed help to break the queen's magic and free White Haven, and Dan and Sally were trustworthy and clever. While Helena spent the day in the shop, the three witches would use their familiars to travel around White Haven, and Alex and Barak would focus on finding a way through the wall.

Helena opened the grimoire and scanned the spells they thought would be the most likely to work. Breaking another witch's spell was always tricky, and could backfire, especially when they knew the original spell to be strong. When the witches were under the spell, they couldn't even see the words on the pages. That was impressive. However, it was heartening that their protection spells on their homes were still intact. The queen still had limitations.

Helena walked to the window that overlooked the street below, noting that snow was still falling. The streets were buried under several feet of it, and it almost reached the sills of the shop windows. Shop owners had cleared paths to their doors, but the roads remained blocked. It seemed this was all part of the queen's plan, though. Even though it was early, sleighs pulled by reindeers transported people around the town, accompanied by the sounds of bells strung on the sleighs and the animals' neck. White Haven had been taken back in time. At least the electricity was back on. Perhaps removing it completely would be one step too far in keeping the town happy and warm.

It reminded her of the White Haven of her own time, except it was bigger and more sophisticated. Perhaps she could go to Penny Lane Bistro, her old house. She could have lunch there and reminisce. Or maybe that would be depressing, and merely remind her of things that she would rather forget.

When she saw Dan on the street below clearing the path in front of the shop, she headed downstairs, trying to look as meek and mild as possible.

Sally was behind the counter, and she looked up at the sound of her approach. "Clea! I didn't expect to see you!"

"Well, it's Yule, so I thought I'd enjoy the festivities. Plus. I'm here to help. Avery stayed at El's home last night, with Alex."

Sally's eyes widened with surprise. "Really? She never said anything."

"It was late notice. The storm caught them out after the fayre, and El's flat was closer."

Helena smiled, wondering if she should appear vaguer. More confused. It was exhausting being someone else, and being a spirit right now would be useful. The ability to go anywhere and spy on the queen, for example, would come in quite handy at a time like this.

Sally, however, seemed more than happy with her reply. "That's fine. She doesn't have to come in at all if she doesn't want to. We can manage." Her face clouded with worry. "That was an odd blizzard last night, though. It whipped up out of nowhere! It had been so calm."

"Well, that's storms for you! Were you there, dear?"

"No, fortunately! We were there early with the kids, and had just arrived home."

Dan joined them, stamping his feet at the door to shed snow before walking to the counter. "Me and Caro had too, Sally. We curled up in front of the fire all night." He turned to Helena. "You say Avery is at El's?"

"Yes. Well, I think so. Maybe they've gone out for the day now?" She shrugged helplessly. "My memory isn't what it once was. Can you remember the details of tonight? The feast?"

Dan rolled his eyes. "The event of the year! Of course. Every single person in the town will be at the palace for the meal. You've been before, Clea," he said reassuringly. "I'm sure you'll enjoy it."

She wrung her hands. "I'm sure I will, too. It's very generous of the queen, isn't it?"

Dan lowered his voice. "Not especially so for those who have to shut down their bars and restaurants and will lose revenue, but it's a holiday, isn't it!" His troubled expression cleared, as if he suddenly remembered he shouldn't criticise. "The Yule parade will start late this afternoon, and then it's off to the castle." He winked at Helena. "Make sure you put your poshest frock and your dancing shoes on!"

"What if you don't want to go? Or are ill?"

Unease swept over Sally's face. "That *never* happens! Why wouldn't anyone go?"

"Silly question," Helena said with a shrug.

She looked through the window when she heard voices and the furious jingle of sleighbells outside. She was glad of the interruption, until she saw that half a dozen guards had arrived in two sleighs, all armed with swords. Leading them was a good-looking young man with snow white hair and dark blue eyes. Helena gave an involuntary shiver. She suspected who it was, and she knew exactly who they were looking for.

"What's going on?" Sally asked, leaping to her feet.

Helena stepped back, rounding her shoulders and trying to appear insignificant as the blond man stepped inside. The Christmas Bunch shivered at his arrival, and his gaze swept around the shop before quickly focussing on the trio at the counter. Four guards entered with him, and two remained outside the door.

"Can I help you with something?" Dan asked, assuming fake cheer. His shoulders and stance, however, were tight.

The man smiled, and Helena shuffled further back into the shadows of the stacks. She feared his sharp eyes would miss nothing. She could certainly feel his power, and an unearthly kind of magic.

"I'm looking for Avery Hamilton and Alex Bonneville. We need to talk to them. It's a matter of some urgency."

"Why?" Dan asked abruptly. "Have they done something wrong? You've brought guards with you."

His eyes travelled from Dan's face to his feet and back again. "It is not your place to ask questions. It is enough for you to know that the queen wishes to speak to them."

"They're not here. They stopped with a friend overnight."

"Is that so?" He stepped closer, menace oozing from him. "Who?"

Helena didn't need magic to tell her that this man was dangerous. She was now sure he was Jack Frost, the powerful sprite with winter in his blood and the ability to freeze anything with a snap of his fingers, but she had to be absolutely certain.

"Elspeth Robinson," Dan said. "She lives close to the harbour."

"It seems you're lying, because no one is answering Elspeth's door, Mr..."

"I'm Dan Fellows, Avery's friend and shop assistant. And I'm not lying. They must have gone out. It's not a crime! Who are you?" Dan lifted his chin defiantly, and Helena wasn't sure if he was brave or insane.

"I'm Jack," the man replied, amused for the briefest moment, before his eyes hardened again. "A very good friend of the queen. And your companions?" Jack stared at Sally and Helena.

Sally stepped forward. "I'm Sally, the shop manager. Dan is not lying. This is Clea, Avery's grandmother. She told us where they are. We have no reason to lie."

"Clea?" Jack ignored her and turned his imperious gaze on Helena.

Her anger was building, and so was her magic. She already hated this sharp-faced, superior man. He reminded her of so many other people who shared that same unwaveringly narcissistic self-belief and lack of compassion for others—particularly Mathew Hopkins, the Witchfinder General. She longed to blast Jack out of the door and wrap him up in spells. At least they still couldn't get past El's protection spell, and that knowledge fortified her.

Helena took a deep breath, looking up at him with her most innocent expression. "Yes, Jack. She's with her friend. I forget the details. Perhaps they're going Yuletide shopping together, or some such... My memory is shaky. Can we pass a message on?"

"Not so quick, Clea. I need to search the shop and the flat above—just in case you're all harbouring them here. I believe this is where Avery and Alex live, is it not?"

The air tightened with malice, but Helena forced a smile. "Of course. I'll show you around."

She half wanted to let him search the place on his own, desperate to keep her distance, but decided she would learn more by being close to him.

Jack turned to the guards. "You two search the shop, and you two come with me."

Helena exchanged a nervous glance with Sally and Dan, hoping nothing untoward would happen to them. *Surely not. They had no magic, and posed no threat.* She led the way through the backroom and up the stairs, aware of Jack taking everything in.

Now that Helena had regained her memories and knew she was a witch, the part of the shop that had books on witches, magic, tarot cards, and other occult objects, were very visible to her, but the day before it was all hidden. The queen's magic had effectively suppressed anything related to witchcraft. She presumed Jack would see it all, however. When they arrived in the flat, the guards opened doors and cupboards—as if anyone would be hiding under the sink.

Jack folded his arms and stared at her. "You live here, too?"

Tricky. *Would Jack know the truth?* In theory, seeing as she had been trapped in the spell here, and Avery had previously believed that she did, she needed to say yes. Besides, she was sleeping in the spare bedroom, and her clothes were there.

She needed to play up her memory loss and decided to mention her daughter. "Yes. Diana is very good and looks after me, because my memory isn't what it was, you know. I used to run this shop. For years, you know! Brought my family up here. Such wonderful times." She gabbled as if she was nervous and dithering.

"Diana? You mean Avery?" His eyes narrowed. "Who's Diana? Someone else lives here?"

"She's, er..." Helena faltered, acting confused, and wondering if a sprite would even understand Alzheimer's. "My daughter."

"Diana lives here?"

"Yes. No. Sorry. I told you, I'm forgetful. No. I live with Avery."

"You are confused, aren't you? Your circumstances must have slipped past us," Jack murmured to himself. "No matter. Let us see upstairs."

Helena became more nervous as she followed Jack to the attic. To her, that room always felt magical. She stood on the threshold, almost holding her breath as Jack stalked the perimeter.

"An unusual room," he observed, casting her a sly glance. "Don't you think?"

"It's just an attic. I don't like it here. I prefer downstairs."

Jack idly turned the pages of the grimoire before searching the bedroom and bathroom. Helena decided to ignore the grimoire. That would be for the best. *Would he know that two were missing?* She stood at the window, watching the street below. Pedestrians were now walking along the lane, in and out of shops, casting a wary glance at the two soldiers at the door. Again, it reminded Helena all too well of the Witchfinder General and his inquisition. She started to feel sick, especially when Jack approached.

She turned quickly to find him studying her, a calculating gleam in his eyes. "You're close to Avery?"

She reminded herself to act like Clea would. "Of course! What a silly question, young man. She's my granddaughter!"

"I think you need to come with us, Clea."

"Why? I have things to do. I was going to help in the shop, and I have knitting to finish! And The Repair Shop is on at lunchtime, if the TV comes backs on." She clucked impatiently. "I haven't got time to go gadding about!"

"What a very interesting woman you are, Clea. You need to come with me because Avery and Alex are missing, along with their friends, El and Briar. They are special to us, and I must find them. And perhaps you are special, too."

"I don't know what you're saying."

He moved in until he was only inches away, and she backed up, the small of her back hitting the windowsill. He was tall, and he loomed over her. She smelled snow and ice on him, and his breath was a cold mist now that she was so close. If he tried to kill her, she would have no alternative but to use magic, and give everything away.

But he didn't. "We are going to have a little party in the square at lunchtime. We will put the word out that unless Avery and her friends come out of hiding—"

"They are not hiding!"

"Oh, they are! Unless they come to rescue you, there will be repercussions. I'm sure they won't want that on their conscience."

He nodded at the guards, who seized her and marched her downstairs. She couldn't resist, not now. She would just have to let things unfold.

# Seventeen

"I am not taking you to the gate on the icesheet," Gabe said firmly to Ben, arms folded across his chest. "They know that we know it's there, and therefore it's either sealed or will be heavily guarded."

Ben rolled his eyes. "If we can take readings from it, it might help us find another one!"

"No way," Gabe said.

They were all gathered in the farmhouse's living room again, deciding on their plans after a hurried breakfast.

Ben was annoyingly persistent. "Then you risk us taking twice as long to find another one. And we don't have time to spare if what Shadow and Estelle have said is right! If that bitch queen is after Briar and the Green Man, and it all happens tonight, *we have to* get in!"

"Risking our lives for a reading is not an option!" Gabe turned to Shadow. "And if you find any more queen sculptures, do not decapitate them!"

"Spoilsport. Maybe the sculptures mark an entrance?" she suggested.

"They didn't in Harecombe," Kendall pointed out. "I mean, there was no wall there. I think Jack is just showcasing his abilities. He seems a complete prick!"

"Unless they have more significance than we think," Ash said, amused at Kendall's outburst.

Nahum was polishing his sword, and he held it up to the light. "I think we have enough theories going on, don't you?"

Ben continued to push, arms folded now too as he glared at Gabe. "Gabe, why don't you just fly me to the gate, and I'll take readings in the air? Then I can join the others on land with useful intel! And after that, you can fly us over Stormcrossed, and I'll take a reading there. It might help us break the spell. *We need all the help we can get.*"

"I'm going there first, anyway," Estelle said. "I have a spell I think will work to get them out. If we're to break the spell to get into White Haven, we need Reuben and Caspian—not just their familiars! I can't do this alone."

The others nodded, and Zee said, "I agree, but it doesn't stop us from searching for a weak point in the wall."

Gabe sighed as he took in Ben's mutinous, tight-lipped expression. He was good at what he did, so perhaps he had a point. "Fine. Just be aware that I will not set you down on the ice. As long as you're comfortable in the air..."

"I'll make it work! Even if I have to do it hanging upside down."

"Let's hope it won't come to that." Gabe turned to Ash and Eli, who were looking through the window while listening to the conversation. "Why don't you two search the perimeter from Raven's Wood and work your way around? Maybe Dylan and Cassie can join you?"

"Totally!" Dylan had already packed his backpack. "I'm ready, and we have spare EMF meters."

Cassie nodded. "Fine with me."

Gabe addressed the others who were all staring at him expectantly, or having whispered side conversations. "That leaves Zee, Niel, Shadow, Kendall, Nahum, and Estelle to tackle the manor. If the sprites attack, you'll need everyone—especially to defend Estelle while she's spellcasting."

Estelle was seated in the armchair, grimoire on her lap, her fingers drumming the cover. She shuffled in her seat, and it was clear something was on her mind. "It's impossible for me to contact the rest of the Cornwall Coven right now. The phones are still down, and I don't use psychic communication like Alex. But I think Reuben was right about Eve. She's a really powerful weather witch. I might need her to get into Stormcrossed Manor. While you are all really helpful, you're not witches! Even if I manage to break the spell around the manor without her, she'll be useful later."

"Let me go, then," Zee suggested. "I've heard Alex talk about where she lives in St Ives. I could fly there now and bring her back—hopefully." He nodded to the window. "The snowfall is still thick. With luck it will be the same across Cornwall, and I can fly the whole way. No one will see me in this."

"And if the snow stops three miles out?" Gabe asked.

"Then I'll catch a cab! I have to at least try."

Estelle smiled at him. "That would be fantastic, thank you. I can't communicate with Caspian's familiar, Eagle, very well, but when he visited me last night, I told him my plans and showed him the spell I'm going to use. Hopefully—if he understood me—he and Reuben can work one from inside the manor, and together we can break the icy spell that's trapped them."

"Excellent plan. Any questions?" Gabe asked the group. They shook their heads and grabbed weapons. Except for Eli.

He stared at Gabe, unflinching. "You know, we have other options as a last resort."

He was talking about Belial's jewellery. Gabe knew someone was bound to bring that up, and wasn't surprised that it was Eli—despite the previous repercussions. He was the one who suggested using it the first time. Eli also worked with Briar and was very close to her. Gabe was surprised someone hadn't mentioned it sooner, actually. He hesitated. *It could be a gamechanger.*

"What?" Cassie asked, obviously confused and looking between them.

Estelle didn't let him answer. She leapt to her feet, fists clenched. "No! That stuff changes all of you. Absolutely not."

"Even to rescue Barak?" Gabe asked her.

"What are you talking about?" Ben asked, eyes narrowing.

*Bollocks.* Now Gabe knew Ben would not stop talking about it for the entire journey. "Nahum found angelic jewellery belonging to the Fallen Angel, Belial. It makes us very strong. Insanely so."

"*What?*" Dylan exploded. "And you didn't tell us? So, it might even get us in there now?"

Nahum intervened. "Woah! Slow down. That jewellery is toxic. You three," he pointed at Ghost OPS, "will not touch it, *ever.* And we don't know if it will help us. Just because it makes us stronger, does not mean that we will be able to break the spell around White Haven. It might even make it worse, somehow. We leave it locked up as we agreed only days ago. And in case you've forgotten, you're all going to be uncles and aunts soon, so I don't want any trace of that poisonous Belial around, okay? Olivia has had enough problems."

Cassie squealed. "Someone's having a baby?" She stared at Shadow and Estelle. "One of you?"

"Fuck no!" Shadow looked horrified. "No offense, Gabe."

"And not me, either," Estelle said, shooting Shadow a look of incredulity at the suggestion. At least there was one thing they bonded over—the horror of motherhood. "My vagina is fine the way it is! It's Nahum who's been busy. He's the baby daddy!"

Cassie's mouth dropped open as she stared at him. "Oh? With Olivia? Who's she?"

"Enough!" Gabe roared. Ben was going to pester him about so many things on their flight. "You can all catch up on Nahum's news later. I agree with him. No jewellery, for now! It's the absolute last resort! Understood?" He didn't wait for confirmation. "Good. Then let's go."

"So, you say there was no sign of El?" Alex asked Avery in Newton's kitchen.

They had all gone to bed very late the previous night after their various searches, too tired to discuss in detail what they'd found, and Alex had let her sleep as best she could. As a consequence, they had risen late.

Avery slumped at the table, her hair tumbling over her face, coffee in hand. "No." Her eyes were bleak as she looked at Alex, Briar, and Barak. "What if she's dead?"

"No! Don't even suggest that!" Briar covered her ears with her hands.

"That witch-bitch tried to kill you!" Avery pointed out, her eyes welling with tears and frustration. "Barak saved you. El had no one! We should never have let her walk off alone."

"She's an adult, Avery, and quite capable of making her own decisions." Alex reached over and squeezed her hand, as much to reassure himself as Avery. She was still angry with him for leaving the fayre without her, and guilt plagued him, too, even though he knew it was irrational. "Let's stay positive. Anything could have happened to make them move her."

"Agreed," Barak nodded. The big man looked none the worse for sleeping on the living room sofa. He had insisted Briar take Newton's second bedroom, citing the fact that he was battle-hardened and had slept in worse places in the past. "Perhaps they realised she would freeze to death overnight and moved her somewhere warmer. Or maybe they saw Raven. He might find her this morning." Raven had left alone to scout White Haven.

Alex released Avery's hand and leaned back in his chair. He hoped some of Newton's calm, investigative instincts would somehow soak into him from his house, but the circumstances were so odd, his thoughts were jumbled and confused. Not helped by his own lack of sleep or failure with Wolf. They hadn't even made it to the wall, because he'd spent all his time searching White Haven.

He sighed. "So, we all failed, then. Barak couldn't find a gate, and I couldn't penetrate the palace at all by scrying. It's like it's a big void. And I couldn't see anything of the outside world, either. I tried for hours. We just have to hope that Helena learns something today."

"I can't sit around and wait all day," Briar complained.

"We're not going to wait. We're going to strategise," Barak said. "I commanded battles and faced armies. I can certainly handle a witch-bitch and her sprite cronies. So can you. We know several things so far. The witch wants Briar's power, that much is clear—and maybe also yours. She also doesn't want you to use your magic against her, hence the spells to make you forget. We know her magic, although powerful, isn't infallible. You broke the spell on you by being angry and scared. That's good, right?"

Alex nodded. "Yes. Her magic has weaknesses. Ours have them too, when someone puts enough work into breaking them. It's like unpicking a lock. Like when Black Cronos broke the protection spell around your farmhouse. They concentrated on one spot."

"Which is what we need to do." Avery smiled for the first time in hours. "We need to reverse engineer a spell. Work out how we could cast a spell like hers—"

"And from there, work out how to break it," Briar finished.

"But everyone's magic is unique," Alex pointed out. "We bring our own strengths to it."

Barak grunted. "And hers is winter and the cold, just like the bastard sprite she works with. Shadow thought she was either fey or part fey. She says sprites are definitely fey creatures. That's what all the guards are, beneath their human appearance."

"That's true," Briar said with a shudder. "I'd almost forgotten that in the excitement of the fight. They look odd. Sharp-faced, narrow eyes."

Avery pulled her grimoire towards her again. "Elemental water. That has to be her strength. That's why there's so much snow and ice here. Didn't Shadow talk about realms in her world? Maybe she's from the Realm of Water?"

"No." Barak shook his head. "She describes that as being subtropical. Hot and humid in some places."

"Damn it." Avery sighed. "I thought I'd suggested something useful then."

Briar started searching her own grimoire. "It's still useful. Working on elemental water as being her strength is good. But we need more. Something to really focus on. We have too many theories and questions. Like how is she here? Where has she come from? Why us? Why now? It's Yule tonight. There's a huge feast that we must attend. It was instilled into us. That must have relevance."

"Maybe we're all going to be sacrificed to some demon," Barak said, laughing.

"Barak!" Briar slapped his arm. "That's not funny!"

"I know. Doesn't mean it won't happen, though."

"Okay," Alex said, trying to ignore Barak's doom-mongering and building on their suggestions. "Yesterday was a shitstorm of emotion and confusion. We were trapped in a spell, then we broke it, leading to fights, hiding, and El vanishing. We ran around like headless chickens last night. But Barak is right. There are things we know for sure. Her magic can be broken. We just need the keys. Undermining that sprite, Jack Frost, has to be one of them. He's clearly a big part of it."

Barak shrugged. "I will happily kill him."

"So will I," Briar said, lips twisting with annoyance. "I knew something was wrong with him. He oozed danger under all that charm, and I instinctively knew to be careful around him. He manipulated me into going to the queen—a willing sacrifice!" She spooned out her herbal tea bag aggressively and dumped it into a saucer. "I had the feeling they had researched me, which was unnerving. And then she detected activity at...what did she call it? The South Gate. That must have been you, Barak. It was like she could see it happening. At least she let Stan go."

"The South Gate?" Barak repeated, eyes widening. "She named it?"

"Yes, didn't I say that before?"

"No. That's interesting. It suggests there's a north, east and west gate, doesn't it?" He raised an eyebrow as he stared at Alex. "It gives us places to focus on."

Hope stirred within Alex. "That's true. Good. Briar, you said Stan was there?"

"Yes. The poor man looked terrified. He had to report on the parade. We bumped into him at the fayre, and I think he wanted to warn me about Jack, but didn't have time. I also think he would have liked to argue about the queen making me stay, but he scurried off. I'm glad he did. I'd hate for Stan to get hurt."

"Stan knows about us, which means he knows about magic," Avery mused. "I wonder if that might make it easier to break the spell on him. He'd help us, I know he would."

"The more I think about it," Briar said, "the surer I am that he knows all this is wrong."

"Ben said he was amazing when they got trapped back in time," Avery said. "We can't endanger him, though. I've been thinking about James, the vicar, too. I wonder how he's finding all this?"

"Wait!" An idea had struck Alex, and he was pretty sure it was a good one. "We broke the spell when we were angry. You were furious with me, Avery, and I was angry, too. What if we can make the whole town angry? What if that undermines her spell?"

Barak huffed. "You'd need a big event to upset everyone at the same time."

"Maybe the feast is the key," Avery suggested. "Everyone is in one place, eating and partying, too happy to see anything underhanded. But if we could switch the mood with a spell..."

Alex laughed. "I like that! But we'd need to be there. That will be hard, considering we're trying to hide."

"We can disguise ourselves. Or work a shadow spell. Something to get us in under the queen's defence systems."

"But," Briar pointed out, "I think that deep down, everyone in this town knows something is different. That something is wrong! I saw it in your pub last night, Alex. Underneath all the happy chat, some people looked furtive. Unsettled. *We* felt it! We knew something was wrong. We're assuming it's because we're witches, but what if everyone can sense it?"

"Another weakness in the spell," Alex said, nodding. "If that's true, then our spell to invoke anger will be more effective."

Avery's fingers drummed the table. "But also dangerous for everyone if we're successful in breaking it. And how the hell do we explain it afterwards?"

Barak gave a dry laugh. "I think you're getting ahead of yourself. The question is, what do you achieve by making everyone see they're in a spell if White Haven is still cut off? Instead, you'll have terrified people and an incensed queen! There's no point, unless you can get rid of her and Jack."

"Fuck it!" Alex's head hurt, his eyes were gritty, and he hated the fact that Barak had just made an excellent point. "You're right. It is senseless unless breaking her hold on everyone breaks the whole spell. And we don't understand enough about it to know that."

Avery held her hand up. "Let's not discount it yet. It might have merit. I need to speak to Sally and Dan. Get a feel for their understanding of the situation. See what Clea has found out already." She checked the time. "It's midmorning. If the guards have searched for us, they must have gone by now. I'll go to the attic using witch-flight."

Alex loved Avery, but often wished she wasn't so headstrong. "What if they're still there? Wait for Raven!"

"I don't know where he is, or how long he'll be. If I can get Dan and Sally on side, that would be huge! And Dan might be able to help us work out who this woman is. The more we know, the more likely we can get rid of her."

"Agreed," Barak said, "but hold on. If we can get everyone outside White Haven inside, we'd stand a much better chance. I know they'll be working on a way in."

"Which brings us back to opening up a hole in that bloody wall." Alex took a deep breath. "I noticed last night that none of the locals go near the perimeter. Something else they've been hardwired not to do. That will make life easier."

"I'm happy to search on foot," Barak told him. "Let's go together."

"Works for me." Alex noticed that Briar's rings of green fire around her irises were bright, and it reminded him of the Green Man that lurked within her. "How's your little green friend after yesterday, Briar? Your eyes are very green today!"

"He's all fired up, actually. He reared up when I fought for my life yesterday. Green vines shot from my fingers! I could barely contain him! He was bubbling right under my skin."

"Is that because it's Yule, or because of the queen?"

Briar hesitated. "I'm actually not sure. I'm so used to him, I didn't even think."

"Maybe you should. This is all about Yule, and he may have a big part to play in it." Alex thought it through. "Traditionally, he's more active in the spring and summer, right? He's dormant this time of year. But after Yule, he'll grow in power again. Have you ever spoken to him?"

"What?"

Alex smiled. "Have you chatted to your resident?"

"Not really." Briar looked around the table nervously. "He just *is*! I mean, I'm aware of him on occasions, but we don't chat over tea and scones!"

"Interesting. I'm pretty sure there's more to his presence than him just lurking around. I think while we're out searching for answers, you need to meditate and connect to him."

"But—"

"No buts, Briar. I can help you begin, but you have to do this. This is Yule. This is his time. And we need him."

# Eighteen

During the night, El was transferred to another cell in the palace's main building, along with half a dozen other prisoners. They had been given no explanations, and she wasn't sure whether to be more worried or less.

It was certainly inconvenient. The raven hadn't found her again, which wasn't surprising, as there was no outside access with open bars for him to fly through. On the plus side, it was warmer, although the cell still left a lot to be desired. She lay on her back on the simple pallet covered in straw, staring at the rough stone ceiling. *Perhaps they had seen Raven and heard her talking? Or maybe one of the other prisoners had caused problems.* She had at least managed to sleep, but her waking hours were preoccupied with Raven's news.

She was a witch. Deep within her was real power. She just needed to unlock it.

The jangle of keys broke her train of thought, and she jumped to her feet as the door swung open. A guard with almost colourless blue eyes wearing a dove grey uniform stepped inside the cell, eyes sweeping over her. "The queen wishes to see you. Follow me."

At first El thought she was going alone, but when she stepped into the corridor, she saw that the other prisoners were being escorted out, too. Manacles were clamped on their wrists, and they were herded along passageways. El studied her companions. They all looked innocuous enough. An old man with wispy grey hair, a middle-aged woman, two teenagers, and a young woman of a similar age to El who she recognised from around town but didn't know. They glanced furtively at each other, but didn't speak.

El's mouth was dry with fear when they were finally led into a rectangular room with bare stone walls, devoid of all furniture except two benches that ran along the long walls, and a throne at the far end. They sat silently for a few minutes until the door banged open and a young man with a shock of white hair walked in with Clea, Avery's grandmother. It was the same man she had seen with Briar.

El opened her mouth in surprise, but Clea flashed her a look that commanded silence, and El stared at the floor. *What the hell was going on? Why was Clea there, of all people? If Avery had broken the spell on herself, what did it mean for her grandmother?* If she let on that she knew her, El might give away her identity.

Fortunately, the man wasn't paying attention to them. He thrust Clea towards the bench. "Sit with the others!"

"There's no need to be aggressive!" she shot back. "Honestly, why am I here?"

His eyes hardened and an icy mist manifested around him, seeming to ooze from his pores. "Clea, I suggest you shut up—before I do it for you, permanently." He surveyed the others, arms folded, one finger tapping his chin. "The queen would normally see you to decide your fate, but she has much on her mind this morning, so I, Jack Frost, her most trusted advisor, will deal with you all instead." His voice dripped with malice. "It seems that some of our residents, like you, are breaking rules and are in hiding. All of *you* will draw them out. In the next few minutes, Clea and one other of my choosing will be escorted to the town square. We will assemble there for one hour. In that time, unless these missing individuals present themselves, they will both be killed."

A ripple of fear ran around the room, and Clea gasped, outraged. "That is utterly ridiculous!"

"Shut up!" Jack slapped her cheek, snapping Clea's head around. Her hair fell over her face, but not before El saw her eyes blazing with anger.

El couldn't contain herself and leapt to her feet, wrestling against her restraints. "She's an old woman! How could you?"

"Easily," he sneered. "Sit down—unless you wish to share her fate."

"Take me! Better me than anyone else." El was furious. She wanted to seethe with anger and break her spell, but perhaps fear was keeping it locked in. No wave of magic rolled over her. No sudden return of her memories.

Jack sneered. "I don't think so. You will provide ample entertainment later – you are insurance. Should these individuals fail to appear in the square, the fate of all of you will be announced to the town." He smiled maliciously. "You will be sacrificed tonight. One by one. Your deaths will be on their conscience." He gave a wolfish smile. "I'm sure all of your relatives and friends will be anxious to avoid that, and having the entire population scouting for them will be another motivating factor. I think we are being very generous with our time. I hope they do not abuse it."

He rolled out the names of the missing, and El didn't blink as she recognised all of her friends' names, including her own. The guards hadn't recognised her, and she was very glad that she had rubbed her makeup off and looked grubby and unkempt. Fortunately, none of her fellow prisoners knew her either, and Clea didn't let on.

"Do any of you know where they might be hiding?" he asked, searching their faces for answers.

Every single one remained mute.

"You may change your mind when death is closer at hand. Now, who to choose?" El wondered whether to volunteer herself again, but then decided that would be too obvious. She could feel the weight of Jack's stare as it ran around the room. Eventually, he picked the middle-aged woman. "You. On your feet now. Your fate awaits."

"My sister is outside with some of the Nephilim—sooner than I expected, actually," Caspian announced to Reuben and Tamsyn as he entered Tamsyn's kitchen. "It's time for us to help her."

"I presume you saw her through your familiar?" Tamsyn asked, deftly kneading dough as she talked. "That must be nice, to see things from so high up. It's a skill I envy."

Caspian laughed. "It's a skill I have yet to master. I'm still not at one with my familiar. Not really. I feel a clumsy passenger most of the time, even though I slip into his form easily enough. But there are no rules, and I struggle with that. And the whole not-speaking thing. It's so frustrating."

Reuben winked as he slid a tray of warm biscuits onto a plate. "You're learning to break the rules, though. That will help. And, well, it seems some familiars don't talk to other people or manifest to them at all. My stallion is very clever." Reuben always loved to mention his stallion, like it enhanced his sexual appeal—and he did it regardless of who he was talking to.

"Shouldn't you be prancing around in him now, being useful?"

"I *am* being useful! Tamsyn needs me for cooking and tasting!" He bit into a sugary cookie and rolled his eyes. "Divine!"

"I do not need you for tasting, young man. Cheeky!" She lifted a floury hand and tweaked his cheek. "If I was fifty years younger..."

Reuben sniggered. "Tamsyn. You devil."

Reuben was incorrigible, and Caspian laughed despite their circumstances. They were still encased in what appeared to be a block of ice, and that morning he and Reuben had cast warming spells across the entire house. Fortunately, they had an ample supply of wood, and Tamsyn was cooking on the wood-fuelled stove as if they would be trapped for weeks. There were already two loaves cooling on the rack on the kitchen table, and the smell of fresh bread was mouthwatering. Caspian was feeling fat just inhaling it.

Reuben brushed crumbs off his hands. "I'm all yours, fully loaded and spell-ready. There's nothing that Silver can do right now."

"I told him," Tamsyn nodded at Reuben, "that he should have called his horse Mr Ed. He hadn't even heard of him."

Reuben huffed. "Mr Ed sounds seriously uncool. My familiar is called Silver, and there's no further discussion!"

"But at least he talks—sort of! I have the silent Eagle. I mean, he's great," Caspian added hastily, knowing he shouldn't insult his familiar, "but, well you know..." he trailed off. There was only one way to truly embrace his eagle, and that was to spend more time with it. He hadn't, and he needed to remedy that.

Tamsyn shot him a sly glance, as if she could read his thoughts. "Silent and deadly, though. Just like you, I would imagine." For a moment, Caspian had a sharp pang of regret that anyone should see him as such, although he knew Tamsyn meant it as a compliment. Her hands kept kneading, but her eyes never left his. "And a deep, true heart beating in its breast. I see someone for you. She's not far away now."

"You what?" Reuben asked, glancing between them. "Who? And I didn't think you *saw* clearly anymore?"

"If you'd listen, noggin head, you would know that now the banshee has gone, the Sight is coming back. You would also know that what we see is not always clear." She smiled at Caspian. "But I know it to be true."

Caspian was suddenly hopeful, which was ridiculous, just because of a few passing words from Tamsyn. He'd carried feelings so long for Avery, and saw how happy Estelle was with Barak, that he could almost taste happiness, too. *Not that he was unhappy, but...* He forced himself to speak. "I'm intrigued, and I may well ask you more later, Tamsyn."

"But in the meantime, Cas," Reuben said, smirking, "let's lay some mojo on those deadly little sprites." He walked to the window. "I've been studying the ice. It's not as thick as it looks. I can see shapes moving through it. Sprites, I suspect, on the other side. Let's hope your sister's spell can penetrate it."

"What type of spell is it?" Tamsyn asked.

"A weather spell, which isn't exactly our thing," Caspian explained, "but the hot air should flush the sprites out. We have to do the same."

"We tried that yesterday," Reuben said. "It didn't work. We nearly suffocated and burnt to death."

"No, we conjured flames—not a weather spell. They're very different. Plus, we were walking through it. Here, we're safely inside. Air is my element. I can direct it in a very controlled way. But we need to get high. I presume there's an attic, Tamsyn?"

She nodded. "And a turret. It's dilapidated, but still usable."

"Of course!" He remembered noticing it in the summer. It was at the back of the house, sitting square at the east corner, with windows on each wall. It looked shabby from the outside, so was likely to be worse inside, but the position was perfect. "Where are Newton and Moore?"

"Calming Rosa down and talking to Beth."

"Any more news?" Caspian asked.

Tamsyn shook her head, clearly disappointed. "Nothing after the Holly King."

That was frustrating. He walked to the door and shouted for Moore and Newton, and from somewhere in the house he heard a response. "Once I've briefed those two, we're heading upstairs, Reuben, and we'll make a window in our protection spell. We'll isolate the turret, leaving ourselves exposed."

"I don't like that idea!"

"But we make a personal protection spell! You wanted to blast sprites?"

"Of course!"

"Good. Now's your chance."

Newton and Moore entered the kitchen, both looking distracted and worried, both with stubble across their chin and cheeks.

"Have you found a way out of this ice cube?" Newton asked.

"We're going to try. But you need to keep everyone safe in the house. The most protected place here. Where would that be, Tamsyn?"

"The cellar. It's dark and damp, but there are no windows, and we can barricade ourselves in."

"Excellent. I have no idea whether this will work, or how long it will take, so go prepared. Take blankets, cushions, food, water, activities..."

Moore smiled. "We'll pretend it's like camping for the kids. They'll love it. Can you make it warm?"

"I'll do that," Reuben said. "You go and set up, Cas. I'll join you soon."

Avery manifested in her attic bathroom. For several minutes she didn't move as she listened for a sign of someone being in the flat.

As the minutes stretched and the silence deepened, she relaxed. *No one was there.* Nevertheless, she cast the shadow spell to disguise herself, and stepped into the bedroom cautiously. Everything looked undisturbed, and breathing easier, she walked into the attic and stopped dead.

A coat of ice was on every window, and crept across every work surface, even encroaching onto Helena's grimoire. Their herbs had withered, and their altar was smashed, their books scattered across the floor.

*He* had been here. The monstrous sprite, Jack Frost. It was his calling card.

*But why hadn't Helena banished it all?*

Avery uttered a spell, and the ice cracked and fell to the floor. She opened a window and with a whisk of air, flushed it all outside and dumped it on the roof. He had been in her private space. A place of magic and happiness, and he had desecrated it. She needed to sort everything out, but it would have to wait.

She stepped onto the stairs and looked down into their living room. Again, there was only silence, but she descended carefully, wary of traps. But the living room and kitchen were untouched. Only the spell room had been damaged. A message. But there was still no sign of Helena.

*What if he was downstairs now, interrogating her friends and Helena in the shop? This was horrible.*

Her anger rose, but she forced herself to be cautious. She listened outside the door to the shop's back room. She heard low voices and someone crying. *Sally!*

Avery didn't care who was in there anymore. She wasn't a coward! She banished her shadow spell and threw the door open, air whipping around her, and fire balling in her hands.

But only Sally and Dan were there, sitting at the table. Sally was sobbing, and Dan's arm was around her shoulders as he tried to comfort her. As soon as he saw Avery, Dan jumped to his feet, standing in front of Sally to protect her. "Avery? What are you doing?"

Avery swiftly decided she was going to break the spell on them. She had to. But Sally was looking more terrified than comforted at her sudden appearance, so she got rid of the fire and calmed the wind before stepping into the room and shutting the door. "What's happened?"

"Not so quick, Avery," Dan said. "What did you just do?"

"You know what I am, Dan. So does Sally. Unfortunately, someone has made you forget. They made us all forget." Dan stepped back, eyes narrowed, and it made Avery's heart ache. He had never looked at her like that. Not once. Fury whipped up inside her again. "Tell me why Sally is crying. Where's Clea? Or rather, Helena. Both!"

"They've taken her!" Sally could barely get the words out. "That man, Jack, and his guards. She'll be at the square at lunchtime, and they threatened her life unless you turn up! We've shut the shop because I'm so upset!" She stood up, hand clutching the table, tears pouring down her face. "They wanted you, Avery! And Alex! What have you done? What's going on? Everything feels wrong!"

Avery's stomach flipped at the news about Helena and her grand-mother. Helena might survive whatever would happen, but not Clea. But she had more immediate concerns. She needed to deal with Sally and Dan first. "It feels wrong because it *is* wrong. This isn't how White Haven normally is. You know me. You trust me. Yes?"

Sally brushed tears off her cheeks and pushed Dan aside, but still clutched his arm. "Of course. You're one of my oldest friends. You're good and kind, and loyal. What's happening? Why is there wind in here? What's that man doing?"

"I'm a witch, and a good one, and deep down, in here," she tapped over her heart, "you know that. White Haven is under a spell, and an evil woman is trying to take this town and everything we love away from us. We won't let that happen."

"We?" Dan asked.

"Alex, El, and Briar. You know they're witches. They're your friends too." Avery raised her hands, casting the spell she'd researched that morning. A spell that would bring their own memory to the fore and banish the manufactured one. She couldn't make it work on a large scale, but with just these two...

But it didn't work.

Sally clutched her throat and fell to the floor, and Dan followed suit. He started to cough, almost uncontrollably. They were choking to death.

Avery fell to her knees in front of them, repeating the spell with urgency and conviction. It only worsened their symptoms. *Was this a counter spell? Or a curse?* She needed another approach.

"Listen to me, both of you! This is all a lie! *All of this*! I am a witch, and you know I am. So is Alex! The queen is not *our* queen. She's taken over White Haven, and she's trying to do something. She's stealing our lives!" She was shouting now, furious and terrified, as her friends writhed on the floor. "You should be as angry as I am! This is your home, and she's turned it into a prison!"

It wasn't working, and their symptoms worsened further. Water gushed from Sally and Dan's mouth, and they started to shiver, their skin turning blue. She needed counter-curse spells. Cures. *Anything*. But she had to focus. She needed to ground her friends, and flood them with clean, elemental magic. She had no idea what the curse was based on, but it must involve water.

Perhaps if she used the opposite of water, which is... *No*. She had a better idea.

She reached over and placed her hands on both of them, immediately feeling the current of water running through their bodies. It was like someone had released a dam. She focussed on stemming the flow and drawing it from them. Afterward, what they needed was more earth, air, and fire to balance them. She was no healing witch, but she could manage that much.

She focussed on the excess water and drew it out of them. She felt it change direction, moving from them to her. It bubbled under her fingers, over her arms, and pooled on the floor. Slowly, she felt them both start to stabilise. As they began to recover, she saw anger building in both of them, quickly surpassing fear.

At first, she thought it was aimed at her, and then Sally coughed, spat water from her mouth, and yelled, "That fucking bitch! I remember everything! Dan!" She reached out and slapped him hard across the face, leaving a red welt on his cheek. "Wake up!"

"Bloody hell, Sally!" He gasped, a hand on his cheek. "Give me a second. I almost drowned!"

"You remember?" She raised her hands, ready to slap him again, and Avery watched in stunned silence.

"Yes, I remember! Keep your hands to yourself!"

Sally sagged back, trying to sit up as she stared at Avery. "How could I ever forget that you're a witch? And what this town means to me? And all of you, and what we do?" And then she burst into tears again.

Sally's reaction stoked Avery's anger. She hated seeing her friends in danger and upset. They didn't have magic to protect themselves or those they loved. They were at the whim of the queen and her vicious sprites who were tearing White Haven apart.

Avery thought she'd been determined to stop the mad witch before, but now she was incensed, and revenge burned in her gut.

She helped her friends up to chairs and sat next to them. "I need you to tell me exactly what's going on so that we can rescue Helena and El, and then we are going to cut this cancerous queen out of White Haven. She will regret ever crossing me. Will you help? It will be dangerous."

They both reached forward to take her hands, and as one said, "Of course we will."

# Nineteen

Kendall's adrenaline rose as she watched Estelle prepare to start the spell at the end of Stormcrossed Manor's Drive.

Shadow, Niel, and Nahum stood by her, and Kendall clutched the short sword she had been given to help her fight. She mentally ran through her self-defence training, glad she kept fit at the gym. She was no match for a witch, a fey warrior, and two Nephilim, but hopefully she could help them get through to the manor.

The snow had stopped falling, and the Wall of Doom around White Haven hadn't progressed any further overnight. It was still halfway down the lane. The whirling barrier of icy, sprite-filled mist that encapsulated the manor was also still there, emanating a polar blast and occasional shrieks of the unearthly beings.

Estelle read through the spell again, placed the grimoire in her backpack, and secured it to her shoulders. "Okay. I'm ready. This is a warm weather spell. I should be using more witches to do this, but I'll do what I can. Caspian and Reuben are doing the same spell from their side, okay? In theory, as I heat the air, the icy mist should be dispelled and the sprites will retreat. But it could take a while, and they'll probably fight back."

Shadow gave everyone her most sneaky grin. "They'll definitely fight back. That's what sprites do. Don't spare them. They won't hesitate to kill you. Kendall, I suggest that you guard Estelle. No matter what happens, she must focus on the spell. Niel, Nahum, and I will tackle the rest. Agreed?"

"Looking forward to it," Nahum said, flourishing his sword.

"Just keep your balance, and don't overextend," Niel advised Kendall.

Kendall swallowed her nerves. She wanted to be more involved in the paranormal world. This was her chance. She nodded, too dry-mouthed to speak.

Estelle took a deep breath and exhaled slowly, faced the manor, and began the spell. Her voice was low at first, her words assured as she chanted, but as the temperature began to rise, her voice grew louder and she lifted her eyes skyward, throwing her arms wide. Overhead, the thick grey clouds started to churn, as if something was about to burst from them.

A shudder ran through Kendall as the magic increased in power, and goose bumps rose along her skin. Warm air began to circulate, and Estelle pushed her hands forward to direct it. As it swelled, Kendall saw the shimmering air—just like a heat haze—move on either side of them down the lane and then surge into the manor's grounds. The hoar frost that coated the hedge's bare branches started to melt, and steam filled the air as the warmth met the icy mist.

Shadow readied herself, twirling her two swords, her violet eyes alive with excitement. Nahum extended his wings, his own sword outstretched, black armour strapped over his bare chest. Niel lowered his head, ready to charge like a bull. They were terrifying. Kendall was glad she was on their side.

A series of bloodcurdling shrieks erupted from up ahead, but Estelle continued to chant the spell.

"They're coming!" Shadow cried, and then roared her own war cry and leaped forward.

Dozens of sharp-faced sprites—human-sized, brawny, and wielding swords and spears, accompanied by blue-skinned imps with icicle daggers—emerged from the mist and charged down the drive. Nahum, Niel, and Shadow met them head-on.

The sound of clashing metal, grunts, and roars fought for dominance over Estelle's voice. Nahum, Niel, and Shadow were whirling blurs, their swords slicing through flesh like butter. Despite the hot air and steamy conditions that the sprites must have hated, they continued to fight, even as the warm air forced the icy maelstrom to retreat, and them with it. Their snarls were terrifying.

Suddenly, to Kendall's left, a sprite vaulted the hedge and sprinted towards her. Up close she saw his unusual blue skin, much paler than that of the imps, his pointed features, inhuman eyes, and fang-like teeth. He carried a huge spear, and he readied to throw it towards them. On his heels were two smaller imps, spitting with fury, ice dancing on their fingertips.

But the hot, moist air around Kendall and Estelle made them sluggish, and the imps hung back.

Kendall saw the sprite hesitate too, his steps slowing, and remembering her role, she didn't hold back. She rushed at him, swiping at his spear with her sword with as much strength as she could muster. He looked as shocked at her attack as she felt, and she knocked the spear from his hand. He charged at her, head down, and crunched into her. They crashed to the ground, and her sword skittered away.

His skin was like ice, and where it met her bare flesh, it burned. But Kendall felt more confident fighting hand to hand. The sprite was bigger and more muscular, but she was lithe and quick. She brought her knee up to push him off her and swung her elbow around as his head lifted. She cracked him hard on the jaw and he rolled off, but he dragged her with him. For seeming endless moments, they rolled, scratched, and scrabbled in the deep snow at the hedge's roots, still too thick to have melted completely. His rancid breath was like poison, and almost retching, Kendall grabbed a rock and swung it at the creature, smashing his head with a sickening thud. Dazed, it fell off her and she scrambled clear.

The imps had seen their chance and advanced on Estelle. She stood imperious, warm air swirling around her like a cyclone, hair lifted, sweat covering her face, continuing the spell regardless of their proximity. When the imps hit the hot air, their daggers melted, but they leaped at her, snapping their teeth.

Kendall lunged for her discarded sword and charged. The imps were small, barely knee-height, and scrawny-limbed. She kicked one with her booted foot, and it sailed into the hedge. The other she grabbed by the scruff of its neck and flung it at the first one. They rolled away in a tangle of limbs.

But the sprite was back on its feet, blood pouring from its head wound, and it stared at her with narrowed eyes, deciding how to attack—or maybe if it should in the increasing heat.

She and Estelle were there alone. Shadow was fighting ever closer to the manor as the icy mist retreated, Nahum was flying and fighting in the garden to the left, and Niel had vanished from view—although, from somewhere in the gardens to the right, she could hear his battle cries. There would be no help from them, and Estelle had to continue the spell.

Kendall decided to help make its mind up. She grabbed an imp and flung it at the sprite, and it staggered back as it struck his chest. She then picked the second imp up, and held it to her chest, her arm pinned beneath its chin so it couldn't bite her.

Kendall held her blade to its throat as it flailed and fought to get free. "One more step and I kill it! Back off!"

Its voice rasped, "Go ahead. I'll kill you anyway."

Reuben had opened as many windows as he could in the tower that overlooked the manor's grounds, and cold, frigid air nipped at his fingers as the icy mist swirled inside the room.

He stood back-to-back with Caspian, repeating the spell that Estelle was using outside. They had lowered the protection spell around them, but kept it on the house. The shrieks and threats of the sprites and imps carried up to them in the turret. *At least that was a good thing*, Reuben reflected. *The sprites couldn't reach them.*

The spell was already working. They had successfully punched a hole in the ice wall, and inch by inch it had grown larger and larger. The tower was now free of the ice encased around it, and it was retreating down the walls of the house—much quicker than they had intended. It was hard to direct the heat from the spell.

As the magic swelled, the steam billowed outwards, and the icy mist retreated. But it was proving impossible to get rid of the mist before the ice wall vanished; the house would be exposed. They just had to trust that Estelle was being as successful. But Estelle was only at the front of the house. Reuben was facing the back.

And then a scrabbling noise drew Reuben's attention, and a clawed hand grasped the edge of the open window frame. And then another, and another.

*Bollocks.*

He couldn't continue the spell, not when sprites were about to lunge into the room. He broke off his chant. "Cas! Incoming sprites. You keep going, I'll handle them."

Ben was not enjoying flying. It was freezing. Cold seeped into every crevice he had, and Gabe was being annoyingly careful.

"Can we get lower?" Ben asked, trying to use his EMF meter while clinging on for dear life.

"No!" Gabe's deep voice rumbled in his ear and through his chest. His hands were gripped tightly around Ben's waist, and he imagined it must have been just as uncomfortable for Gabe to carry him. Shadow was probably far curvier to hold.

"But this is so awkward."

"I warned you! We've been here for ages. Haven't you got enough? That thing's whining is infuriating."

"Tough! This is useful. I can actually see differences from the other parts of the wall that we read yesterday."

"Then what do you need more for?" Gabe's huge wings lifted effortlessly to keep them in place, but Ben still felt like he could plunge to his death at any moment.

"I like to make sure. I'm a scientist!"

"Well, class is over. We're heading to the manor."

"Gabe!"

"If there's a compelling argument to stay in the air, make it good—and quick."

Ben hesitated. Gabe had a point. He had plenty of measurements, although whether he'd be able to decipher his hideous, spidery writing later was another matter. He would learn nothing more, but he always liked to take excessive readings. Variables were important. However, he could feel Gabe's grinding impatience growing by the minute.

"Fine! Carry on," Ben relented. "Take us to the manor."

"Finally," Gabe muttered.

Ben gripped the meter as Gabe wheeled away, heading along the wall's edge and skirting high around it. He managed to take a couple more readings, but his focus swiftly changed. "Gabe. Can you see that?"

Ahead, on the high cliff where Reuben and Tamsyn lived, was a thick cloud of steam.

"Of course I can. That's hopefully good news."

But up close, it was not so good. The house was hidden in a churning mass of mist and steam, and on the periphery, Shadow, Niel, and Nahum fought with deadly grace and skill in a knot of sprites and imps. Bodies were strewn in their wake. Kendall was clearly visible at the end of the drive, a huge sprite advancing on her, as she stood between him and Estelle.

Gabe yelled, "Hold tight. I'll release you as soon as we're close enough to the ground."

Gabe plummeted downward like a fighter jet, and wind whistled in Ben's ears. It was like being on a huge roller coaster, and the force of the descent pinned him to Gabe's chest. Ben was convinced he was going to die. Actually die.

The ground was incredibly close as Gabe swept between Kendall and the sprite, sword outstretched, and before Ben or—no doubt—the sprite knew what was happening, the creature had been decapitated.

Gabe released Ben and he fell the final few feet to the lane, landing with a thump.

But Gabe hadn't finished. Unlike Ben, who had rolled into the hedge in a tangle of limbs, Gabe landed gracefully, spun around, and impaled the imp that was leaping towards him. It slid down his sword, blood spurting everywhere. Gabe shook it off and turned to Kendall.

She stood, wide-eyed and speechless, gaze fixed on the dead sprite. Another imp was wriggling and biting her arms in her loosened grip, and blood poured from her wounds. Behind her, Estelle was still spellcasting, her concentration intense.

Gabe stepped towards Kendall, voice gentle but firm. "Kendall, are you all right?"

She blinked as she focussed on him. "Yes, I think so."

"Would you like me to deal with that?" He pointed his sword at the snapping imp. It was relentless, like one of those annoying, yapping dogs that was filled with self-importance—although far deadlier, if Kendall's injuries were anything to go by.

She looked down as if suddenly remembering it was there. "I don't think I have it in me to kill it."

"Don't worry. I do."

Gabe lifted the struggling creature from her grip. It looked tiny in Gabe's huge hands. He didn't waste time. He slit its throat in one quick movement, and dark purple blood spattered across him. He flung its body on top of the others.

Ben staggered to his feet. There was no one else around. The battle cries of Nahum, Niel, and Shadow were farther up the drive, and more and more of the manor's grounds were being revealed as Estelle's spell was successful. Unfortunately, the manor itself was still hidden for now, but Estelle hadn't faltered, and she continued to chant.

Gabe smiled at a shellshocked Kendall. "Well done. You protected Estelle, and the spell is working. Your arms, however," he glanced at them, "need treatment. But it's not over yet. Are you okay to stay here?

I need to see what's happening at the house. Ben will stay with you to help. Right?"

"Absolutely." He nodded enthusiastically. He had the witches' spells in his bag for protection.

Kendall managed a smile. "I'm fine, thank you. Of course I'm okay to stay. It's not often I fight a sprite and imps, and then see one get decapitated, but now... All in a day's work, right?"

Gabe winked. "That's the spirit."

And then with a beat of his huge wings, he flew towards the manor.

# Twenty

Zee navigated the stormy weather across the tip of Cornwall with ease. It was exhilarating to be flying in violent weather.

He thought he might have had enough of it after fighting in the Pyrenees, but there was something joyous about being surrounded by such elemental energy. They hadn't been wrong, either. The extreme weather system blanketed everywhere. Zee flew just below the clouds, safe in the knowledge that the poor visibility would hide him from anyone on the ground. Thick snow covered everything, making it hard to make out the contours of the land. The villages and towns were chocolate box pretty, ensconced in the wintry landscape, and families walked or played in the snow.

But amidst the pristine beauty was chaos. Cars were abandoned in lanes, and tractors and snow ploughs were struggling to free them. Electricity lines were down, and the steadily falling snow would ensure it would remain chaotic for some time.

As he flew, he considered what Eve had said to Reuben. The weather was supernatural. The knowledge coloured his impressions, making everything seem darker and more malevolent. He had no idea how this queen had done it, but the extreme weather suggested she had researched the White Haven witches and the area, and knew there were other witches to call on. Perhaps that was the plan all along. To cut communication between the covens and isolate White Haven even more, beyond the Wall of Doom she had constructed. *Something to discuss with Eve.*

When St Ives came into view, he circled above it, orientating himself to the layout. Eve lived on the narrow spit of land that jutted into the sea, ending with a mound of green called The Island at the nub. But it wasn't green anymore. It was a greyish-white, blending into the iron grey sea that surrounded it. He could see where Eve lived, though. It was the lane that edged the beach to the northwest.

*But where could he land without being seen?* The Island teemed with families and tobogganing kids, and people strolled along the beaches, huddled in thick jackets. He couldn't land too far away; it would take too long to walk. However, a stiff wind whipped the snow into flurries, providing cover. If he descended quick enough, no one would notice. He spotted a narrow alley not far from Eve's road. He knew the name of the gallery. He could find it on foot.

Zee watched the alley for several minutes, but no one stirred. *It was now or never.* Angling himself downward, wings close to his side, he fell like a stone. Only once he was within the narrow confines of the high-sided alley did he extend his wings and glide to a stop. He folded his wings away and pulled on his sweatshirt in the nick of time.

The hum of a generator marked the back door of a café, and a man emerged from it with a bag of rubbish. He nodded at Zee, dumped the rubbish in the huge bin, and vanished inside again. Zee groaned. *That was close.*

He walked down the main road, looking at the signs. There were many art galleries, just as Alex had said, but he finally saw the one he wanted. It was closed, so he banged on the door. No one stirred, but from above he heard the dull thumping of music. He tried again and again, and then shouted, "Eve!" He was attracting attention, but he didn't care. He fished a coin from his pocket and threw it at the upstairs window. He was rewarded moments later when the music stopped, and a woman opened the window and stuck her head out.

She was pretty, with thick, dark dreadlocks bound back with a bright red scarf, and a mischievous smile on her lips. "Hello, stranger. What light from yonder window breaks... Hold on. Isn't that your line?"

"Are you quoting Shakespeare at me?"

"I might be." She frowned. "Can I help you?"

"I'm Reuben's friend, Zee. He spoke to you last night before the phone cut off. We need your help."

Her humour vanished. "You live in White Haven?"

He nodded.

"How have you got here?"

He glanced over his shoulder at the curious pedestrians. "Long story. Can we talk inside?" She regarded him for a long moment, and he knew she was deciding if she could trust him. He continued, "I work with Alex, actually, in The Wayward Son. I'm about to become his new bar manager." *He hoped.*

"What does Alex look like?"

He smiled. "He's a good-looking bastard with a hot, red-haired girlfriend called Avery. She runs a shop called Happenstance Books. Reuben is a laid-back surfer dude who lives in a big manor house and thinks life is a joke. And then there's Briar, the earthy one, and El who makes jewellery." He remembered the year before, and a fire in the dunes at Spriggan Beach. He had just arrived then, with all of his brothers, and this was the witch who had commanded the storm that helped them banish the mermaids. The Daughters of Llyr. They hadn't lingered by that fire. This world had been alien to them then, and they had kept to themselves. "I met you by a fire on Spriggan

Beach last year. I had only just arrived then." His smile broadened, knowing she would know exactly who he was.

Her eyebrows shot up. "Oh! All right. I'm coming down."

In a few minutes' time, he was upstairs in her spacious, art-filled flat, trying hard not to ogle her. He didn't remember her being this pretty and so...cool. *Why the bloody hell hadn't Reuben or Alex said something?* He supposed he had been adamant on the no-women thing. But Eve was something else. Bohemian. Exotic. Sexy. He focussed back on the conversation. She had been speaking to him.

"So, you're a Nephilim."

"Yep. One of the magnificent seven." *By the Gods...* Was he flirting? *Shut up, Zee.* He decided to stick to the facts. "I've just flown here, using the snow as cover. I know Reu explained some of what's happening last night, but things are worse. We need your help." He ran through the overnight developments and their plans. "We have to get through that wall, and we think your magic will help us defeat her. Them. All of it."

"Of course I'll help, Zee. But how are we getting there?"

"The same way I arrived."

"Flight?" Her eyes widened with surprise and trepidation.

"Yep. It will be an abrupt take off, but smooth after that. You know. Daylight. People."

She looked worried, but nodded nonetheless. "I have a flat roof, if that helps, and spells, of course."

"Great! But bundle up. My wings insulate me, but not you."

"You know, I've been thinking on this ever since I spoke to Reuben. I have several ideas of how we can do this."

"Even better."

"I'll grab my things, then. I can take a bag, I presume?"

"As long as it's not a suitcase!"

She smiled and desire shot through him. "Well, all right then."

Normally, Gabe would never risk flying in the day, especially now that the snow had stopped, but the landscape was deserted, and he needed to be quick.

He circled over Shadow, Niel, and Nahum, but they seemed to be handling their attackers well. Niel and Shadow fought back-to-back, protecting each other as the sprites and imps attacked, but Nahum was further along, fighting sprites in the garden. Gabe flew down to deal with a few stragglers, and then left them all to advance closer to the house. He could still hear shouts and shrieks from within the churning mist, so there were still sprites left to deal with. But it was shouts from the back that drew his attention.

The corner tower was just about visible above the mayhem below. Huge parts of the ice wall had disintegrated, exposing the house. Occasionally, a chunk wobbled free and crashed to the ground, but snarling and shouting drew his attention to the turret. A fiery blast emitted from a window, the air sizzled, and Otherworldly bodies flew in all directions.

Gabe shouted, "Reuben? Caspian! It's me." He didn't dare get closer, fearing he would be hit, too. "Do you need help?"

Reuben answered, his tone clipped. "Yes! Kill the bloody sprites!"

"I'm on it!"

Now that he was closer, he could see them nimbly climbing the walls. Gabe dived under Reuben's blasts, dragging the sprites away or slashing at them—whatever was more effective. He swept around, clearing them from all sides, and then clambered inside, gasping at the intense heat. Caspian was still chanting the spell, face furrowed with concentration, but Reuben was dispatching the final imp who had made it inside the room. He struck it with a blast of power, and it sailed out of the window and vanished into the mist.

"You've made great headway," Gabe observed once he caught his breath. "I think you're safe here—for a while, at least."

Reuben slicked his hair back from his sweaty brow and grinned. "Cheers. But the others are in the basement. Can you check whether any sprites made it into the house?"

"Will do."

The magic in the air intensified as Reuben rejoined the spell work. Gabe focussed on his new task, skirting the spellcasting witches to make his way through the house.

Room after room lay empty and undamaged, until he arrived on the ground floor and found a broken window. He quickened his search, barely taking in the old house with its crumbling rooms. The ground floor was clear of sprites, but a shout drew his attention. A door was open on a back corridor, and stairs led down. He could hear frantic scrabbling, and as he rounded the turn in the stairs, he saw a couple of imps attacking a locked door, deep claw marks raked into the wood. There was silence within, and so far the room was secure.

Gabe killed the imps before they even knew he was there.

"Newton? Moore! It's Gabe."

"Gabe?" That was Newton, his voice tight with worry. "Thank the Gods! Something is out there."

"Not anymore. The house is clear, and the spell is working, but it's not over yet. Stay in there until you hear further."

Gabe didn't wait for an answer. He headed back through the house and exited from the broken window at the back of the building. The cold was less intense than it had been, but the mist was still thick, and ice crystals hung in the air. They eddied and swirled, revealing glimpses of the garden before swallowing it whole again. He progressed stealthily, sword sweeping ahead of him as his eyes adjusted to the murky light. The occasional darting figure appeared and then retreated, and Gabe realised that as the air heated, the imps were escaping. That made sense. The countryside was still cold, and snow lay deep across the fields and hedges. Snow would likely fall again, as the thick clouds showed no signs of going. They would seek the weather they were comfortable in. Or even try to get through the Wall of Doom, as they were all calling it.

If this witch, Eve, was right, then the cold weather was supernatural. It wouldn't go until they had defeated whoever was behind all of this.

*And the imps would know who that was.*

He cursed himself for not questioning the one Kendall had caught earlier. He needed to catch another. Stepping silently through the ghostly landscape, dagger in hand and senses on full alert, a skitter of leaves and the snap of a twig made him turn. He waited, searching for a darting figure. Nothing stirred. Then there was another scurry behind him, and he turned again. Out of the corner of his eye, there was a creeping movement, low to the ground. He followed it.

It was disorientating in here. He wasn't sure whether he was heading to the house, a trap, or deeper into the garden. Something fled ahead of him, a streaking shade of blue. He quickened his pace, and suddenly found himself out of the mist with a huge hedge in front of him. The snow lay thick at its roots, and a pair of scrawny legs were the last part visible of the fleeing imp.

Gabe grabbed them and swung the imp out so that he dangled in front of him, upside down. It spat and snarled and twisted, its razor-sharp teeth snapping. It was an ugly thing. Its bulbous eyes flashed with malevolence, and it was surprisingly strong. Ice bloomed at its fingertips, and it shot hailstones at Gabe.

Gabe tightened his grip and lifted his knife. "Stop struggling, little one, or I will end you right now. Understand?"

Its eyes fixed on the knife and slid back to Gabe again. It fell still, its narrow lips pouting.

"I want answers. Who is the woman behind all this?"

It answered in a flurry of words in a guttural language. An insult. Gabe laughed and answered in the same language. "I know all languages, you idiot creature—including your strong fey dialect. Tell me who she is."

The imp's eyes widened with surprise and then spat more insults.

Gabe lifted his knife. "I'll slice off your scrawny limbs one by one unless you start talking now."

"You will only kill me anyway," the creature hissed.

"If you answer me honestly, I'll let you lead me to the wall and show me the way in. You can return to your people. Sound fair?"

"You lie."

"I don't lie. But I promise if I come across you again, then I will end you."

"My master will kill me for betraying him."

"Not if I kill him first. You refer to Jack Frost?"

"Your name, not ours."

"He is a sprite?"

"The King of Sprites. He commands ice, snow, and the north wind. You will not kill him. He will freeze you with one look!"

"He can try. What does he want here?"

"He wants what the queen wants. He wants winter in the northern lands of our world. Winter forever."

"Not here, in this world?"

It shook its head, ice spraying everywhere, lips drawn back with scorn. "No! Not here. But the queen needs her king to achieve that, and he will die tonight."

"Why will he die? What king?" Gabe asked, confused.

"Her consort, fool! The Holly King. The King of Winter. Her power wains in the north, and she wants to stop it."

Gabe's thoughts were whirling. "You mean in the world of fey. The Otherworld?"

"Where else? We do not wish to live in the world of humans." It shuddered. "Horrible."

"Then why are you here? Why is White Haven cut off behind that wall?"

"No. I have said too much already!" The imp sealed his lips tight, eyes flashing again.

"You have said nothing of use. Fine. I will slit your throat and leave you to rot in the world of men, where no one will mourn you."

"No!"

"Then speak!"

Ice flew from its fingertips again, but Gabe didn't budge. It huffed, defeated. "There is a witch in that place who holds the Oak King within her. In order that the Holly King may live, the Oak King must die—forever. She will use the witch to get him."

The imp could mean only one person. *Briar.*

"How does she mean to do this?"

"There is a feast tonight, and the kings are the guests of honour. They will fight, as always, but this time the Oak King will die. That's all I know."

Gabe was still confused. "Your queen will kill the Oak King?"

"No. The Holly King must defeat him. It is written. He must defeat the Oak King himself."

The myths so far were true. "And then they leave White Haven?"

"What is left of it. The Sprite King will leave behind no trace before we go."

Gabe's gut churned with worry. They had hours left to get inside. Hours before Briar was killed, and White Haven was destroyed.

"Who is the queen?"

The sprite looked confused. "She is the Queen of Winter. She rules the North."

"There is no such thing. My partner is fey. Shadow Walker of the Dark Ways. You must have seen her here."

"Her blade spells death. I have seen her."

"So, who is the queen?"

It shrugged. "The Queen. The Holly King's mate. She seeks to change his fate."

There was clearly a limit to the imp's knowledge. "And now she's found Briar. Are they kind rulers, these three masters of ice and winter?"

"No."

"Would you rather be your own master, little one?"

"Yes."

"Then help me find a way in today."

"My clan is dead. You have killed them all."

"Don't think you fool me. You are vicious, a killer, and I'm sure there are many more of you beyond the wall."

Its eyes narrowed, deciding its fate. Who to play to get the best outcome. Gabe knew he couldn't trust it. *But if it could find them a way in...*

"You will let me go if I open the gate?"

"Yes—in time. But no tricks."

By now, Gabe could feel the heat of the spell reaching them, and the garden was unveiling itself as the coils of mist receded. But over the cliffs and valleys of White Haven, snow lay thick, sparkling with a covering of ice. Snow was falling again, and home was calling the creature. There might well be others hiding in the snow.

It cast a longing look at the wall in the distance. "Agreed."

# Twenty-One

"You can't possibly trust that thing," Newton complained to the group gathered in the chill gardens of Stormcrossed Manor.

He stared at the ugly, blue-skinned creature that was seated in a pile of snow, an iron chain around its legs. It glared at them, occasionally hissing, spitting, and wailing at the iron that burned its skin. Despite Newton's fury at its presence and what it had done, he also felt sorry that the iron was torturing it. But they had no choice at present. Without it, the creature would flee.

The imprisoned house inhabitants had been freed only fifteen minutes earlier. The ice wall and thick mist had vanished, and the ground was a soggy mess, piled with occasional snow drifts. But that wouldn't last long. As the steamy, warm weather spell dissipated, the temperature plummeted and falling snow started to settle again.

Caspian, Estelle, and Reuben were shattered. They were inside, sitting around Tamsyn's kitchen table, clutching steaming cups of hot chocolate, while she plied them with biscuits and toasted fresh bread. The children were with Rosa. Moore had been a revelation. He had entertained the kids and made them laugh, even easing Rosa's fears.

Now, Moore was outside with him and Kendall, Gabe, Shadow, Ben, and Niel. Zee had just arrived with Eve, the weather witch. Nahum had gone to find Ash and the others. They were standing close to the back door, stamping their feet, hands shoved in pockets in an effort to keep warm. Kendall was splashed with blood, a fresh bandage on her injured arms, but had refused to sit with the others. She was tough, insisting her place was with her team. Even so, she clutched her mug of hot chocolate as if her life depended on it.

"Of course I don't trust it," Gabe said, voice brusque with impatience. "That's why it's chained up. But we need it, and now it's our prisoner, we are the only way that creature is getting inside the wall."

"It's a good strategy," Shadow conceded grudgingly as she watched the imp with narrowed eyes. "But it will flee as soon as it gets a chance. We need to keep it on a tight leash. Or you do." She grimaced. "I can't touch iron."

"I could put a binding spell on it," Eve suggested. "It would be better than iron—less painful for it, too. I could even bind it to someone. Just decide who."

"It would need to be strong," Shadow warned. "Fey magic is different, and it might well be able to break the spell. An imp's magic is even different to mine. I suspect that's why it can manipulate the wall, where I cannot. I knew the magic felt familiar!"

"Has the witch disguised it?" Ash asked.

Shadow shrugged. "I don't know if she's done it on purpose, or it's just the type of magic she uses. I haven't heard of her, so it's hard to say. I did not live in the north of our land, or even visit there often, but like many places, there are fey who govern certain areas, some assuming royal titles, and there are the old Royal Houses who keep pretty much to themselves. Perhaps she is from one of those—or is as I originally suggested, part fey and part human. There was much crossbreeding centuries ago. To command the imps and work with the King of Sprites says a lot about her power and her sway, though."

"Or what she has promised them," Zee suggested.

"So, what are we waiting for?" Newton asked, looking at his companions with annoyance. "We need to find that gate! Briar and the others could be in danger right now!"

"We will," Gabe told him. "But we all need to be prepared first, because we don't know what we're going to find in there. The witches are still recovering, and we need to decide who stays here and who doesn't. For example," his lips tightened as he looked at Ben, "I think Ghost OPS should stay here."

Ben looked outraged. "No way! We can be helpful in there! You don't know what you're facing. I detected differences in the wall where you saw the gate. That could be helpful if the imp is lying!"

"True." Kendall nodded, eyeing the imp with suspicion. "What if there are traps in the wall and it leads us straight to one? Corroborating it with what Ghost OPS knows could be valuable."

"Plus, we can fight when we're inside! Come on!" Ben appealed to the wider group. "Have we ever got in the way before?"

"No," Niel conceded, "but you are something else to worry about."

Ben shook his backpack. "We have the witches' spells in here. They made them for us. We won't need your protection."

"What if something comes out of the wall—like Jack," Gabe argued, "and targets this house again? It seems to me they know that the inhabitants are related to Briar. I think the attack was some kind of insurance policy."

"Briar's family could stay at your place," Moore suggested. "The farmhouse is a good distance away. Or Reuben's manor. It's thick with protection spells, and very close. Then Ghost OPS can come." He smiled at Ben. "I think we need as much help as we can get."

Ben beamed at him, but Newton huffed. Like Gabe, he didn't want to worry about anything except defeating the queen and the sprites. But Ben was right. They had always been able to look after themselves.

"Potentially, you could help protect the locals, or rally them—depending on what we find inside. As long as they're still alive."

Gabe groaned and admitted defeat. "All right, come. Just be careful! Let's eat, check weapons, transfer Briar's family to Reuben's place, and plan to move within the next hour or so—depending on what Ash and the others have found."

"I need to pick up my crossbow from the farmhouse," Zee said. "And I'll grab a few extra toys." He grinned. "Like some of JD's weapons. This could be the perfect time for them."

Eve nodded and adjusted her bag over her shoulder. "I'd like to discuss spells with the witches. I need their opinion on some ideas I have. That's assuming you want me? I presume the weather is worse in there."

"Oh, we'll need you," Gabe said with feeling.

The group split up, many heading inside the house. Newton called after Kendall, "Get those wounds dressed properly, or you're staying here with Tamsyn!" Only Gabe, Shadow, and Newton remained outside, and Newton had a nagging question. "What about this Holly King, Shadow? Does he live in your world?"

"I have never heard him called as such, but sometimes people have many names. He could be another nature spirit. A winter one. All myths have their roots somewhere, and our land is as rife with them as yours. Ours are often more deadly."

"Could he really kill the Green Man? It sounds impossible."

Shadow's eyes clouded with worry. "It does, doesn't it? But I've learned never to underestimate the Otherworld. Its magic is strange, formidable, and uncanny. And this Witch-Queen wields it with deadly skill. Whatever is happening on the other side of that wall is going to be bad."

Briar settled in front of the fire in Newton's living room, warm and comfortable, and feeling slightly guilty that Avery, Alex, and Barak were outside. But she had work to do, too. She needed to speak to the Green Man.

She finished the calming tea that Alex had recommended and stared into the flames. She tried to empty her mind of her cares and worries—such as the nightmare that White Haven had become, or the dark, evil eyes of the queen. Her stark, raven tresses against snowy white skin. The hard, sharp gaze of Jack Frost. The horror of a children's storybook that they now found themselves in.

Instead, she focussed on the bright spark of life that was the Green Man deep within her. He had risen to her rescue yesterday, responding to a call she was barely aware of making. She closed her eyes in the curtained, shadow filled room, enjoying the firelight dancing across her eyelids. Briar sank deeper and deeper into a meditative state, her chin falling on her chest as the outside world vanished.

Her heart thumped out its steady beat, and it reminded her of the night they had drummed to summon their familiars. Deer was here somewhere, but it wasn't Deer she needed now. Instead, she pictured wild leaves framing an unruly mop of hair. A wizened face weathered by eons of life. An earthy scent that promised life, death, and rebirth.

"*I need you Green Man,*" she whispered in her head. "*More than I ever have before.*"

Feeling foolish, Briar shook her head. Whenever she needed him, usually during moments of struggle as she cast spells, her call happened instinctively. But it was just as she had told Alex. They didn't chat. He was just *there*.

But then she felt his spark of amusement, and wild, gleeful joy. He darted about as if he were teasing her—in and out of her awareness. *Was it a test?*

"*I need you!*" She repeated. "*Didn't you feel her? The witch? This isn't a joke.*"

She pictured the queen again, and the fight. The thick vines that shot from her fingers. "*Do you remember that?*"

He disappeared for a long moment, and she frowned. *What was he doing?* Maybe he didn't speak. Maybe he couldn't. Or maybe she was asking the wrong questions.

"*Are you the Oak King? Because the Holly King wants to fight you. He wants to kill you.*"

The wild, gleeful presence rippled and then vanished again.

Her eyes flew open, knowing exactly what was wrong. "I'm in the wrong place. I need to be outside."

Briar pulled on her coat and headed into Newton's back garden, barefoot. It was a neat, tidy affair, devoid of wild artistry and wrestled into submission by Newton's need for order, but it was a pleasant enough space. There was a small table and chairs sitting outside the back door, and a trellis that supported clematis to make a shady spot in the summer months.

Hunting down a patch of bare earth, Briar wriggled her feet into it. "Is that better?" she called out. "Stop being stubborn, old man!"

The earth warmed around her feet, and verdant green tendrils once again bloomed from her hands. She directed them at the trellis, and they weaved a pattern, thick and tenacious, leaves sprouting to make dense foliage. They formed a circle. *No, a wreath.* Oak leaves, ivy, mistletoe, beech, birch, and even a sprig of holly with bright red berries. And in the midst of the huge wreath emerged a face.

Briar laughed with joy. "*You're here.*"

His gravelly, rich voice resonated in her mind, "*Always, child.*"

"*When I summon you the right way.*"

His wrinkled, wizened face, eyes dancing with all shades of green, erupted into a smile. "*Exactly.*"

The air seemed to dance between them with dust motes and pollen, and the rich scent of blossoms wafted towards her before vanishing. But then his greenery subsided, and the leaves started to wither.

Briar's smile vanished. "*What's happening to you?*"

"*Nothing that shouldn't. It's winter. In the spring I will emerge again, rising with the sap and the mating of animals. It begins tonight.*"

"*But the Holly King is after you! Didn't you hear me? Are you the Oak King, too?*"

His expression sobered. "*I am the Oak King. Or rather, part of me is. I encompass many things, child. I am a lover to the Goddess. Life giver, life ender. I fall and rise with the seasons. I am but one face of many aspects.*"

Briar frowned. "*I don't understand. Does that mean there is a Holly King?*"

"*My brother.*" He nodded. "*He also carries the spirit of life, but his is the dark, sleeping side that makes autumn and winter. He rises as sap falls. He ripens fruits, gathers seeds, beds down the plants for winter. We will cross tonight. He will wane, I will rise.*"

"*Not if the queen has her way. She wants to kill you! She wants the Holly King to rule all year. To make perpetual winter. And she wants to take my magic, too!*"

"*Do you think the Goddess will allow this, child?*"

"*I don't know! She might not have a choice.*" Briar held her arms out, palms upwards, feeling the soft flakes settle. "*Look at how much snow there is! We are trapped!*"

The Green Man smiled, and his apple red cheeks glowed with life. "*Do you trust me, child?*"

"*Well, yes, but look around.*" Briar was so frustrated at his calm benevolence that she could cry. Her woes in the face of the nature spirit's endless time and immense power must seem minuscule, but to her this was everything. "*My friends are in trouble. The town I love is threatened. Everyone is trapped. El might die! And we are being hunted.*" She stamped her feet, the ground rumbling in response. "*I don't even know who this witch is! And she made me forget who I am.*" This fact was the most terrifying thing. That she forgot she was a witch. Had forgotten Reuben, Newton, Hunter, and even Eli, who helped her in the shop. And worse, she had forgotten her family: Tamsyn, Rosa, and the children. "*She is cruel. Heartless.*"

"*Because she has nothing but ice in her heart. Tonight you must light the Yule log. Do you promise?*"

"*What about our friends who are in danger?*"

"*You will go to the feast and light the Yule log. Understand, child? Offer yourself up.*"

Briar's blood ran cold. "*She'll kill me.*"

"*Remember what I said. It will all become clear.*"

And then the Green Man vanished, leaving her alone in the snow-filled gloom of Newton's midwinter garden.

Dylan was bubbling with excitement as everyone made their last-minute preparations. He always loved it when they were strategising, checking weapons, and collating their ideas.

Everyone had moved from Stormcrossed Manor to Greenlane Manor, Reuben's estate, and the place hummed with excitement. The witches were gathered in the snug, consulting their grimoires. Dylan had a pang of regret as he missed seeing Briar, Avery, Alex, and El, but it was interesting to see the others working together. Especially Estelle. And it was great for Ghost OPS to catch up with Eve. It had been months since they had seen her, and Dylan would never forget how she and Jasper had escorted him and Cassie through the labyrinthine passages below West Haven to escape the vampires. They had saved their lives.

The Nephilim and Shadow were in the kitchen, making last-minute checks of weapons—especially JD's, the mysterious founder and owner of The Orphic Guild. Dylan was yet to meet him, but knew there was something about him that the others were keeping a secret. He didn't pry, though. He was sure he'd find out at some point. They were taking turns to watch the imprisoned imp, who was now chained on Reuben's back terrace and currently under Eli's watchful eye. Tamsyn, Rosa, and the children were exploring the house with Moore, while he made sure they were comfortable. Newton and Kendall flitted between everyone. Dylan, Ben, and Cassie had found themselves a spot at the end of the huge, wooden kitchen table where they compared notes and shared their investigations.

"So," Gabe asked them, "have you found another gateway?"

Dylan shook his head. "No. Nothing like the reading that Ben took from the icesheet's gate. But maybe that's different because it's active and the others aren't."

Niel grunted as he polished his double-headed axe. "Or maybe there aren't any more. What a gigantic waste of time."

Cassie glared at him. "No, it wasn't. We found oddities in the wall. The EMF picked up changes, and it could indicate where a gate might be! But we don't know enough about it." Her eyes drifted to the imp on the terrace. "We should question him."

Ben rose to his feet. "Agreed. Let's do it now. Gabe, when are we leaving?"

"Soon. And you're not questioning him alone."

"We won't be alone! Eli is out there," Dylan pointed out. He bristled at Gabe's controlling nature. He meant well, but he also assumed they were idiots sometimes. He had no idea of some of the weird, paranormal things they dealt with regularly. Only the week before Dylan had been attacked by a poltergeist in a house in Devon that had nearly impaled him on a stag's head mounted on the wall. He was tempted to direct him to their website, but instead said, "Fine. Come and babysit us!"

Gabe and Ash followed Ghost OPS out the door, leaning against the doorframe to watch, hands resting on their sword hilts. The imp was seated at the table, impervious to the cold as he drank a cup of milk, and looking a good deal more comfortable than earlier, even though he had the iron chain around his ankle. Eli was sitting next to him, his relaxed, easy posture belying his vigilant stare.

Dylan pulled a chair out, careful to keep Eli between him and the razor-toothed creature. He wasn't *that* stupid. *How should he address an imp? Did it have a name?* He settled for being direct.

"Hey, imp, we have a question."

The imp looked up at him, its big, blue eyes full of spite, milk dripping down its chin, and said something unintelligible in a grating voice.

Eli smirked. "There's more milk and honey if you're polite. Choose now. And speak English. I know you can."

The imp scowled, its grasping, sharp-nailed fingers closing tightly on the mug. Shadow knew that imps liked sweet things, and it had certainly kept the vicious creature more amenable. "Fine!" It spat out the word childishly.

"We saw something in the wall that we didn't understand," Dylan said, watching its reactions closely. "Our camera picked up odd movements, and what looked like lights. Are they energies? Spells?"

It sipped its drink as it considered its response, sly eyes peering up at him, and then the sword on the table, Eli's strong grip on the hilt. He finally said, "There's nothing there. You can't see anything."

Dylan glanced at Ben and Cassie, amused. If the imp thought he could be put off that easily, he was stupid. "I can assure you that my camera—if you even know what that is—misses nothing. It's special. Like this." He held up the EMF meter and flipped it on. The high-pitched whine almost whistled as he waved it in front of the imp, and it flinched. "It detects different energy signatures—and magic. Like you, my little fey friend. And this made some very odd noises by the wall."

It slurped its drink again, milk sloshing around. "It's magic. The wall is magic! It's obvious."

"I think you're lying. There were shapes in that wall. Or maybe beyond the wall. You see, my camera sees a lot more than I do. What are they?"

The imp hesitated again, and Eli leaned forward, wrenched the mug from the creature's grip, and threw the remaining liquid on the ground.

The creature wailed. "*No!*"

"Answer the damn question, and you'll get more," Eli told it. "Or else I'll start chopping your fingers off, one by one."

The imp hissed, showing a hideous row of razor-sharp teeth, as a wave of icy mist emanated from it like poison. Dylan was pretty sure Eli would do no such thing, but then again, he was a Nephilim no matter how many women he slept with. The imp and Eli exchanged a long glare that Eli ultimately won.

The imp rapped the table. "I want milk."

"Answer Dylan first! What's in the wall?"

"Creatures! Sprites, ice dragons, more imps, ice sculptures that come to life, and lots more. They are on the other side to stop people from escaping."

Everyone leaned forward, and Gabe and Ash no longer rested casually against the doorframe. Gabe marched over and lifted the imp up by the scruff of its neck. "And you didn't think to tell me earlier? That they will attack us on the way in?"

"Not with me. I know a way! Although, maybe... But I will get you in. Can I have some more milk and honey now?"

Dylan slumped back in the chair. "A bollocking ice dragon? Great, just fucking great!"

# Twenty-Two

A lex had finally arrived at the perimeter wall with Barak, after leaving the lanes and suburbs of White Haven behind and trudging across a small section of moor on the northern edge of town.

The roads were filled with people who seemed to be continuing their usual business without a care in the world, and no one had taken any notice of them. If anyone was thinking that something was wrong with White Haven, they were keeping it to themselves.

Before setting out, Alex had contacted his familiar, and now Wolf loped beside them, a barely-there figure, but his presence was reassuring, even with Barak on his other side. Wolf was silent, but with his mental connection, Alex had an expanded awareness of his surroundings. He saw with Wolf's sight, as well as his own. Felt the crisp snow beneath his feet, and smelled the many myriad scents—some that had Wolf on edge.

Now the wall loomed ahead of them. More than a wall, actually, because it stretched overhead, lost behind the thick clouds and falling snow, but he knew it was there because Barak had told him so.

Barak, clad in winter woollens, looked up. "The wall doesn't rise far above the valley. I estimate that it ends not too far above the top of the Queen's palace."

"Really?" Alex squinted up, too. "So it's not like a massive ridge from the other side, then?"

Barak shook his head. "Not at all. It's designed to be as unobtrusive as possible. And as I said, it has a weird, repellent spell on it that turns you around and makes you forget why you're there in the first place."

"But once the gate opened, that didn't happen?"

"No." He pointed ahead. "The thick mist is hiding its solidity. It will be interesting to see what it feels like up close here. I would imagine it has a similar effect to deter people from trying to get out."

"Perhaps some guards, too."

They trudged onwards, Barak withdrawing his sword, and Alex's power tingling on his fingertips. They plunged into the mist before Alex had even realised they were close. It was deceptive—deliberately so, no doubt. The world closed in, and Alex allowed Wolf to move ahead. Every now and again, he detected the odd flash of light in his peripheral vision, but when he turned it quickly vanished.

"Are you seeing the lights, Barak?" Alex whispered.

He grunted. "Like will-o'-the-wisps."

"Or sprites?" Alex fought to quell his rising panic. "I can't see the wall yet. Have we changed direction?"

"I don't think so. What's your wolf think?"

Wolf was still padding ahead, snow appearing to fall right through him. Then he stopped, hackles raised, and lowered his belly to the ground. His voice rang clear in Alex's head. "*Danger. There's something here.*"

Alex's hand shot out and gripped Barak's arm. He held his fingers to his lips.

Both turned, back-to-back, wary of attack. Alex saw nothing, but heard a low, throaty roar.

"It's big, whatever it is," Barak warned in a low voice.

"No shit!"

Blueish lights sparkled in the mist, and another roar that seemed to come from all around them shook the ground. And then a fork of blue-coloured flames shot out of the mist.

Alex yelled, "Down!"

He and Barak dived into thick snow. Blinded and breathless, Alex rolled onto his back and then wished he hadn't as more blue fire rolled over them, bringing sub-zero temperatures. The searing cold was breathtaking, making it hard to think.

However, the huge head and body of a scaly creature with wings emerging from the mist made him focus. It was as white as the snow, but waves of blue flames rippled over it. Still on his back, Alex instinctively threw ball after ball of fire at the approaching creature, but they had no effect. It charged at them, shooting more jets of ice-cold flames.

"What the actual fuck?" Alex yelled, horrified. "Is that a dragon?"

"You tell me," Barak yelled back as he leaped to his feet. "This is not like the fire I know!"

Wolf threw himself at the creature, snapping at its limbs and darting under its long, low belly. Alex felt dizzy with too many images and sensations, and quickly cast aside his connection with his familiar.

Barak was charging forward too, but the dragon whipped around and blasted fire at him again. Barak dived for cover.

Alex didn't know what spell to use, or even if any of them would work, so he hurled balls of pure energy at the creature instead. It howled and roared as Alex found his mark. *At least it experienced pain.* He redoubled his efforts, trying to distract it enough to let Barak get close. Barak's wings exploded from his body, shredding his clothes, and he took to the air.

And then the mist closed in, and the blizzard intensified.

Alex was snow-blind. He couldn't see a thing. He threw a shadow spell over himself, and then a protection spell. Feeling better prepared, he found Wolf again. Through their psychic link, he asked, "*What the hell is happening?*"

But all Alex received back was a flurry of images—thick, scaly skin, claws, and leathery wings.

Alex wanted to strike out, but he couldn't see Barak. If he aimed too high, he might hit him. If he aimed too low, he might hurt Wolf—*if he even could?* He was a spirit animal, after all.

The dragon's long snout lined with razor-sharp teeth emerged from the mist and Alex shot bolts of power at the creature's head. Its snout whipped around, shooting flames again. In his haste to escape, Alex fell over and rolled down a thick bank of snow, at the last second spotting a huge, clawed foot about to land on him.

He rolled again, raised his hand in a slicing motion, and whipped it across the dragon's belly. A line of fire appeared where he'd directed, searing the animal's flesh, and the creature roared in pain. The clawed feet trampled around him. Alex dived one way and then the other, and where he avoided the animal's feet, he was almost crushed by the thick, leathery hide of the dragon's flapping wings.

He could see Wolf now, darting and snarling as he leaped for the dragon's throat. Every now and again he caught a flash of Barak in flight, and the swift sweep of his sword. It was chaos, and Alex knew he needed to calm his thoughts and think rationally.

More by luck than judgement, he scrambled clear of the dragon's underside and dodged a huge wing, the rush of air almost knocking him off his feet. He made a looping motion with his hand and wrapped a loop of air around the dragon's closest back limb. Uttering words of power, he pulled his hand back with a quick snap. The dragon's limb twisted awkwardly, and it stumbled. It wasn't quite as dramatic as what Alex had in mind, but he repeated the action, and this time succeeded in pulling the creature's leg back. It roared with pain, falling backwards to protect its limb, and rolled heavily towards Alex.

Alex jumped away as Barak swooped in. The dragon thrashed its limbs and snow plumed in the air, almost burying Alex. Flames roared towards him, and Alex threw up another protection shield. The flame hit the shield and flashed along it, stopping mere feet away.

But Barak took advantage of the distraction. He flew to the dragon's neck, plunged his sword into the back of its head, and hung on as the creature thrashed back and forth. Blood dripped from its open mouth, pooling like black tar in the snow, before it finally slumped into a defeated heap.

Barak jumped nimbly to the ground, spattered with blood, and hauled Alex to his feet. "Well, that was unexpected."

"A dragon? You don't say!"

"I've faced many creatures over the years, but never one of those. Something to tease my brothers with."

Wolf snarled a warning, his voice resounding in Alexs's head. "*More are coming. Sprites, imps, and another dragon. Too many to fight.*"

"We need to get out of here, Barak. There are more on the way. The queen has no intention of letting anyone out this way."

And without waiting another second, they fled the wall.

"We have a problem," Avery announced to Alex, Briar, and Barak.

She'd just arrived at Newton's place after using witch-flight to leave Happenstance Books, and now she paced in front of the fire in Newton's living room, nervous energy rolling off her.

"That Jack Frost bastard sprite has kidnapped Helena and my grandmother and is using them as bait!"

"We know," Alex told her. He leaned against the doorframe, watching her. "Didn't you hear the town criers? They marched up this street and across White Haven over the last hour, announcing what would happen in the square at one o'clock. They read out our names. We're White Haven's most wanted."

"Not me," Barak grinned. "I'm a ghost! I hope I'm pissing them off as they try to work out who I am."

"That's one positive thing," Avery agreed. "The other good news is that I broke the spell on Sally and Dan, and they're happy to help us. We thought we should try and break it on Stan, too. Maybe even James—as long as I don't put them at risk."

"I'm pleased about Sally and Dan, but we have more problems than Clea and Helena," Briar said, fingers twisting in her lap. "I have to give myself up tonight. Sacrifice myself. I can't believe the Green Man even said that."

"*What*?" Avery had been so preoccupied with Helena's capture that she hadn't thought about Briar's morning. "You talked to him?"

"Yes. I have to take a Yule log to the feast. No, *light* a Yule log. But that means taking one. What am I supposed to do? March up to the gates with a Yule log in my bag? Maybe I should stick it up that bitch's arse!"

Barak laughed. "Way to go, Briar!"

"It's not funny!" She looked outraged.

"No, it's not. We had major problems, too," Alex said, relating their fight at the wall. "White dragons that shoot ice-cold flames from their bloody great mouths. It's like El's ice fire. Nearly froze my nuts off!"

Barak shrugged. "But at least there's one less now. And you still have your balls."

Avery's thoughts whirled with shock. "Dragons? Holy shit. This just gets worse. And the Green Man? Tell me exactly what he said, Briar!"

Briar related everything, her shoulders slumping lower and lower. "We know that the Yule log signifies rebirth. Maybe that's why the Green Man needs it. But it's weird. There's the feast, and before that, the solstice parade. When am I supposed to do it? It's the last thing I thought he'd say."

"Maybe it's a bluff," Barak suggested. "You hand yourself in and I rescue you, later."

"How? You fight your way in through the guards? Alone? With the entire town at the feast? That will risk bloodshed."

"Of course he won't be alone," Alex said. "We'll all help!"

"You two are on the most-wanted list, and we still don't know where El is, other than she's somewhere in that cavernous castle!"

"Wait!" Avery held up her hand to stop the debate. "I'm thinking..."

The room fell silent, with only the crackling fire and the distant peal of the bells from the church in the centre of the town disturbing their thoughts.

Avery sat on the arm of the sofa. "Jack wants one of us—or rather, all of us—in exchange for Helena. Clea..." she faltered. "Both of them. We have to be in the town square soon. I think you offer yourself in exchange *now*, Briar. Sally and Dan will be in the square. I'll ask them to plead on behalf of Clea. Say that they have found out that we have gone to the wall to escape and that we don't know about Clea."

Alex shook his head. "They don't know about the wall."

"Bollocks!" Avery was exasperated trying to remember who should know what. "Okay. We keep it simple. They say that we must be hiding—"

"I'll tell them that," Briar interjected. "I say that when I escaped last night that I found a note you left for me, saying you were trying to escape—because of course I know about the wall now that I have my magic back. I'll say I tried to find you, but couldn't. That's plausible."

"And what about me?" Barak asked. "They'll ask you where I am."

She shrugged. "I will pretend that you're still searching for them. I'll say that I know they only want me and that you guys don't matter. Then I hope they leave you alone."

Avery nodded, exchanging a pensive glance with the others. "That could work, but they will still want to find us. They—hopefully—will search for us at the wall. In fact, news of your fight," she directed this at Alex and Barak, "will have already reached them. They'll have found the dead dragon. I never thought I'd be saying *those* words today. Anyway, then we find a way into the castle later. We know that anger breaks the spell. We do what we planned earlier."

Briar exhaled, flopping back onto the sofa. "So I just hand myself over to the woman who tried to kill me? And that horrible man, Jack Frost."

"She won't kill you yet," Barak reassured her. "It's just like that guard said last night. It's too soon, and she made a fatal error out of hate and panic. She won't make that mistake again."

Avery took a sharp intake of breath. "I know how we get in tonight. We have to be part of the solstice parade! We'll march straight in, right under their noses!"

Alex cocked his head to one side, eyes narrowing. "Interesting suggestion. It could work. But we need Stan for that."

"He'll probably be at the square at lunchtime," Barak suggested. "He'll be finalising the preparations for the parade. We can speak to him after Briar has surrendered herself."

"Which means we should be at the square somehow, too," Alex added. "To see what happens, and step in if things go awry. We can cloak in a shadow spell. It's daylight, but it's still snowing and it's a dark day. A glamour spell too, perhaps."

A screech outside the window announced the arrival of Raven, and Avery jumped to her feet to open the window and let him in. The street outside was quiet, and after a quick glance around she hurriedly shut the window again. Raven was preening himself on the mantelpiece.

"Where have you been?" Avery asked aloud, hands on hips. "Everything has gone mad here and you've been gone for hours!"

"I've been watching the castle, of course. Helena is a prisoner."

"I know. I spoke to Dan and Sally."

"I couldn't track her into the castle, but she was there for the last couple of hours. Now she's on the move again with another woman."

"Already?" Avery said, checking the time. She quickly updated him with all the news. "Was she hurt?"

"Not that I could see. But the square looks grim. There's a rudimentary stage, and—" Raven paused, eyes fixed on Avery. "Gallows."

"Gallows! As if they're going to hang them? No!" Her hands flew to her mouth as white-hot rage erupted. "How dare they!"

"They're putting on a show," Barak said, voice easy as he tried to reassure her. "They want to frighten everyone. It doesn't mean they will."

"But they *might*. They tried to kill you and Briar."

Alex started pacing. "It doesn't make sense. Why terrify people when everyone is supposed to be excited about Yule, and the feast and the parade?"

"They want to remind everyone of what's at stake," Barak said. "To ensure attendance tonight. And it's a common belief that everyone thinks that they'll be immune from whatever's happening to other people."

"But why have a feast at all?" Avery asked. "If the queen wants the Green Man and Briar's earth magic, then why the big meal with everyone there? Surely you'd want as few people as possible around?"

"Big spells require a lot of energy," Alex pointed out. "An excited crowd brings lots of that!"

"And," Raven added, "if she wants to crown the Holly King and defeat the Oak King, she'll want an audience and pageantry. That palace is all about show, and so is she. She likes power and attention."

Barak grunted in agreement. "We're going to have our work cut out for us. I thought storming a Cathar castle was hard enough, but if anything, this will be harder! We need El and we need my brothers."

"But before then," Raven said, "you need to get to the square. It's time."

# Twenty-Three

Reuben had been so relieved to get out of Stormcrossed Manor and back to his own house that he'd only just switched his attention to the next problem. However, now that he was sitting with Eve, Estelle, and Caspian in his warm snug, their next hurdle was all too obvious.

"So, we have two options," Eve suggested. "I can stay outside of the wall and cast a huge spell to get rid of the blizzard and hopefully weaken the wall—that will require at least one of you to help me. I'm comfortable performing big spells and gathering lots of energy, so I'm pretty sure two of you won't be needed. But that won't address what's going on inside—well, I don't think so, anyway." Eve played with one of her dreadlocks, twisting it in her fingers as she talked. "Or I can work the spell from inside. That is where her nexus of power is, therefore that's the best place to target. But of course it's always riskier. She'll probably have more sprites and imps and protection in there. I'll need to find somewhere safe to set up. Outside is fine. But it must be out of sight and defendable."

Estelle shrugged. "If that's the best place to target, then that's what we do. We go in with the others. I think that's the best option, too."

"Also because," Eve continued, "I can best decide the type of spell to use from within. I can assess the magic in there, and tailor the spell accordingly."

Reuben was confused. "Will you be summoning another weather system to chase away hers or his? This could be Jack's doing, after all. I don't get it."

Eve gave a dry laugh. "That's another great question. In theory, yes, I want to bring in another system so powerful that her spell and all this winter weather shatters. And you're right. From what I've seen and what you've told me about Jack, there could well be both of their magic at play here. To erect a wall of ice around Stormcrossed Manor, and an icy storm containing imps and sprites...well, that's impressive!"

Caspian had been listening without commenting so far, but now he asked, "If you can't bring in another weather system, what then?"

"I weaken it from within...somehow. It could create a really weird microclimate. A dangerous one, even. I won't know until I assess it."

"There are no second chances here," Reuben said, despair beginning to grip him again. "I trust you to do the right thing, Eve, and for the best chance, we need to go inside. But once we're in there, I'm sorry, I must find El. I'll be useless to you. I'll be so side-tracked..."

"You don't have to explain," Eve said with a gentle smile. "I understand. And it will be the same for you, Estelle. You will want to find Barak."

She nodded. "And I'm used to fighting with the Nephilim. We work well together."

"Which leaves me," Caspian said, squaring his shoulders. "I am more than happy to work this spell with you, Eve. Anything you need!"

"Thank you, Caspian. Your wealth of knowledge in spellcasting would be fantastic. In fact, your knowledge of curses will help, too. It may be just the thing we need to flip this whole thing on its head."

Briar walked with a determined stride along White Haven's lanes that edged the square, her head held high, confident that her spells hid her from the crowds.

She had been worried about handing herself over to the queen, but the more she listened to her friends' plans, the more she realised that this was the best option. Plus, she had to trust the Green Man, even if she didn't really understand his motivations.

No one gave her a second glance as she walked through the busy streets, allowing her to take in the mood of the crowd. The shops were open, and trade was busy. Everyone bustled about with a spring in their step, and the topic of most conversations was the parade and the feast.

Yet beneath the façade of cheer, there were furtive glances and an atmosphere of unease. Avery and Alex were also in the crowd, also cloaked in spells, trying to glean any information they could. Barak was flying high above them, hidden in the low cloud cover, with a spell to hide him from view. If things went very badly, they would all intervene.

But they wouldn't need to. Briar would make it work.

She emerged into the square and saw Jack Frost standing on the small stage upon which the gallows were raised. Guards lined the square, all armed with swords and spears. The atmosphere here was different. A watchful, quiet group had gathered, eyes darting everywhere, but mainly staring at the two women a short distance from Jack; Helena, or rather Clea, as the crowd knew her, and another woman that Briar didn't know. They stood next to the gallows. Helena held her head high, assessing her surroundings, but the woman next to her had tears running down her face. Helena's arm was around her shoulders, pulling her close to comfort her. Fire sparked in her eyes. Clea was well known and well liked, and Briar heard murmurs of discontent in the crowd. White Haven might have a spell upon it, but the people were fundamentally the same.

Jack had made a big mistake.

Briar clenched her fist. *These bastards would pay for this. What must the crowd be thinking?* Two harmless women paraded onstage for entertainment—and a warning. No one would know that Clea was possessed by Helena, who had faced this before, over four hundred years earlier. *She looked strong, but what was it doing to her?*

Jack addressed the crowd, and Briar pushed her way to the front. "Time is marching on. Where are Briar Ashworth, Elspeth Robinson, Avery Hamilton, and Alex Bonneville? If anyone knows, you should step forward now—or else these two women next to me, these rule-breakers, will hang from a rope."

He waited, his cool, hard gaze that had tried to bewitch Briar now cast towards everyone. Briar caught sight of Sally and Dan. Both looked tense. No one answered Jack. Briar dropped her cloaking spells, suddenly becoming fully visible to Jack, who flinched at her startling appearance. He summoned two guards with a quick jerk of his head.

"Not so fast, Jack," Briar said, stepping forward so that everyone could see her clearly. Keeping the guards at bay with a spell, she raised her voice using magic, ensuring everyone could hear her words. "You wanted me. I'm here. But you need to release your prisoners."

He folded his arms, the elegant cut of his clothes doing little to mask his monstrousness. "I asked for Elspeth, Avery, and Alex, too. Where are they?"

"I don't know. When I escaped from the queen yesterday after she tried to kill me, I couldn't find them." A collective gasp ran around the crowd, and Jack scowled. Briar continued quickly before he could intervene. "But they left a note. They are trying to escape, on the edge of town." He would know what she meant by that. She certainly wasn't going to scare the locals by referring to the Wall of Doom. "They don't even know that you have imprisoned Avery's grandmother, or of course they would be here. They're not cowards or monsters."

The crowd murmured, growing unsettled, and Jack's eyes flashed with annoyance. Ice sparkled at his fingertips, but he had to contain himself with so many people watching. He had to maintain the illusion of normality in this madness.

He shouted at the guards. "Take her! They will all go back to the palace."

"*No!*" Briar snapped, her spell still restricting the guards' movements. The crowd was straining to see what was happening, wondering why the two guards weren't seizing her. But she had to be careful not to overdo it. Already other guards were moving in. Briar sidestepped them and ran up the steps and on to the stage. "I am offering myself in exchange for the two women, as you promised. I am here. Unarmed. Just a harmless woman. Please," she lowered her voice, allowing it to catch and sound vulnerable, "please let them go. What harm can they do you?"

Jack snarled, and for a moment, Briar saw the human mask slip and the sprite appear. "No one can harm me, or the queen. But this is a matter of principle. I asked for Elspeth, Avery, and Alex. And I am interested in one more—you know who."

"I'm sure we can discuss everything in private," Briar answered, gauging the crowd, who were jostling each other, and eyeing the guards with dislike. "Let the women go. You have won!"

Dan's voice carried from the crowd. "Yes, let them go! You have what you came for!"

Sally chimed in, pleading and desperate. "Please! Let me see Clea!"

The crowd grew bolder, shuffling forward, and then Stan shouted out, clad in his Druid's cloak, his face etched with worry. "Please Jack, sir, we have a lot to do this afternoon. The parade will start in a couple of hours. People are excited. There's the feast to look forward to! It's Yule."

Briar could have kissed him for reminding Jack of what was at stake. *Had Avery broken his spell already, or was it just Stan's good diplomacy?* Whatever it was, Jack was losing the crowd, and he knew it. If the group's reasoning was correct and they needed everyone to attend the feast, Jack couldn't risk upsetting the people in the square any further.

Jack clapped loudly, and it sounded like a gunshot across the square. "Enough! As a show of good faith at Briar's arrival, I will release these two women in Briar's stead, but the rulebreakers—Alex, Elspeth, and Avery—are dangerous individuals. They subverted the queen's will, and that will not be tolerated. Therefore, I will extend the timeframe. I ask that they are found and brought to the castle tonight to be dealt with." He released Clea and the other woman's restraints himself. The woman scurried off the stage, but Clea—*Helena*—passed by Briar more slowly. They locked eyes but didn't speak, though it was enough for Briar to know that Helena was furious, and that made her very dangerous.

As the crowd ebbed and Jack and Briar were left alone onstage, Briar cast aside her spell that kept the guards away. Jack lowered his lips to Briar's ear, an icy cold creeping along her skin. "Well played, but you will all lose in the end. Our plans are in motion, and there is nothing that you can do to stop them." He nodded at the guard behind her. "Take her to my sleigh. She will travel with me. Then gather as many men as you can spare and head to the wall. I want the others found—now!"

Shadow eyed the imp standing just in front of her with deep suspicion. She didn't trust him an inch, but what choice did they have?

The wall loomed over the assembled group. All six Nephilim, four witches, the three police officers, and Ghost OPS were armed and ready to fight. The witches had cast a protective spell over them all, and it was helping to counter the effects of the wall. Up close, the strange and unusual magic was overpowering. No wonder they came away from it feeling confused and bewildered. She could feel the powerful sprite's handiwork all over it, and under that the lurking power of the queen.

The imp raised his hand and made shapes in the air, muttering words in his unusual fey dialect. Shadow listened intently, wary of any hidden warning that he might be sending to the other side, but it was just a complicated invocation. The wall directly ahead began to shimmer, and an archway took shape—though not a huge gate as had opened on the icesheet. It was smaller, easier to disguise and manipulate. Within the arch the white wall thinned, shimmered, and then vanished completely to reveal a short tunnel with some hazy whiteness at the far end.

Shadow gripped the imp's shoulder as it made to walk forward. "Slowly, little one. What's on the other side of the tunnel?"

"The town, of course!"

"Where? Is it on the west side? Is the orientation of the town the same?"

It scowled. "It opens on the hill. There are no dwellings around, but it leads to Jack's mist."

"And the creatures that patrol the wall are in that?"

"Close by."

It wasn't a satisfying answer, but it was all they would get.

She kept a firm hold of his shoulder, and Gabe held the iron chain as the imp entered the tunnel, both gripping swords with their free hands. The others followed. Zee and Eli were at the rear. When all had stepped inside, the imp closed the gate with another invocation, and the outside world vanished.

In a few short steps they stood on the threshold of icy mist, and the bluish lights that Dylan had spoken of sparked around them. There would be sprites in this, and imps, and maybe more from the slither of unseen things. Shadow's skin prickled with unease. This was the *fey world she knew. What had this Witch-Queen done?*

She and Gabe exchanged an uneasy glance. There was no one she would rather have at her side than Gabe and his brothers at a time like this—except for maybe her old crew. A gleam of excitement replaced her trepidation. There would be no holding back here. No laws or police or rules. Nothing that Newton could act on, anyway. But they had to keep the humans safe. *Caution first.*

Remaining banded together, they started to cross the mist, the Nephilim and witches loosely ringed around the group, the witches' protection spell helping to mask their crossing. But very quickly the mist crawled over them, obscuring everything. They pushed on, and with every step it seemed to be getting brighter. They were almost there.

And then the snarls and shouts of sprites came from one side, and the unmistakable roar of a dragon on the other. A spear sliced out of the air, whistling past her ear, almost impaling her shoulder.

The imp seized its opportunity and snapped at her hand, his sharp teeth drawing blood. She backhanded its face, sending it sprawling, unsheathed her second sword, and leapt into action.

Caspian was surrounded by mayhem—the cacophony of clashing swords, shouts, the flash of magic, and the roar of something that sounded truly terrifying.

The peculiar energy of the icy mist was playing havoc with their spells, and the thick, coiling vapour clouds wrapped around them like a writhing entity of its own. The group was desperately trying to stay together, to protect the humans without any power in their midst. The Nephilim fought furiously, and Caspian and the witches responded by casting spell after spell at their barely seen enemy.

Using fire was useless here. It sizzled and vanished instantly in their watery surroundings. He could feel ice gathering on his eyelashes and clothes. Water rolled down his neck, and ice pinched his cheeks. Reuben was having a better time of it. He manipulated the water, pulling it out of the mist and creating giant hailstones that he whipped around him like bullets. It was clever, and Caspian copied him, whipping up wind in the process to try to move the mist.

All the time they tried to move forward, but it was impossible. They were floundering and blind.

"Eve!" he shouted, desperate to find her. "We need to get rid of this mist."

She appeared, breathless, at his side. "I know, but it's sticky! I can't shift it. I manage to clear some, and then it's just back."

"I'm having the same trouble trying to move it with wind," Caspian admitted, aiming a huge hailstone at a sprite who leapt out of the mist at him.

Niel emerged behind it, his huge axe swinging, and the sprite fell dead, his head rolling away. The mist swallowed them both up.

"We're as likely to be killed by a Nephilim as a sprite, the way this is going," Eve muttered. "We need to create a tunnel to get us out of here. Or a pocket of space around us. And light! It's so dark in here!"

"A sunlight spell," Caspian suggested. "It's shockingly bright—and hot. It might be enough to get us out of this mist."

Eve grinned. "Brilliant. You cast it, and I'll back you up with another spell."

It wasn't a spell that Caspian used often, but he recalled they had used it against the vampires to great effect. In fact, it had been bottled by Avery for Ghost OPS. He tried to remember it as accurately as possible, and uttering the words, cast his hands high. A spark lit above him, golden for a moment, a promise of warmth, before it guttered out. He tried again, while Eve cast another spell to try to move the mist. This time Caspian changed the words, realising what he'd done wrong before. He directed the spell overhead, and was almost blinded as a brilliant, yellow light exploded above them.

Sunlight burst through the thick mist, illuminating everything around them, and Caspian nearly yelled in fright. It was so much worse than he had imagined. They were surrounded by sprites and imps, all converging on them, and only kept at bay by the furiously fighting Nephilim, Reuben, and Estelle. Even worse, a huge dragon was fighting with Gabe, Nahum, Ash, and Shadow a short distance away. Ghost OPS and the police were battling it out as best they could with their limited abilities.

But the sunlight was rapidly dissolving the mist, and Eve backed it up with another spell. It seemed their enemy did not like the bright sunshine. They cowered away from it.

Caspian saw the way to clear ground, and he bellowed, "Follow me!"

Barak left his perch on the top of a building where he had watched the events unfold in the square.

He had been hidden with the witches' spells, and was relieved that the two women were released without the need for bloodshed. The guards escorted Briar to a large, ornate sleigh, and he watched grimly as Jack settled in next to her.

He was about to follow her to the castle when he saw Raven take after her instead, and Barak swung around to study the town again. They had arranged to meet at Briar's shop once the streets had cleared of the many guards. They figured that after her arrest, no one would search there again, especially as Jack had ordered most of the guards to move along the wall. It would be a good place to plan their next move. Sally and Dan were with Clea, and they joined Stan at the edge of the square. They had to get him on their side. Their next move depended on it.

The best place for Barak to set down would be on the edge of town, and from there he could walk in. But as he circled to find the best spot, a disturbance on the hillside high above the town caught his eye. The snow was falling lightly now, improving visibility, and he frowned. The mist was churning in a far more agitated way than it normally did.

It could just be dragons again—*because, yes, that was so normal*—but it warranted a closer look.

And then suddenly a huge burst of golden light exploded from its midst, and he turned away, dazzled. *What new nightmare was this?* As his vision cleared, he saw shapes in the thinning mist below, a struggling band of people surrounded by sprites and another damn dragon.

It was his brothers and his friends—and Estelle. Barak had never been so grateful to see them in his life.

Unfortunately, the dazzling sunlight was drawing attention. In the town, a few guards were squinting up at the hillside, but they wouldn't be able to see what was happening—yet. A contingent started running up the lanes and would arrive soon.

Barak dived down to help his friends, sword swinging as he cleared a path out of the mist and onto the hill. Caspian was leading them out, helped by a pretty witch with thick, dark dreadlocks. His brothers were spread out, and a slew of dead bodies lay on the ground, but more sprites and imps were running to where the mist still lay thick and deep. Eli and Zee chased after them. The dragon wasn't so lucky. The combined effort of three Nephilim and Shadow was obviously too much to overcome, and it lay dead, blood pooling around it.

"Barak!" Estelle ran to his side, eyes drinking him in.

He swung her up and into his arms, holding her close as he said, "You certainly know how to make an entrance." Before she could answer, he kissed her deeply. "I've missed you."

"And I've missed you, but don't think we won't have words later about that stunt you pulled!" Her voice was stern, but she was laughing.

"You can tell me off all you like then, but we need to move—now. Guards are on your tail." He reluctantly let go of her and studied the gathered group, several of whom were injured and covered in blood. Newton looked winded, Moore had a black eye, and Kendall clutched her arm. Ghost OPS looked barely any better, their clothes ripped and dirty. "Herne's bollocks! You're all here! And you're hurt!"

Niel glanced down at his blood-spattered chest. "More their blood than mine."

"And dragon's blood," Shadow answered, splattered with gore. She spat her own blood at the ground. "But at least we're here, thanks to that devious little imp."

"What imp?" Barak asked, confused.

"Long story," Gabe said wearily, as he kicked a chain lying on the ground. "It's good to see you, brother. What the hell is happening in town? How did you find us?"

Barak gestured around them. "Sunlight is unusual here—especially when it seemingly explodes on a hill. You've attracted attention, and we need to get out of here. Guards are coming."

"Let them come," Niel growled. "We'll kill them all."

"No." Barak shook his head, already assessing the best way off the hillside. "Let's try to keep you a secret."

Zee snorted as he and Eli joined them. "With this body count? They'll know someone did this."

"Let them assume it's me, or the witches."

Reuben shouldered his way forward. "Is El all right? Are they all okay?"

"El is alive, but she's a prisoner."

"A *what*?" Reuben's voice rose with anger.

Barak looked over his shoulder, expecting to see soldiers appearing any moment, but so far the landscape remained empty, settling back beneath the gloomy sky as the sunlight spell vanished. "I'll update you later, but right now we must get off this hill! We need to get to Briar's place, and you guys need to clean up. I suggest we split up, but you all have to keep a low profile. And for Herne's sake, cover up your blood! Use a spell, a cloak, anything—but you can't afford to get spotted. Understood?" They all nodded, mute with confusion. "Good. Let's go. That way."

He pointed away from where the guards would soon arrive, and hoped they'd have enough time.

# Twenty-Four

E l lay on her straw pallet again, staring up at the ceiling and wondering whether Clea and the woman had survived.

After Jack had left with them, the other prisoners had been escorted to their individual cells again, and basic food had been delivered. *That had to mean something.* Or maybe she was just seeing hope where there was none. Jack had said they were bait for that night. *Yule.* And whatever would happen at the feast.

Clea *must* have survived. Her friends would have stopped the execution—hopefully. But still, a nagging doubt remained. She didn't trust Jack. He was sly, and just as dangerous as the queen. If not more so. She couldn't just wait to get rescued. If her captors worked out who she was, they would kill her. And she couldn't hope that memories of her magic would return, or that this weird spell on her would weaken.

Raven had said she needed to be angry, but she already had been. She still was. But she was upset more than that. She still couldn't recall Reuben's face. She said his name over and over again, liking the way the name sounded on her tongue. They would have performed magic together. Planned to spend Yule together. His arms would have held her close and comforted her. He would have made her laugh. Maybe cooked for her.

Tears threatened again and she brushed them aside. This wasn't what she did. She didn't dissolve into tears. She knew that much about herself. She was like her Aunt Oli in that way.

She froze. Aunt Oli. *Where did that come from? Who was Aunt Oli?*

El sat upright, her single, threadbare blanket sliding to the floor, focussing her mind on Aunt Oli. *Why that name? Why had that seeped into her consciousness, of all people? And why could she still not put a face to the name?*

She was important to El, obviously. *But more important than Reuben?* She wracked her brain, filtering memories that were clearly stunted. And that posed even more questions. *Who was she, El? Where had she come from before White Haven?* She knew she hadn't always lived there. *Who had taught her magic?*

*Aunt Oli.*

She still couldn't remember her face, but she knew it, deep down—bone deep, in the core of her soul. *Aunt Oli had taught her magic.*

But the more El chased the strand of knowledge, the more elusive it became. She needed to relax. Let it come to her. Or maybe she should give in to all of her wildest emotions. Be like Avery. Let it all out.

But it wasn't anger that El felt. She was upset. Really upset. She wanted to cry and wail and sob and lament for her lost memory. She wanted to surrender to all of it for the first time in her life. So, she lay back on the bed, pulled the blanket over her, and let everything overwhelm her.

And much later, it was there, in her deepest, darkest, loneliest moment, that her memories and her magic returned.

Avery watched Stan, hoping he wasn't about to freak out as his memories returned.

"Just take deep breaths, Stan," she advised him, pushing a cup of Eli's soothing herbal tea in front of him. "The panic will pass, and the tea will help."

He blinked a few times, eyes wide as he stared at Sally, Dan, Alex, and Clea—or rather, Helena—who were all in Briar's herb room at the back of her shop, seated around the table.

Stan cleared his throat. "I'm really not sure it will, actually. We're trapped in a giant spell that has been cast by some crazy witch and self-proclaimed queen, and now I have to pretend I don't know?" His voice rose. "This is insane!"

Alex grinned. "But better than going back a millennia or so in time, right? And you get to meet more fey! You liked them."

"I liked the woodland fey and their wolves. I do not consider meeting murderous sprites and imps a good thing!" He reached for his tea and sniffed it suspiciously. "Is it safe?"

"I'm not about to poison you, Stan!" Avery huffed. "We need your help. You're on Team Witch now, and you like that, remember?"

The familiar twinkle returned to Stan's eyes, and he adjusted his cloak with a flourish. "Of course. It's just a shock to find guards in White Haven, and a huge palace on the hill. And the wall, of course. Very interesting."

Dan shook his head. "Always the master of understatement, Stan. Well? Can you get them in the parade?"

"Absolutely. I have spare costumes. I can't remember what kind, exactly. Dryads and nature spirits, I think. Lots of green wigs and leafy headgear. That would mean we could put paint all over your faces. A few jugglers' outfits. Drummers, too!" He nodded to himself and checked his watch. "Yes. They're at the council. The parade will start at four o'clock, when it's getting dark. We'll begin in the square and walk through the town and end up at the palace for the feast. There's time to get you ready."

Avery sighed with relief, flopping back in the chair. "Can you bring the costumes here? We can't risk being seen."

"Absolutely. Lots of people will get ready at home and meet in town. Can Sally or Dan please assist?"

Sally nodded. "Of course. Anything. And then me and Dan will line the route, cheering them on." She glanced at him for confirmation. "But do I have to take my kids?"

"No," Helena said, steely-eyed. "If anyone questions it, and I doubt they will, say they're sick. Caro too, Dan. We have no idea what could happen later. It's best they're safe at home. Tonight, we're just going to have to play it by ear."

"Which is risky," Stan said, scratching his chin.

"But inevitable. We'll judge things in the moment. And the first chance I get, I will kill Jack Frost."

Avery squeezed Helena's hand, feeling horribly guilty for risking her grandmother's life and bringing up bad memories for Helena. "I can't imagine what it must have been like for you in the middle of that crowd. I'm so sorry, I never for a moment—"

Helena cut her off. "It wasn't your fault, and I'm okay. It brought back some unpleasant memories, but if anything, it was cathartic. At least I knew I had the power to get out of it, unlike back then. I should have thought it through more. I honestly didn't think he would use me as bait. But the crowd wasn't behind it. They were just scared of Jack and the guards. Modern sensibilities aren't easily swept away, and White Haven is full of good people."

"The crowd hated it," Stan confirmed, and Sally and Dan murmured their agreement. "It was stirring things up for me because it felt so wrong. You could see it in people's eyes. Maybe it would have been better if the spell had broken then?"

Alex shook his head. "Absolutely not. They need to achieve something tonight, so they would have reacted badly. The guards might have killed people, or at least arrested everyone. That's why Jack had to back down. Briar played it well, and you helped to remind him of his priorities."

"But Briar is now in a far worse place than I was," Helena said, hands clenching around her mug.

"She's in the perfect place," Alex said. "As long as we can get to her."

"That's the big issue, though, isn't it?" Dan pointed out. "And what about El?"

Avery shrugged. "One of us has to get away and find her."

A knock rattled the front door, and they all froze.

"I'll go," Dan said, rising to his feet. He peered around the edge of the door and then turned back to them with a big grin on his face. "It's Barak, and he's brought back-up."

It was a joyful, if crowded, reunion in Briar's shop, and Newton could barely keep track of what was going on.

Multiple conversations were taking place at the same time as everyone caught up with the latest news, made plans, and drank copious amounts of coffee and tea. Eli, Estelle, and Caspian healed and dressed wounds in the middle of it all, while everyone cleaned blood off themselves.

Newton had his own plans, though, and he was determined not to be left out of the action. And he had questions. Lots of questions. He cornered Stan. "I need costumes, too. For all of us, actually." He gestured to Moore and Kendall, who were talking to Helena.

"If I have enough," Stan said, looking doubtful. "You can always enter the castle after the parade, just like everyone else. We might be better saving costumes for those guys!" He gestured to the Nephilim.

Newton grimaced. He couldn't argue with that. "Where are Hamid and Kev, the community police officers?"

"They're under the spell, just like everyone else, Newton. They're doing what they normally do. Dealing with community issues and keeping the peace."

Newton seethed with frustration. "This is infuriating. I need them on our side. They need to protect everyone. Get them out of the castle later!"

"If the witches break the spell," Stan said calmly, "that's exactly what they'll do. You haven't seen half of what's going on here. How could you? The spell is..." Stan paused to find the words. "It's powerful, but it goes against everything we know, and consequently, while we know things such as: The queen rules us; We always celebrate Yule with a huge feast at the castle after the parade; That it's normal to have guards in the town, perpetual snowfall for months, and travel by sleigh and reindeer — it still feels odd. Even now that we've lost radio and TV. That's something I barely thought about! We know it, but we don't *feel* it. But we also know that to question it would be insane. The spell has instilled in us that life here is great—*if* we follow the rules. So, we do."

Newton massaged his temple, another headache brewing. He could barely believe that only just over twenty-four hours earlier he'd woken with a hangover after the Christmas party. *What the hell must his boss be thinking?* His entire team hadn't checked in since yesterday. This would take a lot of explaining. *Or maybe it wouldn't.* If he ever got out of this, maybe he should pass it all off as something far less—*weird.* "What do you know about the queen and Jack Frost? You must have some knowledge of them."

"I know that the queen has ruled us forever. She is benevolent and generous—when obeyed. Jack is her right-hand man and beneath his smooth ways we know he is as dangerous as a wild boar. It's odd, though," he acknowledged, "because the witches didn't know about Jack—like she deliberately hid him from them. I have no idea why. Paranoia, perhaps? And we also know that rulebreakers are taken to the palace and punished. They could lose money, business rights, status...rarely their lives, though." Stan huffed, patting his portly belly beneath his Druid's robe. "Now that I'm free of the spell, it's hard to believe that this has been only, what? A day and a half? It's crazy."

"It's terrifying," Newton said, grimly. "What about the witches? Could *you* remember them?"

"Not as witches, no, and I never once thought of magic. It didn't exist. I didn't remember going back in time, either."

"What about the Holly King, who the queen wishes to save. Did you know about him?"

"Well, that's the thing," Stan mused. "I don't remember much about him at all! I don't remember seeing him, or even what he looks or sounds like." Stan spotted Dan and called him over. "What do you remember of the Holly King? Newton was just asking me, and I can't remember much at all."

Dan frowned. "No, nor me. He's elusive. I mean, I know he exists, but that's about it."

"But according to you, that's what this situation is all about. Why can't you remember him?"

"Maybe we're not supposed to know anything about him," Dan suggested. "I guess for the queen, the less we know about him the better."

"That makes no bloody sense to me," Newton admitted, "but she must have her reasons. So, that's it, then? That's as much as we have to go on. She wants to kill the Green Man in Briar to change the balance of nature and save her lover. To make a perpetual winter. And we have to stop her." He snorted. "Not much then, really."

Dan grinned. "Glad to see you still have your sense of humour, Newton. Anyway, we need to go. Want to come with us and find costumes? It will give you a chance to get a feel for things."

Newton downed his coffee with a grimace, eager to get out and walk the streets of White Haven. "Hell yes."

It was with a sense of disbelief that Briar entered the palace again, Jack right next to her.

It had been a silent drive up the hill, and would have been romantic in many ways if not for her companion and circumstances. The ever-present snow, the jingle of the bells, the stunning views of White Haven glimpsed from the curving lanes, and the Winter Fayre once again plying its trade to customers. Not to mention the glorious castle that rose above it all, its pennants streaming in the breeze.

Briar remained resolutely silent, despite Jack's attempts to engage her in conversation. She ignored him, always turning away, thinking of ways to outwit the queen—and hoping no one would find the small, blackened Yule log from the year before that was wrapped in a scarf and hidden at the bottom of her bag. At one point on the ride, she spotted a deer, and then realised that it was actually Deer, her familiar. Overhead, wheeling above them, was Raven. They comforted her, making her feel less alone.

Jack's growing frustration amused her, and she felt his mood turn ugly. Cold emanated from him, and ice crystallised in the air. He had clearly overestimated his charm, and his ability to mask his inhuman features. Once seen, they were not easily forgotten.

But once she entered the grand palace courtyard, all thoughts of Jack were forgotten.

Much had changed from the day before. Huge banners bearing the queen's emblem had been unfurled down the castle walls that lined the courtyard, and torches, already blazing with flames, had been planted in the ground to form a ceremonial walkway to the ornate double doors that were the castle's formal entrance.

It was easier to appreciate its scale during the day. It was big enough to admit an elephant, and the large reception hall was enormous. Jack directed her to the left, through another antechamber to the Great Hall. She knew what it was, and had memories of how it should look, but they didn't prepare her for the reality of it.

She paused on the threshold, mouth open, as she took it all in. It was a long, high-ceilinged room, with stone walls and floors, but again, rich tapestries of deep reds and greens lined the walls, and columns stretched to an ornate ceiling bedecked with spectacular chandeliers. As well as the ground floor level, there were three staggered levels around the periphery, edged with balustrades. All were filled with tables and chairs. But it was the table decorations that caught her attention. There was an array of endless cut-glass crystal goblets, sparkling silverware, enormous candelabras, and snowy white tablecloths. Greenery dressed the tables—sprigs of pine, holly, and mistletoe—and the walls were dressed with big, looping swags and wreaths between the tapestries. At the far end was a raised dais set with a table for the guests of honour, and higher up, set into the wall, a minstrels' gallery. It was hard to know where to look first. And it wasn't even finished yet. Staff still bustled around making final touches and additions.

Jack gave a mean laugh at her obvious shock. "Oh, yes. The queen knows how to make a statement. I thought you should see this, so you can appreciate what tonight means. Do you not remember the previous feasts, Briar?"

She turned to face him for the first time since the square, and found his eyes fixed on her with greedy intensity. "There were no previous feasts, you odious man. It's an illusion planted by the queen."

He tutted. "Not true. There have been feasts in this hall for as long as I can remember. A tradition that we all honour. The turn of the wheel as the longest and darkest night passes, and the Holly King gives way to the Oak King. Of course, the feast doesn't happen *here*, but in our own home that is so far away right now." A trace of regret crossed his features and his gaze turned inward. "The northern lights will be dancing now, and our celebrations would last all night." He smiled spitefully again as he focussed on her. "And will again, after tonight. But we will no longer have to subject ourselves to the rules of nature. Not once we defeat the Oak King."

"I thought you were from the Otherworld. Are the northern lights seen there?"

"Of course. The northern lights reach to the ground there. They dance on the snow. We live on the edges of that world, an icy world that few like—except us, of course. But even there we're subjected to thaws and summer. Admittedly, it lasts a short time only, but still the king dies, and the queen must mourn her love—alone."

"And what about you? What do you do while she mourns?"

"I flee the summer with my sprites and imps, and inhabit other winters. Icy retreats, where the days are short and the long nights promise mischief and revelry." He wiggled his fingers; spikes of ice grew from his fingertips, and frost coated his eyebrows and hair.

"And from that your myth was born," Briar said, musing on the tales of Jack Frost who spread ice and cold wherever he went.

Jack leaned close again, frozen mist blooming from his perfect mouth, ice crystallising on his skin. "You could come with me. It has a beauty all its own. We could dance beneath the stars together. It will be magnificent in an endless winter. The stars are brighter, and I swear, Briar, that you can hear the celestial bodies singing. There are mysteries there that you would never believe. Wonders that I could show you. Bridges of ice over frozen rivers. Caverns of delights. My own ice palace that dwarfs this one. And the queen would like your company, I think." He ran a finger down her cheek, so cold that it burned. "As would I. You are very beautiful, Briar, and powerful. An enchanting combination."

Jack had his own magic and weaved his own spells. Staring into his deep blue eyes, she could see the stars burning in endless nights, and thick, white snow that ran to the horizon. She could even hear the distant strains of music that threatened to enchant her. Jack almost made her feel sorry for the queen, for both of them, and almost made her want to see his wintry northern kingdom—until she remembered what they had done. And were planning to do.

She recoiled and stepped away from him. "If you kill the Oak King, you kill summer for everyone. You will kill us all."

He blinked and the images vanished. "Not my concern. When you have lived for as long as I have, you have little tolerance for rules and other people."

"But I do have concerns, Jack. I care deeply about other people. I have seen enough. Take me to the queen. I wish to know my fate—from her alone."

She turned away, glimpsing the anger that swept over him—and maybe a touch of regret. Out of the corner of her eye she saw a swooping bird leave the hall and fly down the palace passageways.

Raven had found a way in.

# Twenty-Five

Z ee adjusted his costume that was adorned with what seemed to
be a million scratchy, fake leaves, and checked the camouflage
makeup on his face in the window of Briar's backroom.

He turned to Alex. "What do you think? I feel like I look like
Rambo."

Alex sniggered as his eyes ran up and down him. "You look like an
oversized woodland spirit, but you'll do. I'm not sure about the sword,
though," he added, smirking.

"Well, I'm not leaving it behind. I need to sneak the crossbow in
somehow, too."

Stan tutted from behind him. "You need a cloak! I think there's
a feathered one somewhere. Your costume will be a mishmash, but
that's okay."

"Don't worry," Alex reassured him. "We'll disguise your weapons
with spells. Let's just hope they're not searching people."

"We all look a bloody mishmash," Niel complained. "Although, I
do look magnificent." He lifted his chin, preening. "And hunters are
meant to have axes." Niel was dressed in animal skins and leather, and
with his hair pulled up on his head exposing his shaved sides and strong
jaw, he looked deadly.

All of the Nephilim and most of the witches, Newton, and Shadow
were dressed up to join the parade, and the Nephilim had been able to

remain bare chested, which would make flying easier later. Stan, Sally, Dan, Kendall, Moore, and Ghost OPS were going to line the route and enter the palace in the general crowd. Stan would be towards the front. It seemed that even in this reality, the queen had kept his role the same as everyone was familiar with it. Their plans were loose. They had no other choice. All they knew was that Briar and the Oak King were going to be sacrificed so that the Holly King could live. If it was going to take place elsewhere in the palace, they were in big trouble.

They also had to find El. It was odd not to have her with them, and Reuben had lost his normal bounce. Once he saw the palace on the hill, it seemed to absorb his every thought. Although, to be fair, it was dominating Zee's thoughts, too.

"We need to find a way to search the castle when we get inside," Zee said, voicing his concerns. "We have to free El as quickly as possible." He raised his voice so Reuben could hear him. "I'll search for El with you, Reu."

Reuben flashed him a smile. "Thanks. We can use shadow spells and others to confuse the guards. I want to find her before the queen decides to use the prisoners for leverage. And then we'll help her to find her magic."

"I know where I saw the prisoners earlier today," Helena said, as she adjusted her costume. "I think I can get there again. It was on the ground floor. But we should keep our group small. Reuben, me, and Zee. The less of us there are, the easier it will be to sneak through the passages."

By now the room was falling silent as individual conversations stalled to listen to the plans.

Eve leaned against the bench top, still wearing her normal, hippy-style clothes, arms crossed. The more Zee saw of Eve, the more he liked her. "I half wish I was going in with you, but I must stay outside of the palace. The queen's power is rooted in the freezing cold weather. She's brought it with her. I can feel it. This is the source of the weather system that is over Cornwall."

Caspian, also wearing his own clothes, was helping Estelle with her costume. "Let's hope you're right, and that breaking the spell will make them more susceptible to whatever you guys can do inside." He looked over at Avery. "Eve will need to set up somewhere private. Can we use your garden, Avery?"

"Of course!" She smiled at Eve. "It's big, with high walls and a gate. You should have plenty of privacy there."

"Excellent." Eve ran her fingers across the top of her lip, deep in thought. "I know what spell I want to use, but like any weather spell, it can take time."

"A warm weather front?" Estelle asked. "Like the one I used?"

Eve shook her head, eyes sparkling. "No. Something much more dramatic. I'll keep it a surprise."

"Are you sure you only need Caspian with you?" Zee asked, wishing he hadn't volunteered to find El. He'd like to spend more time with the enigmatic Eve. "If the queen detects that someone is working magic to undermine her spell, she'll send guards."

Barak nodded in agreement. "According to Briar, she knew as soon as we were at the South Gate, and dispatched Jack and the guards."

"It depends on what Eve needs me to do," Caspian said. "I can join in the spell with you, Eve, or defend you?"

"I'm pretty confident I can do this one alone. You can keep watch and repel anyone who attacks. Whether you think you need help, though, is up to you."

"I can manage," Caspian reassured Zee. "Keep your numbers for the hall, I have a feeling you'll need them. Speaking of which, Eve, we should probably get going. We can travel by witch-flight. But I have a question first. The palace, obviously, does not belong here. The queen brought it with her, somehow. I presume, when she leaves—hopefully in defeat—it will vanish, along with Jack and all of the guards and the palace staff. The last thing we want is for anyone to be trapped in it when that happens. And potentially, that could happen at any time this evening. Maybe dawn, at the latest."

"Oh shit," Alex groaned. "You're right. It's not like she'd want to hang around if she loses the battle with the Oak King. Damn it. This makes everything far more complicated."

Niel snorted with amusement. "Okay. Let me get this right. We have to get into the castle, stop the queen and Jack from killing the Green Man—and maybe Briar—so we're not stuck in perpetual winter. Find El and the other prisoners, and then get the entire population of White Haven out of the palace before Eve either boots her out, or she leaves anyway." He stared at the gathered group. "Maybe we should iron out a few more details before we head in, because I, as sure as Herne has big hairy bollocks, do not wish to end up in the Otherworld and stuck with the queen forever."

The parade members gathered in the town square, and Alex found a place among them, not far from Avery and Estelle.

The mood was raucous, and far higher-spirited than it had been earlier in the day. If anyone had fears or misgivings about the Yule celebrations at the palace, no one was showing them. Alex was buoyed by it, and he laughed with the crowd as he shuffled into place, directed by Stan and a few other council members who were overseeing the parade under the watchful eyes of the guards. They, unfortunately, were everywhere, but Alex stayed away from them, even though he knew he blended in well.

The drummers were already beating time, and the pipers struck up an unearthly, haunting tune that made the hairs stand up on Alex's neck. Eli, dressed as Herne, with huge horns attached to his head, grinned at him. Eli was enjoying the bacchanalia, and Alex hoped his small harem of women wouldn't recognise him. With luck, the queen's spell would ensure they wouldn't even remember him. *There were some advantages to the spell, after all.*

Just when the square was full to bursting, and the parade was getting restless, a shout heralded the start, and the drumming changed from a lively beat to one that set a march. The square started to empty, and the participants jostled onto the main road, starting their slow march down to the harbour. Once there, they would turn and take the long road up to the palace. Alex glanced up at it as it came into view through a break in the buildings.

A line of burning torches lit the way to it—a beacon on the hill that blazed with light. Alex hoped that their plans would work. If they didn't, life as they knew it might change forever.

Briar was forced to wait for hours to see the queen.

It wasn't what she had expected. She thought she would be escorted to the queen upon arriving at the palace, but obviously she had other things to do. Or just wanted to keep Briar waiting. Instead, she was escorted to the room she had been in the night before, and guards had been positioned outside. Fortunately her magic had not been restricted by a binding spell. The queen knew she was a witch, but obviously trusted her not to escape. Briar hadn't even tried. The sprites who masqueraded as guards had magic, and to risk anything now would mean that their plans for that night would be ruined. It seemed the queen had her own timeline, too—and her own demands.

A spring green dress made of silks and velvet had been laid on the bed. It had a tight bodice and a full skirt, much like one the queen had worn the day before. Briar had been instructed to wear it, and a young woman, pale and quiet, had helped her into it and arranged her hair into elaborate coils. It was unnerving. *What new nightmare was this for?*

Finally, after she was dressed and left alone with her thoughts, Briar went over her plans and reviewed alternatives. But it was hard to plan for anything when they didn't know what the agenda was. The Green Man, curled inside, wouldn't respond at all. And what was she supposed to do with the Yule log? Should she put it on the fire now, or take it with her, somehow? Briar groaned. *This was a nightmare.* Glad that she'd only brought a small piece with her, she put it into the pocket of her gown, confident the fold of the skirt would hide it.

Eventually, a knock at the door interrupted the silence, and a guard stepped into the room. His eyes swept across her, and he nodded as if she'd passed his inspection. He gestured her to follow, and heart racing, Briar was finally escorted to the queen's chamber that she knew only too well. It was the place where the queen had tried to kill her.

Briar paused on the threshold, taking everything in. The broken window that Barak had crashed through had been repaired, and like the Great Hall below, this room was also dressed with garlands of greenery. The room was full of shadows, cast by the wavering candle-light, but the darkness within allowed the glittering beauty of White Haven and the scene below to be fully appreciated. The queen stood on the balcony, taking in the view.

The guard that had escorted her pushed her fully into the room, and then stepped inside too, shutting the door behind them. He crossed the room with long strides and opened the door, a blast of cold air carrying music to Briar. She followed in his wake, her finger stroking the silk covered chairs and polished wood surfaces. The snow had stopped falling, leaving everything pristine white. The sea and the harbour below were frozen solid, the distant view cut off by the wall. Down the hill, she could see the snaking line of the parade as it wound upwards, bringing her friends—and an end to this, she hoped...

The queen turned to her with a whirl of her skirts, sharp eyes boring into hers. Briar tried to hide her shock. The queen was obviously fey, and whatever glamour she had used yesterday was gone now. She seemed taller, more ethereal, and far more deadly.

"Briar, the earth witch who shelters the Green Man, you are back. Come closer."

"If I must," Briar complained, and pulled the thick cloak she had been given around her shoulders as she joined the queen on the balcony.

"You are here of your own free will, Briar. Don't complain now."

Briar snorted with derision. "I am here because I didn't want anyone to hang. It's hardly free will. You and Jack have a very interesting interpretation of that phrase. Are you going to leap upon me? Attempt to kill me, like yesterday?"

"Not yet. My guards have been scouring White Haven and have searched the wall without finding a single trace of your friends—including the one who crashed through this window to save you. All they found were dead sprites and two slayed dragons. Impressive, if annoying. And very suspicious. The deaths occurred in two different places."

*Two? Had the others got inside?* Briar remained expressionless. "Hardly suspicious. They want to get out. I would imagine they'd have tried several places. And they're not likely to just surrender."

The queen wagged a finger. "Oh no, Briar, I know there was another group at the wall who were led inside by a foolish imp who is now dead. A very peculiar group." She stepped closer to Briar so quickly that Briar stepped back. "I don't like any of it, and I will find every single one of them. I still have prisoners, and later, before the fight, I will sacrifice them one by one until your friends surrender." She smiled, maliciously. "I have no doubt they will enter the palace tonight. I will find them, no matter how hard they try to disguise themselves."

Briar didn't respond. She didn't want to say anything that might give them away.

"Besides, my brother will help. Jack is very good at seeing through deception."

"Jack is your brother?"

"Half-brother. But we are very close. He has taken quite the interest in you. I think I should take you home, once all this is done. My home, that is."

Fear lanced through Briar. "I don't think so. And if you think I'll stand by and let that happen, then you're the fool. Or if you think my friends will let you."

"They are no match for me."

"Or me," a voice said from the deepest shadows at the end of the balcony. "Neither will they stop our plans from coming to fruition." Startled, Briar turned, trying to discern a shape in the darkness. "Yesterday, my darling queen was premature in the execution of our plans, out of concern for me, but events must proceed as they are written. To a degree."

Briar squinted, still unable to see him. But the shadow was bulky. The voice deep. "The Holly King, I presume? Show yourself. Or are you a coward, to hide in the shadows? Scared, perhaps, of the Green Man?" Briar knew her tone was risky, but she was sick of waiting, and sick of this couple who had turned her home into a nightmare.

He laughed. "Scared? No. Wary of his power, yes. I would be a fool not to be. He wants his portion of the year, but I want to keep it. I want my brother to die."

Briar's pulse quickened at the confirmation of what they all had feared. "That's ridiculous. You will subvert all nature. Life itself!"

The queen merely laughed. "But what is that to us? We who live in the wintry north have no need of sunshine and summer."

"So you'll condemn everyone else?" Briar's power was building with her anger. "Besides. It's impossible."

"No, it's not." The man stepped out of the shadows, and Briar stumbled back at the sight of him.

He was huge, broad-shouldered, and dressed in layers of greenery. His thick, dark, curly hair was silvered in places, and it framed wild eyes that glowed like coals. Corded muscles rippled on his arms, and he wore a crown of holly leaves and carried a staff that writhed with living vines. He towered over her and the queen. Briar had imagined that he would be weak at the end of his reign. But far from it. He was robust, with an intensity that rippled off him. He bristled with...*life*. That was the only word for it. And he emitted the rich, earthy scent of forests. But that wasn't surprising. His crown of holly housed a small robin, and the vines from his staff curled around his arms and legs, actually growing on him. However, within the vibrant greenery was evidence of death—withered leaves, brown stems—and a dusting of snow covered everything.

And more than that, he was part of her Green Man. She knew it.

"You feel him, don't you?" Briar asked him. "My Green Man. But you know, I have only a tiny part of him. I don't understand why you need me. It's just as you said. Every year, you fight. That's tonight. He's due here anyway—or wherever it is you duel to the death."

"Oh, child," the queen sighed as she stood next to the Holly King, resting her hand on his arm. "In our world, it is only ever symbolic. As Jack has told you, for six months I am alone, while the Oak King rules. But in this world, things are different. We can kill him for good."

"But you are a part of a whole! Don't you see?" She appealed to the Holly King. "You will only weaken yourself!"

"No. I will grow stronger. Our power will not be split between the two of us!" The Holly King's eyes flashed with anger. "You think you understand, but you do not." He uttered words that Briar couldn't discern, and a wrenching feeling from deep in her core made her cry out.

"What are you doing?"

"Calling my brother."

Briar doubled over in pain, almost falling to the floor, but the sensation didn't last long. The pain vanished as the Green Man unfurled like a fresh leaf deep in her core, and the air shimmered around her. She felt as light as a feather as a summer breeze gusted through her, carrying the scent of blossoms. The promise of spring.

In seconds, another man stood next to her. He was as tall and broad as the Holly King, but the leaves and greenery that clothed him were a pale, fresh green, and acorns nestled in his huge crown. His hair was golden brown, like sunshine on a forest stream, and when he looked at her, she felt all her fears evaporate. There was no grey in his hair, though, and he looked different to how he had looked in Newton's garden only hours before.

Ignoring his brother and the queen, he bowed low and lifted her hand to his lips. "Briar. You look as enchanting as always. You will allow me to escort you to the feast, I hope."

"Escort me? Well, yes, of course." *Were they actually going to participate in the feast? Was the fight to take place in front of everyone?* It certainly didn't sound like she would be killed if the queen wanted to take her to her home. She couldn't comprehend it. It was madness.

If the Oak King had any idea of her confusion, he didn't address it. Instead, he smiled, and only then did he turn to his brother and the queen. "My brother and his Winter Queen. I wish I could say it's a pleasure, but instead we go through the rounds again. I much preferred other years, when we merely pretended to fight. But thank you for arranging the perfect companion."

The Holly King laughed. "We haven't pretended for many years. And this year you hide in a witch!"

Briar froze, staring at the Oak King. Her Green Man. "You hid in me? I don't understand."

The queen smirked, eyes dancing with malice as she stared at Briar. "You thought he was helping you? No. He saw his chance to hide and took it! Trying to avoid defeat."

"Not true," the Oak King shot back. "They are trying to confuse you, Briar." He turned to his brother. "I was always going to face you. It is written in the Wheel. It is inevitable. I didn't hide at Litha, did I? I could have avoided you then, sought to extend my own reign, but I didn't. Your thoughts, Holly, have been poisoned by the witch. Enough of this. I am hungry, and the feast awaits. We will fight, as always, before midnight." He extended his arm to Briar. "Time to greet our guests. We will await you two, in the hall."

Helena marched in the parade, confident that the voluminous layers of her green dress, cloak, and green makeup under a crown of leaves would disguise her enough that no one would recognise her.

She could barely recognise the others in their group, so the guards would have no chance, especially with only flaming torches to offer illumination. Only the Nephilim were more recognisable because of their height, but even so, it was unlikely the queen or Jack would know about them—unless the imp had told them; they hadn't found him after the fight. Besides, they had all minor glamour spells cast over themselves to add confusion. Not that Shadow needed one. Her own fey glamour meant she blended in all too well. Helena admired her. She was far from her own world, yet in a very short time had made a place for herself here.

And yet, right now, Shadow must have divided loyalties. She might hate the sprites and imps, and might profess to want to stay with Gabe, but now she had a real chance to return to her own world once they rid White Haven of the queen. Would she go? Helena had watched her with Gabe and his brothers. Shadow loved Gabe, she was sure of it. *But would it be enough?*

Helena shook her head to dispel her thoughts. They were not her business. She had her own objectives here. Ever since Jack had taken her prisoner and then paraded her on the stage for entertainment, she had wanted to kill him. She hadn't lied when she told Avery that she was all right, because she was—unlike Meg, the woman who had been with her. However, men like Jack, and their presumptuous attitude that everything was for the taking, ate at her. Many men were like that in her time, and some women, and there were still people like it now. Arrogant and entitled, with a need to control or oppress whoever showed the slightest spark of individuality or spirit. When she was young, she had been foolish enough to fall in love with such a man—before her husband, of course. *Thaddeus Faversham*. The man who had created the circumstances that had led to her death.

She saw him in Caspian, even all these centuries later. His looks though, not his actions. And now he was working with Eve to free White Haven of this monstrous woman. When she had wanted to inhabit Clea's body, it had been for fun—not for this. So yes, she would find Jack, and she would have her revenge and stop him for good.

She cracked her staff on the ground as she walked, ignoring the cheering crowds on either side of the road who stood in front of the snow drifts. The roads were easy to navigate as the constant passage of sleighs up and down the road had compacted the snow, making it comfortable to walk on. However, in Clea's body, Helena struggled, even though the pace was slow. As the palace loomed ahead, dazzling with lights that glistened off the ice and snow, it was the thought of Jack that spurred her on.

Then the horn blew, the drumming stopped, and a deathly silence fell. From the huge balcony high above came a fanfare of trumpets, and then a blaze of lights. Above them was the Winter Queen, her ice crown glistening, and next to her an enormous man who could only be the Holly King.

Her voice boomed around them. "Welcome to the Yule Feast! Let the festivities commence."

El lay on her back, eyes closed, pretending to sleep should any guards check on her.

However, she was far from sleepy. She was searching for Bear, her familiar. The relief of having her memories and magic return was overwhelming. She had felt ridiculous for continuing to cry, but she had obviously needed to. When she had finished, she was clearheaded and resolute.

She needed to escape from the cell and find the other prisoners, and then she would locate her coven and find a way to destroy the queen.

It was dark now, she could tell from the flare of torchlight down the passageways and the sound of distant drumming. The Yuletide parade, she presumed. However, she turned her thoughts inward and called to Bear. It didn't take long. Within seconds he appeared in her mind, and his deep, rumbling voice helped to stir her power. Then, with astonishing speed, he was prowling around her small cell, making it seem even smaller by comparison. His musky scent washed over her, fuelling her magic even more.

"I am very pleased to see you again," she told him aloud as she sat up. Although, she had a trace of guilt, too. She had only contacted him once since Samhain. She wasn't as comfortable with her familiar as the rest of her coven was.

"Even though I unnerved you?"

"It was not you so much, it was everyone else I could hear at the same time. It can be too much!"

"But it doesn't have to be that way. Just you and me, then?"

"Yes, please. Although, if you have news of the others, that would be good."

"Why don't you travel with me, and we'll explore together? You remember how to?"

"I doubt I am ever likely to forget."

El closed her eyes and lay on the bed again, and suddenly found herself in Bear. He passed through the wall as if it didn't exist, and paced down the corridor. Everything looked different. The flames seemed brighter, and she could see the queen's magic woven through everything.

After hours being cooped up, she relished the sensation of freedom. "*Show me everything*," she instructed.

Caspian sat in Eve's protection spell, safely cocooned from the inclement weather, a fire burning merrily between them.

Eve's spell was well underway. He had watched her with admiration as she controlled so much power with ease. She had laid out a pentagram on the ground, set candles on each point in the appropriate colour, burned a myriad of herbs, calling to the four elements as she did so, and then layered incantations, one upon the next. Already, the sky was changing above them. The thick pall of cloud was turning dark purple and black, and the air was thickening like soup.

"I don't understand how another weather system can get in here if she's sealed the whole town?" he asked, puzzled.

"It can't, is the simple answer. I realised that as soon as I arrived. This place exists as if it's in a vacuum. The walls—the bubble—ensures that. But fortunately, I can do things others can't." Eve smiled mischievously. "I can make weather systems from scratch. It's not as if we're missing an element. And I'm making a big one. It's gathering power, and combined with your mastery of air, it will blow her walls apart."

"And White Haven?" Caspian asked, as the repercussions became clear.

"That's where it gets tricky. I need to keep it to the outskirts—and her palace."

"You didn't mention that earlier."

"I think they all have enough to worry about, don't you?"

# Twenty-Six

A s soon as Reuben entered the huge courtyard where the snaking line led to the grandiose front doors of the palace, he and Helena cast the shadow spell over themselves and Zee, and they retreated to a dark corner away from the flickering torches.

It was easy enough to fade into the background in the huge space, despite the heavy presence of guards. Everyone was still filing into the palace, and a large group still gathered behind them, waiting to get in. The atmosphere was festive, excitable even. In any other circumstances Reuben would have loved it, but he filed it away to recreate when they weren't ruled by a power-crazed queen and her malignant sprites. Now, he needed to find El.

"We need to get through that door on the right," Helena whispered.

"There are half a dozen doors on the right," Zee pointed out.

"The one in the corner," Helena said. "It's the one Jack led me through earlier. There's a long corridor beyond it, and a few turns, but I think I can remember the way."

They followed Helena's barely visible body through the crowds, and with a whispered spell, the door opened, and they slipped inside. Instantly, the babble of conversations and strains of music vanished, replaced by the weighty silence of endless stone.

Reuben grimaced. "This place already feels like a prison."

"There are worse places here," Helena informed them as they hurried down the long corridor that ran deeper and deeper into the palace. "Raven said the main prisoner cells are in the working courtyard at the rear. That's where he found El before. The barracks and stables are there, and the entrances to the kitchen and storerooms. But I didn't see any individual cells. Just a kind of holding cell. A big room."

They passed various utilitarian rooms that looked like offices along the way. Reuben supposed that even in the Otherworld there would be need of staff to organise various things. The queen sounded—and looked, from the brief evidence he'd seen of her—demanding. But there were no staff around now, and no signs of the guards.

"This is the room we were all held in earlier," Helena said, pausing before a heavy wooden door to listen for voices before opening it on an empty space. "Damn it. Not surprising, really."

"But I hear noise from down the corridor," Zee said, and Reuben heard rather than saw Zee adjust his stance and ready his crossbow. "Let me go first."

The corridors in this part of the palace were narrower, with low ceilings and zero ornamentation, but they carried sound easily. Screams and shouts echoed down the passageways from some distance ahead, but Reuben couldn't understand a word of the sibilant language.

"It's a fight!" Zee said, breaking into a run.

They eventually rounded a corner into a square area with chairs around a small table, but it was a scene of chaos. Three sprites in guard uniforms lay dead, and half a dozen others were fighting a huge bear that had reared up on its back legs. It roared and swiped with its huge claws, but the guards danced away, jabbing the creature with long spears. It was bloodied and injured, but it didn't stop it from raking the closest guard's chest into ribbons of skin and bone.

"It's El's familiar!" Reuben yelled, blasting the guards with a ball of fire, and he cast off their shadow spell so that Bear could see him easily.

Zee took aim and shot down three guards in quick succession, and Helena finished the final two off by throwing them against the wall with a bone-crunching crash. But another guard disappeared down a side corridor, already shouting for help.

"Leave him to me," Zee said, sprinting after him. "And don't wait! Get out if you can."

Bear was already limping off down the main corridor, past a row of doors. Reuben's heart pounded. *If Bear was injured, what did it mean for El?* He didn't know if he could face what was to come.

"Why are we seeing Bear?" he asked Helena. "He should be invisible!"

"We're straddling worlds here, Reuben. It's probably some kind of fey magic. What are you waiting for? Go follow him." Shouts erupted from behind the locked doors. Helena pushed him after Bear. "Go find El, I'll sort these."

Bear had rounded a corner and was slumped outside a door, looking up at him with pain-glazed eyes.

Heart pounding, Reuben yelled, "El, I'm coming in!"

He cast a spell to unlock the door and eased it open. El lay inside on the bed, unmoving.

Gabe seated himself at the end of a long table, next to Shadow, and close to the entrance.

They aimed to prevent more guards entering the hall later.

Nahum, Avery, Alex, Estelle, all of Ghost OPS, Sally, Dan, and the three police officers were all inside the Great Hall, all seated in various places, all masking their tension under bright smiles. Barak, Niel, Ash, and Eli had not entered with the others. They had taken advantage of the crowd to hide and make their way to the rear courtyard where the main barracks were. Gabe hoped they hadn't been seen. Their plan was to stop as many guards as they could from responding to the potential chaos later.

So far, there was no sign they had been discovered. The guards, although vigilant, looked generally unconcerned—until trumpets summoned everyone's attention, and two figures appeared at the entrance to the hall. The guards rapidly stood to attention as a courtier announced loudly, "The Oak King and his consort, Briar Ashworth, The Oak Queen."

Gabe gasped at Briar's appearance, her hand on the arm of a virile, muscular man dressed in green leaves and vines, who bowed deeply to the hall. Briar gave a brief nod, and then both progressed in a stately manner down the central space between the towering pillars. Gabe wasn't the only one surprised. The gasp rippled around the entire room, and Avery and Alex, who were seated a short distance away, froze, but then quickly masked their surprise.

Briar looked spectacular in her spring green dress and coiled hair, her bearing regal. Her eyes darted everywhere, alighting on her friends briefly, a warning in her smile, as the band in the gallery struck up a tune. Everyone watched their progression to the table on the raised dais at the end of the room.

Gabe leaned close to Shadow, mouth to her ear. "What the fuck is happening?"

"Our Winter Queen has decided to enact the full rites of Yule tonight, and it seems she has decided Briar must play a part."

"As the Oak Queen? Is that a thing?"

"It seems it is now." Shadow's face creased with concern. "The Green Man's consort would normally be the Goddess—in summer, at least. But this Winter Queen is the Holly King's consort. Perhaps she seeks to even things out. She likes a spectacle, that's for sure."

"But what does this mean for later?"

"I suspect the fight between the Holly King and the Oak King will be a real one, but as for Briar's role..." She shrugged. "The queen likes games. This place has all the attributes of one of the feasts of the Royal Houses. They like games, too. I'm now wondering if that's who she is."

Shadow had explained all about the Royal Houses of the fey; the princes, dukes and duchesses, and other noble titles of the ancient ruling fey class, and the fact that they lived in magnificent under-palaces under great green mounds, keeping to themselves and dancing their long lives away. Her gaze was distant as she drank everything in, her hand clutching her goblet of wine.

Gabe swallowed, needing to ask what he had been putting off for hours. "Does this make you want to go home? I mean, we're hoping to send her back—palace and all. You could go."

She turned to him, violet eyes serious for once. "Is that what you want? You want me to leave?"

"Of course not! That's the last thing I want. I love you, and of course I want you to stay here. But equally, I know that you miss your home—despite what you've said." He floundered, horrified at even the thought that she would go. She could be credited for everything that was good in his life, including their business. She was the original driving force behind it. "But I desperately want you to stay."

"You could come with me."

"You mean you're thinking about it?" *Would he follow her? Could he leave his brothers...and his future niece or nephew?* Nahum would never leave now. And he was pretty sure the others wouldn't, either. "Shadow? Answer me!"

But before she could speak, the trumpets resounded again. Gabe didn't turn around. He didn't care to. Instead, he stared at Shadow, drinking in her wild beauty—especially tonight, dressed as a hunter. However she wasn't looking at him. She was looking at the door, and reluctantly he turned as the courtier announced the Winter Queen and her consort, the Holly King. *Interesting. A switch of consort roles.*

In the entrance was a spectacularly beautiful woman, with pale white skin and raven dark hair, and her Otherness rolled off her. She wore a dress of white and grey feathers, a huge crown of ice crystals on her head. She was undoubtedly fey. Next to her was another virile, huge man, dressed in dark green and browns, and crowned with dark green holly leaves and bright red berries.

The queen took a step forward, an imperious smile hovering on her lips as if a full smile might crack her perfect façade. "I would like to say a brief word of thanks before the feast commences. Thank you for joining us for our Yuletide celebrations. I know we do this every year, but I feel I still must extend my thanks. It is important we join our energies together as the Wheel turns and the Holly King gives way to the Oak King. Today the fight will be even more spectacular, and once the victor is proclaimed, he will be anointed with a new crown as befits the King of Winter. In the meantime, enjoy the first few courses before we break for entertainment."

After the flash of a jubilant smile, they proceeded down the aisle to join Briar and the Oak King at the head of the table.

Just as Gabe was hoping the feast could actually get underway, there was another fanfare of trumpets, and the courtier announced, "The King of Ice and Snow."

A slim man with a shock of white hair and deep blue eyes stepped into the doorway. He was youthful and good-looking with a dangerous smile that assessed everyone as he studied the room, striking a pose in a well-cut grey suit with a long-tailed frock coat. He was looking for the witches or Barak, Gabe was sure. They had all been studied closely as they entered, but no one had been questioned or detained.

Excited chatter followed the latest arrivals as they progressed to the table at the far end, and from the conversation to Gabe's right, there was only excitement at the coming night ahead. Already, the smell of food was intoxicating.

But Gabe cared for none of it. He turned back to Shadow, but her gaze followed them down the hall, almost greedily, and Gabe had the feeling that he had already lost her.

Barak and his brothers had successfully evaded the guards, and they flew to the roof of the palace, settling on the edge that overlooked the rear service courtyard to watch the activity below.

Barak, like Niel, was dressed as a hunter, while Eli and Ash were portraying Herne. They had painted themselves with camouflage markings for their costumes, extending it over their upper body as well as their face, and it helped them now, even though it was much darker here, away from the flare of the hundreds of torches, and the fanfare of the feast and the parade.

"There's the kitchen entrance," Barak said, pointing. "There will be a way into the Great Hall from there. But from what the witches have said, most of the cooks are from White Haven—Jago, Alex's chef, included.

"So, we need to get them out, too," Niel said, nodding. "I presume that is the barracks." He gestured to the long building at the rear of the courtyard. Although a couple of guards stood at the back gate, the barracks looked mostly empty. "All the guards' attention will be elsewhere—hopefully."

"Where did Raven say he saw El the first time?" Ash asked.

Barak shuffled around. "Down through that door."

Ash drew his sword. "If we take out the two guards on the gate, I'll head there and make sure there are no other prisoners."

"Where is that damn bird?" Eli asked, annoyed. "He's supposed to be relaying information."

"He's been gone for hours," Barak said, worried. "Perhaps he's stuck somewhere."

"Or imprisoned, too," Niel suggested.

Eli shook his head. "I doubt that a familiar could be imprisoned, but the queen and Jack have unusual magic, so I guess it's possible. But if he doesn't appear soon, how are we to know what's happening? We're presuming there'll be some kind of ritual, but how will we be alerted?"

"We improvise by spying through the kitchen," Barak said. "There will be passages that lead to the main hall. That's the only way. Then we know when to start evacuating or fight, or whatever else is needed." He looked up, feeling a change in air pressure. "Eve's weather system is kicking in. Have you noticed the sky over there?"

Above the town, the thick, snow-laden clouds were darker, and it felt warmer, too.

"We're very close to the wall here," Ash observed. "This could be either a really easy way out, or an absolute disaster. If the queen's magic breaks down here, we might end up anywhere."

"Not anywhere, brother," Niel said softly. "The Otherworld. Come on. We're wasting time. Let's do what we can before the madness begins. Kill the guards on the gate, and then we attack the barracks."

Barak hadn't forgotten the sharp spears of the sprites as they tried to stop him from rescuing Briar. He was looking forward to killing as many as he could get his hands on.

El was breathless, her wounds were on fire, and her limbs ached, but the stone was cool beneath her as she slumped on the floor.

She barely took in the fact that a blond man dressed in some mad costume was rushing towards her, before he blasted the door next to her and ran inside. It was *her* Reuben. The man she loved, and he'd come to save her. *But where was he going?*

"*El,*" a deep voice growled in her head. "*Get out of me now!*"

"*What? I don't understand.*"

"*You are making me too real! It's a trick of the queen's magic. We have bonded far too strongly. Get out, now!*"

El couldn't think straight. She was cold and she was aching, and her wounds throbbed from the sharp ice spears the sprites used. "*But we are one. I am you. I mean, this is me.*"

"*No! You are El, I am Bear. Your familiar. Get out now! You are killing both of us. And do not try to bond with me again here!*"

El experienced a weird mental shove that sent her hurtling out of the huge, aching body on the floor, and with a shock she landed back in a body that felt quite different. Lighter. Smaller. And much colder. Not to mention, someone was shaking her.

"El! Wake up. It's Reuben. Please come back to me."

Despite her bone-deep weariness, she felt herself smile, and she struggled to speak. She licked her dry lips. "Reuben?"

Suddenly, she was pulled into a familiar broad chest, and strong arms wrapped around her, his hand pressing her head to him. She inhaled deeply, smelling the sea, and the unique scent that was all Reuben. She wasn't a bear. She was El. A witch who mastered fire and metals. *But why did she feel so bad?*

"It's Reuben, El," he whispered in her ear, "and I swear I'll never leave you again. Just open your eyes and tell me that you're okay."

"I think I am. I'm thirsty." She forced her eyes open, blinking in the light of the torch outside her door, and lifted her head to look up at him. "Look at you. You're so gorgeous. How could I have ever forgotten what you looked like?"

His blue eyes filled with tears. "You remember me now, though. And who you are?"

"I do. I'm a witch. Like you and the others. That bitch made me forget."

"That's my girl, but ignore her. What happened with Bear?"

"I bonded with him to go exploring once I regained my memories and my power. I thought it would be safer with him until I knew what was happening. But something happened with the guards. Bear said we bonded too strongly." She struggled out of his embrace, even though it was the last thing she wanted to do, and sat up. "He's injured. Where is he?"

"He's gone." He nodded to the door. "You two somehow must have become too real. He's hurt, and that means you are, too." He stroked her hair. "Look at what they did to you. I've never seen you so filthy."

"I did this to myself. Or some of it, at least. Raven told me to disguise myself."

"You're still beautiful." He cupped her cheeks in his hands and kissed her gently. "Are you strong enough to move? We have to get out of here."

"Yes. I'm okay." She flexed her fingers. "I have magic, so I'm good."

Helena appeared at the door to the cell, a broad smile on her face. "Hey, El. Good to see you again. I've freed all the prisoners. It's time to get them out!"

Newton fretted at the ridiculous farce that was being played out around him, all the time wearing a stupid fake grin on his face and trying not to stare at Briar's spectacular beauty. Or the big, handsome lug that sat next to her, bristling with vitality and sex appeal. *Bastard.*

"Guv," Moore said, leaning in close. "You looked crazed. Stop staring at Briar."

"I'm not."

"You're practically salivating, while looking like you want to rip the Oak King's head off. He's on our side, remember?"

"Is he? He's sitting very close to Briar."

"As her consort! She doesn't look particularly thrilled, either. I'd save your anger for the blond twat sitting next to her on the other side.

If you're not careful, he'll spot you staring and the last thing you want to do is to make him suspicious."

Briar was sandwiched between the Oak King and Jack Frost. Moore was right. If anything, Jack—the King of Ice and Snow, apparently, otherwise known as Bastard Sprite Number One—was paying her even more attention. The good thing was that she was ignoring him as much as she could. However, the whole event was wearing thin. They had been eating and drinking for almost an hour as the first courses were brought out by a small army of serving staff. The dishes were tiny things that barely assuaged his hunger. There was no doubt that the food was magnificent, but as the time advanced, the more the food tasted like cardboard.

The rest of their group looked similarly strained. Kendall was making polite conversation with her neighbours, and Ghost OPS, seated a short distance away down the long table, were fidgeting. Newton had spotted the community police officers, but hadn't had a chance to speak to them. They looked happy though, laughing and drinking with the rest of White Haven.

Newton generally thought the event was going smoothly, and the queen looked at ease and thoroughly in control. That was a good thing, as far as Newton was concerned. That meant she had no idea what was going on—unless her guards had already caught the rest of the team. Every now and again a courtier would come and whisper in her ear, and she would nod and pass on an instruction. Only once did she look annoyed, and whatever she said had the courtier scurrying down the hall.

Finally, a huge bell rang out, summoning everyone's attention to the table at the front as the Winter Queen stood up. Her voice carried clear across the hall as she made a short speech about the pleasure of Yule and the fight between the Oak King and the Holly King and the passing of one season to another. She made it all sound very reasonable. A proper Yuletide celebration.

Until she said, "But there are still a group of individuals who must be found tonight. Right now, in fact." It seemed as if her gaze fell on every single one of them. "Over the past twenty-four hours they have sought to undermine this feast and the ritual that will take place. An attempt to subvert our traditions. We were driven to perform actions we would rather not, when we had to threaten to kill two women in the square today." A trace of regret crossed her face, and Newton had to admit she was a good actor. "Fortunately, Briar stepped forward to save them, and being crowned Oak Queen is her reward." The crowd cheered, but Briar remained emotionless as she watched the queen. "But as the King of Ice and Snow, my brother, warned then, we still expect them to hand themselves in. And now is your chance, because I have no doubt that they are here now! You have five minutes in which to declare yourselves, the time in which it will take for the prisoners to be brought in here. For every minute after that that you make me wait, a prisoner will die."

All excitement from the crowd vanished, and a deathly silence fell.

"Yes," the queen acknowledged, a trace of sympathy in her voice as she acknowledged the difficulty of the situation. "It's hard to celebrate once death is amongst us, which is why I urge you to give up those individuals now. Look to your neighbours for Alex Bonneville, Elspeth Robinson, and Avery Hamilton. I also urge you to find any strangers amongst you, for I have become aware that there are people here who trespass upon our celebrations, and are only present to cause trouble. There is no point sheltering them. To hand them to me now will save bloodshed. For have no doubt, there will be bloodshed should they not be found, and the ones to die will be your relatives or friends, those who are detained right now. Their misdeeds will be forgiven—*if* those individuals are found. I urge you to do the right thing."

A wave of unease and murmurs ran through the room as people shuffled to look at those around them, eyes narrowed, and the guards positioned on the periphery started to move closer.

"It's easy!" the queen declared breezily. "We will take them away now and the feast can continue as planned. The Holly King and the Oak King are ready to entertain you with their fight. But first, we must have justice!"

Newton didn't dare look at where Avery and Alex were sitting, but he found himself under scrutiny from his neighbours, and he knew that one way or another, the time for action was imminent. They had hoped to take advantage of the fight between the kings, but that was clearly not going to happen.

A man on a far table shot to his feet and pointed to a woman dressed as a piskie. "I think that's Avery Hamilton!"

The woman shrieked. "I am not! I am nothing like her!" She stood up and pulled off her wig and headdress.

More rumblings followed, and Newton exchanged a glance with Moore and Kendall to ready their hidden weapons. Their role in all this was the same as the other humans on their team—they were to evacuate everyone and get them away from the palace, and that might involve fighting for their lives. Then a guard hurried to the queen's side, a look of pure fright on his face. The queen's response was swift.

Ice crackled from her fingertips and the temperature in the room plummeted as veins of ice crept along the walls and around the room, icicles formed overhead, and an icy mist bloomed around them.

Her voice screeched like broken glass. "Seal the palace!" She marched around the Oak King and dragged Briar to her feet. "Change of plans. I will find new people to sacrifice, and the first one to die will be Briar, unless someone answers my questions, now!"

However, Briar did something no one expected, and the room erupted into chaos.

## Twenty-Seven

Briar had anticipated what the queen would do to her, and opted to attack in the way she would least expect.

She reared back and punched the queen hard in the face. Blood exploded from her nose, splattering across her feather dress and pale skin. She may be fey, but she still experienced pain. The queen reeled backwards, arms flailing. Knowing Jack would attack in seconds, Briar grabbed a plate off the table and smashed it over his head as he stood to respond, and then kicked his chair out from under him, sending him sprawling.

She rounded on the queen again, grabbed a knife off the table and stabbed her, aiming for her chest. Despite her shock and pain, the queen reacted quickly, twisting to her side. Briar stabbed her in the shoulder instead, and followed it up with a blast of magic that propelled her over the table and into the exhibition ring where the fight was to take place.

At any moment she expected Jack to attack, and she whirled around to defend herself, but he was already fighting for his life against an enraged Nahum. She had no need to worry about the Holly King, either. He was already brawling with the Oak King, and the roar of their encounter and the clash of their swords was almost louder than the screams of the crowd.

Briar scrambled over the table, sending glasses, plates and food flying, and sent a wave of fireballs at the queen.

But the queen, despite being covered in blood, was making a swift recovery. She countered Briar's magic with her own, shooting darts of ice towards her. Briar threw up a protection shield with a sweep of her arm and batted the darts away. If the queen thought Briar was left weakened by calling the Green Man from her, she was gravely mistaken. Briar was surrounded by her element in the Great Hall. The thick branches of greenery that decorated the space and the huge, stone building that surrounded them all spoke to her.

Briar kicked her shoes off, planted her feet firmly on the ground, and cast a spell that shattered the flagstones beneath them. A deep crack opened up, ripping the space between them into a jigsaw of cracks and crevices, and a deafening boom cut through all the shouts. A jagged hole opened up beneath the queen, but with speed that made Briar blink, she sealed it with ice.

And with horror, Briar saw that the ice around the room was thickening as its icy fingers tried to close off the entrance.

Shadow was in her element. Guards were converging on the crowd in all directions, but she and Gabe had positioned themselves in the doorway, keeping as many of them at bay as possible, and maintaining a way out for the locals.

A huge stone plinth that displayed a bust of the queen was just outside the huge doors, and Shadow pushed the bust to the ground and nimbly leapt onto the plinth. Once up high, she fired on the guards with her bow and arrow, killing many before they even knew she was there. Gabe ploughed through the others at ground level, often fighting several sprites at once.

Alex and Avery joined them, casting spell after spell at the sprites and the advancing ice. Dylan, Stan, and Cassie had fought their way to the Great Hall's entrance, urging the crowd to race home as they managed to keep the doorway open. The locals didn't need much encouragement. They rushed out in a stampeding horde.

Shadow took advantage of her elevated position to check her surroundings. Unfortunately, many of the White Haven locals were still marooned in pockets around the Great Hall, especially on the upper levels, with guards blocking the way out. Sally and Dan were with one group, throwing chairs and grabbing anything they could to escape, but they were pinned in as a ring of guards tightened around them. Newton and Kendall were similarly engaged on the other side of the room, but Moore was leading a group through the upturned tables and chairs with Hamid and Kev, the two community police officers.

Estelle couldn't help anyone because she was fighting sprites that were trying to attack Nahum and Briar while they were battling Jack and the queen. The two kings were meanwhile locked in their own battle. At least there were no more guards arriving through the servants' doors at the rear of the hall, or any other staff, either.

Shadow focussed her attention on the stranded humans. She couldn't aim at the guards with all the locals in between, but high above was the now deserted minstrels' gallery. She yelled, "Gabe. I need a ride!"

He extended his wings and she leaped into his arms.

"You didn't answer me earlier, Shadow," he said as he flew across the room.

Guilt nagged at her, but she didn't need any distractions. "Gabe, this is hardly the time to talk about our future."

"Are you fucking kidding me? This is the perfect time! Or were all those whispered sweet nothings in my ear exactly that? Nothing! Was I just a distraction until you could get home?"

"Will you stop being an idiot and put me down? I'm in a killing mood, not a chatting mood."

"Will we even have time to talk later?" He deposited her into the minstrels' gallery, glaring at her with a fiery fury she had never seen directed at her.

"Of course we will. Now go and kill more guards and let me do the same! Estelle needs help."

The truth was, she realised as she fired on the unsuspecting guards below, especially the one dragging Sally by the hair, was that she had missed the feeling of fey Otherness. Seeing the sprites and imps, and feeling Jack and the queen's magic was intoxicating—even though they were clearly sociopaths. The feast, the palace, everything was so Other, it left her confused.

And she didn't have time to think about what it all meant now.

Zee pursued the fleeing sprite. He was quick, sprinting down the narrow passageways. Zee took aim a couple of times but missed, and the sprite gained valuable ground.

Zee was being led deeper into the palace complex. Although there were no windows to help orientate him, he was sure he was moving towards the back of the building. He passed offices and areas lined with ceremonial weapons and realised he must be close to the barracks.

He had to kill the sprite now before he alerted the others. Fortunately, the corridors were getting wider and longer. Zee skidded around a corner, just in time to see the sprite a long way ahead. Zee took a breath, brought the crossbow up and shot him in the back. The sprite dropped to the ground, blood pooling around him.

Wary, he waited, listening for any signs of other guards, but this area of the palace was deserted. He stepped over the dead body, and found himself at an intersection of passages. If he didn't go back, and he wasn't even sure if he'd find his way, he needed to find his brothers and help them. If he carried on, he might find the barracks or the kitchen, and reach them that way. But as he stood in the quiet, he heard a frenzied screeching and a flapping of wings. Throwing open a door, he was almost battered by a huge, black bird that flew over him and into the corridor, scattering feathers everywhere, before perching on a mounted shield on the wall.

Zee frowned. "Raven?"

"Of course I am!"

"You bloody cantankerous bird! The queen might keep a menagerie, for all I know. What happened?"

"I got locked inside, what do you think happened? I've been stuck here for hours! Why are you here? What's going on? I found El!"

"Don't worry, so did we. And Bear, although he didn't look too good. Forget them for now, Reuben and Helena are dealing with it. Where are we? Can I get to the barracks? Or even the Great Hall from here?"

"The kitchen is close, and there's a way to the hall from there. Follow me."

Barak wiped his bloody sword on a discarded jacket belonging to the queen's guard, and left the barracks filled with a dozen dead sprites to join his brothers in the courtyard.

It had been a hard and bitter battle. The sprites were good fighters, and he and his brothers were all injured with cuts, grazes, bruises, and broken feathers. Barak winced as he walked, sure he also had some broken ribs.

Niel was studying the sky as Barak stepped into the courtyard, and he asked, "All done?"

"Done. No one will fight for the queen in there anymore." He grimaced at the scene of carnage in the courtyard. "Or out here, by the look of it."

"Good, because we need to get moving." Niel pointed upwards at the ominous clouds. A strong wind was already twisting around the courtyard. "Eve's spell is taking effect. Ash and Eli are evacuating the kitchen, and from there we attack the hall. Ready for the next round?"

"Always."

Helena stood in the main courtyard, draped in the shadow spell, just outside the door that led them to the prisoners. Reuben and El waited in the corridor with the captives they'd freed.

She was waiting for an opportune time to let the prisoners escape from the palace, but so far it was impossible. A dozen guards were split between the entrance to the courtyard and the grand doors that led to the Great Hall. Any attempt that she made to kill or incapacitate the guards would be seen by the others. She either had to wait for a distraction, create one herself, or use a spell big enough to lay them all out. The last thing she wanted was to create panic and draw even more guards out.

She fidgeted and shuffled her feet, casting a warming spell to keep away the cold. The scent of food drifted to her, and she heard the strains of music and the sound of laughter. It sounded as if the feast was going well.

But out here, things seemed tense. The clouds churned, and occasional flashes of lightning punctured the sky. The guards started to shuffle, talking together in low voices, and one of them pointed to the sky behind her. Helena crept to the edge of the courtyard and stood at the gate to see what they were staring at.

In a corner of White Haven that she knew to be Avery's garden, was a column of swirling air that pierced the clouds above, making them rotate slowly too. On the periphery of the town, where the wall sealed them all in, things looked even weirder. The thick mist was evaporating into thin tendrils that drifted up on currents of air. They were caught up in the vortex, sweeping around the entire town in slow motion. Now that she was at the gate, she could see the wall that cut the sea off and butted up against part of the castle. It was a seething mass of warm and cold air, and it was doing very odd things to the castle. Ice was already melting and dripping down the walls, and the resulting mist was hanging over the battlements. They didn't have time to wait; Eve's spell was taking effect — if only she could continue it without the guards attacking. Unfortunately, the root of it was all too obvious. A squadron of soldiers was already making their way into town on sleighs, and Helena knew exactly where they were going.

She raced back to the door, intending to warn the others, when a roar erupted from inside the palace, and the guards started to close the huge gates to trap them inside.

Helena threw the door open. "Reuben, El, time to go! We need to stop the guards now!" She addressed the frightened men and women who had patiently waited for their chance to escape. "Wait for a moment, and then join the crowd. Run home, stay inside. Do not linger out on the streets! Tell everyone to do the same."

Not waiting for a response, or caring that they would see her perform magic, she whirled around, flinging her arms outwards and casting a spell. She caught three guards in a wave of power that threw them out of the courtyard and into the deep snow outside. She was still covered in her shadow spell, but the other guards were already advancing on her.

Reuben and El ran to help, as the townsfolk who had been at the feast rushed through the huge doors on the other side of the courtyard, trampling the guards in their way. The guards on the gate redoubled their efforts to shut them inside, but El was unleashing fire on them, and Reuben was blasting them out of the doors and against the walls. The sheer numbers of people forced the gates back open again, and the guards were either dead or running away to the rear of the castle.

But Helena wasn't ready to leave yet, and neither were Reuben and El. Forcing their way through the tide of people, they headed to the Great Hall.

Caspian was perched on Avery's garden wall, half an eye on the lane below, and half watching Eve.

He was mesmerised by her spell and her power. He had never seen magic like this, and she had complete mastery of her art. After her initial spells, she had placed a huge cauldron on the fire, suspended by chains from a tripod, and had concocted a potion within it. Once her initial incantations were complete, she had watched and stirred it, adding herbs, roots, feathers, and other natural ingredients as she worked. Then she would chant again, taking up a ladle and stirring clockwise. With every turn of the ladle, and every chant, a column of writhing yellow smoke rose from the cauldron.

Only half an hour ago, she had looked up at him, deadly serious. "This will get bigger—much bigger—and will eventually be seen above this wall. It will attract attention. I hope you're prepared."

"I am, don't worry about me."

She hadn't been exaggerating. The column of smoke had connected to the sky, and with every turn of the ladle, the sky would churn even more. Eve's concentration was now intense. She didn't look away from her potion, except for brief intervals when she looked up at the sky and extended her arms, repeating words of power as she invoked the Gods.

The bitter cold had given way to a muggy, turgid air, and the wall had taken on a sickly hue. The snow was melting, and water trickled down walls and off rooftops. Her spell was effective. Caspian also had a clear view of the palace from his position, and it was looking even murkier up there.

The jingle of sleighbells made him focus closer to home. He called down to Eve. "We have company. You focus on the spell. I'll keep them away."

There was only one way onto Avery's lane behind her shop, and that was down the entrance between her shop and the next one. He used witch-flight to get to her roof, and looked down on the dozen guards disembarking from their sleighs.

All were armed. And all had shed their human illusions. But he was used to fighting them now, and he had the advantage of height. Caspian grinned to himself. *Time for some fun.*

He cast a shield spell at the end of the lane that would prevent them from reaching the garden, and then waited for them all to enter the space. They were moving quietly, and they definitely looked scared. A couple were watching the column of yellow smoke, looking uncertain as to whether or not to proceed. The captain, however, summoned them with a hissed instruction.

Once they were all in the narrow alley between the buildings, Caspian sealed the other end too, trapping them inside. The roofs of both buildings were thick with snow, and he manipulated air to send the snow tumbling from the roofs. Inch by inch, the thick sheets slipped forward until with a rumble, they cascaded onto the sprites below.

Most were buried completely, but others had their arms and head free and were struggling to dig themselves out. A couple pointed upwards, and one or two managed to throw spears at him. But Caspian was too high up, and their aim was poor. Caspian was torn with indecision. To kill them during a fight was one thing, but to kill them while they were trapped and helpless was something else entirely.

He called down to them. "Your time here is ending, and will come swiftly now. You can see we are destroying the queen's power. It is inevitable." At least he hoped it was. "You can leave now, and head back to your home by any way you can manage, or you die here. Your choice."

"The queen is powerful, and you cannot destroy her magic, or ours," one sprite answered boldly. He raised his hands as Jack had done the day before at Stormcrossed Manor, trying to raise an ice wall.

He succeeded for a short while, until the ice crumbled only a few feet above his head, and he lowered his hands in dismay.

His companions were having hushed conversation as they frantically dug their buried companions out of the snow and didn't try to help him.

Caspian continued, "You see? Already we are making you weaker. Is her battle your fight? Or do you choose your own destiny?"

"She will kill us for abandoning her."

"Not if she dies first. If you return to the palace to fight, you will die there, too, at my friends' hands. Choose wisely." Caspian was taking a big risk. If they did return to the palace, they could hurt his friends and undermine their attack, but he could already sense the change in them.

Another sprite shouted at him in his broken English. "Release us. We will return home." He pointed away from the palace. "We have another way."

"I'll watch you go," Caspian warned. "I will stop you if you're lying."

"We do not lie."

Caspian lifted the spell, and watched the guards mount their sleighs and take off towards the wall. They must have a way of creating their own way through the wall, but he would watch them until he was sure.

A sudden wind whipped around him, and he stared at the palace on the hill. Huge chunks of ice were now falling from it, and it seemed that parts of the palace were vanishing, too. He blinked. *Was it an illusion?*

His mouth was suddenly dry. If parts of the castle were already vanishing back into the Other, then his friends and his sister could vanish, too. But he had promised to protect Eve here. If another group attacked and her spell was cut off, then all of their hard work would be for nothing.

Caspian just had to wait and hope.

# Twenty-Eight

Avery wielded strong wind with deadly efficiency as she threw a couple of guards against the wall, and watched them crunch to the floor, unconscious.

The Great Hall was mostly empty of the White Haven locals who were attending the feast, and to her relief, all of her non-magical friends had managed to get out. But there was still stubborn resistance from the guards fighting to get to Briar and the queen, the duelling kings, and Jack and Nahum. Barak, Niel, Ash, Eli, and Zee had all recently arrived through the servants' doors at the rear and had immediately joined the fighting. Some were flying as they fought, others were on the ground, and the rest were fighting on tables, like Shadow. She had abandoned the minstrels' gallery and was fighting two sprites on one of the long tables, crunching through glass, plates, food, and greenery.

Alex was fighting next to Estelle, blasts of power slinging back and forth as they beat back the guards and a group of imps who had joined the fight. Helena had arrived with El and Reuben, and they had also jumped head-first into the fight. Avery had managed to catch El's attention as she ran past. She was relieved to see her friend, but horrified at her appearance. It magnified Avery's anger and determination to get rid of the queen and everything she stood for.

Helena, face etched with fury, fought her way to Nahum's side with Gabe, and was fighting Jack, who was proving a formidable adversary.

The same was true for the queen. Guards were ensuring that no one could get near her and Briar. The women were using anything to hurt each other. Chairs, knives, plates, and even the fallen weapons of the guards. But the queen looked to be wearying, and with every minute that passed the thick ice that had crept around the walls receded.

As for the Oak King and the Holly King...well. Their fight was the most dramatic of all. Vines shot from their hands to choke and smother each other. The garlands sprang to life at their touch, and as the ice receded, the plants took over the hall. The entire place was turning into a forest. Chunks of masonry were falling, and cracks appeared in the stone columns. Avery was debating who she should help when Raven landed on her shoulder.

"You all must leave now. Eve's spell is powerful, and the palace is vanishing."

"What?" Avery thought she was hearing things. "Vanishing?"

"Going back through whatever portal she created to get here. But other things are coming through. The veil between worlds is thin, Avery. Dragons are close. I can hear them. If we aren't out of here soon, we'll all be sucked into the Otherworld."

"But the Oak King has to win!"

"And we need to go."

"If he dies, it will have all been for nothing!"

The bird cocked his head, fixing her with a bold stare. "Whatever the outcome, you will be stuck in the Otherworld. The queen's power is waning, and her spell won't hold. We must leave."

Avery made a snap decision. "Fly around, tell everyone. I'm heading to Briar."

"Don't kill the queen!" The bird screeched. "It might mean the spell collapses when she does! We could go to the Other instantly!"

Avery grabbed one of the huge spears the sprites wielded that was discarded on the floor. With a whirl of air, Avery manifested behind the queen, lifted the spear, and swung it wildly. With an immense crack, she smacked the queen's head, knocking her off her feet. She lay insensible on the ground, blood pooling from the head wound.

Raven screeched. "Are you deaf? You might have killed her!"

Briar looked at Avery in shock, but Avery was staring at the walls of the palace as they shimmered in and out of vision. Beyond them, she could see a vast desert of ice, with peaks curled like frozen waves. "Oh, shit."

Briar had a moment of shock as the Oak King, her Green Man, roared. "Briar! Don't forget your promise!

*The Yule log.*

Briar felt in her pocket and panicked. "The Yule log, Avery. I've lost it!"

"Bollocks to the log. We need to leave!" Avery yelled, "Everyone, get out now!"

She didn't need to tell them twice; it was already obvious. The sprites and imps had made up their own mind. They abandoned their fights and dived through the shimmering walls, back to the Otherworld, and the Nephilim and the witches were preparing to leave, too.

But Jack and the kings kept fighting.

Jack roared with fury. "What have you done to my sister?"

It was all the distraction that Nahum needed. He threw a dagger at Jack, and it sank deep into his chest.

Jack looked down in shock, eyes wide, as he dropped to his knees, then stared at Briar. "I would have given you everything."

"You would have given me nothing but heartbreak and broken promises." She addressed Nahum. "Take Helena and go. All of you!" she raised her voice to the stunned group—her closest friends. "Make sure everyone is out!"

Briar turned away. She needed the sliver of Yule log, and she dropped to her knees, searching amongst the rubble and cracks around them. "Avery, go! I'll find it."

"I'm not leaving you."

Briar snapped her head up and glared at Avery. "Take Alex, now! I will deal with this. All this is because of me, anyway."

"Briar!" Avery's face was twisted with anguish.

"I will find a way out. Go!"

But Avery joined her, regardless. "Briar Ashworth, if you think that I am leaving a member of my coven behind, then you don't know me at all."

"You're a stubborn mule!"

"I'm a loyal friend," Avery spat back. Her long, red hair streamed over her shoulders, and she looked as wild as the dryad she was dressed as. She scrabbled on the floor. "There it bloody is!"

She pointed to the chunk of blackened wood beneath a chair. *Excellent.* It would have fuel to burn.

Briar cast the spell with the invocation she had prepared, and flames flickered along the log. Avery blew a breath of wind at it, and the flames caught hold and ignited the whole log, and then the chair it was next to. In seconds, a massive fire was blazing, and it seemed to renew the Oak King as he fought his brother.

Alex gripped their shoulders. "Ladies, now is not the time to be warming your hands around a fire."

Reuben shouted from behind him. "We're not leaving without you!"

Briar scrambled to her feet, annoyed to find everyone there except for Shadow and Gabe, who seemed to be arguing on the far side of the hall—and the fighting kings, of course.

The Holly King seemed to be losing now, retreating before his brother.

She tore her gaze away, back to her friends. "What are you all waiting for? You need to go!"

A wild wind was howling through the palace now, coming from the world beyond the vanishing palace, and Briar could feel it tugging her closer. Wild songs were calling to her, and she remembered Jack's words about hearing the celestial bodies, and lights that would dance along the horizon.

Any second now she could be pulled through. "All of you, leave now. I'll join you soon."

"Briar!" Avery was clearly furious and upset—a dangerous combination.

Briar only smiled at her. "You can't use witch-flight for both of us. Don't worry. You'll see me soon."

"I'll take Briar," Eli said, shouldering the others out of the way. "The rest of you, go!"

"There, you see? I'll be fine," Briar said, as if she was soothing a child.

Avery trembled. "You have a family here. And friends!"

"I know. *Go!*"

Reassured that someone would make sure Briar could leave, the Nephilim vanished, whisking the witches with them, and with one final glare, Avery used witch-flight to take Alex.

Now there was only her, Eli, Gabe, and Shadow remaining to watch the Yuletide fight.

"You're waiting to speak to *him*, aren't you?" Eli said softly.

"Yes." Briar suddenly felt tearful and afraid. She had the horrible feeling she might not have the spark of the Green Man inside her anymore. She had become used to his presence. She wanted to say a proper goodbye.

Eli gently gripped her upper arms and turned her to him. "Briar. Don't be me. Don't get caught up with dryads and nature spirits. They are far too different from us to make any kind of meaningful relationship work. And besides, he's the Green Man. He will find you anywhere. Let me take you home. We belong in this world, not that one."

"And what about Shadow?"

"That's for Gabe and her to talk about. I just hope it's not the last time I see either of them."

He opened his arms, and she stepped into his warm embrace, ready to fly.

Gabe thought his heart was breaking. "Shadow. We have to go. Or is this it? Is it all over?"

She didn't answer him, eyes steady on the vast, snowy landscape beyond them. He stared too, feeling the pull of its wild magic, and then he turned to the queen spreadeagled on the floor. She wasn't dead yet, but it was moments away. Beyond the palace walls that faced White Haven, he could see the churning skies and the thinning mist as the final wall around the town vanished. All around, the old foundation of White Haven Castle was coming into view. They were straddling worlds, right now, as the Oak King fought his brother.

"I feel it too, you know," he continued. "I can see why you would want to return home. It's wild, like you." He took a breath, not sure what she might say. She was so enigmatic sometimes. So hard to read. But he knew his decision. "If you want to go, I'll understand. You've lived there for hundreds of years, and here for only one. An eventful one, at that. But if you want to go, I'll go with you."

She turned to him, eyes full of sorrow. "You'd leave Nahum, and his child, and your brothers...for me?"

"Yes. Because that's how much you mean to me. I'd miss them, but I'm not letting you go alone. Your ridiculously handsome-sounding partner, Bloodmoon, and the rest of your motley crew will just have to get used to me."

She cupped his cheeks in her strong hands, and he thought he'd drown in her violet eyes. "Gabe, you have no idea what it means to me that you would do all that. But I would never ask you to. It's too much."

"It's my decision, not yours."

She smiled and kissed him. "No wonder I love you. I better decide quickly then."

But the landscape was already shimmering, and the world rocked violently. Gabe found himself in a freezing place, ice waves towering over them, where the stars glittered in a too close sky, and the roar of something large sounded nearby.

White Haven had gone. They were too late. It had happened. This was it; there was no choice anymore. He had abandoned his brothers. And to be honest, Shadow looked just as shocked. The queen's palace towered over them, and next to it was what appeared to be a whole city of ice.

A voice boomed behind them. "Did you intend to come here?"

They turned to find that both kings had vanished, and in their place was one Green Man, a huge, towering giant who was even taller than Gabe. At his feet were the dead bodies of the queen and her brother, Jack Frost.

Gabe looked at Shadow. "I don't know. Did we?"

"No! I was going to say no! That I wanted to stay in White Haven, with you and your stupid brothers!"

"Well, perhaps you should have decided a bit quicker!"

The Green Man laughed. "You two would make a good life here."

"We had a good life there," Shadow shot back, shivering with the cold.

"But you hesitated."

Her voice dropped. "It was good to feel this place again. To smell the Otherworld air, and feel the wild magic. But it was an illusion. That was the past. Gabe and his world are my future. *Was* my future. That's how the fey and the Otherworld plays tricks with you."

The Green Man nodded. "That it does. My brother knows how the world works, and still he listened to the queen's wild plans. See, the Wheel is already turning." He pointed upwards at the stars that seemed to realign before their eyes.

"Who was she?" Shadow asked.

"One of the Royal Fey who abandoned her kind a long time ago to live here. They have grand ambitions, and hers were grander than most. I did not foresee the lengths she would go to in order to achieve her desires. But all is as it should be now. Even here, the snow will melt, and spring will come."

"And your brother?" Gabe asked.

"Defeated for six months, until his time returns. This time without madness guiding him."

Gabe sighed. *So, it was over.* He looked at the bleak landscape, wondering how long it would take them to travel somewhere warmer. Friendlier. He felt an acute sense of loss. That he would never see his niece or nephew. But at least he still had Shadow.

But the Green Man continued. "You and your friends helped me today. Risked your lives and futures for many people you hardly know. It's a noble thing that you did." He smiled as a squirrel shot out of his sleeve, bounded up his arm and settled on his head. An acorn appeared between his finger and thumb, and the squirrel snatched it from his hand. "I can send you back, but know this, Shadow. Your chance will not come again. The Raven King and I said so before, but we never expected this. The world is changing, and even the old, hidden portals are closing now. The old magic cannot sustain them. What do you choose?"

Shadow looked at Gabe and laid her hand on his heart. "I choose this man and White Haven."

"So shall it be, sister."

And while the world once again whirled around them, Gabe wrapped Shadow in his arms and kissed her.

"Everything feels wrong," Cassie said to Dylan and Ben as they wandered the roads leading to White Haven's square. "The streets are too empty, there's no electricity, and the whole town seems abandoned. Do you think it will ever be the same again?"

Dylan shrugged. "I reckon it will. I assume some people might still be caught in the queen's spell—or they're recovering from it. There are definitely aftereffects. I think that's what has stalled the electrics. I can feel it. Can you?"

Cassie paused, head lifted, as she sniffed the air. "Sort of, but the mugginess is all Eve's spell."

"That's already going though," Ben said, shivering. "Feel that wind. The natural winter weather is coming back. We might even have snow—again."

"Not bloody supernatural snow, I hope!" Cassie said with feeling. "For once, I've actually had enough of all that."

It was almost midnight on the Yule solstice, and they had escaped from the castle only an hour or so before, although she had lost track of time. The whole night—no, the entire past twenty-four hours—had been so weird that it all felt like a dream. Except that the fight and the palace and the queen and everything associated with her had been far too real.

A short distance ahead, Sally and Dan were walking through the melting snow with Moore; Newton, Stan, and Kendall were a little way behind them. They had all raced down the hill from the palace, urging the townsfolk on in the stolen sleighs. They didn't need much encouragement. The spell on them was already starting to break. Families sheltered their children and elderly relatives in their hijacked sleighs and raced home. There was no celebrating on the streets. In fact, they had discouraged it.

For a short while they too had sheltered in Briar's shop, until it became clear that the wall around the town had gone, and that there was nothing to fear anymore. Except the fear for their other friends' safety—specifically, the witches and the Nephilim. They hadn't planned to meet up anywhere, as their retreat had been so frantic. There had been some vague mention earlier that day of going to Reuben's place, but that was up on the hill and hard to get to without transport.

"Where are Caspian and Eve?" Ben asked. "We should go to Avery's. They might know what's happened."

"What if everyone vanished with the palace?" Cassie said, voicing everyone's concerns as they glanced up at the old castle. At least they could see Ravens' Wood now.

"Let's get to the square first," Dylan suggested, quickening his pace.

As they advanced, the streetlamps suddenly turned on, as did all of the Christmas decorations, and the lights within the shop windows.

Cassie gasped with delight. "Look! Everything is so pretty!" She paused to take in the festive scene. Normality was returning to the town.

"Bollocks!" Ben exclaimed, pointing down the street. "I think I can see a fire up ahead. Bloody hell! Is the town on fire? Don't tell me there's *another* problem."

But when they arrived in the square, they found Caspian and Eve chatting next to a bonfire in the centre.

"You're okay! Thank the Gods!" Cassie said, rushing over and hugging them. "You did it! You're so clever! And how did you start the fire?"

"I decided we should use the gallows and the stage more productively," Caspian admitted with a wink. "I thought a Yule fire was what we all needed to unwind. Least I could do, after all of Eve's hard work."

"It was teamwork," she remonstrated. "He kept the sprites away. It looks like you all did a great job of getting everyone out of the castle. We watched from Avery's house." She frowned at Caspian. "I had to stop him from flying up there. I was worried he might get whisked away into the Otherworld."

Caspian shrugged. "I wanted to help."

"There was enough going on up there," Moore said as he stood next to the fire, eyes haunted by the evening's events. "You were best staying out of it."

Sally huffed. "And we really didn't do much to help the locals escape. They didn't need much persuasion, to be honest. It was terrifying. We ran for our lives." She shook her head, exchanging a nervous glance with Dan. "It's the others that worry me. Where are they?"

Newton pointed overhead. "I've just seen someone flying, but I couldn't tell who it was. They should have spotted the fire. Let's hope they'll come and find us."

Even as he said it, they heard cars approaching, and the beating of wings, and within a few minutes, the Nephilim and the witches arrived. Their voices and the fire drew the attention of a few locals too, and it wasn't long before it seemed that most of the town was coming to see what was happening. The closest restaurants and pubs started opening, as well as a few street vendors, and drinks and food began circulating around.

Cassie grinned as she accepted a bottle of beer. They were well on the way to another Yuletide party, and this one would have nothing to do with the wicked queen.

# Twenty-Nine

The atmosphere in White Haven the next day felt as wild as the Yuletide party the previous night, Newton reflected as he strolled down the street to Briar's shop.

Everyone was shouting to each other with good-natured banter across the narrow lanes, the cafés were full, shoppers were laden with bags, and fabulous scents of Christmas food assailed him from all directions. Even the snow had returned, thankfully a gentler snowfall than the previous few days had seen.

Newton had enjoyed the party, for once casting off the restrictions of his demanding job. That morning he slept late, catching up on much needed rest and dealing with a mild hangover. Everyone had partied long into the night, from the confused locals who weren't sure what had happened and were happy to leave it that way, to those who had lots of questions about the palace on the hill.

Stan had been bombarded with inquiries about the reality of the show the council had put on that year, and he took the easy route and admitted it was one of their more ambitious, immersive experiences that they probably wouldn't repeat. Some of them accused him of drugging the water supply, while others had accepted that it was all part of living in White Haven, and therefore whatever happened, happened. They mostly shrugged it off, enjoyed the party, and went to bed happy.

Hamid and Kev, the two police officers, had received a full breakdown of events, and were spending the day patrolling the streets and looking in on local business owners to make sure that everyone was okay. They were annoyed they had been caught up in the spell, too and had missed out on the fun—despite Newton assuring them it hadn't been much fun at all. But at least they coped with the news well. It had been a good idea to bring them in on White Haven's secrets.

The witches and the Nephilim had formed their own party in the corner of the square with everyone else who had helped them, including Tamsyn. The Nephilim had flown to Reuben's house after the fight, and once they shared the news of the party in the square, Tamsyn had wanted to join them. She had taken the Nephilim in her midst in her stride—in fact, she was downright gleeful about them—and happily left Rosa and the children at home to join them. Gabe and Shadow, like Reuben and El, had remained at each other's side all night. That was unusual for both couples. Newton knew why Reuben and El would act like that, but wasn't quite sure what was behind Gabe and Shadow's behaviour. *Not yet, anyway.* After leaving the palace, El went home with Reuben first and cleaned up, and then returned looking as glamourous as ever.

Those who had participated in the parade stayed in costume. That had added to the surreal, carnivalesque nature of the party. Now, as Newton looked back, he realised that the fire, Christmas lights, alcohol, and gaudy, Otherworldly costumes had also enhanced the atmosphere of the previous night. With luck it would confuse everyone, helping the normal events blend more seamlessly with the paranormal. Although, that may prove to be a harder pill to swallow for the locals who had worked in the kitchen.

Newton entered Briar's shop, taking a moment to appreciate the well-ordered space, and Briar and Eli behind the counter. The shop was busy, but Briar spared a moment to smile at him. "Head on through the back, Newton, and put the kettle on. I'll be with you soon."

*Soon* turned into ten minutes, but Newton didn't mind. He took their drinks to them along with the cakes he'd brought as gifts, and then returned to the herb room to wait patiently. When Briar did finally arrive, she looked flustered, with a flush to her cheeks. She sat down at her table opposite him.

"Thanks for the cakes. What are they for?"

"Do I need a reason?" She looked gorgeous. Her dark hair was loose around her shoulders, contrasting with the dark red dress that suited her colouring so well. "I'm just glad you're okay. You and Eli, of course. He was the one to get you out of there, after all."

She sipped her tea, one hand playing with the remnants of Newton's cake crumbs. "I never had any intention of going anywhere, you know, but I did want to speak to him. You understand who I mean."

"Of course. The big green fellow with virility pouring out of every orifice."

Briar sniggered. "You do have a way with words."

"I know."

"But Eli made me see sense. He'll come by when he can. I miss him already, though." She patted her chest. "It feels kind of empty, here."

Newton wished it was him who had made her see sense, but at least someone had. "You lived most of your life without him. You'll be fine. Sounds like he was hiding in you, from the weird conversation I heard last night." He hadn't had a chance to have a proper conversation with Briar during the party, unfortunately.

Briar shook her head. "No, he wasn't. Not really. The Green Man is everywhere and nowhere. You can't pin him down. Even in a human form, he's still not everything that he is. Just a part he can show us. Do you understand?"

"Yes, of course. But why did the queen need you? That's what I don't understand. That's sort of why I'm here now. Trying to get my head around all this."

Briar paused, thoughtful. "It goes back to the Crossroads Circus last year, when he made Ravens' Wood. As you know, he left a bit of himself in me, because I had helped him manifest. I helped give him form in this world by becoming a vessel for him, and I hadn't fully appreciated it back then. He has shape and a human figure in the Otherworld. That's how we know what he looks like. From when our worlds used to cross. Now we see him in trees and leaves and wild places. The queen knew about that because of the Holly King, and thought that if she came here, and the Holly King—one half of the Green Man—fought him here, that they could actually kill him."

"That's nuts," Newton said.

"I know. She thought that his human form here would be more vulnerable. Their fight in the Otherworld is symbolic, and really does happen every year. Jack told me about the Yule feasts they had. Every year and at every Litha, one submits to the other, and vanishes for six months. But love does funny things, doesn't it? She loved the Holly King. He existed in their world, in physical form, and she wanted him all year. Jack Frost, her half-brother and the King of Sprites, wanted to help her. They cooked up this mad plan together."

"So the Holly King, as part of the Green Man, knew all about you and White Haven." Newton shook his head. "Weird. But he should have known that it would never work. They're the same!"

"But I had the Oak King half of the Green Man. It was Imbolc when he raised Ravens' Wood." Briar raked her hand through her hair and laughed. "Nuts, completely nuts, right? That he could be two people and still be the Green Man as a whole."

"So, all this time, you had a bit of the Oak King in you?"

"Yes. It seems so. That's the best I can explain it, Newton. And the queen was from one of the Royal Houses of the fey. Shadow told me all about them last night. They're absurdly powerful, when they bother to be, but they're not interested in us anymore. Luckily."

"At least that bastard Jack is dead," Newton said, thinking of all the follow up he had yet to do with the families of the deceased.

"Are Moore and Kendall okay?"

"Fine. It seems to have whetted their appetite for more paranormal weirdness—especially Moore. You know how fey-obsessed he is. And I think it's helped prompt Kendall's decision making."

"What do you mean?"

"She's gone to see Alex with a special request."

"So, you see, Zee," Alex said, polishing glasses behind the bar at The Wayward Son, "I need you to start the bar manager job sooner than expected."

Zee was freshly washed and showered and seemed not the slightest bit perturbed about the previous night's events. Unlike his old bar manager, Simon, who brought his resignation forward with a phone call that morning.

"He's not coming back at all?"

"No. I would imagine that he's left the county already—if not the country."

"Wow." Zee leaned against the counter, arms folded. "Well, I suppose it was quite a big twenty-four hours, and some people clearly have better memories of it than others."

"It seems so." Alex scanned the late morning crowd who'd come in for one of Jago's famous breakfasts. Jago seemed none the worse for his time spent in the palace kitchen, and had given Alex a long, knowing look when he arrived. Alex was planning to have a private conversation with him later. As far as the customers went, the hum of conversation was loud and generally good-natured, and if anyone had noticed Alex performing magic, no one was mentioning it. "Maybe they're just conditioned to the paranormal now. Like those three."

The Ghost OPS team were sitting in the corner, paperwork spread all over the table, no doubt planning how to document the latest events.

Zee laughed. "Well, you'll be very glad to know that I am extremely happy to take on the position immediately! In fact, I can't wait! I've already asked Gabe to leave me out of everything except the absolute worst cases."

A squeal from behind them almost made Alex drop his glass. It was Marie, running over to hug Zee. "You said yes! I'm so glad, Zee. You're going to be brilliant."

"I am?" He wrestled her off him. "How do you know? I have no experience. I could be awful."

She tutted and gripped his cheek with her finger and thumb. "Don't be ridiculous, you big, handsome devil. Everyone thinks you'll be brilliant. Just make sure you organise the staff lock-in for Christmas—with games—and you'll be fine."

"I have to do that?"

Alex laughed. "And so much more, besides."

He left Marie to inform Zee of all the finer points of staff management, and went to meet Kendall, who'd just entered the pub. "Hey, Kendall. You recovered after last night?"

"After a long, hot bath and a big sleep in one of Reuben's fabulous beds, I'm just dandy."

Alex frowned. "Are you here for breakfast? I would have thought he'd have fed you an epic after-party brunch."

She patted her stomach. "Of course he did. I'm positively bursting. I'm here for something else."

Intrigued, Alex set down the glass he'd been cleaning. "Go on."

"I gather you're renting out the room upstairs. Or will be, soon. I just wondered if it was still available? Because I'd like it, if that's okay? I'm a responsible tenant!"

"I should think so, Detective Sergeant," Alex said, laughing. He shot a quick glance at Zee. "The thing is, Zee is taking my manager's job, and I'm not sure if he might want the room, or if he'll continue to live with his brothers at the farmhouse. Not that he needs to stay onsite, of course!"

Zee looked their way. "Did you mention me?"

Alex explained what Kendall had asked. "I just thought I'd give you first option, that's all, although I realise you'll probably stay at the farmhouse."

Kendall looked at him anxiously, hands twisting on the countertop. "No worries if you want it, Zee. I just like being close to the action." She looked sheepish. "Can't get much closer than this." She realised that Marie was listening. "You know, all the fun, White Haven action that might go on above a pub."

Marie was oblivious to Kendall's floundering. "It's a beautiful flat. I don't blame you. Have you seen it?"

"Actually no, but Avery said it was nice."

Zee was clearly wrestling with the decision. "I must admit that it had crossed my mind. It would be great to get some space from the madness up there, but then again, I don't want to leave Eli on his own. The others are away so much. You know what? It's fine. You have it, Kendall."

"Oh, can I?"

"It has got two bedrooms," Marie reminded them. "You can be flatmates! Or occasionally, anyway."

"Marie!" Alex glared at her. "And what if Kendall doesn't want a flatmate? With big Zee leaving his size twenty boots on the floor?"

"I do not have size twenty feet," Zee said, appalled. "Or leave my boots all over the floor!"

Kendall laughed. "I can handle a flatmate. Especially an occasional one. Bags the biggest room, though."

Zee gave it a moment's thought and then offered his hand. "Deal. We shall discuss the details later."

Kendall shrieked with joy. "Agreed! So, I've got the flat?"

Alex laughed. "Let me show it to you first, and then if you're happy, it's all yours. Well, both of yours, in whatever way you organise it."

Marie nudged Alex as she went to take an order. "That could be fun, right?"

Alex groaned. It was something he'd rather not think about at all.

Reuben had never been so nervous in his life.

He had debated his decision all night and that morning while he was cooking breakfast for his guests—the three policemen and Ghost OPS. Briar's family had returned to Stormcrossed Manor to have breakfast at home, and Zee had flown Eve home in the early hours of the morning. Despite the late night, El had headed into work early, eager to make sure her shop was fine, and root herself in her job.

Having made his mind up, he couldn't wait any more.

Reuben walked into El's shop and found Zoe lost within a mountain of tissue paper. "Are you okay in there?"

She snorted. "I'm in wrapping hell, but at least I have a break between customers."

"Then who are you wrapping for?"

"Returning customers who have gone for coffee." She rolled her eyes. "I would kill for coffee right now."

"So, where's El?"

"Finishing stock."

"Let me through then, and I'll rustle you up a cup."

"I'd kiss you if you weren't already taken."

He winked. "Like I haven't seen your other half lately." She was dating his friend Nils from Viking Ink, the tattoo shop. A huge, shaven-headed beast of a man who was covered in tattoos.

She swung the counter up. "Thanks for introducing us. He's the best thing since sliced bread."

"Make that black bread, and he'll be happy you said so."

The levity helped reduce his anxiety, but it all came rushing back when he entered the backroom and saw El sitting at the counter, at work on one of her latest creations. The place was a mess. Jewellery was on every flat surface, candles burned on shelves, and incense filled the air. He heard her cast a spell as she worked.

He deliberately shut the door loudly, so she knew someone was there, and crossed the room to turn the coffee machine on.

She finally looked up. "Hello, gorgeous."

His heart filled. There was no woman who compared to El. None were more beautiful or brave, or clever, or hot. No one who understood him more. He'd talked to Silver about his decision, and he had backed him up completely.

El frowned. "What's the matter? You're looking at me all funny."

"Am I?"

"Yes. Like your brain flew out the window and left an empty space in your skull."

"You're hilarious!"

She sniggered. "I know."

He took a deep breath and decided to just get on with it. He was a very confident man, but right now, his confidence had vanished. He dropped to his knee in front of her and took her hands in his, hoping she wouldn't laugh at him.

"El, I've always known that I loved you, ever since I met you. You were the wildest, sexiest woman I'd ever laid my eyes on. And you still are. You know that I love you, right? I mean I don't say it that often, but you know, don't you?"

"Of course I do, but what are you doing?" Alarm had filled her eyes.

Reuben persevered, determined to finish his speech. "When I couldn't get to you the other day, I was beyond horrified. I was numb with fear. I shoved it down, and I kept going, but honestly if something had happened to you...the thought of never seeing you again..." He was losing it. "Well, I couldn't cope. Then finding you, and seeing what those bastards had done, well, it just made me see sense. I want us to be more than just girlfriend and boyfriend—which, by the way, sounds completely juvenile. You are my life partner." *By the Gods, he was rambling, and her jaw was clenched. Shit. Just do it.* "Will you marry me?"

El took a sharp breath in and tears filled her eyes. "Are you serious?"

"Yes, but don't freak out! I know we said we're not the marrying kind, but honestly, yesterday changed everything for me, and—"

She cut him off. "You really mean it? You're not going to wake up in a week and say, 'El, you know—'"

"*No*!" Reuben cut her off right back. "I'm not that flaky! I'm sweating, I'm so nervous!"

El smiled and kissed him. "Yes."

"Yes! You're serious? We're getting married?"

"That is what you wanted, right?"

"Yes! But not a proper church wedding. I want a handfasting, in my garden, with all of our friends. Does that sound good? Although, of course, if you want something else, that's okay. And you know, we can even keep living separately, if that suits you!"

"Good grief, Reuben," El said, laughing and crying at the same time. "Slow down! Yes. A handfasting ceremony sounds like the most perfect thing I could possibly imagine. Honestly, life without you was awful, and the queen making me forget you—well, she really couldn't. Not properly. There was a big hole in me." She teared up again and sniffed, and once again, Reuben's anger flared. "Let's not wait too long. Beltane is too far away. What about Imbolc?"

Reuben's panic receded. "Too soon! I have things to organise. What about Ostara? It will be warmer too."

El laughed. "Ostara then. Perfect."

"But I want everything. Flower girls, a best man—Alex, obviously. Your crazy Aunt Oli—all of it."

"Wow. When you do things, Reuben, you don't hold back."

"No, I don't. Not when it matters." He kissed her again. "It's going to be the best handfasting ever."

Avery ended the call with El, squealed, and ran out of the kitchen and into the shop, almost crashing into Dan.

"What's happened?" he asked, grabbing her arms to slow her down. "Is everyone okay?"

"Yes! Everything's perfect. El and Reuben are getting married! He just proposed."

"Are they? Wow!" Dan grinned. "That's brilliant. What a sly old dog Reuben is! Well, maybe not quite as sly as Nahum, who impregnated a woman after one night of sex, but you know..."

The rest of his response was drowned out by Sally. "Did I just hear you properly?" She emerged from the stacks. "Reu and El are getting married! When?"

"Ostara! In Reuben's garden!" Avery hadn't felt so excited since moving in with Alex. "I'm so happy for them."

"I'm going to find champagne," Dan announced. "I'll be back soon. Sally, break out the mince pies."

"If there are any left," Sally grumbled. "I think he has hollow legs."

He headed outside, not even bothering with his coat, and Avery looked around. "Where is Helena? Sorry, Clea." Other customers were listening and laughing at her excitement.

"At the counter, regaling Mary with stories about last night."

Avery froze. Mary was an old and regular customer who embraced the old ways, but even so... "What kind of stories?"

"Just about the parade, I think." Sally lowered her voice and looked over her shoulder, then pulled Avery into the corner. "Why is no one more freaked out this morning?"

Avery had spent a lot of time pondering that, and had discussed it with the other witches the previous night while everyone was partying in the town. "I think some people remember it and don't want to admit it, because they think they've gone mad. Others are either in denial or think it was a giant event planned by Stan. I think, at some point over the coming days, there'll be more questions, but for now, everyone is happy it's over. You said your family is okay?"

"Yes, but they were at home." Sally sighed. "I'm so glad I persuaded Sam to stop there with the kids and Caro. What a night."

"And you're sure you're okay?"

Sally shrugged. "It all got a bit more up close and personal than I was comfortable with, but I'd do anything for this place, and you, so I'm fine. I'm just happy to be rid of that bitch. Let's forget her. She doesn't deserve our time." Sally visibly shook it off. "Now tell me, are you going to be a bridesmaid?"

"I might be!"

"And can I come?"

Avery laughed. "Of course. By the sound of it, Reuben is inviting all our friends, family, and anyone *in the know*. It's going to be fun! Standby for your official invite."

Avery left Sally to warm the mince pies and found Helena at the counter, wrapped up in layers of cardigans—some of Avery's modern ones, rather than Clea's. Helena had decided that if she was going to be inhabiting an old woman's body, she was going to make the best of it. A new wardrobe was on the way. She was leaning over the counter, fully made up, her hair perfect, looking like she hadn't got a care in the world.

"Excuse me for interrupting you two," Avery said, "But I have news!"

"Oh, don't mind me," Mary said, grabbing her bag. "I've got to go, anyway. See you for drinks later, Clea?"

"Of course. Seven sharp." Helena waved her out the door.

"Dinner plans?" Avery asked.

"Yes, and pub quiz at The Kraken." She held her hand up. "I know it's a young person's pub, but don't judge me. I *am* young."

"I wouldn't dream of it. Now, shut up and listen!" Avery told her the news.

Helena smiled. "How lovely. I expect to be there—in Clea, you know."

"You will be. Now, how are you after yesterday?"

"This is the millionth time you've asked me. I'm fine. Honestly. I'm a bit achy, but nothing a few spells can't ease."

"And your time in the square hasn't left you with nightmares?"

"No. Helping to defeat Jack helped, although I'm annoyed Nahum was the one to kill him."

"He's very efficient."

"And handy." Helena squeezed Avery's hand and lowered her voice. "Being able to use my magic, to actually be a proper witch again and inhabiting a body, has been a complete blessing, Avery. Thank you for agreeing to this. I know I've been a bit of a handful before, but I promise that's all behind me now. Mostly."

Avey laughed. "It's lovely to see my grandmother out and about again, so thank *you*!" Avery meant it, too. It was nice to have her around again, even though it was only her in body, not mind. It was still plenty to celebrate. "I'm glad you're around for Christmas day, too. Or part of it?"

"Yes, I'll be in the pub for a couple of hours, but then I'm home. We'll have a proper celebration now all this is done. And we're celebrating the solstice too, yes?"

"Of course, tomorrow with Cornwall Coven, now that the roads are passable."

"Excellent." She nodded at Sally and Dan, who converged from opposite ends of the shop. "And here are the mince pies and champagne, just in time! Now," Helena's eyes sparkled, "tell me more about this wedding."

Thanks for reading *Midwinter Magic.* Please make an author happy and leave a review. There will be another book in this series coming soon.

*The First Yule*, a Yuletide Moonfell Witches novella, is on pre-order now, out on December 12th if you order through Happenstance Books, my online shop:

https://happenstancebookshop.com/products/the-first-yule-moonfell-witches-novella

If you enjoyed this book and would like to read more of my stories, please subscribe to my newsletter at tjgreenauthor.com. You will get two free short stories, *Excalibur Rises* and *Jack's Encounter,* and will also receive free character sheets for all of the main White Haven witches.

By staying on my mailing list you'll receive free excerpts of my new books, as well as short stories, news of giveaways, and a chance to join my launch team. I'll also be sharing information about other books in this genre you might enjoy.

Read on for a list of my other books.

# Author's Note

T hank you for reading *Midwinter Magic*, the twelfth book in the White Haven Witches series.

I was due to write a book about Yule as I follow the Wheel of the Year, and I was itching to write a fairy tale-based story with a twist, and start the book in a different way than usual. It was also great to revisit the Otherworld and see how Shadow might respond, as well as the rest of my cast. Getting dragons in there was fun! I also wanted to have all of the Nephilim participate as a sort of end of year finale. I hope I didn't disappoint!

As you can gather from the ending, there are more adventures to come. I love writing about the witches, so there will be another book next year – 2024. It's also—I said this last time—my biggest book to date.

I'm currently working on a novella for another witch series, this one is called Moonfell Witches. If you've read *Storm Moon Rising*, Storm Moon Shifters Book 1, and *Immortal Dusk*, White Haven Hunters Book 6, you will have met them there. I will write a full story in that series next year, in the meantime, a Yuletide novella will be out in December 2023. It's called *The First Yule*. As requested by you, my readers, this series will be set in the present day with past flashbacks of other Moonfell witches, and of course, there'll be plenty of mystery and magic too.

This month, October 2023 as I write this, celebrates five years since I released *Buried Magic*, book 1 of this series. It has changed my life. I was able to become a full-time writer in October 2020, and so the White Haven witches have enabled me to do the job I love the most – create worlds and write books. Thank you, my fabulous readers, for making this happen.

If you'd like to read a bit more background on the stories, please head to my website, www.tjgreenauthor.com, where I blog about the books I've read and the research I've done for the series. In fact, there's lots of stuff on there about my other two series, Rise of the King and White Haven Hunters, as well. I also now have an online shop called Happenstance Books, where you can buy all of my eBooks, paperbacks, audiobooks, hardbacks, and merchandise:

https://happenstancebookshop.com/.

I also now offer a subscription community called Happenstance Book Club. I offer early access to work in progress chapters and so much more. Check it out here:

https://reamstories.com/happenstancebookclub

If you love audiobooks, you can listen to all of my audiobooks on my YouTube channel. Please subscribe here: https://www.youtube.com/@tjgreenauthor

Thanks again to Fiona Jayde Media for my awesome cover, and thanks to Kyla Stein at Missed Period Editing for applying your fabulous editing skills.

Thanks also to my beta readers—Terri and my mother. I'm glad you enjoyed it; your feedback, as always, is very helpful! Thanks also to Jase, my fabulously helpful other half. You do so much to support me, and I am immensely grateful for you.

Finally, thank you to my launch team, who give valuable feedback on typos and are happy to review upon release. It's lovely to hear from them—you know who you are! You're amazing! I also love hearing from all of my readers, so I welcome you to get in touch.

If you'd like to read more of my writing, please join my mailing list at www.tjgreenauthor.com. You can get a free short story called *Jack's Encounter*, describing how Jack met Fahey—a longer version of the prologue in *Call of the King*—by subscribing to my newsletter. You'll also get a free copy of *Excalibur Rises*, a short story prequel. Additionally, you will receive free character sheets on all of my main characters in White Haven Witches series—exclusive to my email list!

By staying on my mailing list, you'll receive free excerpts of my new books and updates on new releases, as well as short stories and news of giveaways. I'll also be sharing information about other books in this genre you might enjoy.

I encourage you to follow my Facebook page, T J Green. I post there reasonably frequently. In addition, I have a Facebook group called TJ's Inner Circle. It's a fab little group where I run giveaways and post teasers, so come and join us.

# About the Author

I was born in England, in the Black Country, but moved to New Zealand in 2006. I lived near Wellington with my partner, Jase, and my cats, Sacha and Leia. However, in April 2022 we moved again! Yes, I like making my life complicated... I'm now living in the Algarve in Portugal, and loving the fabulous weather and people. When I'm not busy writing I read lots, indulge in gardening and shopping, and I love yoga.

Confession time! I'm a Star Trek geek—old and new—and love urban fantasy and detective shows. Secret passion—Columbo! Favourite Star Trek film is the *Wrath of Khan*, the original! Other top films—*Predator*, the original, and *Aliens*.

In a previous life I was a singer in a band, and used to do some acting with a theatre company. For more on me, check out a couple of my blog posts. I'm an old grunge queen, so you can read about my love of that on my blog: https://tjgreenauthor.com/about-a-girl-and-what-chris-cornell-means-to-me/. For more random news, read: https://tjgreenauthor.com/read-self-published-blog-tour-things-you-probably-dont-know-about-me/

Why magic and mystery?

I've always loved the weird, the wonderful, and the inexplicable. Favourite stories are those of magic and mystery, set on the edges of the known, particularly tales of folklore, faerie, and legend—all the narratives that try to explain our reality.

The King Arthur stories are fascinating because they sit between reality and myth. They encompass real life concerns, but also cross boundaries with the world of faerie—or the Other, as I call it. There are green knights, witches, wizards, and dragons, and that's what I find particularly fascinating. They're stories that have intrigued people for generations, and like many others, I'm adding my own interpretation.

I love witches and magic, hence my second series set in beautiful Cornwall. There are witches, missing grimoires, supernatural threats, and ghosts, and as the series progresses, weirder stuff happens. The spinoff, White Haven Hunters, allows me to indulge my love of alchemy, as well as other myths and legends. Think Indiana Jones meets Supernatural!

Have a poke around in my blog posts and you'll find all sorts of posts about my series and my characters, and quite a few book reviews.

If you'd like to follow me on social media, you'll find me here:

facebook.com/tjgreenauthor/

pinterest.com/Mount0live/

tiktok.com/@tjgreenauthor

youtube.com/@tjgreenauthor

goodreads.com/author/show/15099365.T_J_Green

instagram.com/tjgreenauthor/

bookbub.com/authors/tj-green

# Other Books by T J Green

Rise of the King Series
A Young Adult series about a teen called Tom who is summoned to wake King Arthur. It's a fun adventure about King Arthur in the Otherworld!

Call of the King #1
The Silver Tower #2
The Cursed Sword #3

White Haven Hunters
The fun-filled spinoff to the White Haven Witches series! Featuring Fey, Nephilim, and the hunt for the occult.

Spirit of the Fallen #1
Shadow's Edge #2
Dark Star #3
Hunter's Dawn #4
Midnight Fire #5
Immortal Dusk #6

Storm Moon Shifters

This is an Urban Fantasy shifters spin-off in the White Haven World, and can be read as a standalone. There's a crossover of characters from my other series, and plenty of new ones. There is also a new group of witches who I love! It's set in London around Storm Moon, the club owned by Maverick Hale, alpha of the Storm Moon Pack. Audio will be available when I've organised myself!

Storm Moon Rising #1

Moonfell Witches

Witch fiction set in Moonfell, the gothic mansion in London. If you love magic, fantastic characters, urban fantasy and paranormal mysteries, you'll love this series. Join the Moonfell coven now!

The First Yule, a Moonfell Witches Novella.

Printed in Great Britain
by Amazon